A DISTANT DAWN

They were the best of friends, as close as sisters.
Would the winds of war tear them apart forever?

"HER STRONGEST WORK TO DATE."
—*Publishers Weekly*

FAR HORIZONS

From the bustling streets of England to the golden
shores of Australia and Hawaii, three women from
different worlds would have the courage to
dream—and never to surrender . . .

"EXCELLENT . . . FAST MOVING . . .
HARD TO PUT DOWN!"
—Bestselling author ROBERTA GELLIS

VISIONS OF TOMORROW

A night of tragedy changed the lives of
two friends. Now Megan and Joanna would have to
make the heart's hardest choices . . .

"ENGROSSING . . . AN EXCITING JOURNEY
OF DISCOVERY."
—Bestselling author LAURIE MCBAIN

A DIFFERENT EDEN

Fleeing a dark destiny, Eleanor surrendered to her
heart's passions—within the treacherous shadows
of a rambling Welsh estate.

"A VIBRANT TAPESTRY . . . STRONG
AND COMPELLING."
—ELIZABETH KARY, author of *Midnight Lace*

DARE
~TO~
DREAM

KATHERINE SINCLAIR

BERKLEY BOOKS, NEW YORK

DARE TO DREAM

A Berkley Book / published by arrangement with
the author

PRINTING HISTORY
Berkley edition / June 1993

ISBN: 0-425-13718-X

A BERKLEY BOOK ® TM 757,375
Berkley Books are published by The Berkley Publishing Group,
200 Madison Avenue, New York, New York 10016.
The name "BERKLEY" and the "B" logo
are trademarks belonging to Berkley Publishing Corporation.

PRINTED IN THE UNITED STATES OF AMERICA

10 9 8 7 6 5 4 3 2 1

Part I

Chapter 1

• •

THE PALLID MOON vanished behind scudding rain clouds.
A dog howled, his mournful cry almost lost amid the
clattering hooves and grinding wheels of a carriage rattling
down the cobblestoned street.

Emily cast a frantic glance over her shoulder as she ran.
The carriage was gaining on her; she could hear the swish of
the driver's whip. She had to get off the gaslit street, find a
dark place to hide.

A lamppost loomed ahead. Breathless, she dodged the
amber pool of light, turned the corner, and sped down a
narrow alley.

Too late she realized her mistake when she was confronted by a blank brick wall. She beat against the rough
brick with her hands in numb frustration. Turning, she saw
the carriage had come to a halt, blocking the alley. She was
trapped.

She watched in silent terror as the carriage door yawned
open and the gaunt frock-coated figure of the doctor's
assistant, Martin Crupe, stepped out. He walked down the
middle of the alley toward her, his heavy walking stick
beating a tattoo on the rain-glistened cobblestones.

Emily shrank back against the dank wall, anticipating the
blows he would surely lay about her. But whatever punishment he inflicted for her attempt to run away would be
nothing compared to the horror of being dragged back to
that house of evil.

Her terrified gaze swept the few closed and barred doors
and windows on either side of the alley. No glimmer of
light, no sound indicated the presence of anyone who might

take pity on her. The rain slashed down, drenching her, and
undoubtedly adding to Crupe's anger.

"You've caused me a great deal of trouble"—his thin,
peevish voice penetrated the sound of wind and rain—
"dragging me out on such a foul night. You are going to pay
dearly for my inconvenience."

Emily ran to the nearest door and pounded on it with her
fists. "Please! Somebody—help me! Help me, I beg of
you!"

Her only response was the patter of raindrops against the
iron-barred glass of a darkened window.

The next moment she felt Crupe's bony fingers bite into
her arm, spinning her round to face him. Her sodden shawl
slipped from her shoulders. She caught a glimpse of his livid
face beneath the dripping brim of his tall hat, then his
walking stick landed a stinging blow along the side of her
head.

She sprawled on the ground, stars dancing dizzily in front
of her eyes. The stick descended again, and she attempted to
roll out of its path, raising her arm to deflect the blow. Pain
exploded in her wrist as the stick connected, and she fell
back, gasping.

"Damn you for an ungrateful little wretch," Crupe said.
"Where would you have been if the doctor hadn't taken you
in? I'll tell you where, in the workhouse, that's where, or
worse, on the streets." He punctuated every word with a
prod of his stick, causing an involuntary whimper of pain.

A clap of thunder exploded overhead, and the rain came
down in a solid sheet. Crupe bent and grabbed her long hair
to pull her to her feet.

Feeling faint from the pain of his blows, Emily could
barely stay on her feet as he dragged her back along the
alley to the carriage.

She thought perhaps she did indeed faint during the
journey back to the house on River Court, as later she had
no recollection of traveling through the deserted streets as
the storm battered the seaport and its citizens retreated
behind closed doors at the approach of the midnight hour.

Emily came to her senses as a cold gust of rain wafted

into her face, and she found herself standing on the pavement in front of the doctor's house.

For a moment she swayed dizzily, expecting Crupe's stick to prod her forward. Then she realized their carriage was not the only one arriving at the house. A second brougham, handsomely appointed and pulled by a fine pair of horses, came to a halt behind them, and a young man leapt out.

An educated voice called out, "Mr. Crupe? Is that you? I need the doctor right away. My sister has been taken ill."

"Sir Edward?" Crupe peered through the misty rain at the visitor. "Come along inside—I'll fetch the doctor at once."

For one hopeful second Emily thought she might be able to take advantage of the diversion to slip away again, but Crupe seized her arm and propelled her up the steps to the front door.

Godfrey opened the door almost the second the brass lion's head knocker fell, as though he had been waiting in the cavernous hallway for their return. As always, Emily shivered at the sight of the powerfully built manservant, who frightened her even more than the spiteful Crupe, since she had no doubt Godfrey could probably kill a grown man with a single blow, let alone a sixteen-year-old orphan.

They stepped into the hall, shedding puddles of rainwater, and Crupe said shortly, "Take Faraday to her room, Godfrey. I'll go and wake up the doctor."

"Wait a minute," Sir Edward said, looking more closely at Emily. Gently he pushed aside a long strand of dark gold hair from her forehead. "I think the doctor had better take a look at the young lady first. Her head is bleeding. Let me help you to a seat, miss. Here, take my arm."

She looked up into a youthfully handsome face that was creased with concern, undoubtedly for his ailing sister, but words of sympathy in this dreadful house were so unexpected that she was overcome with gratitude. After the mistreatment she had received at the hands of Crupe and Godfrey, a stranger's kindness was almost more than she

could bear. She stammered, "Oh, thank you, sir, for your
concern."

Sir Edward looked at her with surprise. "Are you related
to Dr. Stoddard, miss?" He had undoubtedly been expecting her to speak with a Liverpudlian whine and was taken
aback by her accent, which did not match her servant's
attire.

Crupe stepped forward immediately and said, "Faraday
is a housemaid here, Sir Edward. There is no need to fret
about her, Godfrey will awaken one of our live-in students
to bandage her head."

For one instant Emily considered begging Sir Edward to
help her escape, but the last time she had attempted to enlist
the aid of an outsider . . . merciful heaven, had it been
only two days ago that she had tried to slip a note to the
butcher's delivery boy? Crupe had explained that she was
suffering from delusions, a poor demented charity patient
who earned her keep as a maid but imagined herself to be a
prisoner and that the doctor's teaching and research facility
was some sort of torture chamber. Crupe added that if her
behavior didn't improve, they would be forced to commit
her to a lunatic asylum.

The memory of that threat, and the punishment later
administered by Crupe, flashed through Emily's mind in the
instant before Godfrey took her arm to lead her away.
Crupe's explanation had been made even more plausible by
the presence at the time of poor Dudley, who really was
mentally deficient. Dudley had the body of a strapping
young man, but the mind of a six-year-old, and earned his
keep by helping the doctor with the animals he kept for his
experiments.

Godfrey dragged her straight up to the attic room she
shared with the scullery maid. As he pushed her into the tiny
room he muttered, "I'm not waking any of the lads up to
bother with a bit of a cut like that. Consider yourself lucky
you didn't get worse."

He closed the door with a thud, but the sound didn't
disturb the sleeping scullery maid. Doris was so exhausted
at the end of her long day that she slept like the dead.

Emily lay down on her pallet on the hard floor, shivering as the shock of the evening's events set in. Too weary and defeated to remove her wet clothes, she huddled under a threadbare blanket, unable to sleep for worrying about the inevitable confrontation with the doctor the following morning. Her fear was so great that it almost—but not quite—eclipsed the tight knot of grief that enclosed her heart. There had been no time yet to deal with the loss of her beloved father.

Chapter 2

....

LADY BRIONY FORESTER faced her husband with shoulders squared. "I sent Edward for the doctor because I fear that without immediate medical attention Mrs. Winthrop will not survive this night."

Sir Rupert Forester tossed his overcoat and hat into the waiting arms of his butler and dismissed the man with a wave of his hand. Rupert gestured toward the drawing room door, and Briony preceded him into the room, where a blazing fire banished the chill of the night and sent golden images dancing on brocaded walls.

He stood with his back to the fire, and despite her anger, Briony felt a familiar, if somewhat reluctant, thrill at the sight of him. She recalled her mother's reaction upon meeting Rupert Forester for the first time. "Too demanding, too tall, too handsome, too dark, too sure of himself, too *everything*, Briony. He'll need a wife who obeys his every command, anticipates his every whim. Darling, that isn't you! You're cut from the same mold as he is! My dear, you're too beautiful to be subservient enough, and far too opinionated to be acquiescent. Men like Rupert need docile little women, and women like you need timid men."

How right her mother had been. Their seven-year marriage had been turbulent from the start, but so filled with passion that despite two still births, somehow it had prevailed. Until now. But this was not the time to discuss Rupert's perfidy, for now she must concern herself with her housekeeper.

"In any event," Rupert said, "Dr. Stoddard is hardly

likely to come out on a night like this in order to treat a servant.''

"I told Edward to say I was ill."

Rupert's eyes glittered like dark mirrors. "The devil you did. Surely your brother will have more sense than to blatantly lie to the good doctor."

"Perhaps," Briony said in a deathly quiet tone, "I should instead have sent word that your mistress is ill."

For a second his eyes locked with hers, but there was no change in his expression. "Ah," he said softly, "so that's it."

She glared at him, wanting to feel his flesh tear under her fingernails, to scream at him that she would kill him. Her fists tightened in the folds of her burgundy velvet gown, as if fearing the thought would produce the act.

Rupert moved closer, rested one hand on her shoulder, and with the other pushed a strand of auburn hair back from her brow. "Your eyes turn a steely blue when you're angry, Bri, and grow so large I could drown in them."

He allowed his hand to drift down to her neckline, and his fingertip caressed the soft hollow between her breasts. Briony suffered his touch for only a split second, although her treacherous flesh responded instantly. Seizing his hand, she jerked it away. Too many arguments had ended in erotic bliss. But not this time. Damn him, this time he had committed the unforgivable sin.

At that moment there was a knock on the door, and the butler entered the room. "Excuse me, Sir Rupert, but Dr. Stoddard is here."

"I'll speak with the doctor before you take him to the sickroom, Mathers," Briony said, sweeping past her husband.

As always, Briony felt a quiver of distaste at the sight of Dr. Stoddard. A great gorilla of a man, with a small bald head, colorless complexion, and enormous, pale hands, he seemed to her to be a creature emerging from some netherworld, rarely exposed to sunlight, glorying in decay and despair, feeding on it. But of course, she had always detested the man and perhaps judged him unfairly. He had, after all, saved Rupert's mother from almost certain death by performing an experimental operation. The Foresters were one of only a handful of families he continued to treat, having given up his practice in order to pursue his medical research and teaching.

Stoddard's almost transparent eyes, which had an odd yellow cast, regarded her in surprise. "Why, Lady Forester, for one at death's door, you look remarkably healthy."

"Did I say my *sister* was ill?" Edward exclaimed in innocent surprise. "I must have been so rattled at the sight of that lovely housemaid of yours, Doctor, that I got mixed up. I meant to say my sister requested that you come and look at her housekeeper."

"Mrs. Winthrop has great difficulty breathing, Dr. Stoddard," Briony said. "I fear she might have pneumonia."

Stoddard stared at her, mouth compressed as if to keep from soundly chastising her.

Briony said quickly, "Mathers will show you up to her room. I'll join you in a moment."

The doctor wordlessly shifted his black bag from one hand to the other and followed the waiting butler to the servants' quarters.

Briony squeezed her brother's arm. "Thank you. I know you hated to do that, but he wouldn't have come otherwise. This is really a rotten welcome home for Oxford's most distinguished graduate, isn't it? I haven't even had a chance to congratulate you. I really am so proud of you. Rupert's in the drawing room. Why don't you join him while I go up to Mrs. Winthrop?"

Edward smiled. "Anything for you, sis. I hope the old girl will be all right."

He watched as she walked quickly across the hall, thinking that she grew more beautiful with every passing year, yet a nagging suspicion, born when he arrived earlier that evening, persisted. Since he had visited her during the summer holidays, something had happened to kill her former *joie de vivre*.

Pushing open the drawing room door, he went into the room to greet his brother-in-law. Perhaps Rupert could shed some light on those haunted shadows that lingered in Briony's twilight blue eyes.

"Ah, Edward, old chap, there you are." Rupert shook his hand warmly. "Good to see you again. University days behind you now, I hear. You must stay with us as long as you wish, but I expect you're eager to begin your grand tour."

"Well, I shan't be sorry to leave this foul weather behind for a while."

"Bound for warmer climes then? Italy? Spain?"

"Haven't decided yet."

Rupert poured two brandies and handed him one. "Let's warm the cockles, shall we? I suppose Briony has gone up to the sickroom? She really shouldn't have asked you to lie to the doctor for her. We may need him sometime, and he'll refuse to come." There was a hint of a rebuke in his tone. "But then, you and your sister have always been prepared to sell your souls to the devil for each other, haven't you?"

"Briony is only six years my senior," Edward responded quietly, "but she's always been both mother and father to me. Yes, I'd do anything for her, and she for me. Rupert . . . she seems awfully downcast about something. I mean, it's Christmastime, and she's always loved the season, but this year—"

"Oh, I expect it's because of Mrs. Winthrop's illness. She's been with your sister for a long time, after all."

"Perhaps you're right." Edward settled back into an easy chair beside the fire and sipped the warming brandy. He stared into the leaping flames.

"You're frowning fiercely, Edward," Rupert said after a few minutes. "You're not really worried about Bri, are you? I assure you there's absolutely nothing wrong in her life."

"No, no, I'm sure you're right. I'm imagining things. Actually, I was thinking about a young girl I saw at the doctor's house. I can't get her out of my mind."

"Aha," Rupert murmured. "Now we're getting somewhere. Bri is giving her usual party on Christmas Eve— shall we invite the young lady in question?"

"She's a housemaid."

Rupert laughed. "In that case, I could send Mathers to offer her a position here. Seduction of the servant class is always more readily accomplished under one's own roof."

Edward knew he was blushing with embarrassment, but he managed to respond, "Miss Faraday spoke like a lady, not a servant, and I saw Crupe drag her into the house. Furthermore, she had a nasty cut on her head that was bleeding. I wish I'd insisted that the doctor look at her before I left, but Crupe said one of the students would take care of her. Rupert, the more I think about it, the more I believe Crupe had been abusing her."

"Even so, there's not much you can do about it, is there? You don't know all of the circumstances. Perhaps she was a thief."

"I don't believe that for a moment. Perhaps when Dr. Stoddard is finished with Mrs. Winthrop, I should simply demand an explanation."

"Now, wait a minute, let's be discreet about this. The storm is raging worse than ever. Why don't I invite the good doctor to spend the night here, then tomorrow morning we'll find some excuse for you to ride back into town with him. You're obviously smitten with the young lady. Why not speak to her in person? Find out if she really is a damsel in distress ready to fall into your waiting arms?"

"Don't make fun of me, Rupert."

"Wouldn't dream of it, dear boy."

The drawing room door opened, and Briony walked into the room. The two men looked at her questioningly.

"Pneumonia, just as I feared," she said. "Dr. Stoddard will be down in a minute. He's preparing a draft and a poultice for her and ordered a kettle to be kept boiling on the hob in her room. He says the steam will help."

"Sounds as though the doctor has the situation well in hand, then," Rupert said.

Edward was immediately aware of the undercurrent between his sister and her husband. It was evident in Rupert's wary gaze and in Briony's studied avoidance of him. She took a chair as far away from Rupert as she could get and didn't look directly at him. They'd quarreled over something, that was certain. But then, their marriage had always been stormy.

Rupert said, "Apparently a thunderbolt struck Edward over at the doctor's house, Bri. He saw a young housemaid and is convinced she's a princess in disguise."

Briony looked questioningly at her brother.

"It's just that the girl spoke like a lady and . . . well, I think she'd been beaten by the doctor's assistant."

Shocked, Briony exclaimed, "The minute the doctor comes downstairs we shall certainly ask him about her!"

"Perhaps he's unaware of it?" Edward said. "Crupe appeared to be manhandling her. Don't say anything to the doctor yet. I'd like a chance to talk to her first."

"Why not invite the good doctor to spend the night?" Rupert suggested. "Then the young Sir Galahad can ride back with him in the morning."

"I'll speak to Mathers and have him prepare a guest room," Briony replied. "Now, if you two will excuse me, it's been a rather trying day and I'm tired."

She kissed Edward's cheek and murmured, "Good night, Edward. It's so good to have you here." She didn't look at Rupert.

Edward sat with his brother-in-law in uncomfortable silence for a few minutes, then also excused himself in order to retire.

An hour later, as Edward was drifting off to sleep, he was jolted awake by the sound of loud knocking nearby. Slipping out of bed, he went to the door and peered down the gaslit landing. Rupert stood in front of Briony's bedroom door, his fist raised.

"Damn you, open this door or I'll break it down. Briony, do you hear me?"

Before Edward could react, his sister's voice called out, "If you force your way in here, Rupert, you'll regret it. I have your shotgun pointed squarely at the door."

Edward drew back inside his own room and closed the door. Whatever they were quarreling about, it was not his place to interfere. Besides, it sounded as though Briony had the situation well in hand.

He heard Rupert's boots go stamping past his door and descending the staircase. Silence again claimed the house. But sleep eluded Edward. The pale frightened face of the young housemaid lingered in his mind. How had a refined young lady managed to find herself in such circumstances? Had the pretty Miss Faraday no mother, no father?

Chapter 3

• •

"ASHES TO ASHES, DUST TO DUST . . ."

The smell of raw earth overpowered the subtle scent of hothouse lilies, nodding their waxy heads as a chill breeze swept through the cemetery.

Fletcher Faraday remained composed as the coffin of his only daughter was lowered into the ground. One or two of the mourners glanced in his direction, perhaps repelled by what they perceived to be his coldness. But he had spent a lifetime disguising his feelings, cultivating the carefully aloof countenance of the diplomat, maintaining tight control of his emotions under the most chaotic circumstances. His first superior officer had put it to him bluntly: Never let the native see you're ruffled, rattled, or wrong. Having spent most of his adult life dealing with the native in various far-flung outposts of civilization, Fletcher had long ago acquired a steely reserve that now masked the depth of his grief over the loss of Emily.

At his side his new wife Antonia—Tonia, as she liked to be called—sighed softly and wiped away a tear. Her gloved hand slipped into his, but for once he felt no comfort from her touch.

The small circle of mourners were waiting for him to drop the first handful of earth on the coffin, but he remained frozen to the spot, unwilling to see the earth cover her. Emily had been so young, so vibrantly alive. The shock of her death had seeped through his body to his very bones, creating within him a numbness that he knew had been fused there forever. It was his only protection against the memory that welled up so agonizingly of Emily's lovely face so destroyed that the coffin had been sealed immediately after he identified her; from her bracelet, her diary, and her mother's ring, now being buried with her.

An image leapt into his mind, unbidden, of a little girl, golden ringlets flying, robin's egg eyes wide with delight, flying into his arms and clinging to him, making him feel like the most powerful and important man on earth. Surely no other accomplishment could bring the joy one felt in seeing the love in a child's eyes?

"Darling . . ." Tonia prompted him gently, and reluctantly he picked up a handful of the cold earth and let it fall. Oh, God, the sound of it rattling on the coffin . . . Emily, oh, my beloved daughter, all the sunlight is gone from my world.

He turned away quickly and strode to the carriage. At least he would be spared the awful ritual of the gathering of the mourners after the funeral, as he had been in England for such a short time and had not bothered to rent a house, preferring to stay at a hotel while awaiting his next assignment. His possessions, except for clothing, remained warehoused at the docks. Tomorrow he and Tonia would board the ship for the long voyage to Mexico, where he would take up his duties at the British Embassy.

As the hired carriage led the somber procession from the cemetery, Tonia tugged at his sleeve. "We really should invite them into the hotel dining room for a glass of port at least."

"I will not celebrate my daughter's death in any way." He attempted a level tone, careful not to vent his agony on his wife.

"Of course, dear, I understand," she whispered, but her eyes narrowed slightly at this breach of etiquette.

"I just wish . . ." he said savagely, "that we didn't have to sail tomorrow. I would have liked to be present at the trial—I would have liked to see the swine hang."

"Oh, my dear, you must put such violent feelings out of your mind. The poacher surely didn't intend to kill Emily. He was after one of Lord Barlow's deer."

"I should have kept closer watch on her. I should have

recognized how unhappy she was about being separated from us. I shouldn't have insisted she go to Switzerland,'' he said for the hundredth time.

"Don't dwell on it, Fletcher. Who could have foreseen that she would run away? You mustn't blame yourself.''

Her hand found his again, and he looked at his bride, at the perfection of her heart-shaped face, accentuated by a widow's peak of blue-black hair. Her slightly oblique eyes, fringed with lustrous lashes beneath high arching brows, seemed to hold all the mystery of the ages. She had told him little about her past, other than that she had been widowed before she was twenty. Her quick wit and lively conversation had attracted him, her beauty mesmerized him, but there was also a dangerous quality to her charm that intrigued him. There had never been another woman quite like her, although the distant memory of another exotic beauty he had known sometimes came back to haunt him, and he'd wondered more than once if Tonia's resemblance to her had been what attracted him in the first place. Still, he hadn't expected to be swept away by passion again in his maturity.

"Are you sure your years of loneliness and your imminent departure are not combining to cause you to act impetuously?'' the newly appointed ambassador had asked when Fletcher announced his forthcoming marriage, a scant two months after meeting Tonia, by which time she had woven a spell so compelling that it was impossible to leave her behind. Knowing, not immodestly, that he was far too valuable to have his plans interfered with, Fletcher had simply ignored the query.

Still, he realized that for so long it had been just him and Emily, coping with the loss of Emily's mother as best they could. Had he been so swept away by his obsession for Tonia that he had neglected his daughter? That was the question that tortured him now.

He had worried somewhat about Tonia's influence on Emily. He was not so besotted by his new wife that he did not recognize that Tonia was, in polite parlance, a woman of the world. He'd expected a certain antagonism on his daughter's part toward a stepmother only a few years her

senior, but Emily had shown none. She had seemed eager to
welcome Tonia, to offer friendship and even love, confiding
to her father that although she had always adored him, she
had missed the companionship of an older woman of her
own race.

Tonia had been amused but slightly horrified. "Darling,"
she'd said, rolling her eyes heavenward. "Isn't your daughter something of an ingenue for her age? She's sixteen, isn't
she? Most young women are thinking of marriage by that
age, but she seems . . . charmingly, of course . . .
childish."

"I suppose I've sheltered Emily," he answered, almost
apologetically. "She was barely two years old when her
mother died; perhaps I was excessively protective of her.
Then, too, my profession kept her insulated from the outside
world. Since I was stationed in China and never chose to
return home on leave, except for the few Europeans we met
at the embassy, she had little contact with her own race."

"She needs to go away to boarding school, Fletcher."

"School?" He'd been aghast at the suggestion. "But
she's never even had a governess—I always tutored her
myself."

"Exactly, and—forgive me—it shows."

He'd bristled. "If I do say so, there's little more any
school could teach her."

"A good finishing school could teach her the social
acumen she lacks, give her confidence and feminine grace.
I went to an excellent one myself, in Switzerland—I can
highly recommend it. Then later she could join us abroad.
Why don't we let Emily decide for herself?"

He never knew what argument in favor of the finishing
school Tonia presented, but to his surprise, Emily agreed to
go. She did seem somewhat subdued, but nothing she had
said or done had even hinted that she was planning to run
away rather than go to the Swiss school. Where, in fact,
could she run to? She knew no one in England.

While Fletcher had believed she was safely ensconced in
the boarding school in the Alps, where was she hiding?
Only when a curt note arrived from the headmistress of the

school, chiding him for not letting her know his daughter
would not be arriving, did he frantically notify the police of
Emily's disappearance.

A scant week before he and Tonia were due to sail for
Mexico word had come of the body found in Lord Barlow's
woods after his gamekeeper had routed a poacher. Around
the wrist of the young girl was a silver bracelet, engraved:
To my dear Emily, Peking, China, 1839. On her finger was
her mother's ring, and in her pocket they found a miniature
leather-bound diary, with brief entries in Emily's handwrit-
ing.

If only he had not agreed to send her away to school, if
only Emily could have confided her desperation . . . if
only . . .

"Darling," Tonia's voice interrupted his reverie. "There's
our hotel. Won't you please change your mind about
inviting the mourners—"

"I don't even know these people, except for a slight
acquaintance with a few minor officials and civil servants
no doubt coerced into showing their respect. Who are the
others?"

"They're friends of mine, with whom I hope to renew my
friendship when we return to England." There was a slight
edge to Tonia's voice he had not heard before. "I know
you're racked with grief, Fletcher, but we can't simply turn
these people away."

"Do as you wish," he said wearily. "But I won't be a
part of it."

He didn't say so to Tonia, but he knew he would never
return to England. He had said his last goodbye to his
country at the same moment the earth rattled down on his
daughter's coffin. The memories here were too painful, first
Emily's mother, now Emily.

Chapter 4

● ●

EMILY HAD JUST finished scrubbing the chamber pots when Martin Crupe sent for her. Pushing her chapped hands into the pockets of her apron to keep them from shaking, she went to the anteroom adjacent to the doctor's study where Crupe spent most of his time.

This surely was the summons she had been expecting, to face her punishment for running away. As she knocked on the door, Emily hoped she would not have to face the doctor himself.

She scarcely recognized the raspy voice that called for her to enter, but once inside the gloomy room, with its dark, oppressive furniture and shuttered windows, she saw that Crupe was alone, huddled under a plaid blanket behind his mahogany desk.

"I hope you're satisfied. I've caught a terrible cold that will surely turn into pneumonia, and all because you dragged me out on such a filthy night." His voice was a hoarse whisper, his eyes red-rimmed, and he held a damp handkerchief to his nostrils.

Emily murmured, "I'm sorry."

But he wasn't listening. "You're fortunate, indeed, that the doctor was called away to treat Lady Forester, but don't think for one minute that he won't punish you severely when he returns. Where, pray tell, did you think you were going? Who would feed and clothe you, if not the doctor?"

She hung her head, fearing that if she spoke she would enrage him further.

"Get it into that stupid mind of yours that if you leave this house you will meet a fate out on the streets far worse than starvation. Do you wish me to describe that fate to you?"

She shook her head.

He leaned forward. "You are an orphan. Your father was killed, run down by a carriage and most horribly mangled. Now it pains me to repeat this to you again, Faraday, but obviously it is something you have not yet grasped. Your father's only bequest to you was to leave a number of—very substantial—debts."

"If I could just speak with Tonia—my stepmother."

"Apparently his poor bereaved bride has left the country and is beyond the reach of debtors' court. No, Faraday, you are not only dependent upon the doctor's largess for your daily bread, but your wages will help pay off your father's debts."

Was it all a horrible nightmare? she wondered, staring at the Persian rug on the floor until the colors swam, a medley of reds, the red of rust, the red of blood. But she knew there was no waking up from the grim reality of this house. How she had looked forward to returning to the land of her birth, of seeing for herself the gentle meadows her father had spoken of so fondly but which she did not remember. Instead, they had come to this teeming city, where her father had all but abandoned her in his obsessive pursuit of Tonia.

Emily had been in a carriage taking her on the first part of her journey to Switzerland to Tonia's finishing school when a rider caught up with them, crying out that he had come for Miss Emily Faraday. There had been an accident, he said, and she was to be taken to the man who would explain what had happened, and what was about to happen. That man was Martin Crupe.

He was speaking again, his voice rasping with the effects of his chest cold. "Now, since I am too ill for the task, today you will clean the operating theater."

Emily blinked in surprise. Except for poor witless Dudley, who was needed to move heavy objects and deal with the animals, she had been warned that the rest of the household staff were never allowed inside that evil place the doctor called his theater, not even to clean, a task that fell to the doctor's assistant.

Crupe went on. "No one is to know I sent you into the theater, do you understand? You will go in and sweep the floor and scrub down the operating table while the staff and the students are having breakfast so no one will see you. If anyone finds out you were there, it will be the worse for you, do you understand?"

She nodded, wondering if Crupe had not yet told the doctor about her running away the previous night. Perhaps if she performed the task of cleaning the theater well she would be spared the ordeal of facing him.

Crupe produced a large wooden ring containing three keys, one of which he slipped from the ring before handing it to her. "This key is for the outer door, and this one for the vestibule door. You'll find what you need in the cupboard near the door. Look sharp, now." He slipped the third key into his waistcoat pocket. "Return the keys only to me."

Emily took the key ring and hurried from the room. She had not yet eaten breakfast herself, and since the doctor was away, he would have no need of the theater today, but Crupe clearly wanted the cleaning done immediately.

Usually the doctor's students came to the theater in the mornings for their ghastly lessons, and he worked there alone in the afternoons and often in the evenings, too, doing what was referred to in hushed tones as his "research." The doctor rarely treated patients himself nowadays, except for a few important families he had served for years, like Sir Edward and his family.

The house consisted of two wings, connected by a short hallway, with the theater set off by itself and reached through a heavily studded door which led into a small vestibule. She used the second key to enter the theater and stood on the threshold, staring at the cavernous room before her.

Her eyes went immediately to the most sinister item of furniture. A long table, sturdily built, was bolted to the floor in the center of the room. The table was surrounded by benches, all on a raised dais, from which the students could observe as Dr. Stoddard carved up a cadaver and lectured on the proper way to do it.

Emily had heard it whispered belowstairs that the bodies were those of executed murderers, and she wondered fearfully if their spirits lingered behind in that evil room.

Her worst nightmares had always been about the poor animals—the living, breathing creatures who were sacrificed on that table. Dudley had said the animals were kept in the cellar, which perhaps could be reached through the door on the far side of this chamber. She remembered the third key that Crupe had removed from the ring, and wondered why he did not want her to enter the animals' quarters. That was Dudley's domain, of course, but the precaution of removing the key troubled her.

Despite its atmosphere of death and the musty odor of decay that hung in the air, the theater was the lightest, brightest room in the house, with a huge skylight overhead spilling a cascade of sunlight down onto the table with its ominous stains, some of which were repeated on the surrounding floor. She dared not imagine what the room looked like at night, when the lamps weren't lit. Pinpricks of stars and a thin crescent moon would create just enough light in the canopy of the night to produce shadows. Oh, the grotesque, ghastly shadows there would be in here at midnight!

There were cupboards along one wall of the theater, floor to ceiling, broken by a wide counter upon which were neatly laid out an array of tools. Rows of knives and hacksaw blades, several handsaws, even an ax with its handle wrapped in dirty bandages, as though it were wounded, but she guessed the bindings were to soak up the blood from an amputation, which might make the handle slippery.

The sunlight slanting down from above reflected on a glass-fronted cupboard that contained various potions in apothecary jars, whose rainbow prisms exchanged blinding rays of light with the blades of the arsenal of cutting tools.

Another wall was filled with bookshelves, tightly packed, and in one corner of the room was the doctor's desk, carved in majestic proportions of mahogany.

She was aware of other items in the operating theater, but as she removed a broom from the cupboard and began to sweep between the spectators' benches, she could not take her eyes off the gleaming knives. She glanced at them frequently as she swept the floor and scrubbed the operating table, then got down on her hands and knees to scrub at the stains beneath the table.

Waves of weakness washed over her, and she remembered she had not eaten since supper the previous evening. Resting for a moment, she heard the muffled sound of dogs barking. The animals were kept beyond that other locked door, which she believed opened to a flight of stairs descending to the cellar. Doris had told her that there was an outside entrance to the cellar, from the back alley, but that door was always locked and barred.

Forcing her aching limbs to obey, Emily finished scrubbing and rose to her feet. The apothecary jars and bottles and the knife blades all gleamed and appeared not to need any further cleaning or polishing, so she put away the bucket and brushes and fumbled in her apron pocket for the keys to lock the doors behind her.

As she passed by the third door leading to the cellar, she heard a sound that caused the wooden ring to slip from her fingers and clatter to the floor. Above the muted barking of the dogs came a faint cry that was almost, but not quite, human. A long-drawn-out wail of anguish like the lament of a lost soul that caused her heart to leap into her throat.

Emily hesitated, her gaze fixed in fascinated horror on the cellar door. Surely that sound could not have been made by an animal. She listened intently, but the cry was not repeated. Still she was reluctant to leave. Had poor simple Dudley somehow been locked in with the dogs? But surely someone would have missed him. No, she must have mistaken the howling of a dog for a human cry of pain.

She started to walk away, and the cry was repeated.

Heart thudding, she ran back to the cellar door and pressed her ear to the heavy wood. "Is someone there?" she called.

The sound of her voice set the dogs off barking again,

drowning whatever response could have been made, and also masking the opening of the vestibule door and a footfall across the wooden floor of the theater.

Emily gasped as a heavy hand descended on her shoulder and a deep voice growled, "What do you think you're doing?"

Chapter 5

BRIONY POURED A small quantity of milk into a delicate china cup, then picked up the teapot.

Across the breakfast table Rupert stabbed a sausage with his fork. "Isn't it punishment enough to lock me out of your room? Am I also to be given the silent treatment?"

She paused, teapot in midair. "Mrs. Winthrop seems to have passed the crisis. Dr. Stoddard and Edward had an early breakfast and left for River Court before I came downstairs. Your newspaper is on the sideboard. Shall I ring for a footman to pass it to you?"

"I'd really prefer one of your screaming rages to either the silence or the sarcasm."

"The time for that is past, Rupert. I told you I would not stand for another infidelity and I meant it. I shall maintain the facade of our marriage for the sake of appearances, but you lost the right to expect more from me when you chose to flout your marriage vows."

"Bri . . . a moment of weakness . . . she meant nothing to me, I swear."

"And obviously I mean nothing to you, either, or you wouldn't have hurt me a second time. I forgave you once, but never again. If you prefer to maintain separate residences, so be it. Otherwise, I wish to be left alone."

Rupert stood up, his face livid. "Dammit, I won't be treated like a lodger in my own house, nor will I put up with a marriage in name only. May I remind you that refusal of conjugal rights is grounds for divorce?"

"Then divorce me, Rupert," Briony responded quietly. "I don't fear the stigma of divorce for the simple reason I shall never wish to marry again. You, on the other hand, might find your political career in gravest jeopardy should you decide to drag us through the divorce courts. The wives of your constituents may not be able to vote, but you can be sure they will influence their husbands' selection of candidate. And may I remind you that, under the law, adultery is also grounds for divorce—and if you institute divorce proceedings, I shall file a countersuit and name your whore as co-respondent.''

He clapped his hand to his forehead and groaned, ''God's truth, Bri, what are we doing to each other? And where in the name of all that's holy did you get such radical ideas? Look, this whole situation is getting out of hand. Please . . . forgive me. I swear I'll never look at another woman as long as I live.''

''That's what you said last time. I warned you then I would not tolerate a second betrayal. There's nothing more to be said, Rupert.''

He stared at her for a moment. ''I'll be at my club when you come to your senses.''

Briony sat for several minutes staring at his empty chair, feeling desolate, bereft. Then, knowing she must occupy herself with other matters in order to maintain her sanity, she went to see how Mrs. Winthrop was feeling.

She had just left her housekeeper when Edward returned. She followed him into the library, where he stood warming his hands before a blazing fire. It was obvious from his troubled expression that his visit to the doctor's house had not gone well.

''Did you speak with the girl, Edward?'' Briony asked.

He shook his head. ''The doctor appeared genuinely surprised to hear I had seen his manservant drag her into the house and that her head was bleeding. He told me that he left the matter of the household staff to Crupe, who is a sort of general factotum rather than a butler—and that housemaids come and go. Stoddard himself rarely encounters them about the house, that at best they are faceless creatures who perform certain tasks as unobtrusively as possible. He wasn't aware of a maid who sounded educated, refined.

When we reached his house on River Court, he immediately sent for Crupe and asked him in my presence about the incident the previous evening.''

"And what did Crupe say?"

"That the girl in question—Faraday—had sneaked out of the house to meet a man and that undoubtedly the man caused her injury. That he, Crupe, had merely found her on the street and brought her home.''

"Did you ask to see her?"

"Yes. But Crupe said she had been troublesome from the start and that after having one of the students treat her, he had given her a month's wages and sent her packing. He had no idea where she had gone.''

Briony squeezed her brother's hand. "I'm sorry, Edward. But you did all you could.''

"Ah, but there's more. As I was leaving the house, another young skivvy was whitewashing the front steps, and I asked about Faraday. The girl seemed very frightened but whispered to me that she shared a room with Emily Faraday, who had told her she had lived most of her life in China.''

"China? How interesting. . . . How did she come to be a servant in the doctor's house?''

"Apparently she returned to this country with her father not long ago. Her father was killed, leaving unpaid debts— apparently some owing to Crupe, who gave her the house-maid's job. I asked the skivvy where Emily Faraday might have gone now that she'd left the doctor's employ, and she gave me a baffled look. I was about to question her further when Crupe came out of the house and ordered her inside. Bri, I'm convinced the man was lying and Emily Faraday is still in that house. He just didn't want me to talk to her.''

Briony sighed. "And you're determined to find out if she's still there. I'd try to talk you out of it, but I keep remembering all those bedraggled puppies and kittens—yes and beggar children, too—you used to bring home. What do you intend to do?''

"Go back to River Court and get inside the house.''

"Edward, you can't simply break in! Why not speak to Dr. Stoddard again?''

"He made it clear that he has nothing to do with the household staff and that Crupe's word is his bond. But don't worry, Bri, I shan't break in. Stoddard is teaching medical students there—I shall enroll as one of his students."

Briony blinked in astonishment. "Medical training? You, Edward? Forgive me, dear, but you're far too tenderhearted. Besides, people of our class simply don't enter the medical profession, and Stoddard knows it. Wouldn't he be suspicious?"

"Not necessarily. He knows I have nothing but an inherited title, no income beyond a small trust fund and what Rupert provides."

Her brows creased as she contemplated the present condition of her marriage to Rupert. How long would he continue to support either of them if she refused to be a wife to him? "But why on earth would you toss away your Oxford degree to enter such a disgusting profession? You might just as well become a butcher."

Edward grinned. "You make it sound as though I'm actually going to become a doctor—I'm not."

"What you should become is an actor—you do so love to dramatize everything. You'll probably discover the girl in question has a brutal lover and doesn't welcome your interfering in her life."

"We shall just have to see, won't we?"

The doorbell rang, and from out on the street came a chorus of children's voices singing Christmas carols. As the sweet strains of "The Holly and the Ivy" filled the frosty air, Briony considered the irony of all of the problems that beset her in this, the season of peace. First her housekeepers' illness, then her husband's unfaithfulness, now her quixotic brother's quest to rescue one Emily Faraday, who spoke like a lady, worked as a skivvy, and claimed to have spent her life in the mysterious Orient.

Chapter 6

PHIN TSU AWOKE in the clammy darkness, her mouth parted in the silent scream that had jolted her from her dream.

Her narrow bunk swayed with the motion of the ship, timbers creaked, and the sea slapped gently against the hull. A faint glow of starlight defined the small circle of the porthole.

Her breathing gradually returned to normal, although her heart continued to pound. A moment passed before she remembered that she was aboard a trader out of Hong Kong, bound for Singapore on the second part of her long journey to England.

By the time she readjusted to the confinement of the tiny cabin and considered again the enormity of her quest, she had forgotten the details of the dream that had awakened her. But her nightmares now were all variations of the same theme, and that was her urgent need to find her half sister, Emily Faraday.

The dreams had begun shortly after the night the chief eunuch came to tell her of her mother's death. Phin had been thirteen and had known no world other than the House of Delights within the Forbidden City.

She remembered the smooth, hairless face of the chief eunuch, floating moonlike above her as he told her that the children of favored concubines usually were allowed to remain, but that in her case he feared what would become of her, because of her mixed heritage.

"To create a mixed-race child is to violate the sacred

trust of one's ancestors,'' he had said, ''for what is different and unique to each people is lost.''

There had been no need for him to remind her of this, for throughout her childhood she had been tormented about her round eyes, big feet, and extraordinary height (she was five feet five) by all who saw her, except for her mother and the chief eunuch, who had taken pity on her. Perhaps he, being only half a man, had understood the tribulations of a child only half Chinese.

Now he lowered his voice and said, ''Only your mother's position as most favored concubine has saved you thus far, but now I fear for your life, child. Therefore, I shall risk my position here and perhaps my own life to see that you leave immediately. But before you go, I must tell you that you are not alone in the world.''

''But you said my mother has gone to the happy place. I *am* alone in this world,'' she protested through her tears.

''Your father still lives, and you have a half sister.''

Phin listened silently now.

''He was an important man, an Englishman of high rank, named Fletcher Faraday. He was recalled to England shortly after your mother found herself with child, and there married a woman of his own race, who also gave birth to a daughter, Emily. When he returned to China, several years later, he attempted to find your mother again, but she had fled to the Forbidden City, beyond his reach. Your father never learned of your birth.''

''My mother feared he would have me killed because I was female?'' Phin knew well the fate of so many female babies throughout most of China.

''Worse—a half-foreign female,'' the chief eunuch responded. ''It is a tribute to your mother's beauty and sensual skills that she became a favored concubine, burdened as she was with a mixed-race child. And it is also a tribute to your own charm, little one, that you were allowed to live. I was beguiled by you and would allow no one to harm you, although to my regret I was not always able to shield you from the taunts of the others.''

"But why did not my mother tell me about my English father—or about my half sister?"

"Shame, little one," the chief eunuch replied sagely. "Your mother felt deep shame that she had lain with a foreign devil."

"So they do not know I exist," Phin said, feeling a faint stirring of connection to someone other than her mother. Now at last the mystery of her round eyes was solved. A distant, unknown world beckoned. "But *I* know of *them*. Uncle, tell me what shall I do with this knowledge?"

"Child, I do not know what the future holds for you. But if our society shuns you, perhaps you can find a place in your father's world, and if he rejects you, then there is the slight hope that your half sister will help you. You will know when the time comes for you to seek your father and half sister, which will either be when all other resources have failed you, or you have received a sign telling you to go to them."

"But how can I leave the Forbidden City—where can I go?" she asked, suddenly afraid.

"Word of your mother's death will travel slowly through the labyrinth of palace passages—I shall see to that," he replied. "By the time the emperor learns she is dead, you will be gone."

He helped her dress in the black pajamas, straw hat, and sandals of a peasant. Then he folded his arms and regarded her sternly. "You will never see me again. My presence in your life has ended as surely as that of your mother. But what we have taught you will be our gift to you forever. Our voices will caution and guide you. The skills you have recently learned from me will be your main means of survival. Do you understand?"

She nodded. Her lessons in the pleasures of the flesh had begun shortly after her mother became ill. The chief eunuch had devoted many hours to her initiation into the erotic arts, and now she saw that he had been teaching her how to survive.

"Always remember the power women wield over men, and how to use it," he said. "What you have learned from your observations of the concubines and your mother, but above all what I have taught you, will set you apart from other women, making you irresistible. Despite your round eyes and unbound feet, you are very beautiful. There is about you an exotic appeal, a mystical allure that even I am unable to define. If the emperor had not been in poor health for so long, doubtless you would have come to his attention. Now take this pouch, which contains some of your mother's jewels. With these you can pay for food and lodgings until you find a safe haven.''

To her surprise, he then embraced her, urged her to pray to the goddess Kwan Yin to watch over her, and bade her farewell.

She was spirited out of the Forbidden City that night, concealed in a large basket strapped to the back of the donkey of a departing priest, who stole her pouch of jewels and delivered her into the hands of a wandering fortune-teller, who in turn sold her to a wealthy silk merchant. By the time she was fourteen, Phin Tsu had had ample practice in the sensual arts taught by the chief eunuch and was almost as proficient as her mother had been in the delights of the flesh.

Phin missed her mother terribly but tried not to grieve for her, because her mother had told her many times that she was tired of living at the whim of an aging and infirm tyrant and longed to join her ancestors in the happy place.

Shortly after leaving the Forbidden City, Phin began to dream about her half sister, Emily. Her father, whom she pictured in the kaleidoscope of her mind as a figure shrouded in shadows, did not enter these dreams at first. But it seemed that a hundred lanterns lighted a pathway through her dreamworld to guide her to her half sister, whom she saw bathed in golden light, with tawny hair and azure eyes but without the ugly long nose of the foreigner.

Phin's daytime dreams brought her half sister into even sharper focus. Like herself, Emily would have long, high-arched feet, and Phin thought how nice it would be not to be the only woman striding when the others tottered on their mutilated ''lily'' feet. Emily would be tall, too, perhaps even taller than Phin. But Phin dared not hope that Emily might share her own burning ambition of autonomy, to be mistress of her own unfettered fate. To have the freedom to pick and choose, come and go, like any man, yet retain all the feminine powers and gifts and secret strengths. Ah, was it possible?

For several years Phin lived as one of the silk merchant's concubines, a role she was trained for and regarded as an honorable profession. Since the silk merchant was elderly and frequently impotent, her duties were minimal. During this period she merely dreamed about and imagined her father and half sister. Some inner wisdom advised that the time was not yet ripe to seek them out. She still had much to learn about their world. Was she not a woman of two worlds with knowledge of only one? Besides, she was reluctant to give up her life of perfumed ease. Few Eurasians ever aspired to such luxury.

But the dreams continued, and when another, more sinister, symbol appeared in them, she went to a spirit woman to ask their meaning. Phin described to her the dark water surrounding her sister in the dream, and how she always awoke in terror of what was about to happen.

The spirit woman listened closely, her tiny black eyes in her wrinkled yellow face lighting up with comprehension when Phin mentioned the dark water, then told her that her dreams of a lost sister were easily explained.

"Are you yourself not only a despised female but also of mixed blood? A double burden," she said. "It is a miracle that you were allowed to live."

The spirit woman explained that Phin's dreams represented not, as she imagined, dark water threatening her sister, but her own escape from being drowned as an infant, when perhaps other sisters had not been so lucky.

But Phin knew her dream had nothing to do with the ghosts of drowned baby girls—and everything to do with Emily. As time went on the desire to meet her grew from a tiny seed to a rapidly opening blossom.

Phin had already begun to make plans to go to Peiping to see if her father and Emily were still there, when the Opium

Wars broke out in the south. Instantly her life of ease ended. The silk merchant fled, abandoning her to the confusion and terror that followed.

Yet she had survived, thanks mainly to a man who had saved her from becoming part of the spoils of war. He was Caucasian, a soldier of fortune who fought a river bandit for her.

Brent Carlisle was an enigma in a land where inscrutability and face-saving were fine arts. At first Phin had been terrified of him, with his flashing steel-silver eyes and wild mane of dark hair that curled and waved about broad shoulders. He towered over her, fully six and a half feet in height, and brought the river bandits to their knees with such swift efficiency that Phin feared what her own fate at his hands would be. However, he did not kill the bandits; he merely incapacitated them. Three men lay on the deck of the junk, bleeding and resigned to their fate. But the foreigner merely swept her into his arms and leapt aboard his own boat, which he had brought alongside the bandits' craft in order to board it.

He took her to a magnificent house built beside the river, where apparently he lived alone, and showed her to a room. Trembling, she sank to the floor and covered her face with her hands, expecting she knew not what. But he spoke gently in his incomprehensible foreign tongue, which later she would learn was American, and left her.

All night long she waited for him to come and claim his reward, and just before dawn, unable to bear the tension, she crept out and prowled through the deserted rooms.

When she could not find him in the house, she went out into the garden, which was built in terraces down to the river, and there saw him silhouetted against a pink gilded dawn. He stood motionless, his head raised toward the heavens, his arms hanging at his sides with the palms of his hands turned upward. Unsure how to interpret the barbarian's strange pose, although it appeared to be an attitude of despair, Phin quickly withdrew.

For two weeks he did not approach her. He provided food and clothing and, when he left the house, a Chinese guard named Liang Wu, with whom he conversed in fluent Manchu. Brent Carlisle rarely addressed Phin directly. Still she felt safe, as if she were on a peaceful island, while all around the conflict raged.

As her gratitude grew, so did her curiosity about this foreigner. Was he not like the other men she had known? Perhaps he preferred boys? But he brought neither boys nor pleasure women to the house, and on the rare occasion she had caught him looking at her with lust in his eyes, he had quickly turned away.

For her part Phin was bewildered by her feelings toward this man. Although she had been brought up to revere Oriental physical beauty and knew she should feel a natural revulsion for his alien Caucasian features, still his courage and his kindness moved her deeply, and she was drawn to the inner man, if not yet to his looks. But he puzzled her. Why had he saved her from the river pirates if not to make her his concubine? She decided she must learn if he felt desire for her.

She waited until he was asleep, then crept into his room. Naked, her body perfumed with jasmine, she slipped into his bed.

Her touch was silken soft, as light as the flutter of butterfly wings. She brought his manhood to pulsing life before he came fully awake, then stifled his muttered exclamation with her lips, her tongue darting between his teeth.

There was a moment when she thought he might fling her away, when his huge body grew as stiff and unyielding as an oak. Then with a swift intake of breath, his arms clasped her, pulling her on top of him and impaling her on an organ as hard as jade.

She gasped, her own pleasure as intense as his. Rising and falling like the moon-drawn tides, she felt enchantment for the first time and with it the startling realization that, like her mother, if she was not careful, she might fall under the spell of a foreign devil. As they came floating back to earth, Phin vowed to zealously guard against such foolishness.

Afterward, he appeared angry, although at himself, not her.

He rose from the bed and paced about the room for a while, then returned to where she lay. Taking her hands in his, he spoke to her in her own language, revealing that he spoke at least two Chinese dialects fluently, since she had heard him speak Manchu to Liang.

"I never intended to keep you here, only to save you from the river pirates. But it is not safe for you to leave yet. When it is, I will take you wherever you wish to go. You have a family somewhere?"

She shook her head, dismayed that she had not pleased him.

He said, "Very well, you can stay here for the time being. But this is a temporary arrangement only, and there will be no repetition of what happened between us tonight, do you understand?"

Phin did not understand, but it didn't matter, because although he seemed to fight some inner battle with himself every night, she always ended up in his arms, and he seemed to take as much pleasure in her body as she did in his.

Early one morning as they lay entwined in each other's arms she said, "You speak my language so well. Yet when you first brought me here you addressed me only in your own language. I am puzzled by this."

His steel-silver eyes seemed to focus on a place only he could see, and he replied, "I wished to keep distance between us. If there was no conversation, there could be no closeness. Or so I thought. But once again I did not pay enough heed to human frailty or to the unrelenting power of human desire."

The meaning of his words escaped her. She decided that barbarians' minds did not work in the same way as Oriental minds. Besides, she had brought up the subject of language for a specific reason and so decided to ignore his odd ramblings. She said, "I would like to learn your language. Will you teach me?"

He was surprised at how quickly she mastered English, and at her interest in Western culture.

Would she have begged him to allow her to stay with him, she wondered, if she had not had that most compelling dream about Emily and their father?

Emily appeared in the dream first, and again Phin saw her across a black stretch of water. But now her half sister was surrounded by daggers and a dark mist that closed in, entombing her. As Phin struggled through water that foamed and raged, she was caught in a deadly current that prevented her from reaching Emily.

At this point in the dream Phin was caught in a violent whirlpool and sucked down. As the whirlpool tossed her free, she looked down into the dark water and saw, clearly for the first time, the face of her English father. He regarded her sadly, his lips moving in a silent plea as he slowly sank to the bottom of the river.

Phin did not have to go to a spirit woman this time. She knew she had received a sign that she must go at once to her father and Emily. Strange, she had always believed that when she finally began her quest to find them, it would be because she needed their help; never once had she imagined that she would be the rescuer.

She asked Brent to inquire about them, although she did not tell him who they were, or about her dream, and he brought her the news that the Faradays had returned to England a few months earlier. She knew then what she must do.

How sad she was, the last night she lay in Brent's arms and he made love to her so tenderly, as if his body, if not his mind, suspected it might be the last time.

She lay curled against him, his arm encircling her like the strong branch of a tree, his breath creating warm eddies against her brow as he spoke softly, "Where are you, Phin? You just left me."

"Ah, no, my love. I am still here." She caressed his firm pectoral muscles, pressed her lips to his warm skin, marveling that she who had never been moved by any man, who had always believed she generated her own sexual energy and response, now trembled with need at the mere sight of this man, whose touch excited her beyond ecstasy. "But . . . I must soon leave you."

He exhaled slowly. "I knew this moment would come. I suppose I hoped it wouldn't be for a while yet. The time we could be together was always destined to be fleeting; it could not be otherwise. Tell me what you need, and where you must go. I will help you."

She was taken aback that he accepted this so easily, and more than a little chagrined that he could let her go without a word of protest.

He rolled over, so that he was above her, and pushed aside the curtain of her long black hair. "I shall miss you."

"And I you," she whispered, her voice husky with desire. He had taught her his language, and perhaps because it was a part of him, when she spoke English it became the language of romance, of love that was more than sex, of loyalty and devotion that was offered without thought of reciprocation. Despite her best intentions, she had allowed him to become too important to her and now would have to tear herself free of him. At the thought of leaving him, tears welled up and slipped down her cheeks.

Brent caught her tears with his lips, their mouths connected again, and the kiss was filled with urgency and yearning. Their flesh fused again and moved in dearly familiar ways. They lingered in that realm of the senses they had made their own until the first pink streaks of dawn lit the skies. Then Phin rose and made tea, needing to perform some mundane task in order to hide her pain at having to part from him.

He watched her, his eyes brooding. At length he said, "We could not have let this idyll continue much longer, because I can never marry you."

She looked at him in surprise. "I have never expected you to. We are from different worlds. A marriage is not just between a man and a woman. It involves all of their ancestors and generations of the unborn."

"But part of you is from my world, Phin. The impediment is not with you, it's with me, with my way of life. An expatriate soldier of fortune living by his wits in a country where his very appearance makes him an enemy surely has no right to ask a woman to share his life.''

"My love, I am far more of an outcast than you. I am neither Chinese nor Caucasian.''

"You are the most beautiful woman on earth, and if it were not forbidden, I could learn to love you, Phin," Brent said. "But the truth is . . . I was married before I met you.''

She looked bewildered. "But you can have concubine, yes?'' A favored concubine in China often had more power than a wife, so she did not understand his concern.

"No, Phin. Legally and morally, in our society a man can have only one wife. I am bound for life by the vows I made, and to my shame I violated those vows when I made love to you.''

Bending her head to hide her tears, she poured the tea into delicate china bowls, knowing that she had secretly hoped they would not have to part, that he would accompany her on her quest to find her half sister.

Placing the tea before him, she whispered, "Our time together has come to an end, then. We must accept what is our fate, for we cannot change it.''

He stood up so suddenly the fragile tea bowl before him crashed to the floor. Catching her tightly in his arms, he held her so close she could scarcely breathe. "Where are you going, Phin? Is there another man? Someone to whom you will now return? I would be relieved to know you have a safe haven to return to.''

She raised her head to look deep into his eyes so that he would know she was speaking the truth. "You mean another lover. No, there is no other lover. I must travel to England to find my English father and my half sister.''

"Fletcher and Emily Faraday? The people you asked me about?''

She nodded.

Cradling her face between his large hands, he looked down at her so intently that she knew he was imprinting her face in his memory. "I hope you will find great happiness with your family.''

He brushed her forehead with his lips and added softly, "You have given me far more than you will ever realize."

She clung to him until he said heavily, "I must go to see about a cargo for the general." He didn't have to explain this, as Phin knew Brent hired out to fight as a soldier.

He added, "I shan't return. I would find a second parting too painful. But I will make arrangements for you to sail to England as soon as possible. Liang Wu will accompany you to the ship and will see you have everything you need. Goodbye, Phin."

There was a terrible finality to his words, despite the anguish in his eyes. She was too proud to beg him to accompany her.

Phin left Kwangchow the following day.

Her heart ached for all she was leaving behind, but somewhere across the dark waters her half sister was in terrible danger and needed her.

Chapter 7

· ·

EMILY TURNED FROM the cellar door to look into the angry stare of Crupe's manservant. Godfrey's position in the doctor's household was something of a mystery to her, certainly he was too uncouth to be a butler, yet he instilled fear into the rest of the staff and answered to no one but the doctor and Crupe.

Godfrey shook Emily roughly before pushing her away from the locked door leading from the operating theater to the cellar steps.

"What do you think you're doing? Mr. Crupe told you to clean the theater, not go poking into places where you've no business."

"I heard a sound coming from behind that door," Emily said.

At that moment a muffled chorus of barking rose from the cellar below. Godfrey's gargoyle-like features twisted into an expression of derision. "You heard the laboratory animals, stupid wench."

"But I'm sure I heard a person, too. I was afraid Dudley might have locked himself in."

Godfrey's eyes went immediately to the keyhole, and Emily followed his gaze. For one eerie instant she had the unnerving feeling that behind that keyhole an eye watched them.

"Dudley's not allowed to use that staircase. He enters the cellar from the backyard."

"Perhaps I was mistaken," Emily said uncertainly. "I've finished cleaning. I was just leaving."

"Give me the keys and go, then."

Emily glanced down at the large wooden key ring in her hand. "But Mr. Crupe told me to return the keys only to him."

"Mr. Crupe is very poorly. He's taken to his bed." Godfrey drew himself up to his impressive height and added pompously, "I shall be assuming his duties until he's well."

Hesitantly Emily handed him the key ring. She wondered if in view of Crupe's illness he had not reported to Dr. Stoddard that she had again tried to run away. Perhaps she would be spared the doctor's wrath. She hurried from the theater, glad to leave the icy chill of the vast chamber, not to mention that disembodied eye behind the keyhole.

At noon she had finished her other morning chores and, ravenously hungry, went to the kitchen for her first meal of the day. As a mere housemaid, she was not allowed to eat at the table reserved for the senior household staff. Instead she ate with Doris and Dudley in a cramped pantry.

As usual, Dudley stared in glassy-eyed concentration at the food he transferred rapidly from tin plate to slack mouth. Doris was already too exhausted to do more than nibble a few bites of bread and cheese, but she looked up in surprise as Emily appeared. "I thought you'd got the sack, Emily. When I was doing the steps this morning, a toff asked me where you'd gone."

"A toff?" Emily reached for a thick slice of bread.

"Nice-looking young man with reddish-gold hair."

"Sir Edward? How kind of him to inquire, but what made him think I'd been sacked, I wonder?" Emily scraped a patch of blue-green mold from her cheese.

Doris shrugged tiredly, her head drooping over her bony chest. "Dunno. But he was sure Mr. Crupe had sent you packing."

The bread was at least two days old and required a great deal of chewing. What a far cry this fare was from the delicate and subtle dishes of China to which she had been accustomed, Emily thought, but she knew she had to keep up her strength and so doggedly gnawed on the stale bread.

Snatches of conversation at the main table in the adjacent room drifted through the open pantry door.

". . . and the doctor put Mr. Crupe in a room next to his. Very concerned he is, and no wonder. Mr. Crupe is very poorly indeed. He won't be back on his feet soon, you mark my words."

Godfrey's voice put in, "We'll all have to pull our weight while he's out of commission. I shall have my work cut out for me, and no mistake."

"What about me?" Cook demanded petulantly. "The doctor's taken in another student. A live-in. That means more work for me and my girls."

One of the parlor maids giggled. "A lovely-looking chap he is, too. I shan't mind doing Sir Edward's room for him."

"Seems a bit odd that a titled toff would want to learn medicine," Cook said.

"Not only a title," Godfrey put in, "but an Oxford degree too, I heard Mr. Crupe say."

"Here . . ." Cook called shrilly, looking through the open pantry door. "Haven't you three finished eating yet? There's work to be done, so stop your dawdling."

Dudley, who was terrified of her, jumped to his feet and ran. Doris followed. Emily remained to finish her bread and cheese, knowing it would be a long time until supper, and even then she would not eat until after everyone else in the household had been fed, the tables cleared, and the dishes washed.

As she was about to leave the kitchen, Godfrey stopped her. "You, Faraday, you'll clean the operating theater until Mr. Crupe is well. Come for the keys tomorrow morning."

For the rest of the day Emily was too busy to wonder about Sir Edward Darnell, but before she fell into an exhausted sleep that night, she allowed herself to consider the fact that he had inquired about her, and to hope she might enlist his aid in leaving this terrible house.

The following morning Cook informed her that Godfrey had not returned from his "night work." He and the coachmen were often gone at night, according to Doris, who had seen them depart in the shuttered carriage at midnight and sometimes did not return until dawn.

"I'm supposed to clean the theater," Emily said. "Do you know if he left the keys for me?"

"The theater keys?" Cook asked incredulously. "He'd not leave them lying about. The doctor would have a fit."

Emily was busy with her other chores when Godfrey returned, his mud-spattered boots leaving a damp and dirty trail across the floor she had just polished with beeswax. He wore a dark caped overcoat, a muffler swathed about his thick neck, and a black cap pulled low over his forehead. He seemed to bring a cemetery chill with him, and Emily shivered, remembering that Doris had hinted that not all of the doctor's cadavers were acquired legally. Had he been out robbing graves? She shrank back as he approached.

Looming over her, he dropped the distinctive wooden ring that housed the operating theater keys with a clatter on the floor beside her. "Get the theater cleaned and be right quick about it. The doctor is giving a lesson this morning." He gave an evil grin. "His lads are in for a rare treat today."

It was only when Emily unlocked the theater door that she realized Godfrey had left the third key, which unlocked the door leading to the cellar, on the wooden ring.

As she dusted the apothecary jars, she glanced several times in the direction of the locked door. The dogs were quiet this morning, and the silence was oppressive. After a moment Emily nervously began to hum as she worked, a Christmas carol in honor of the season, and before long she was singing the words.

Halfway through "Good King Wenceslas" she thought she heard a deep sigh from the direction of the locked door. The words of the carol faltered and died on her lips.

The sound was repeated.

Emily raised her head and listened.

For a few seconds only the sound of her own breathing broke the silence. Her gaze fixed on the door, she began to sing again. Seconds later a low voice, little more than a whisper, joined in.

The feather duster slipped from Emily's fingers. Whoever was singing was directly behind the door and . . . yes, *there was an eye at the keyhole!*

But as she stopped singing, so did the accompanying voice. The eye had also disappeared. Had she imagined both the voice and the eye? Somewhere down in the cellar a dog howled mournfully, but there was no human sound.

Nervously she resumed dusting, backing farther away from the locked door as she did so. There was no doubt now that there was someone there, watching her through the keyhole. Every nerve in her body tensed. She wanted to run from the theater but had not yet scrubbed the operating table.

She carried her bucket and scrubbing brush to the table, but before she could begin, the vestibule door opened and Godfrey appeared, carrying a rigid, sheet-wrapped object that could only be a body.

Emily gasped, feeling all the blood in her veins turn to ice. Godfrey made straight for the table and dropped his burden with a dull thud. Before Emily could gather her wits, he yanked the sheet away, and to her horror she found herself looking down at the body of an adolescent boy. There was a bluish cast to the waxy skin, and the eyes were wide and staring.

Godfrey gave her a malicious grin. "Never seen a corpse before, is it? Well, you'd better get used to it while you're working for the doctor. Now get yourself out of here before the lads come for their lessons."

Emily hastily gathered her cleaning materials, but before she could make her exit, the first of the medical students began to file into the theater and take their places on the benches. She had to stand aside and wait for an opportunity to pass through the small vestibule.

Suddenly she looked up into the warm gaze of Edward Darnell. "Hello—Miss Faraday, isn't it? How are you? I was concerned about the cut on your head."

"Sir Edward . . ." Emily didn't know what to say. She wanted to beg him to help her escape, but two other students pressed close behind him, gazing at them in amusement. She murmured, "I'm all right, thank you." At the same time she implored him with her eyes to disbelieve her.

He bent close to her ear and whispered, "We must talk."

She nodded in the instant before he was swept into the theater by the tide of students. As she went back to the kitchen, she wondered how Sir Edward would deal with the postmortem on the youth's body. It seemed a ghastly introduction to the world of healing for a brand-new student.

All day long she hoped she would see Sir Edward again, but the opportunity did not arise. She heard later that Dr. Stoddard kept his students in the theater most of the day and then sent them to their rooms to write reports on the dissection of the cadaver.

The following morning she approached the theater with much trepidation, not knowing what she might find. Mercifully, the body of the youth was gone, but she closed her eyes as she scrubbed the table, imagining the corpse still lying there.

When she had finished with the table, she began to scrub the floor around it, glancing from time to time in the direction of the locked door. The dogs were noisy, and it was impossible to detect any human voice above their barking and whining.

The distressed cry of the dogs began to play on her nerves, and almost without thinking, she again began to sing. Before she finished the first line of "God Rest Ye Merry, Gentlemen," the voice joined in.

Emily stopped singing.

Then, distinctly, she heard the words, "Ah, dear God!" uttered with such soul-wrenching anguish that her heart turned over.

Dropping the scrubbing brush, she ran to the door and pressed close. "Is someone there? Are you all right?"

There was no response.

"Don't be afraid," Emily called. "I want to help you. Are you ill? Do you need something?"

A sound like a muffled sob was her only answer.

She was shaking with fear but felt compelled to say, "I know you're there. Why won't you answer me? Tell me what's wrong."

After a long pause she heard a hoarse whisper. "Go away."

Some of her fear dissipated. The voice did not sound like that of a madman. Who was he, and why was he locked in the cellar with the dogs? The key to the door was still on the ring, but she did not feel brave enough to unlock the door and face whoever lurked behind it. She went back to finish her work. There was no further sound from behind the door.

During her midday meal she studied Dudley. When he spoke he sounded like a child, and it had definitely not been his voice that spoke to her from behind the door. But he must know who it was who lurked there.

"Dudley," she said gently, "tell me about your charges in the cellar."

"Dogs," he said, munching a cold bacon sandwich. "Cats and rats and mice and guinea pigs in cages. Don't like them. Like the dogs." A tear trickled down his cheek. "Don't like it when they don't come back."

"From the theater, you mean?"

He nodded. "Don't like it when they're hurt, neither."

Emily shivered, not wanting to hear more about the experiments on the animals. "Tell me about the man in the cellar, Dudley. Does he stay with the animals?"

Doris kicked her under the table, and her frightened eyes darted in the direction of the main table, but Cook and Godfrey were laughing together about something, and Emily was sure they were not listening to the conversation in the pantry.

Dudley regarded her blankly.

"You know—the man who lives down in the cellar," Emily prompted.

He shook his head. "No."

She wasn't sure if he meant there was no man, or if he was refusing to tell her about him.

Doris muttered under her breath, "There's always an extra tray. The doctor takes it himself."

"What does he do with it? Does he take it to the cellar?"

"Dunno." Doris bent her head over her food again, and it was clear she believed she had already said too much.

That evening Emily waited until just before the doctor and his students were due to eat dinner and then slipped into the dining room carrying a copper coal skuttle, as if to bank the fire, although this was Dudley's task, and it had clearly recently been performed.

There were no footmen in the doctor's house, and the table was being set by a parlor maid who glanced at Emily but did not question her, as with the loss of Crupe's services, everyone was doing extra work.

Emily crouched in front of the fireplace, stirring the glowing coals with a cast-iron poker. A moment later Godfrey entered the room carrying a tray of covered dishes. He was followed by Cook, who carried a tray draped with a towel.

Godfrey growled, "All right, you wenches, get out of here. The doctor's coming."

Disappointed that she would not see what became of the extra tray of food, Emily followed Cook and the maid from the room.

Late that evening Emily and Doris were in the kitchen scouring the pots and pans as Dudley cleared the table just vacated by the senior servants, who had now departed for their quarters.

Dudley peered under the lid of a vegetable dish. "They left us plenty of spuds."

"Any gravy?" Emily asked hopefully.

Doris, as usual, drooped wearily over her task, unable to muster any enthusiasm for the prospect of eating dinner.

"No gravy," Dudley answered gloomily.

"I hope there's some beef left. I'm so hungry," Emily said. Her chapped hands bled as she scraped the baked-on residue of the Yorkshire pudding from a pan.

Dudley gave a sudden yelp of fright, and Emily dropped the pan with a clatter on the tile floor. She spun around.

Sir Edward stood in the doorway. "I'm sorry. I didn't mean to startle you. Miss Faraday, if I could have a word with you in private?"

Wiping her hands with a dish towel, Emily hastily ushered him into the pantry and closed the door. "Oh, I do so want to talk to you, but if Godfrey catches us—"

"Miss Faraday, what happened the other night? Did someone hurt you?"

"I ran away," she whispered. "It was my own fault."

"But that's outrageous. You're not a slave; you have the right to leave if you wish."

"My father—" Her voice broke and she had to compose herself. "My father was killed. Mr. Crupe said there are debts I must work to repay. I believe perhaps the doctor treated my father, as I can't imagine he incurred debts in any other way. But I know my father did not die a pauper, and there would have been more than enough in his estate to pay a doctor's fee. Mr. Crupe told me my stepmother left the country, and so I'm responsible for the debts. But my father would have left me adequately provided for, I know. But I don't know what to do, where to turn."

"Then please allow me to help you," Edward said at once. "However, my inquiries as to the disposition of your father's will might take some time, and a young lady of your refinement cannot continue this menial work. How much would it take to buy your freedom from servitude? Have you seen the bills?"

She shook her head. "Please, Sir Edward, you must go now. If Godfrey returns and finds you here, we'll both catch it."

"Find out the extent of your indebtedness. Perhaps we could talk again? Could you come to my room? I assure you I would behave like a gentleman. Miss Faraday, I want very much to help you, to be your friend."

She cast a frightened glance in the direction of the kitchen door, sure that Godfrey would materialize at any moment. "I'm not allowed in the students' quarters. Please . . . Doris and Dudley are hungry, they need to come in here to eat."

"Good God, you haven't had dinner yet? It's eleven o'clock. Very well, if you won't come to me, I'll come to you. Where is your room?"

"Up in the attic. I share a room with Doris."

"I'll come up to the attic tomorrow night." He took her hand in his. "Doris will be our chaperone. In the meantime, ask the doctor how much you owe. You have the right to know." He paused. "May I call you by your first name?"

"Yes, of course. It's Emily."

"And you must call me Edward."

To her complete astonishment, he raised her hand to his lips and kissed her red and swollen fingers. "Until tomorrow then."

Emily stood in the pantry after he left, thinking about their conversation, until Dudley brought in the food.

The memory of the handsome young student's visit was very much on her mind the following morning when she again went to clean the operating theater. When she picked up the keys from Godfrey, she overheard him telling the coachman that Crupe's condition was worse. Godfrey had added, with an evil leer, "If he declines any further, he'll find hisself in the theater being carved up for the edification of the students, won't he now?"

Shuddering, Emily took the keys and hurried away. With Crupe incapacitated, she wondered how she would learn the total of her father's debts. Godfrey wouldn't know, and she was reluctant to approach the doctor, whom she had never met face to face.

Still pondering this dilemma, she got down on her hands and knees to scrub the floor, gradually working across the room until, without realizing it, she was close to the locked door.

The low whispery voice suddenly spoke. "You are very pretty."

Her scrubbing brush fell from her hands, splashing into the bucket. All of the hairs on the back of her neck stood up. Slowly she turned to look into the eye framed by the keyhole. "It's very rude of you to watch me through a keyhole." Her own voice shook so much she could not say more for a moment.

He did not reply, but the eye remained.

Emily said, "But perhaps you cannot show yourself? It occurs to me that your door is locked. I have a key. Shall I unlock the door?" She rose to her feet, her heart beating madly, but curiosity conquered fear.

"No! Do not touch the lock." There was a panicked edge to his tone now, tinged with anger. "Does it not occur to you that locks work two ways? I am not locked in. I have my own key; if I wished to leave I could do so, but I do not."

"But why would you want to stay in there? Surely you are at the top of a flight of stairs leading down to the cellar. Not a comfortable place to spend your time."

"But I do not spend all my time crouched behind this door. I have a comfortable room in the cellar. I come up here only to observe what takes place in the operating theater."

"Are you a medical student?"

"No. I am nothing."

"You are a man, are you not? Why do you live in a cellar? Do you ever come out and show yourself?"

"You ask too many questions."

"Answer just one—what is your name? I am Emily."

For a moment he didn't respond, then said shortly, "Kane."

"How do you do, Mr. Kane."

"Quite well, Emily, all things considered. At least I am having a conversation with a pretty girl. Don't call me Mr. It's just Kane."

Emily, feeling bolder, impulsively said, "When the skylight is uncovered, a beam of sunlight strikes this side of your door and your eye appears golden."

There was a long pause, followed by a strangled gasp. His eye vanished from the keyhole.

"Wait—don't leave," Emily called. "I didn't mean to offend you. Your eye is beautiful. I believe you must be a very warm, compassionate person, Kane, and I can't understand why you hide yourself away. . . ."

Her voice trailed away as faintly she heard footsteps descending the stone stairs to the cellar. A moment later there was a chorus of excited barking from the dogs, undoubtedly greeting the return of their fellow prisoner.

He was a prisoner, she was sure of it, despite what he had said about having his own key. No one would willingly live in a cellar with a research doctor's sacrificial animals.

A chilling explanation entered her mind. Was it possible he, too, was a sacrificial animal? She had heard of condemned felons who, in order to postpone the hangman's noose, volunteered to be human guinea pigs, offering themselves for various medical experiments. Was that his purpose here, and was that why he was locked away? Could he be unfit to associate with his fellow man, perhaps a murderer?

Chapter 8

BRIONY FROZE, HER fingers tightening on the delicate stem of her wineglass. Around her the murmur of conversation and laughter continued unabated, the candles twinkled on the Christmas tree, and the Yule log blazed cheerfully in the hearth. Several guests clustered about the grand piano waiting for a volunteer to begin playing carols for them to sing. That task usually fell to Edward, but he had elected to remain at the doctor's house on this Christmas Eve.

For a split second it seemed that only Briony had noticed the new arrival who stood at the double doors of the drawing room, then Rupert detached himself from a knot of guests and moved toward her. Briony watched in stunned disbelief as he took the woman's hand and raised it briefly to his lips in greeting, then led her into the room and began to introduce her to the other guests.

The late arrival was a handsome woman of at least Briony's age, with raven hair and heavily kohled eyes. She was clad in stark black but adorned with so many jewels that Briony's first impression was of glinting diamonds and the coldly reflective quality of white gold, so that the overall image suggested the aurora borealis set in the dark sky of the endless arctic night.

For several minutes Briony stood immobile as her husband led the woman from group to group, watched him present her to their friends, smiling as if he were welcoming a treasured friend. As she watched, Briony's numb disbelief turned to anger, and soon it grew to a bursting point.

How could Rupert do this to her? He had actually brought his mistress into their home.

Briony whirled around and flung her wineglass at the marble fireplace. The sound of shattering glass startled those standing nearby, and she heard several gasps. Then she was striding toward Rupert and his black widow, pushing aside anyone who did not move out of her way fast enough.

As she drew closer to Rupert, she saw the faint derision on the face of his mistress, the smug expression that said *He is so enamored of me that he has flung caution to the winds, defied convention for me, and what can you do about it?*

"Ah, Briony," Rupert said smoothly, "may I present an old friend, Mrs. Ursula Markham—"

"No," Briony declared in ringing tones, "you may not. I do not entertain whores in my home."

The silence that fell upon the assembled guests seemed to resonate throughout the room. Rupert's face flushed a furious red, and Briony had the satisfaction of seeing Mrs. Markham's mouth fall open, giving her a slightly moronic look.

"Briony—" Rupert began in a low, warning voice.

But she had already turned on the woman. "Get out. Now. If you linger another second, I shall drag you out of my house by your hair." She took a step closer to the woman, who hastily backed away.

Mrs. Markham turned to Rupert, but before she could speak, Briony screamed, "Don't look at my husband. I don't care if he did invite you, I don't want you here."

The red haze that obscured her vision blocked out the shocked faces of the guests. She didn't even see the look of rage on Rupert's face any longer. She sprang toward his mistress and pushed her violently backward. She was screaming, she was unsure what, and then the Markham woman was scrambling out of her path, fleeing through the double doors.

Flushing with victory, Briony pursued her, calling out every derogatory name she could think of, punctuating each

scathing comment with a push, until all at once Briony was
captured in strong arms that lifted her bodily into the air.

"Rupert, put me down this instant!" she cried, but he
slung her over his shoulder like a sack of potatoes and
carried her up the stairs.

In her room he dropped her onto the bed and stood over
her, his expression livid. "Have you taken leave of your
senses? How could you make such a scene in front of all our
friends?"

"*You* ask *me* that? You, who brought your whore into our
home?"

"Mrs. Markham is the widow of a former client, who—"

"Whom you are sleeping with," Briony finished for him.
"Do you take me for a complete fool?"

"It's impossible to have a rational conversation with you
when you're in such a state," Rupert said shortly. "Since
one of us should maintain some semblance of decorum in
front of our guests, I shall go back downstairs and explain
to them that you are indisposed."

Before she realized what he was about to do, he crossed
the room and disappeared through the door. A second later
she heard the key turn in the lock.

She jumped from the bed and sped to the door, pounding
on it and attempting to twist the brass knob. "Rupert, come
back! You can't lock me in here. Rupert . . ."

But he was gone and there was little likelihood that
anyone would come and unlock her door, even if they heard
her cries, which was doubtful since her room lay above the
east wing of the house and the guests were assembled in the
west drawing room. Of the household staff, only Mrs.
Winthrop would have had the courage to defy Rupert and
come to her aid, but the housekeeper was still confined to
her bed following her bout with pneumonia.

There was a sheer drop of some thirty feet from her
bedroom window to the flagged courtyard below. For an
instant Briony considered knotting her bedsheets, but then
reason prevailed. How could she possibly face anyone at the
party after attacking her husband's mistress and publicly
berating her? Unfair as it might be, it was a greater social sin

to create a scene than it was to parade a barefaced home wrecker before one's family and friends.

Briony went into her dressing room and began to unbutton her basque. After a moment she couldn't help but smile at the memory of the look on Ursula Markham's face as she was thrown out of the house.

After the last guest departed, Rupert sat in the library staring into the dying embers of the fire, oblivious to the damp chill creeping through the house.

Everyone had left early after spending an uncomfortable couple of hours pretending nothing had happened. He had merely told them that Briony was indisposed, hinting that she had drunk a little too much wine and was suffering from delusions about the widow of one of his clients, whom he had invited to come tonight to ease her grief. They had all nodded sympathetically, and one dowager had discreetly inquired as to whether Briony might be in a "delicate condition," since this often precipitated such attacks of jealousy.

Normally he and Briony would have accompanied their guests to church for the midnight services on Christmas Eve, but tonight he was in no mood to celebrate the season. The problem was that Mrs. Markham had contributed large sums of her late husband's money to Rupert's political campaign, with the promise of more to come, and he needed her financial support. That it came as a reward for his copulating with her seemed, in his mind, a minor detail. Why couldn't Briony realize that men didn't regard their peccadilloes in the same light that women did? They were inconsequential, meaningless, and had nothing to do with their wives. Certainly Ursula Markham was no threat to his marriage. But Briony's behavior tonight was very definitely a threat to his political aspirations, and he would have to act quickly to dissipate that threat.

He reached for the bell cord. His butler appeared instantly. "You rang, sir?"

"Come in, Mathers, and close the door."

He paused until the butler did so and then said, "You

were in the room this evening during Lady Forester's outburst?''

Mathers nodded. ''Very distressing for you, sir, I'm sure.''

''A regrettable incident, but not entirely unexpected,'' Rupert went on. ''Dr. Stoddard had warned me that such irrational behavior might be the next phase of her break-down.''

The butler looked surprised by this announcement but made no comment.

Rupert continued, ''I have, of course, tried to conceal my wife's illness. Indeed, most of her outbursts have, merci-fully, taken place in the privacy of our chambers. But tonight's ugly scene, and the embarrassment of my guests, in particular Mrs. Markham, forces me to face the fact that I can no longer ignore my wife's malady, nor continue to hope that it will go away. I am telling you this, Mathers, since we must keep her confined until I can have Dr. Stoddard examine her again. Naturally, all that I am telling you must remain in strictest confidence. Now, wake up my coachman. He is to deliver a message to the doctor.''

Mathers looked surprised. ''Tonight, sir?''

''Immediately. Move, man. Don't stand there like an idiot.''

Rupert went to his desk and scrawled a brief note to Dr. Stoddard, a plan formulating in his mind as he wrote. Briony had to be brought to her senses, convinced that it was in her best interests to overlook his association with the Markham woman. He needed Briony at his side, beautiful, intelligent, high-born, the perfect wife for a noted barrister on the threshold of a political career. But it would be best to keep Briony out of sight for a while, until the memory of tonight's unpleasantness had faded. Later he could say she had a nervous breakdown, perhaps due to yet another stillbirth. Rupert's plan required Stoddard's cooperation, which would not be difficult to obtain, since as his lawyer, Rupert had knowledge of the doctor's activities that he wouldn't want divulged to the community.

* * *

Briony had fallen into a troubled sleep, punctuated by fragmented dreams that made no sense, so that when she first felt herself lifted from the bed, swathed in a smothering mantle, and carried from her room, she believed she was still dreaming.

But as the freezing chill of the night air penetrated the imprisoning cloak pulled over her face, and she heard Rupert's muffled voice instructing someone to open carriage door, she realized this was no dream.

Although she attempted to cry out, she could only choking sounds and realized a gag had been tied about mouth. Outraged, she attempted to raise her arms, but corb bit into her flesh. She had been bound and gagged, and was now pushed into the carriage and borne away.

What was Rupert doing? Where was he taking her in the dead of night? Undoubtedly this was her punishment, and he intended to humiliate her in response to the embarrassment she had caused him over Ursula Markham. But how? She felt his presence beside her in the carriage as it rattled over cobbled streets and although her restraints were uncomfortable she felt no real fear. He was her husband, after all, and would not physically harm her.

At last the carriage came to a halt, and she was again lifted into Rupert's arms and carried into the freezing night. She heard a door creak open and then thud behind them, followed by the hollow echo of footsteps along a flagged corridor. Then they were descending, going down a long flight of stairs. Voices, muffled by the cloak, floated over her head.

She began to shiver, partly from the dank cold and partly from apprehension. This was too much, Rupert was going too far. But it was important not to let him know she was frightened. That was what he wanted.

Another door opened, ancient wood groaning in protest. She was lowered to a hard wooden bench, and the cloak was pulled away from her face.

Sickly yellow light from a single oil lantern attached to a bare brick wall illuminated a small windowless room containing only the narrow plank bed upon which she sat and an ominous bucket in one corner whose purpose she did not dare imagine. A small grating in the stout iron-studded door framed Rupert's face for an instant, then he disappeared into the gloom.

Briony felt rough hands seize her, and a shadowy figure materialized at her side. She would have screamed but for the gag in her mouth. The man removed her bonds but left the gag in place. She recognized him now. Dr. Stoddard's coachman, the gargoyle-like Godfrey. Dear Lord, was she at the doctor's house?

"Nah, then," he said. "Yer might as well know that screaming and shouting will do you no good. All that'll happen is that you'll set the dogs off barking. Nobody's going to come and let you out, see. So you be a sensible girl and behave yourself."

He yanked the gag from her mouth, and she tried to speak but could only manage a hoarse whisper. "Why am I here? What has my husband told you?"

"Why, lovey, that we've got to keep you locked up 'cos you're stark raving mad, that's what."

Chapter 9

EMILY FINISHED CLEARING the Christmas dinner of the senior household staff, who were now gathering in the family drawing room for the annual distribution of gifts from the doctor, and turned to Doris. "For once they've left plenty of food. Look, there's chestnut stuffing and Brussels sprouts and giblet gravy and even some of the roast goose."

"Plum duff, too!" Dudley exclaimed excitedly.

Doris merely collapsed into a chair and propped her head on her hands. Her bloodless face, listless pose, and dull gaze told their own grim story. She was wasting away from overwork and her starvation diet. Emily had heard her coughing at night, a tight, dry sound that did little to ease her labored breathing. Emily had tried to take on some of Doris's chores herself and to save her the choicest of the leftovers, but Doris continued her inexorable decline.

Emily squeezed Doris's scrawny shoulder. "You just sit there and rest, and I'll fill up a plate for you. Dudley, leave that pudding alone until we've eaten our dinner."

The festive meal had been served earlier than usual, in midafternoon, and the servants would have the rest of the day off, to visit family and friends if they wished. The three waifs in the pantry had no one to visit, but at least Doris would be able to rest, and for once Dudley would get enough to eat. He was happily gobbling up his scraps of goose so that he could get to the plum duff.

Emily harbored her own secret hope, that Sir Edward would slip away to see her. She knew he hadn't gone home for the holidays, as he and several other students had joined the doctor for Christmas dinner. Unfortunately Edward had been caught trying to slip up to their attic room. Emily and Doris had overheard Godfrey castigating him outside their door, warning that if Edward were to attempt such a thing again, the doctor would be informed, and the young gent would undoubtedly be sent packing.

"You did remember to feed the dogs, didn't you, Dudley?" Emily asked, fearing he may have forgotten in the excitement.

He shook his head. "Mr. Godfrey said not to go down to the cellar today. He took food."

"I'm amazed that he'd do your chores for you, even if it is Christmas."

"Two trays went down today," Doris said unexpectedly. "I saw Cook getting them ready, and I heard her tell Godfrey that the doctor wanted him to carry one."

"Perhaps they're both for Kane—maybe all the extra holiday food wouldn't fit on one tray," Emily suggested. She had told Doris of her conversation with the mysterious man in the cellar.

But Doris's brief animation had already faded, and she merely shrugged tired shoulders.

They were about to divide the remaining Christmas pudding into three portions when there was a tap on the pantry door and Edward appeared. He beckoned to Emily to step out of the cramped pantry, and when they were alone, he said, "Sorry I couldn't see you the other night. I expect you heard Godfrey bellowing at me?"

He pressed a small package into Emily's callused hands, and as she murmured in surprise, he added, "What I'd really like to give you for Christmas is your freedom from servitude. Did you learn the extent of your late father's debt to the doctor?"

"Mr. Crupe is still confined to his room, and I didn't dare ask the doctor." Emily opened the tiny box Edward had given her and exclaimed in delight as a gold and sapphire brooch was revealed. "Oh, Edward! I can't possibly accept such an expensive gift! I hardly know you. It's not proper. It's beautiful, but—"

His face fell. "I had the jeweler make it from a pair of

cuff links I owned. Please. Emily . . . I want you to have
it. Accept it as a token of my deep regard for you, or my
hope that one day I shall be able to tell you all that is in my
heart. Just to know that you have something I once wore
would forge a bond between us. Oh, Lord, am I being
impossibly sentimental? The truth is, I think about you
constantly—I can't think of anything else. I want so
desperately to take you away from here. When you learn the
extent of your father's debt I shall pawn everything I own in
order to buy your freedom.''

She held up the brooch, and the sapphire sparkled in the
gaslight. It seemed so long since she had worn anything
pretty. All of her belongings had vanished after she was so
unceremoniously taken from the southbound coach, and she
had no idea what had become of her trunks and bags. She
had been given a maid's ''uniform,'' a gown of coarsely
woven material and two cotton pinafores—''one to wash
and one to wear''—and the latter were threadbare, as they
quickly became soiled and required daily washing.

''I really shouldn't . . .'' she began, then looked at his
crestfallen expression. He had sacrificed his cuff links for
her. It seemed cruel to refuse his gift, despite the fact that
propriety decreed jewelry could only be accepted from
one's betrothed. She smiled at him. ''Thank you, I love the
brooch. I shall treasure it always. But I have nothing to give
you in return.''

''Your smile—your presence—is all I need to fill my life
with sunshine. But, Emily, these furtive meetings are
crumbs to a starving man. Do you get a day off? I should
love to take you away from here for at least a little while.''

She shook her head. ''Godfrey says I can't have a day off
until at least some of my debt is repaid. He said most of
what I earn goes for my keep.''

''I'd hoped to take you to meet my sister, that's why I
stayed over the holidays. I'm sure you and Briony would
like each other, and if my resources were insufficient to pay
your debts, I thought perhaps Bri might help.''

''Oh, Edward, I feel quite overwhelmed by your concern
for me. I fear I may have led you to believe I care for you

in a way I am not yet ready to consider. We barely know each other for one thing, and for another I am mourning my father. I simply can't make any promises about the future.''

''My dear, I know that. I ask nothing more than that you allow me to be your friend.''

Emily pinned the brooch to the rough material of her bodice, positioning it just above the top of her pinafore. ''I'm honored to have you for a friend, Edward. I do hope I shall be able to meet your sister one day. When are you going to see her?''

''Before New Year's Eve, I expect. I do wish you could come.''

''So do I. But you must go now, as I have to clear our dishes before the senior servants return.''

''I don't suppose Cook hung any mistletoe in here?'' he asked wistfully.

Emily chuckled and, standing on tiptoe, planted a brief kiss at the corner of his mouth. She felt his swiftly indrawn breath, but before he could speak, she slipped back into the pantry and closed the door.

On Boxing Day Emily could not arouse Doris. Peering through the dawn gloom, Emily gasped. Doris's pinched features looked tranquil, but there were streaks of dried blood on her lips, and her eyes were wide and staring.

Emily stumbled down the narrow stairs and burst into the kitchen where Godfrey had just returned from his night's work. ''Quick, fetch the doctor. I think Doris is . . . I think she might have passed away.''

Godfrey finished peeling off his greatcoat. ''If she's dead, then what do you expect the doctor to do? Resurrect her?'' He gave an evil chuckle.

''I'm not sure—perhaps she's fainted. Do people keep their eyes open when they faint? But she felt so cold. Oh, please, we can't leave her lying there.''

''I'll send up that new student. He was eager enough to get into your room and get 'is filthy hands on you two wenches, wasn't he? As for you, you'll have to do Doris's work as well as your own, so you'd better get started.''

That day proved to be the hardest Emily had ever spent. It was impossible to do all of Doris's work as well as her own, despite taking only minutes for her meals and skimping on the cleaning. The brasses weren't polished, the chamber pots only hastily rinsed, the grate didn't get blackleaded. When Cook ordered her to peel the potatoes for dinner, Emily said, "But I haven't cleaned the theater yet."

"Never mind the theater. They won't be using it this week. Get the potatoes done."

"Please, ma'am, have you heard how Doris is?"

But Cook ignored the question and berated Dudley for not wiping his feet properly before he came into her kitchen.

When Emily at last crept wearily into her attic room late that night Doris was gone. In her place Emily found a note.

My Dear Emily:

I am so sorry. There was nothing I could do for Doris. I believe she must have slipped away peacefully in her sleep. She is at rest now. Try not to grieve for her—she has left behind the burdens of this world.

Your devoted friend, Edward.

Emily was too exhausted even to cry. She said a brief prayer for Doris's soul and then fell into a deep slumber.

During the following days there was no respite from the endless chores and constant demands of Cook and Godfrey. Emily did not see Edward, nor did she go into the theater. When she asked if another scullery maid might be hired to take Doris's place, she was told curtly that the doctor did not want any new servants brought in until Mr. Crupe was able to select them himself.

On New Year's Day she saw Edward briefly as they passed in the hall. "Did you find your sister well?" Emily whispered.

"I didn't see her. Apparently she's gone to visit her husband's sister up in Scotland. I can't understand why she didn't let me know. Are you all right, Emily? It must have been a dreadful shock for you, to find Doris like that.''

At that point Cook came looking for her, ending the conversation.

The following day Godfrey instructed Emily to clean the theater as the doctor's lessons and research would resume after Twelfth Night.

Since she knew none of the other servants would observe her while she worked in the theater, Emily couldn't resist pinning her sapphire brooch to her shoulder before beginning the task of scrubbing the operating table. The sparkling stone would surely cheer her and lift some of the deep winter gloom.

A great deal of dust had accumulated during the Christmas hiatus, and cobwebs festooned every corner of the room. She worked quickly, resisting the urge to glance at the cellar door, yet curious as to whether the mysterious Kane was watching her.

She did not have to wait long to find out. He called to her. ''Why do you not sing today, Emily?''

''I have nothing to sing about,'' she answered shortly, without looking in his direction.

''Not even that beautiful—and rather expensive-looking— brooch you are wearing? A Christmas gift, no doubt, from your beloved? Tell me, did he rob a jeweler for you?''

Angry, she whirled to face the cellar door. ''You think that because I am only a skivvy I could not possibly know anyone who could afford to give me such a gift? That I associate with thieves? How dare you make such assumptions?''

The golden eye peered at her through the keyhole. ''I thought perhaps you had enchanted one of the good doctor's students, and since I know they are all penniless louts who are too stupid to embrace any other profession—else why would they enter the disgusting field of medicine?—I could only deduce that your smitten swain must have stolen the brooch.''

''He had it made from his own cuff links,'' Emily blurted out before she could stop herself.

"The fool. He should have kept them to pawn when he starts his own practice. I've seen more than one fledgling physician starve while waiting for patients to knock on his door."

Emily angrily scrubbed the operating table surface. "What would a prisoner in a cellar know about medical students or doctors or . . . or anything."

"But I've already told you. I am not a prisoner. I choose to be here."

"I don't believe you."

"Suit yourself."

The ensuing silence lengthened unbearably. Emily finished cleaning but lingered in the theater, even though Kane's eye no longer watched her through the keyhole.

She put away her cleaning materials, took the keys from her pinafore pocket, then hesitated. The third key, which would unlock Kane's secret hiding place, hung temptingly from the wooden ring.

Suddenly the theater was filled with music. The most exquisite sound she had ever heard drifted through the locked cellar door, surrounding her with magic. She stood, spellbound, listening to the haunting strings of a violin, playing a melody that brought tears to her eyes. Only a master violinist, using a rare and wonderful instrument, could have produced such a melody.

Almost in a trance Emily moved toward the cellar door. She placed her hand on the stout wood, as though to touch Kane's music, to feel it flow through her very being. She did not recognize the piece, but it conjured all of her own lost and stolen dreams, promised joy and peace, but was born of tragedy. It expressed a longing that had no name, a searching for something unattainable, a quest for happiness that might be denied.

When the last perfect note faded away into the bleak and empty air, Emily held her breath, too overcome to speak.

Almost at once she became aware of another sound. A muffled sobbing that surely came from a woman, not Kane, and seemed to rise from deep within the cellar. A dog began to howl in accompaniment.

"Kane?" Emily called. "Are you there?"

But he was gone.

Briony clapped her fist to her mouth to stifle her sobs. She had been too angry to cry during the terror-filled hours she had spent in this dismal cell, but the music had moved her to tears with its sheer beauty.

The unseen violinist knew isolation far worse than hers, yet reached beyond it to a dreamworld where he might cast off mortal shackles, touching bow to strings to speak with the gods.

She shivered as a dog began to howl. The sound was such a mournful contrast to the lilting strings of the violin.

Then a voice spoke on the other side of her door. "I did not realize you were a woman. Who are you?"

The voice was male; low, sonorous. But his face did not appear in the grating, as Godfrey's did so frequently.

"Please . . . I am Lady Briony Forester, and I am being held here against my will. Could you . . . could you get word to my brother? He's a student here."

"You don't sound demented. Yet you must be, or you wouldn't be in there. The last denizen of that room believed himself to be Napoleon. He ranted and raved about his armies freezing to death in Russia until I thought I, too, would become insane. The good doctor tried to cure the poor wretch but without success."

Briony peered up at the small grating, twisting her head from side to side to try to see her unexpected visitor, but he kept out of sight. "Please believe, sir, that I am not insane. I am here only because I embarrassed my husband."

"Great Scot, woman, how dare you commit such a crime?"

"Please don't mock me. I am desperate. My brother is Edward Darnell. Will you tell him of my plight?"

"I have no contact with the students."

"Are you also a prisoner, then?"

"Not at all. But I do not leave the cellar."

"You take care of the dogs, is that it? I suppose those poor beasts are used for the doctor's research?"

"Would you have him experiment with living humans instead?"

"I beg you, tell my brother I am here."

"I will learn more about you, Lady Forester, and decide then what I shall or shall not do."

The household was in an uproar. Mr. Crupe had been taken away to the hospital, and everyone knew what that meant. He was near death, and very likely his disease was contagious. Not bronchitis or pneumonia, as everyone had believed, but probably galloping consumption. Had poor Doris succumbed to the same malady?

Emily hurried to the theater the following day, anxious to speak to Kane about his music, but as she pushed open the door she saw at once that a draped cadaver lay on the operating table.

She recoiled, a scream caught in her throat. Why hadn't Godfrey warned her? She crept around the perimeter of the room to the cellar door, keeping as much distance between herself and that grim object on the table as possible.

The smell of death permeated the room, and Emily found herself taking shallow breaths. As she made her way along the uppermost row of benches, the far side of the operating table came into view, and she saw that the sheet covering the body did not cover one dangling arm. Thin gray fingers trailed on the floor, and Emily gasped as she saw the livid scar on the palm of the hand. Doris had grasped the red-hot handle of a stewpot only days earlier.

Emily stumbled backward, staring in horror at Doris's dead fingers trailing in the dust.

"Don't clean today," Kane's voice urged. "Go on, get out of the theater before the students arrive. You don't want to be here when they lift that sheet. You don't want to hear their coarse comments or witness their callous jests."

She spun around. Kane's amber eye regarded her unblinkingly. "Go on, leave," he ordered, his tone more commanding.

"I cannot," she whispered. "I must clean—Mr. Godfrey—"

"Can go to hell where he belongs! Don't worry, I'll speak to the doctor."

"You?" She was incredulous. "What can you possibly say to the doctor on my behalf?"

"Trust me. You will not be punished."

Emily cast one last frightened glance at Doris's body. Would that also be her own fate? Then she was stumbling back through the student benches, desperate to reach the vestibule and leave the horror behind her.

Chapter 10

THE CELLAR ROOMS occupied by Kane were a sharp contrast to the isolation cell, one of a trio used to confine mental patients, where Briony was held.

A chimney had been cut from Kane's quarters to the ground floor and a fire blazed in a raised brick hearth. The stone floor of the cellar was covered with thick wool rugs, and comfortable armchairs flanked the fireplace. A gate-legged table of polished walnut matched a sideboard containing china and silver, and the rough walls were hung with tapestries and paintings. Had it not been for the lack of windows, the room could easily have fitted into the main house. A smaller adjacent room contained a four-poster bed on a raised dais, a chest of drawers, a washstand, and a wardrobe.

As usual, as the dinner hour approached, Kane sat in an armchair, his long legs sprawled in front of the fire, a notepad on his lap, pen in hand. He dipped the nib into an inkpot on the side table next to him and drew a treble clef, following it quickly with several notes. Except for the firelight, the only illumination was a small oil lantern next to him, shedding a meager pool of light on his notepad.

He glanced at his violin, lying in an open leather case beside him, as if seeking inspiration. The violin had been made by the master, Antonio Stradivari, and Kane loved it with a passion he was sure he could never feel for any woman. Still, as he composed, he could not keep the image of Emily Faraday's lovely face from intruding into his thoughts, and the music he created began to take the form of homage to her gentle beauty.

A tentative tap on his door announced the arrival of his dinner tray. As usual, the doctor himself carried it into the room and silently placed it on the table. He unwrapped the cutlery from a linen napkin, poured wine into a crystal glass. The chores were his penance, performed nightly while his own meal grew cold, and in addition to the food he frequently brought small gifts. A book, sheet music, some delicacy such as Turkish Delight or hothouse fruit.

"How are you this evening?" the doctor asked. He did not expect a reply. Kane rarely spoke to him. It was part of the grim ritual played out each evening.

But tonight Kane responded, "Tell me about Lady Forester."

The firelight flickered on the walls, and the doctor's shadow grew huge, grotesque. "I told you about her when she arrived. She is demented. A threat to herself and anyone who goes near her. I would prefer you to stay away from her."

"That woman did not sound insane."

"She is suffering from delusions, imagining all kinds of things. She attacked a guest in her home, flew at her like a wild woman. If you do not believe me, you can ask her if it is not so. Like many lunatics, she has her rational moments. But she is also subject to fits of violent rage."

Kane laid down his music and approached the table. The doctor pulled out a chair for him. "Roast pork with plenty of sage stuffing, and a fine apple dumpling."

Kane sat down. "I sent the girl Emily from the theater today. Godfrey had put the dead skivvy's body in there before Emily had a chance to clean. Be sure you chastise him soundly and warn the great lout what will happen to him if he says a word to Emily about not cleaning the theater. Did you learn where Crupe found her and how she came to be in such reduced circumstances?"

"Crupe is on his deathbed. I sent him to the hospital. He's in no condition to tell me anything. But when I first asked him about her, he said her father is one of the legion of paupers who owes me or my hospital large debts. That she was working—willingly—to pay off her father's debts."

He paused. "She has another champion, you know. I suspect young Sir Edward Darnell decided to study medicine simply to be near her."

"*Sir* Edward Darnell?"

"An inherited—and worthless—title from an impoverished family. He and his . . . He is penniless, but he has an Oxford degree. I, too, thought it was odd he would wish to apprentice himself to me. At first I thought perhaps he was one of those idealistic young men who feel compelled to serve humanity and believe they can alleviate the suffering of the sick—"

"You and I know how foolhardy that belief is, don't we?" Kane interrupted. "At best doctors merely preside over their patients while their own bodies heal themselves and at worst . . ." It was not necessary for him to finish.

The doctor avoided meeting his eye and busied himself ladling a thick vegetable soup from a tureen to a bowl.

"Wheels within wheels," Kane mused. "This Edward Darnell is also the brother of the woman confined to the insane cell, isn't he? Tell me, do you think insanity runs in their family?"

"Some forms of derangement, yes, certainly can run in families. But I attribute Lady Forester's breakdown to her childlessness. I don't believe she has a lesion on her brain. I shall have to keep her under observation until I can be sure."

"Does her brother know she's here?"

"No. Her husband naturally is keeping her whereabouts secret."

"Get rid of her brother."

"He's an excellent student. Far more educated and intelligent than any of the others, and he doesn't faint at the sight of a scalpel."

"I want him out of the house by tomorrow evening." Kane waved his fork, dismissing him.

"As a matter of fact, I had already decided to send him packing at the end of the week. His room and board is paid until then."

The doctor started for the door, then turned. "If you find the girl appealing, I could send her to you."

"Get out," Kane growled.

Emily spent longer than usual cleaning the theater, hoping that the music of Kane's violin would again fill that grim chamber, but the silence was broken only by the occasional whining of one of the dogs or the soft scraping of her scrubbing brush against wood. She glanced frequently in the direction of the cellar door, but he was not watching. Then, just before she reluctantly decided she must get back to her other chores, the golden eye appeared in the keyhole.

Dropping her scrubbing brush, she sat up on her haunches. "Oh, Kane, your music was so beautiful it broke my heart. Where did you ever learn to play a violin with such skill? Why are you not on a concert stage, playing for an audience?"

An explosive snort was his only response.

"Will you play for me again?"

"Did you think I played for you? You vain creature. How many hearts must you capture? Is not the heart of your poor student who sacrificed his cuff links for you enough of a trophy?"

"Why do you answer my question by asking another one? Are you—were you a concert violinist?"

"No. I am a Cimmerian, a mythical creature living out my days in the darkness of my tomb world."

"But why? Why do you hide yourself from the sunlight? Why do you deprive the world of your music? Have you committed some crime?"

"No. Why do you ask all these questions? Why do you care who or what I am?"

"I do care. I feel you must have some tragic secret, and if we could just air it out, then you would be able to leave the cellar."

"What a little fool you are. Don't you understand, you find me appealing because I am inaccessible. You cannot see me or touch me. You can imagine me to be anything you want me to be. Probably young and tall and handsome. But perhaps I am old and ugly and mad as a hatter. Have you considered that? And if I am, would you still wish to unleash me on the world?''

''No one who plays such music could be ugly. Your music reveals beauty of spirit.''

''Mad, then? Surely only a madman would choose to live as I live?''

''I believe you are hiding down there. I haven't quite decided the reason yet. If, as you say, you have committed no crime, then perhaps you are hiding from some indiscretion, or maybe you have lost someone dear to you and are in deepest mourning, so choose to live as a hermit in a dark cellar.''

A sardonic laugh greeted her remark. ''What impossibly romantic notions! The truth is far from what you believe, but please, continue to entertain me with your theories.''

Emily had been so engrossed in her conversation that she had not been aware of the passage of time, and now the vestibule doors burst open and the students began to stream into the theater, forcing her to leave.

Edward regarded Dr. Stoddard in stunned disbelief. ''But why? What have I done?''

The doctor's pallid face hovered above his white surgical robes like an arctic moon floating above the frozen tundra. His large pale hands moved with curious grace, almost like separate entities, as they efficiently dissected the body of a white rat.

Edward had been summoned to the doctor's laboratory adjacent to the theater, and he had been flattered but apprehensive that he should be allowed to enter the inner sanctum. Now the reason for the summons became clear. He was to be dismissed.

Some perverse streak of determination surfaced, provoking him to plead his case. Although Edward had never had any intention of pursuing a career in medicine, and had come only to rescue Emily, now that he was to be denied the doctor's instruction, he felt deprived. Not only that, but he had already begun to see that there could be more to the healing profession than lancing boils and hacking off diseased limbs.

"I was concerned about you from the beginning, Sir Edward," the doctor replied, still concentrating on the dissected rat. "You must realize the other students are hardly of your class. Let's face it, my profession does not usually recruit members of your class. After all, we doctors are somewhat below merchants in the hierarchy of occupations. Yet there are a few of us—I myself am one—who entertain the hope that some day we can elevate the medical profession to one of greater respect."

"I have studied endlessly, I have passed every test. I have not flinched from any lecture, any demonstration—unlike many of my fellow students. This simply is not fair."

"Allow me to finish what I started to say. I have no complaints about your performance as a student. I am unable to keep you on for a more mundane reason. Your financial support has been withdrawn. Sir Rupert has informed me that he will no longer pay your tuition and room and board. I doubt your own small trust fund can meet the most meager of living expenses, let alone the cost of your books and tools—even were I to forgo my fees. So there you are. I'm sorry, but I must ask you to leave at the end of the week. Your room and board is paid until then."

"Would you consider allowing me to work in some capacity in return for tuition? I would be willing to do the most menial task if I might be allowed to stay."

"No. That's out of the question, and please do not embarrass yourself or me by suggesting I offer you some sort of scholarship. Besides, you can get all the training you need by applying to a charity hospital. I'll give you a fine recommendation. Now, please leave me, I wish to study the internal organs of this rodent. This rat lived in a sewer in a neighborhood ravaged with cholera, and it occurred to me that since only the human animal is subject to this disease that perhaps something in the physiology of the rat protects it. Is it possible? And would I recognize the protection if I saw it? Then, the larger question, could we duplicate the rat's protection in human beings?"

Interesting questions, Edward reflected, but he was too shaken to ponder them for long. Why had Rupert withdrawn his support? When Edward visited him on Boxing Day, his brother-in-law had seemed somewhat cold and distracted, perhaps because Briony had so abruptly left for Scotland. Rupert had said he would be joining her within days. Probably by now he had already left. The blighter might have had the decency to inform him that he was cutting off all financial support.

Edward returned to his spartan room to pack his belongings. He would have to find Emily and tell her of his departure. How he wished he could take her with him.

The instant Dr. Stoddard's face appeared in the grating of the cell door, Briony leapt to her feet and cried, "At least open the door and talk to me. You stare at me through that grating as if I were a caged beast. What are you afraid of? That I will attack you with teeth and fingernails?"

There was a moment's hesitation. Briony held her breath. Her only hope was to have someone unlock the door. She had dug and chipped at the walls and floor under the door to no avail. When Godfrey brought her food, it was handed to her through that same grating, which was far too small for her to climb through.

Dr. Stoddard said, "You won't have to remain in there much longer. Tomorrow you will be taken to the theater."

"The theater?" Briony asked in alarm. "You would not subject me to an examination in front of your students?"

"They will be present to witness your treatment. You will be fully clothed, so have no concerns in that regard."

"Treatment? What treatment? I am not ill!"

"Nor, madam, are you well. Your mind is beset by demons who must be driven out."

The icy chill Briony had felt before intensified to raw fear. "Please—at least come in and talk to me. I fear I really will become insane if I don't see another human being soon."

Another pause, then to her great relief she heard the key slide into the keyhole and turn.

Knowing she would have only a split second to catch him off guard, as the door yawned open she ducked her head and darted under his arm.

She immediately collided with the unyielding bulk of Godfrey. He seized her around her waist and, snickering, lifted her into the air.

Briony could have wept with frustration. She beat Godfrey's chest with her fists and screamed at him to put her down. He merely laughed and gripped her more tightly.

Behind her the doctor said grimly, "Shackle her to the bed. I should have remembered how cunning such patients are. And as for you, Lady Forester, your treatment would have been quite mild had you not behaved like the madwoman you are. Now I regret we shall have to resort to more severe methods of shocking you back to reality."

Chapter 11

• •

PHIN TSU STOOD in the cemetery before the simple marble gravestone proclaiming this to be the final resting place of Emily Faraday, who had been sixteen years old at the time of her death, the only daughter of Fletcher and Priscilla Faraday.

A cold drizzle threatened to turn to sleet, and the winter-bare trees quivered in anticipation. Phin felt herself shrink into her layers of clothing, but the ice in her veins had little to do with the inclement weather. She murmured softly, "Ah, but she was not his *only* daughter."

She had not been aware that she had spoken aloud until the grave digger who had brought her to the spot asked, "Beg pardon, miss?" Despite the rain, he twisted his cloth cap in his hands and regarded her with that expression of open-mouthed admiration she was growing accustomed to seeing on Caucasian faces.

"The stone is new—there are still flakes of marble where her name was chiseled—and the mound of earth is still bare."

"Oh, yes, miss. We just put up the headstone. Poor young thing was buried only weeks ago. Very tragic it was. She was shot right in the face, an accident y'know. Sealed the coffin, they did. I 'eard tell her own father didn't even know 'er. But he recognized some personal effects she 'ad."

"He was here—her father? You saw him?"

"I did indeed. A fine-looking gentleman. Newly married, too. His bride was on his arm at the funeral."

The officials she had contacted regarding Fletcher Faraday had not mentioned his recent marriage. All she had learned was that her father had buried his only daughter and then departed immediately for a new post in Mexico. A pinprick of curiosity about the new bride now joined Phin's list of questions about the tragic shooting of her half sister.

Turning to the man beside her, Phin gave him a beguiling smile. "Thank you for being so helpful. Emily and her father were dear friends of my family. I had hoped to see them while I was in England. This is a terrible tragedy. Do you know who shot poor Emily?"

"A poacher, I 'eard. Somebody said that he'd be charged with murder, on account of he was committing a crime when she was shot—even though he didn't mean to kill 'er.''

"A poacher? Here in the city?"

"No, milady, at a big estate in the country. Seems the poor lass ran away from 'ome. The new stepmother was prob'ly the reason. Young, she was, and striking looking, y'know. Black hair like yours, quite foreign-looking. . . . Oh, excuse me, miss, I didn't mean to offend.''

"I'm not offended. Thank you again for being so kind.''

She turned up her coat collar and thrust her hands deeply into her fur muff as she walked away. She had known cold weather in China, but it seemed the damp chill of the English winter was particularly hostile.

There would be a record of her father's marriage, giving the maiden name of his bride. She would have family or friends somewhere who would know how and where to contact the embassy in Mexico. Phin would have to be very discreet, a skill she was honing every day, so as not to give away her relationship to Fletcher Faraday. Phin had long known the stigma attached to mixed-blood progeny. And now she was learning that in English society a child born outside of marriage was equally reviled. A concubine's children were considered illegitimate, referred to as bastards.

Perhaps, too, there would be newspaper accounts of the trial of the man who shot Emily. Phin's mind was racing. An accidental shooting by a poacher that coincided with her father's remarriage after sixteen years of widowerhood was ringing warning bells. Was it possible her half sister's death

was not accidental? Phin had observed the disappearance of
favorite concubines and their children in the House of
Delights and heard whispers that "accidents" had befallen
them. She and her mother had been fortunate indeed to have
the protection of the chief eunuch, or else such a fate might
also have befallen them. The jealousy of second wives and
lesser concubines was a well-known fact. Perhaps Fletcher's
new bride had no wish to share her household with her
husband's daughter, who would be a constant reminder of
his first wife.

Phin decided that if her inquiries resulted in even a hint
that the shooting was not accidental, then she would not rest
until Emily had been avenged. It was the least she could do
for her sister, after arriving too late to save her.

Emily was aroused from exhausted slumber by Godfrey.
He shook her arm roughly. "Get up. Come on, the doctor
wants to see you."

Struggling to come fully awake, Emily tried to grasp what
was happening. Since she had not retired until after eleven,
it must now be well past midnight. "Wh-what have I
done?"

"Hurry up. Don't keep him waiting, or it'll be the worse
for you." He carried a candle in a pewter holder and
shielded the flickering flame with his hand. He made no
move to leave the attic room while she dressed.

Emily grabbed her Sunday frock and pulled it on over her
nightgown. Her fingers were shaking, more from terror at
the prospect of finally coming face to face with the doctor
than from the midnight chill of the air. She slipped her feet
into her shoes and followed Godfrey out onto the landing.

He led her down the stairs, out of the servants' wing, and
along the corridor leading to the theater. Fear welled up
within her as her imagination ran riot. Was she to be the
object of some horrible experiment? The memory of poor
Doris's ashen fingers trailing in the dust came back to haunt
her.

By the time they reached the theater wing of the house,
her teeth were chattering and she couldn't stop trembling.

Mercifully, their destination was not the theater itself, but the doctor's study, a smaller room that adjoined his laboratory, which in turn connected with the theater.

Godfrey pushed her into the study and departed, closing the door firmly. She stood in a pool of yellow gaslight coming from a ceiling fixture, and a second lamp on the massive desk in front of her illuminated the doctor's face.

He was an extraordinarily large man, with broad shoulders and powerful arms, yet his head was small, his features compact, and he was completely hairless. No hint of whiskers, or even eyebrows, sprouted from his smooth pale skin. At first glance the effect was gnomelike, but when Emily forced her frightened gaze to meet his eyes, she realized there was nothing ugly about his face. It seemed merely unexpressive, like that of a puppet's; and there was a curiously sterile quality to his hairlessness that added to the impression.

His eyes flickered over her. "Come closer," he ordered.

She took a step nearer, and he tipped the desk lamp in order to cast more light on her face. He nodded, satisfied. "Tell me about yourself."

Emily began a fumbling recital of her life in China, their return to England, and being plucked from the southbound coach to be told of her father's death. Recalling the shock of that news, her voice shook and she tried to blink back the tears.

Stoddard interrupted. "When did you return to England? When did your father incur his debts—was he treated at the hospital, or did I see him personally? I cannot recall treating you, so I assume your father was my patient?"

"My father was never ill. I thought perhaps he had had some business dealings with you. Or . . . well, he was married recently; perhaps his wife was your patient? I mean, before they were married, and my father pledged to pay her debts? Mr. Crupe would not explain to me, but I think he must have an accounting somewhere. I should be most grateful to learn the extent of my indebtedness, if you would be so kind as to ask Mr. Crupe."

"Mr. Crupe passed away earlier this evening. I will, of course, have an accountant go over our books."

Crupe was dead. Emily tried in vain to feel sorry.

"Your stepmother—where is she?"

"According to Mr. Crupe, she has left the country. He didn't tell me where she was going. If my father hadn't been killed, she would have gone to Mexico with him." Emily paused. "I hardly knew my father's bride."

"What was her maiden name?"

Emily thought for a moment. "I don't think I ever heard it. She'd been married before, you see, and so was introduced as Mrs. DeWitt."

"Ah, the lovely Antonia. I believe we have solved the riddle. You were correct in your assumption that your father took on the debts of his new bride. But those debts were to Crupe, not to me."

Emily digested this news silently. "But you said Mr. Crupe passed away. Does that mean—"

"That you are no longer responsible for the debt? We shall see. Crupe has relatives who might wish to pursue the matter, and you, Faraday, are more available to them than is the wily Tonia. Besides, it appears you are all alone in the world, so it would be prudent to remain in my service until you have somewhere else to go."

Unsure whether her situation had just improved or had grown more precarious, Emily made no comment.

The doctor rose suddenly, and Emily cringed. What a huge man he was! But he spoke quietly, if dispassionately. "Come with me."

Now she was led into the theater, which, as she had expected, was even more forbidding at night. Only a dim gaslight in a wall sconce lit the vestibule, and since the night was stormy, no moon- or starlight entered through the skylight. The doctor walked quickly to the cellar door.

Some of Emily's fright was replaced by a curious sense of anticipation. Kane was in the cellar somewhere. Would she meet him face to face at last? Then the dogs began to bark a warning, and her fear returned a hundredfold. Was she to be imprisoned down there to await who knew what

horrible fate? Even though she now knew she owed the
doctor nothing, he was still a greater menace than Crupe,
what with his gruesome medical research and experiments
and his dealings with grave robbers.

The doctor unlocked the cellar door, revealing a cramped
stone landing atop a long flight of roughly hewn steps. An
image of Kane crouching in the confined space with his eye
to the door flashed into Emily's mind as the doctor picked
up an oil lantern and turned up the wick. Another lantern,
halfway down the stairs, did little to dispel the darkness.

There was no rail or banister, and as they descended,
Emily trailed her hand down the clammy wall, fearing she
would lose her footing. The doctor, however, moved with
the surefooted ease of one accustomed to the cellar stairway.

A corridor led to a larger chamber that appeared to have
been used at one time as a wine cellar but now housed the
laboratory animals. Small cages lined one wall, in which
rats, mice, and guinea pigs were kept. The dogs, half a
dozen or so, were confined by an iron grating in a long run
on the opposite wall. They leapt excitedly at the grating,
tails wagging, and Emily wanted to reach in and pet them,
but the doctor kept walking, and she had to follow his
lantern. She had noted that the cages and run were clean,
and the animals, although desperate for human contact,
appeared healthy and well cared for. Dudley was to be
commended for that at least.

Another corridor, which took a sharp turn and undoubtedly followed the H shape of the house, led past three
heavily studded doors with tiny openings in the upper
panels covered by iron gratings. A faint light emitted from
one of the doors, and as their footsteps approached, Emily
was startled when a woman's voice cried out, "Please!
Whoever you are, have pity on me! At least stop and talk to
me."

The doctor quickened his pace and muttered, "A mental
patient. Very sad. She will be receiving her treatment
tomorrow, and then I hope she will be able to return home."

The echo of the woman's cry lingered in Emily's mind.

She certainly hadn't sounded insane, merely lonely and frightened.

Then, abruptly, they passed into another chamber, and the doctor stopped beside a door lit on either side by oil lanterns. He knocked, then pushed open the door, motioning for Emily to precede him.

She stepped into a room that was almost cozy, if ill-lit. A fire had diminished to glowing coals, and a single lamp, the wick turned low, illuminated only the surface of a gate-legged table and the hands of the man seated beside it. His face was in shadow.

Emily's heart thudded against her ribs. Kane! It was he—she would have known even if she had not caught a glimpse of the violin case lying on a chair nearby.

Chapter 12

. . . .

"DAMMIT, I TOLD you I didn't want you to bring he
here." Inexplicably Kane's hand darted to the lamp to turn
down the wick still further, plunging the room into nea
darkness.

Emily stood frozen to the spot. There was no doubt tha
the man in the shadows was the same one whose golden eye
had regarded her through the keyhole. She recognized
Kane's voice.

The doctor said, in a mildly rebuking tone, "Try to be a
little more sociable. A short visit wouldn't hurt. If you can
speak to her through the theater door, why not here? She is
quite intelligent, educated, and well traveled. True, she is an
orphan and a servant in my household, but she is not the
lower class waif Crupe usually hires. You've been too long
alone, Ambrose. It would do you good to spend some time
with a companion closer to your own age."

Ambrose? Why had he told her his name was Kane?
Questions whirled through her mind.

"And did you ask Emily if she wished to descend into my
tomb world to visit me? Of course you didn't. Furthermore,
if you intended her merely to converse with me, why did
you wait until midnight to bring her to me?"

A good question, Emily thought, a knot of apprehension
tightening inside her.

Kane went on, "The bewitching hour itself suggests that
this is an assignation. Damn you, how dare you set yourself
up as my procurer?"

"And how dare you speak to me so disrespectfully? Mind
your tongue, or I shall leave you to rot down here. I'm well

aware that you rarely sleep before dawn, and I know the hours between midnight and dawn are the most difficult for you. That was my reason for bringing her now.''

"Get her out of here. Return her to her bed. Has she not worked at least a sixteen-hour day? Do you want her to come to the same end as the unfortunate Doris?''

The doctor's reply was only mildly chiding. "Doris had consumption. There was nothing to be done for her; the disease is incurable.'' He paused, then went on in a more persuasive tone, "Spend half an hour with Faraday. You can be civil to her for that long. If you will agree to this, I will see to it she is promoted to parlor maid.''

Hope leapt in Emily's breast. A parlor maid's lot was far, far easier than that of scullery maid. She silently willed Kane to acquiesce, the forbidding darkness and his unpredictable behavior notwithstanding.

"Half an hour, then," Kane growled.

"I shall return for you shortly, Faraday," the doctor said. "Have no fear; my son's bark is worse than his bite.''

His son. Emily was so startled by this revelation that she was scarcely aware that the doctor had departed, leaving her alone with Kane.

She peered at his silhouette. He had broad shoulders like his father, but his head appeared better proportioned, and she could see that he had an abundant growth of hair. The firelight created copper glints in tousled locks badly in need of trimming. She couldn't distinguish his features, but the low light of the table lamp illuminated his hands, and she saw he had long fingers like his father, but smaller palms and wrists. A violinist's hands, she thought, expressing delicacy of touch rather than the brute force required to accompany the precision of movement of a surgeon's hands.

The silence lengthened. She could hear the dying coals of the fire settling into their bed of ash. A clock ticked. The wind moaned softly in the chimney.

"You may sit by the fire," Kane said at last.

Emily walked carefully toward the dull red glow in the grate and sat down. Her eyes were becoming accustomed to the darkness, and she could see several pieces of furniture in the room, a bookcase filled to overflowing, shelves laden with periodicals, three music stands. She turned to peer at Kane, but his features were in almost total shadow.

"Your father called you Ambrose. Why did you say your name was Kane?"

"Kane was my mother's maiden name. I use it because it is appropriate. Are you a student of the Bible, Emily?"

"My father is . . . was an agnostic. But he had me read the Bible as an example of Western literature. He also suggested I read the Koran and the teachings of Buddha. He said he believed in good and evil, but that they were creations of man, not God and the devil."

Not knowing where his question was leading, she added helpfully, "I was allowed to make up my own mind about religion. I believe in God, but I'm not sure about the Church of England. I found much to admire in the teachings of other cultures. Why do you ask if I've read the Bible?"

"To explain why I use my mother's maiden name."

Kane? No, *Cain*, Emily thought, feeling a thrill of horror. She unconsciously drew back, pressing herself to the smooth leather of the armchair. *And Cain slew Abel.*

"What? No questions?"

She cleared her throat. "I'm not sure I want to know any more about your chosen name. I'd thought of you as K-A-N-E and shall continue to do so."

"*Kane* with a *K*. Interesting. I like it."

"But your name is really Ambrose Stoddard."

"Don't ever speak that name again." His voice was an angry hiss. "That man is dead. He no longer exists."

"If I may . . ." Emily said shakily, "I would like to ask you about another . . . resident of the cellar. There is a woman down here. She called out to us as we passed by, and she sounded so desperately lonely."

"A madwoman. My father is going to attempt to treat her, since she's of the aristocracy. If she were not high-born, she'd be thrown into a lunatic asylum, such as Bedlam, at the mercy of violent inmates. Believe me, she's better off here."

"Do you think we could go to her and just visit for a few minutes? I feel so sorry for her."

"Out of the question. Besides, you're here to converse with me. Make conversation if you wish to rise to the lofty heights of parlor maidhood."

Even as he spoke she saw he had picked up a pen and was writing on a sheet of paper. He pushed it across the table toward her and motioned with his hand that she was to read it.

He had written:

My father is listening at the door. Do not mention Lady Forester again. I have spoken to her and will do so again.

The message registered only fleetingly on Emily's brain because in the split second that Kane pushed the note toward her, he leaned into the meager light cast by the lamp, and his features, although not clearly illuminated, came into view sufficiently for her to see a parody of a face, a human gargoyle so cruelly scarred that now she understood why he hid himself from the world.

She felt instant, overwhelming pity. But he must have heard her swiftly indrawn breath and mistaken the reason for it, because he snarled, "Get out. Go on, get out of here now."

"Kane, I—"

"Did you hear me?" he roared, leaping to his feet as if to physically remove her. "Get *out!*"

She turned and stumbled to the door, which opened before she reached it.

In the dank corridor the doctor motioned silently for her to follow him.

He did not speak until they reached the theater. As he locked the cellar door behind them, he said, "You saw his face, I presume?"

Emily nodded, biting her lip.

"Would you believe he was once a very handsome young man?"

"What happened to him?" Emily whispered.

"There was an explosion in the lab. A vial of acid and some other chemicals ignited. His face was burned. Mercifully he did not lose his sight."

"How dreadful. But surely locking himself away in the cellar isn't the answer? He is such a gifted violinist, his music should be shared with others."

"Can you imagine the reaction of a concert audience to seeing him onstage? He is my son and I am devoted to him, but even I can scarcely bear to look at him. His face would horrify grown men and send frail women and impressionable children screaming into the streets. Besides, he will never leave this cellar. He allows no one but me to see him. Oh, I've tried to force companions such as yourself on him. The results are always the same. They cringe from him in horror, and he flies into a rage and sends them away."

"Dr. Stoddard, I did not cringe in horror. I admit I gasped, but I felt pity, not horror. I would be glad to return to talk to him." Even as she uttered the words, Emily was unsure if she really wanted to speak with Kane again, to perhaps be forced to look into those cruelly scarred features in a bright light; or if her real reason for wanting to return to the cellar was the pathetic plea of the imprisoned Lady Forester.

"We shall see," the doctor murmured. "You may go back to bed now, Faraday. Tomorrow you will report to Cook, and she will tell you what your new duties will be."

"Lady Forester—are you awake?" The voice at first seemed to be a part of Briony's tortured dreaming, but as her eyes flickered open, she realized that someone was speaking to her through the locked door. There was no face peering in through the grating.

"Lady Forester," he said again. She recognized the low-pitched voice now. He had been here before.

"Yes, yes, I'm awake. Who are you?"

"My name is Kane."

"Are you a prisoner like me?"

"No. Why don't you tell me how you came to be here."

"Not until you tell me why you are asking such questions," Briony declared, some of her spirit returning.

"I wish to determine the extent of your dementia."

She forced herself to speak in a level tone, despite her exasperation. "I am not insane, nor did I have a nervous breakdown. I am being punished by my husband. I shan't tell you any more than that unless you unlock the door and treat me like a human being."

There was a long silence.

"Are you still there?" Briony inquired at length.

"Yes. But I do not have a key to your door. I might be persuaded to help you if you would tell me honestly why you are here. The doctor would not lock you in without a good reason."

"The doctor," Briony said with icy contempt, "would do anything my husband asked of him. The doctor treated my husband's family for many years, and they pretend to be close friends, but I've long suspected there is more to it than that. My husband is a barrister—" She broke off, realizing she had better not give voice to her suspicion that Rupert might have provided legal services to Dr. Stoddard. There had been nasty rumors about the origin of some of the cadavers the doctor used for teaching, but neither he nor his frightful manservant, Godfrey, had ever been called to account. She suspected Rupert's legal prowess had ensured that Stoddard was never charged with grave robbing. She had also learned of other sinister possibilities. On the morning after Stoddard treated her housekeeper, Briony overheard two of the servants whispering about him, and even allowing for the exaggeration of gossiping servants, what she had heard had troubled her greatly. It seemed there was much speculation about the exact nature of Stoddard's research, and gruesome hints that it was conducted on humans as well as animals.

"Why do you not finish what you started to say?" Kane asked.

"I would be repeating gossip. Please, will you at least look through the grating? I feel unnerved speaking to someone I cannot see."

"You don't want to see me, believe me. Now, when I spoke with you last time, you mentioned you have a brother studying here. Surely if your husband had evil designs, he would not send you to the same doctor who is teaching your brother?"

"How would my brother know I was imprisoned? The students don't come down here. The only people who come near me are Godfrey and the doctor. Godfrey told me that even if I could get out of this room, I would find myself in a maze of corridors and chambers, many of which are unlit, and if I were to find the stairs, the cellar door is kept locked."

"That's true. But someone is now aware of your plight. One of the servants heard you call out. Perhaps your brother will now learn you are here, and I can put you out of my mind."

"Oh, please don't do that! Please speak to my brother yourself. His name is Edward Darnell. Just ask him to come and see me, that's all I ask."

"I don't mix with the students."

"Send him a note. Just say, 'Briony locked in the cellar.'"

"And how is he supposed to breach our locked sanctuary? If what you say about your husband and the doctor conspiring against you is true, they aren't likely to allow him to see you, are they?"

"If, as you say, you are not a prisoner, you must be able to roam freely throughout the house. You could bring Edward to me."

"No. I can't do that."

"Why not? For God's sake, *why not*?"

"Don't question me." There was a dangerous edge to his voice.

"I will question you! What would it cost you to merely speak to my brother? Have you no compassion? Are you not a member of the human race?"

A low moan that sounded like anguish echoed in the hollow reaches of the corridor outside, followed by an exclamation of anger. "No, no, by God, I am *not* a member of the human race! See for yourself."

She looked up at the grating, a small cry of alarm escaping her lips. The face that appeared there truly belonged to the creature of her worst nightmares.

Chapter 13

· ·

EMILY FOUND THE note from Edward tucked under her pillow that night.

> My dear Emily:
> I am being forced to leave today. No time for explanations. I will keep in touch with you, but since I fear any letters may be intercepted I will send them to a fellow student (John Carruthers) whom I can trust, and you may reply in the same manner.
>
> > In haste,
> > Your devoted friend, Edward.

As she began her new chores as parlor maid under the ever watchful eyes of Godfrey and Cook the following day, Emily felt a sense of loss. Even though she had seen Edward only infrequently, his presence in the house had been a comfort. But there was no time to wonder about his sudden departure from the medical school as she was measured for a new uniform and ordered to begin her new duties. Now she would polish silver rather than scrub chamber pots and dust the fine rosewood furniture in the drawing room instead of applying beeswax to the floors. She would also change linens and make beds in the students' quarters, and this would make it easier for her to receive Edward's letters if he kept his word and wrote to her. Since she had been kept busy all day, there had been no time to clean the operating theater, and she assumed this task would now fall to someone else. She was disappointed and wished she could have continued her conversation with Kane in the sanctuary of the theater, with the locked door safely between them. The possibility that she would again be taken for a midnight visit to Kane hovered like a specter beside her throughout the day. She rehearsed in her mind what she would do and say if this came to pass.

But by the time Cook at last dismissed her for the day, Emily was too weary to think about Kane, or Edward's departure, or anything else. She started up the stairs to the attic room, but before she was halfway, Godfrey called after her. "The doctor wants you in 'is study, Faraday."

Emily hurried downstairs, then knocked on the door to the study. Once she was inside, Dr. Stoddard said only, "You said you felt pity. Show some toward my son and perhaps I will settle your debts with Crupe's estate."

Once again she was taken down to the cellar.

Kane was standing in front of his fireplace, and a blazing log illuminated the room. His father said only, "Faraday is here, Ambrose. She has something to say to you."

Emily stared at Kane's back, at his broad shoulders and long legs, the abundant head of hair, and thought that anyone approaching him without seeing his face would immediately decide they were about to meet a very attractive man.

He didn't turn around. "What is it you want to say to me, Emily?"

She hesitated, glancing over her shoulder to be sure the doctor had departed, then she drew a deep breath and walked to the fireplace. She had the satisfaction of seeing him start visibly as he looked down at her standing beside him.

"I wanted to tell you I'm very sorry about your accident, but I don't think your appearance should keep you sealed away from the world," Emily said fearlessly. "You play the violin so beautifully. I've never heard such spellbinding music, and I feel sad that you do not enchant many people. Do you know how many lives would be brighter for it?"

She wasn't prepared for his reaction. Suddenly she found her shoulders seized in a vicelike grip that made her wince. He held her in front of him, bending his face close to hers so that the leaping flames of the fire fully illuminated his scarred features.

At close range she saw that only one eye—the one he had undoubtedly used to peer at her through the cellar door— had been unscathed by the explosion and fire. The other was cruelly distorted by the granulated tissue left in the wake of his burns.

She looked up at him, willing herself not to blink or lower her eyes.

"Well done," Kane said sarcastically, releasing her so abruptly that she staggered backward. "You rehearsed very well—I did not see you flinch. Now, before I send you back where you belong, let me tell you why I shall never leave this cellar. I am incarcerated here as punishment for my sins, and my sentence is for life. Ah, your expression tells me that you believe my disfigurement surely must be punishment enough for any sin I have committed. Not so."

"Please . . . don't—" Emily began.

"But I must. I'm sure my father told you that my face vanished in a flash of fire when I was seventeen years old, and that the being known as Ambrose Stoddard disappeared that day. What my father probably did not tell you was that my younger brother died in the explosion. So you see, I am a murderer as well as a monster."

"You are neither," Emily whispered. "It was an accident."

"It was I who caused the explosion. I who lured my brother into our father's laboratory and instructed him to mix certain substances. I was always the instigator, the troublemaker. The whole thing was my fault. He died a horrible, lingering death, while I quite literally had my face burned off. God, how I wished I could have gone with him! I would have killed myself, but a swift death would have been too easy. I have served thirteen years of my sentence and intend to willingly endure my pain and isolation for as many years as my miserable life lasts."

Emily thought she had never heard a human voice express such soul-wrenching anguish. She was too overcome to speak. Her pity for him choked her, and tears streamed down her face.

Kane saw them and gave a hideous, manic laugh. "Spare me your crocodile tears! You think I want pity from you? I'd rather have your scorn, your taunts, your hatred! Dear God, anything but pity!"

"I cannot help myself," Emily murmured, her voice breaking.

He turned away. "Go now. And don't come back. Ever."

"At least tell me what became of the woman who was locked up. She did not call out to us as we came by this evening."

"If you don't leave at once, I shall forcibly remove you!"

Emily stumbled to the door and was glad to find it was unlocked. The doctor stood outside in the shadows. Silently he led the way back to the stone stairs. He made no mention of what had transpired with Kane, and she wondered tiredly if he had listened at the door to their conversation. The doctor's parting words were, "Tomorrow you will resume cleaning the theater. Perhaps Ambrose will be more comfortable talking to you through the keyhole."

Kane's voice, mercifully disembodied, awoke Briony from a troubled sleep. Since her cell was windowless, illuminated only by an oil lantern attached to the wall beside the door, she had no idea of the time of day. "Lady Forester, I have persuaded the doctor to speak with you again rather than give you the shock treatment he planned for today."

"Thank you," Briony said, a wave of shame washing over her as she recalled her reaction to Kane's hideously scarred face. She was wondering whether to apologize or if it would be kinder not to mention the matter when he spoke again. "You mustn't become hysterical, do you understand? No matter how he may try to goad you, stay calm and rational."

"Yes, yes, of course. How can I ever thank you?"

But her only response was the fading echo of his footsteps retreating down the stone passageway.

She did not have to wait long for her interview with the

doctor. Godfrey brought her breakfast within minutes, a bowl of lukewarm porridge and a pot of tea, and announced, "Hurry up and finish. The doctor will be along directly."

Briony was too nervous to do more than sip the tea.

Godfrey remained with her.

When the cell door opened a little while later and Dr. Stoddard entered, Briony was seated stiffly on her plank bed, ankles crossed, hands folded upon her lap. She hoped he couldn't hear the thunder of her heartbeats.

"Now, Lady Forester, I understand you have undergone a remarkable recovery. Is that so?"

Keeping her tone low and, she hoped, submissive, she replied, "I was never ill, Doctor. I was angry and perhaps acted in an unladylike manner. I certainly have had time to mull over my actions and assure you I will never embarrass my husband again."

"Good, good. Now tell me exactly what transpired with your husband's client Mrs. Markham. I must be sure you are not suffering from memory lapses, which might indicate the onset of dementia."

At the mention of Rupert's mistress, Briony felt her blood begin to boil again, but she managed to maintain her decorum. "I acted hastily, I realize now. I should not have behaved like a fishwife in front of our guests."

"You do understand that a public apology to Mrs. Markham and all of the guests who were present that night will be necessary?"

A red haze obscured all rational thought. Leaping to her feet, Briony declared, "I will never apologize to that slut! I'll scratch out her eyes if I ever see her again, and as for Rupert I will—"

Too late she realized the trap she had fallen into. She clapped her hand over her mouth as though to stop the angry torrent, but the doctor had already turned to leave. Godfrey stepped forward and seized her.

She was borne from the cell, through the maze of dank passageways, up the stairs, and into the large room she knew from Edward's description to be the operating theater.

Thin winter sunshine streamed from a skylight onto a

sturdy wooden table bolted to the floor, surrounded by benches on ascending levels to afford a clear view for observing students. Struggling in Godfrey's powerful arms, Briony was carried to the operating table and dropped like a sack of potatoes.

Gasping for breath, she looked around. The theater was empty. There seemed little point in screaming, but she did so anyway—a shriek of terror and rage at her helplessness. Godfrey merely pulled a leather strap across her arms and body and buckled it. A second strap secured her ankles.

Godfrey looked down at her, assured himself she was immobilized, then slowly and deliberately ran his hands over her body, caressing her breasts, insinuating rough fingers between her thighs.

"Dr. Stoddard, if you are watching," Briony screamed, "know that I will have the law on you for this!" She spat in Godfrey's face and received a stinging slap on her cheek.

Stars danced dizzily in front of her eyes, and Godfrey's image blurred and then vanished.

She wasn't sure how long she was left strapped to the operating table. In her weakened state the blow to her face almost caused her to faint, but she hovered in that half-conscious state without slipping into merciful oblivion. Her thoughts became fragmented, and she tried desperately to find some shred of hope to cling to but could find none. Would students come streaming into the theater to fill the benches and observe whatever horrors Stoddard had in store for her?

In the midst of her panic she remembered that Edward was one of Stoddard's students. Of course, Edward would stop this horror.

But the minutes ticked by and no one came into the theater. Her body grew stiff, her head ached abominably, and she felt she might vomit at any second.

At length her eyelids began to flutter, and she drifted into an uneasy sleep.

Suddenly she was aroused by a deafening cacophony of sound: cymbals, drums, shouts. Her eyes flew open, and she screamed as she saw she was surrounded by dancing,

leaping figures that surely came from hell. Some wore the
garb of demons; others trailed ghostly mantles and chains.
All wore hideous masks, and one thrust a grinning skull
toward her. They shrieked and yelled, blew bugles, and
pounded cymbals and drums. If she could have covered her
ears, she would have, but her arms were fastened to her
sides.

All at once the din stopped, and she became aware of Dr.
Stoddard's voice. "You may step back now. Take your
seats."

The demons, ghosts, and goblins discarded their masks
and became ordinary medical students, filing in an orderly
manner to their benches.

Dr. Stoddard appeared beside the table, and his huge
hands went to her face, pulling up her eyelids firmly but
gently. He peered into her eyes and asked, "Do you know
who I am?"

"You are a fiend incarnate," Briony responded. She was
trembling violently, her body straining against the leather
straps.

He turned to face the students. "We rarely find that one
shock treatment is sufficient, even in the mildest cases of
dementia. We shall repeat the shock treatments at intervals.
Each treatment will be different and, of course, unexpected.
The purpose of these shock treatments is to jolt the patient
back to reality and teach them that it's better to be healthy.
Now, as soon as Godfrey has returned the patient to her
room, we will discuss the various treatments for mental
disorders. We shall cover everything from the ancient
method of trephining—that is, opening the skull—to such
modern theories as the fever treatment, in which an infec-
tion, such as a boil, is introduced to the patient's neck and
a curative fever produced. . . ."

Briony's senses left her, and when she came to, she was
again lying on the hard wooden plank of her cell.

Chapter 14

• •

THE DOCTOR HAD departed amid a great deal of noise and confusion with Godfrey and the footmen rushing about carrying luggage and passing along orders to underlings. The school would be closed for at least two weeks while the doctor attended a gathering of physicians in London, and some of the students left to go home for an unexpected midwinter break.

Afterward the household settled down to a less arduous routine, and Emily received her first letter from Edward, hurriedly given to her by Carruthers before he, too, left to visit his parents in Preston.

Edward had written:

My Dear Emily,

I am studying at a charity hospital in the dock area and cannot begin to describe the misery and suffering our fumbling efforts do little to ease. Most of our patients are seamen suffering from a variety of injuries and diseases (many of a tropical nature—malaria, beriberi, and so on) and street women, whose ailments I cannot disclose to a gently bred girl such as yourself. Nevertheless, I feel intense pity for all of them, but especially the innocent children, who for the most part come to the hospital under a sentence of death. Surely we humans with our superior brains are capable of understanding more about how our own bodies function and what causes them to sicken and die. Physicians seem to become impervious to the agony of their patients, seeing them only as a specific disease rather than a living, breathing fellow human being. I hope to God I never become so inured.

Emily brushed aside a tear, thinking of the kind and compassionate Edward. He would never become hardened to suffering, she was certain. She read on.

But my dear, I do not wish to burden you with the shortcomings of the medical profession, as I am more concerned about how your sweet self is faring. Have you now learned the extent of your indebtedness to Dr. Stoddard? If so, please let me know, and I will find a way to acquire the funds to set you free.

I am also concerned that none of my letters to my sister (who as I told you is staying with her husband's sister in Scotland) have been answered. But perhaps Briony is ill and unable to write. The weather this winter seems to have been particularly severe, does it not?

Now, as to my abrupt departure from Dr. Stoddard's establishment, it seems my brother-in-law stopped paying my tuition. I have not contacted him in regard to this but will be forced to approach him soon if I don't hear from Briony, as I am becoming more and more concerned about her silence.

Duty calls, my dear, so I will say goodbye for now.

Your devoted friend, Edward.

Emily considered the implication of Edward's offer to pay her debts. Would she then be indebted to him? Of course she would. Since he continually expressed his devotion to her, there was the distinct possibility that he might one day propose marriage, and then she would be obliged to accept. But although she liked Edward very much, her feelings were sisterly, and the idea of marriage was not appealing. Not that she wished to remain in the doctor's service; far from it, since even her elevated position as parlor maid entailed endless grinding chores that left no time for the pursuit of other activities. Emily had been accustomed to accompanying her father to the theater and concerts and social gatherings that he as a diplomat attended. They had visited museums and art galleries, and she had had unlimited time to read or work on her watercolors and embroidery. She missed all of these activities. Her life had become a gray blur of work. She felt her mind atrophying as her once pretty hands grew calluses and burned with chilblains. But if she were to escape, where would she go? Penniless, without family, how could she survive? In moments of despair the prospect of marriage to Edward became more tolerable.

As she tried to shape her thoughts to accept what seemed to be her only escape from servitude, a troubling seed of a thought began to wend its way through her mind, growing and becoming more imperative. Despite her own predicament, the fate of Kane and his violin locked away in the lower reaches of the house began to be more important to her. If only there was a way to release him from his self-imposed isolation.

But his golden eye no longer appeared at the keyhole when she cleaned the doctor's operating theater, and she missed his presence.

As the day for the doctor's return approached, Emily found time to write a brief letter to Edward so that she would be able to give it to Carruthers after the school reopened. In her letter she thanked him again for his concern, told her debts were now complicated by the fact that they were owed to the late Mr. Crupe's estate, and then, instinctively knowing that Edward would feel happier if he felt needed, she asked if he could find out where her father had been buried so that she could visit his grave.

Except for Godfrey's twice daily visits with her food, Briony had been left alone. On the one hand she was relieved that she had not been dragged up to the theater for another "shock" treatment, but her complete isolation was beginning to take its toll. She was lethargic; both body and mind seemed numbed from her ordeal. How much longer would Rupert make her suffer? Why had the doctor not returned to see her? Questioning Godfrey was useless. He pushed her food through the grating and departed, ignoring her pleas for news of the outside world.

She desperately tried to keep track of time, scratching a record of the meals she received in order to count the days. She also began to chip away at the stone wall in the corner of her room in the hope of making a tunnel through to the next chamber. It gave her something to do and a faint hope that one day she would escape.

In spite of her best efforts to remain hopeful, one day she succumbed to utter despair. She had heard the dogs barking earlier, but then they grew quiet, and faintly she heard someone whistling. Her hearing was becoming more acute, she'd noticed, perhaps due to the darkness that seemed akin to blindness.

Could it be the man with the scarred features who was whistling? She called out, "Kane! Kane, is that you?"

There was no response, and the whistling gradually faded away. It was more than Briony could bear. She screamed and sobbed and beat on the door until her fists bled.

At last, exhausted, she sank to the cold floor and buried her face in her hands.

"If you are quite finished with that hysterical outburst, perhaps you will explain what precipitated it?" The calm, resonant voice belonged to Kane.

"I have been left alone for . . . I think it is almost two weeks. I cannot bear it. I heard you whistling . . ."

"I do not whistle. You probably heard Dudley as he fed the dogs. He is a half-wit and cannot help you."

"You promised to give my brother a message."

"I made no such promise. I could not have kept it even if I had, since your brother is no longer one of the doctor's students."

"Then he must have returned to Rupert's house. I can't understand how Edward can tolerate my incarceration here. Why, he hasn't even been to see me. Has everyone deserted me?"

"My father has gone to London to a meeting of physicians. He goes to such gatherings in the hope of meeting a doctor who—like himself—is experimenting with methods of removing scar tissue and rebuilding faces such as mine. But of course it is a futile hope. Still, it keeps him going. He'll be back in a day or two, and then no doubt you'll be released and sent home to your husband.''

"Do you think I would ever return to that blackguard? Please, Kane, let me go. I swear I will never go near my husband—that no one will ever hear from me again. Just unlock my door and show me how to get out of the cellar. I beg of you to have pity on me."

"I cannot let you out, even if I wanted to, since Godfrey has the key, and this door is far too stout to be battered down."

"You could order Godfrey to give you the key."

"His allegiance is to my father. He would never disobey him."

"Then for God's sake overpower him and take the key away from him!"

Kane seemed to smother a chuckle. "You must imagine my physical strength to be great, indeed, if you think I could overpower Godfrey. However, I will speak with my father again and see if he'll send you home, if only because you disturb my peace with your raving. Now, will you promise to be quiet?"

"Please don't leave me alone! Stay and talk for a while."

His footsteps echoed down the corridor and faded into silence. Briony sighed and returned to her bed.

Then, miraculously, the footsteps returned.

A moment later she thought she surely must be dreaming as the air was filled with the sound of a violin. She didn't recognize the melody, but the music was almost too beautiful to bear. Spellbound, she held her breath and listened, feeling her spirit transported far from her grim surroundings to a place of serenity and hope.

When the last sweet strains of the music ended, Briony felt uplifted, filled with hope that life would be good again. Before she could find the words to express her wonderment, Kane's footsteps retreated down the passageway.

The staff lined up in the hall for Dr. Stoddard's return, and Godfrey, who seemed to have taken Crupe's place in the hierarchy of servants, stepped forward to take the doctor's greatcoat, hat, gloves, and muffler. Stoddard looked gray with fatigue and out of sorts. He barely glanced at the maids bobbing curtsies.

"I shall retire immediately," he told Godfrey.

"Begging your pardon, sir, but there's a matter of importance I must inform you of," Godfrey said with unaccustomed pompousness. Listening, Emily wondered what couldn't wait until morning, as the hour was late.

"What is it, then?" Stoddard asked, frowning.

Godfrey's small deep-set eyes gleamed as he motioned to the servants that they were dismissed. He waited until they were out of sight before speaking.

"It's Sir Rupert Forester, sir."

"He hasn't paid his bill, is that it?" Stoddard said testily. "For heaven's sake—"

Godfrey said quickly, "I took him to your laboratory, sir. He didn't want anyone else to know of his visit, so I thought it must have to do with 'is wife. He's been waiting for hours."

The doctor followed Godfrey to the laboratory adjacent to the operating theater, where Sir Rupert paced back and forth, still wearing his coat. The room was as cold as a crypt.

As soon as Stoddard entered the room, Rupert said, "No one must know I came here tonight. I assume you can trust Godfrey to keep his mouth shut? Especially since a word from me in the right quarter could send both of you to jail?"

"What is it we can do for you, Sir Rupert?" Stoddard asked.

"Dismiss your man, and then we'll talk."

"You may go, Godfrey."

When they were alone, Rupert said, "There's been an accident. I was cleaning my pistol, and it accidentally went off. . . . Mrs. Markham was with me at the time. She's dead."

Stoddard digested this startling news silently for a moment, considering the implications, then said, "I see. You sent for the police, of course, and a doctor to sign the death certificate?"

"Don't be a fool. I left her in my bedroom and came straight here. I want you and Godfrey to take care of matters for me. I can't be involved in a scandal—it would ruin my political career."

"Let me see if I understand you, Sir Rupert. You're asking me to conceal a death by gunshot and dispose of a body—is that it?"

"It wouldn't be the first time you or your students have dissected a cadaver of dubious origin, would it? Look, we've got to go and get her immediately. I've been waiting for you all evening, and I'm afraid one of the servants might discover her. We'll need Godfrey to . . . clean the room."

"Godfrey will return to your house with you. He will clean the room and then bring the body back here. You should remain at home. You're sure none of your servants saw her arrive?"

"Absolutely. She always entered the house through the French doors in my study."

"Does Mrs. Markham have anyone who will report her absence?"

"A housekeeper and a lady's maid. But she's frequently gone for several days at a time. I doubt they'll sound the alarm immediately."

The doctor rang the bell, and Godfrey returned. He was given instructions swiftly and briefly. Minutes later he and Rupert were in a carriage rattling through the almost deserted city streets.

The moment they turned the corner of the street where Rupert's fine old Georgian mansion stood, he knew they were too late. Constables and neighbors swarmed around his house, which blazed with lights. He saw Mrs. Winthrop standing in the doorway, in conversation with a man Rupert recognized as the coroner. There was no doubt that they had discovered the body.

"Stop!" Rupert struck Godfrey a sharp blow with his stick. "Turn around! Go back."

Godfrey didn't need telling twice.

Back at the doctor's house Rupert ordered Godfrey to awaken the doctor.

Stoddard, clad in his nightshirt, came stumbling into the study a few minutes later. "What is all this now? The body has been discovered? Then you must face the music, Sir Rupert. There's nothing to be done."

"Nonsense. I've thought the situation through, and there is something to be done. We will give the police Ursula Markham's murderer . . . my wife."

Dr. Stoddard, who had long ago steeled himself to accept the imperfections of humanity, now stared in horror at the man standing before him. "Surely you don't mean that? You can't blame your wife. You must tell the police it was an accident."

"I'm not sure it will look like an accident."

"What do you mean?"

"I shot her twice."

The chill creeping along Stoddard's veins warned that he was dealing with a man who would stop at nothing to protect himself. It was now obvious that Sir Rupert had deliberately killed his mistress. Probably because in Briony's absence Mrs. Markham had foolishly demanded that he divorce his wife, using insanity as grounds, and marry her. There may have been a threat of blackmail to cause Sir Rupert to resort to murder.

"Look, man," Rupert went on, "everyone knows my wife had a mental breakdown. You and Godfrey can testify that you had to confine her here, that you gave her shock treatments. All because of Ursula. I will have to admit that she was my mistress, of course. I'll say that Briony burst in upon us and shot her. Anyone who knows Briony is aware of her temper."

"But your wife will deny it, and she can be quite rational at times. Besides, she was here, in my care, at the time Mrs. Markham died."

"She escaped, of course. Godfrey was careless and left the door unlocked."

"But the cellar is also kept locked."

"Don't trouble me with details—somehow she escaped, returned to my house, and caught me in flagrante delicto. After she shot Mrs. Markham, she fled from the house and

I pursued her. This will explain why we were both gone when the body was discovered.''

''And where did Lady Forester go?''

''To her brother. You said he's studying at that charity hospital near the docks, didn't you? We'll deliver her to him, and then I'll go and tell the police my story, let them arrest her. I won't even have to go to her trial, since a husband cannot be forced to testify against his wife.''

''But Edward may be charged as an accessory, or at least with harboring a fugitive. He's a good chap, and I believe he has the makings of a fine doctor. I'd hate to see his chances ruined. God knows we need better educated physicians.''

Rupert shrugged. ''His career is the least of my concerns at present.''

Stoddard, who had always deferred to Sir Rupert's higher rank, stared at him. ''What a cold bastard you are.''

''We're wasting time. Can you give Briony something that will put her to sleep? Preferably something that will make her groggy when she wakes up, so she won't remember what happened. That's all you have to do. We'll put her in my carriage, and I'll deliver her to the hospital.''

The doctor hesitated for only a moment. Ever since the day the lab exploded into flames, there had been one driving, yearning goal that he had pursued. To find a way to eliminate scars, to discover a way to regenerate tissue and skin. Most of his secret experiments had been a means toward this end. In order to restore Ambrose's features the doctor was more than willing to sacrifice his own soul. Nothing must be allowed to prevent his experiments. Besides, if Sir Rupert were crossed, he would press grave-robbing charges, just as he threatened. No, the doctor simply couldn't risk being implicated in Sir Rupert's tangled web. The sooner both he and his wife were out of the house the better.

Emily awoke with a start, her heart pounding. She couldn't recall having had a nightmare, yet something had called her from deep sleep. She was alone in her attic room, as Godfrey had not yet hired a replacement for Doris.

Something was abroad in the night, something evil. Emily knew it with a certainty. She slipped her feet into her shoes, wrapped a blanket around her shoulders, and crept down the stairs.

A faint sound in the hall below stopped her in her tracks. A low moan, as though someone were hurt or ill.

Emily quickly descended the staircase, moving toward the sound. She almost collided with two men at the foot of the stairs.

Godfrey held a limp body in his arms, long hair streaming loose. Emily had never seen the woman before but knew instinctively it was the woman who had been locked in the cellar. Behind Godfrey a handsome, well-dressed man uttered a curse and grabbed Emily's arm.

"Dammit, where did you come from?" Without waiting for an answer, he turned to Godfrey. "Give me Briony. I'll take her out to the carriage. You'd better lock this one up until we decide what to do about her."

Emily tried to pull free, but they were too quick for her. The unconscious woman was transferred from Godfrey to the well-dressed man. Emily found herself being propelled along the corridor by Godfrey.

Somehow she knew, long before they reached the locked and barred door, that she was being taken to the cellar, perhaps to occupy the same room the unfortunate woman had just left. Emily also knew that the images of the well-dressed man, with his dark good looks, and the beautiful auburn-haired woman were etched in her memory forever.

Chapter 15

• •

PHIN LOOKED AT the black pearl dangling from a slender gold chain and murmured, "It is very beautiful."

"No more beautiful than you, Lotus Blossom." Giles Whittleford lifted the silken curtain of her hair and slipped the chain around her throat. The black pearl lay against the lily-petal softness of her skin in the hollow between her breasts, and he stared at it for a moment. Then he bent his head and pressed his lips to the pearl, moved sideways to find her nipple and eagerly lick it, suck on it gently, and take it fully into his mouth in the way she had taught him.

She sighed and lay back against the cool linen of the bedsheet while his mouth made hungry forays between her breasts. His manhood swelled and grew against her thigh until she opened herself to him and felt the pulsing shaft penetrate her secret places.

Although to Giles she was now completely engrossed in the pleasure they shared, murmuring her delight in his skill, her admiration for his physical attributes, and her everlasting gratitude that he found her own humble person appealing, even as she writhed beneath him, gripping him tightly with inner muscles so carefully trained by the chief eunuch, until poor Giles was mindless with ecstasy . . . even so, Phin's thoughts were removed from her body. She was carefully examining the information he had given her.

She found it necessary to do serious analytical thinking during lovemaking with a Caucasian, as otherwise it was impossible for her to keep her thoughts from straying to that most treacherous of territories where lurked sensual memories of her magnificent barbarian, Brent Carlisle.

Not that any other Caucasian affected her as Brent had. Phin told herself that white skin, blue eyes, a long nose, or perhaps broad shoulders and great height would naturally remind her of Brent, causing his memory to insinuate itself into her thoughts. But she knew her problem was far more complex than the troubling similarities between Caucasians. It had to do with some mysterious spell Brent Carlisle had woven that ultimately she must find a way to break, or she would never again be able to enjoy a man's body.

So she moved her hips in erotic circles and caressed Giles's pectoral muscles and in her mind fitted together the pieces of a puzzle concerning her father and her half sister.

Phin's painstaking tracing of Fletcher and Emily Faraday's movements after they returned from China resembled an incomplete map, with paths that led nowhere and blank spaces where inhabited settlements should be.

Giles Whittleford was a shipowner whose vessels traded with China. She had met him on a visit to the consulate, made expressly for the purpose of becoming acquainted with any officials who might tell her more about her father. Giles had been an easy target for the exotically lovely Eurasian. He was a rather bland individual with a staid wife and dull children who nevertheless saw himself as a daredevil adventurer, despite the fact that he had inherited his ships and never once had sailed on them. Indeed, he seemed astonished when she asked if he had ever been to China. Phin thought that perhaps having an affair with her was the most rebellious thing Giles had ever done. He had been shocked at her wickedness when she persuaded him to remove his nightshirt before making love to her, and amazed when she initiated him into only a fraction of the infinite varieties of coupling in which she was proficient.

Tonight he had brought her the news she had waited to hear. Her father and his new bride had sailed to the New World. Their journey would take months, but eventually Fletcher Faraday would arrive at the British Embassy in Mexico City and assume his duties. His daughter Emily had, as Phin already knew, been accidentally killed by a poacher.

But Giles had heard rumors in diplomatic circles that

Fletcher's new bride, Antonia, was an adventuress who had banished Emily and that Emily had run away to avoid being sent to a finishing school abroad. Furthermore, Antonia was a little too fond of the gaming tables and had been heavily in debt at the time of her marriage. A puzzling rumor that Giles passed along concerned Antonia's connection to a man named Crupe, who was an assistant to a prominent doctor, about whom even more sinister rumors swirled.

Giles had hinted, red-faced, that some of Antonia's acquaintances—perhaps out of jealousy or spitefulness since she was apparently a very beautiful woman—believed she might have approached Crupe or the doctor for an illegal operation. He clearly did not want to discuss the matter further.

Later, as he reluctantly rose from her bed to return to his family, Phin unhooked the clasp of the chain holding the pearl pendant and handed it to him. "I cannot accept this, Giles. Give it to your wife."

"Wh-what are you saying?" he stammered.

"I am saying goodbye. I have found our brief acquaintance to be pleasant, but it is time for me to move on now."

"But—what have I done?"

"Nothing. We both knew our affair was temporary. Let us part now and remember each other fondly."

His face had begun to slowly crumble, and she feared he might become maudlin, so she quickly opened her hotel room door. "Go now, my dear. I shall soon be leaving the country. If I ever return, I will come to you."

She almost pushed him from the room, closed the door, and leaned against it. He had been generous during the short time she had known him, and she didn't need his black pearl, an unlucky gem. Giles had served his purpose. Phin felt little remorse about ending the affair. Did not men use and discard women at will? Why, then, should they complain if they were treated in the same way? There was no longer time to dally with him, even if she'd been so inclined, as she needed time before setting sail for Mexico to investigate the connection between her father's bride and the man named Crupe, who worked for a reputedly brilliant

doctor who taught students and engaged in extremely
advanced research.

"Turned his back on me, he did." Hortense Crupe
sniffed into a soggy handkerchief. "Didn't come to the
funeral, and not a penny have I received from the doctor
since my brother passed on. Now, wouldn't you think
there'd be back wages? If I had the means, I'd get a solicitor
to look into the matter, that I would. Why, he hasn't even
had the decency to return Martin's belongings."

"Your brother was your sole support, was he?" Phin
asked sympathetically.

Hortense nodded, dissolving again into her ruined handkerchief in a torrent of self-pity. She was a reed-thin spinster
clad in unrelieved black, and they sat in her unheated parlor.
A gray bloom coated the furniture, and little light penetrated
the shuttered windows, which proclaimed the house to be in
mourning. Phin's teacup rattled against her saucer when she
picked it up, and she realized she was shivering with the
cold, although Hortense appeared to be impervious to it.

"If we could return to the subject of Mrs. Fletcher
Faraday," Phin prompted gently. "I would be most grateful. You said she visited your brother here—were you
present?"

Small glittering eyes behind gold-rimmed pince-nez regarded Phin speculatively. "Oh, yes, I was here all right.
Not in the room with them, you understand, but—" She
broke off.

Phin murmured encouragingly, "If I'd been you, I'd
certainly have listened at the door to any conversation my
brother had with a woman like Antonia. One can't be too
careful, can one? After all, her reputation alone must have
given rise to concern. I'm sure only the fact that Mr.
Faraday had been abroad for so long kept him from being
aware of his bride's tarnished past."

Her eavesdropping vindicated, Hortense gave a thin
smile. "You didn't say *why* you're asking about my brother
and Dr. Stoddard and that woman."

"Miss Crupe, I find it appalling that Dr. Stoddard has
ignored you since your brother's death. As I told you when

I arrived, I am prepared to help you financially, but in return I must have some answers about your brother's—or the doctor's—dealings with Tonia Faraday. The amount of your compensation will depend on how honest you are with me. Know first that I shall be going abroad shortly, and nothing you tell me will go beyond this room. But before I leave I must learn all I can about Tonia. You see, she had a step-daughter who died under rather mysterious circumstances—"

Hortense gasped and clutched her throat. For a second Phin was afraid the other woman was having some sort of attack, but then realized she was cringing in abject fear.

"No, no! You mustn't accuse my brother of having any part of Tonia's evil schemes! I won't have his memory besmirched. He only said he'd do it because she threatened to spread lies about the cadavers the doctor used and implicate my brother."

The floodgates had opened. Phin leaned forward, her expression understanding, as Hortense first made her swear never to repeat anything she said, and then told her story.

"My brother was one of Dr. Stoddard's students years ago, but Martin wasn't cut out to be a doctor. He had more of a business mind, so the doctor let him run the household and the school. Martin dealt with the students and the patients and tradespeople—everyone."

Sensing that she was about to begin a long recital of her brother's accomplishments, Phin asked, "And Tonia was a patient?"

Hortense snorted indelicately. "Wanted to be. She was in the family way and wanted to get rid of it. Martin sent her packing, of course."

"Of course," Phin agreed.

"But she was persistent. She said she knew the doctor dealt with grave robbers and . . . well, that was the start of the blackmail, you see. But as it happened, she didn't need an illegal operation; she miscarried. Martin didn't see her again until she suddenly appeared a few months ago and again threatened to go to the authorities and accuse him of being a grave robber unless he got rid of her fiancé's daughter for her."

Phin froze. She spoke very softly, to disguise her agitation. "Got rid of? You mean . . . kill her?"

The pince-nez slipped from Hortense's thin nose as she nodded her head. "Antonia had it all planned. The girl would be aboard a southbound coach on her way to a finishing school abroad—nobody would miss her for days, maybe weeks. Tonia wanted Martin to take the girl from the coach and do away with her. Tonia said the body could be given to the doctor, and he could be told she was a street waif bound for a pauper's grave with no family to miss her."

"Emily was used . . . in the doctor's medical school?" Phin felt a sharp inner pain. Little wonder her dreams of the danger to her half sister had propelled her on her quest. Phin had thought there was little human depravity left to shock her, but this was so sickening she recoiled.

"That is indeed what Tonia suggested. I was listening at the parlor door, and I can tell you, I was shocked . . . couldn't believe my ears when I heard Martin agree. The minute Tonia left, I confronted my brother. He said at once that he had no intention of having the girl murdered. He had agreed to the wicked plot only so that he and the doctor could be free from Tonia's threats forever. Martin pointed out that if he had refused Tonia's request, some thug somewhere would kill the girl for a price. My brother's plan would not only rid himself of Tonia but save the girl, you see."

"But he didn't save her, did he? Emily was shot in the face and the blame put upon a poacher."

Hortense's expression became crafty. "A *poor orphan* who ran away from the workhouse was shot by the poacher. My brother saw at once that he could use the body of the orphan to save Tonia's stepdaughter."

Phin let out her breath slowly. "So Emily did not die? What became of her?"

"You must understand that a certain amount of white lies were necessary. I mean, if you get in touch with her, she'll tell you that Martin said her father was dead. He had to, you see, or she'd have gone back to him and, of course, to Tonia.

And Martin needed to keep an eye on her until they left the country. So he took her to the doctor's house and got her a job there.''

"She's still there, then—working for Dr. Stoddard?" Phin asked, hope leaping in her breast. Her half sister was still alive, and they would meet after all! She said a silent prayer of thanks to Kwan Yin.

Phin didn't doubt that Hortense Crupe had sanitized the story, but she felt the basic facts were probably true. There would be no reason for Crupe to murder Emily, risking being caught, when he could substitute a nameless body. She did wonder what else he'd told Emily in order to keep her in servitude, but for now all she needed to know was that Emily was alive.

Phin stood up. "Rest assured that what you've told me will be kept in confidence. Now, perhaps this will tide you over until your brother's estate is settled?" She took several bank notes from her reticule and placed them on the sideboard.

Emily huddled in the dark cell-like chamber into which she had been thrown, trying to make sense of her imprisonment. Since she hadn't done anything to precipitate punishment, the only explanation must be that she had seen something she wasn't supposed to see, namely the well-dressed man and Godfrey carrying the beautiful auburn-haired woman from the house.

The sound of the dogs barking a greeting interrupted her search for answers. She called out, "Dudley? Dudley, is that you? Can you find me? Please, it's Emily—come here, Dudley."

But he didn't come.

How far away was Kane? She remembered a long corridor and a sharp turn before reaching his basement quarters. She doubted he would hear if she called to him unless he happened to be passing by. He'd told her he spoke to the other prisoner in the cellar. Emily hoped he would return to do so again.

She thought she had become accustomed to the cold, but

her unheated attic room had been cozy compared to the
dank chill of the cellar. She forced herself to pace back and
forth in the confined space to keep her circulation going,
fearing that the numbness might reach her brain and she
would succumb to it, drifting away to oblivion.

A memory flashed into her mind, lingering for only a
moment, yet complete and, in retrospect, disturbing. Emily
and her father had always been so close—an island of two,
he used to say, afloat on the great continent of Asia. She had
adored him, and he was her dearest friend as well as a
devoted parent. He had never been too busy to listen to her,
to laugh with her, or to comfort her. Until the advent of
Tonia.

The first time her father suggested she join him and Tonia
at an afternoon concert in the park followed by high tea,
Emily had accepted with pleasure. She had felt she wouldn't
be in the way, since she would excuse herself before dinner,
leaving them to spend the evening alone.

Emily had gone to her room to put on her bonnet, and
Tonia had slipped into her room behind her. Black eyebrows
arched over Tonia's green-gold eyes, and she spoke in a
tone of amused condescension. "Emily, dear, I realize
you've been brought up without the benefit of an adult
female influence in your life other than those heathens you
associated with in China . . . so your lack of manners is
quite understandable. Therefore, I am taking it upon myself
to remind you when you fail to observe the niceties of polite
society. Now, when your father suggested you join us this
afternoon, the appropriate response was for you to say that
you had other plans for the afternoon or that you had a sick
headache and needed to rest. You see, your father followed
a little rule of etiquette by inviting you, but you broke one
when you accepted. He didn't really want you along, you
know; he wanted to be alone with me. Do you understand?"

Emily had never again made the mistake of accepting an
invitation to join them on any outing, even though Tonia
herself—in Fletcher's presence—asked her to do so. Still, it
had not been enough to keep Tonia from insisting she go to
finishing school. There had been one of Tonia's private

lectures about not intruding upon her father's honeymoon, and Emily, who wanted her father to be happy far more than she dreaded going to finishing school, agreed. Oh, if only she'd known how little time she had left with her beloved father! She would have defied Tonia in order to spend those precious minutes with him.

Now as she recalled her brief acquaintance with her father's bride, Emily at last asked herself the question she had not previously dared contemplate. Was it possible that everything that had happened to her, from servitude to her present imprisonment, was Tonia's doing?

"Lady Forester—are you awake?" Kane's face suddenly appeared at the grating in the door.

Startled, Emily gave a cry of alarm.

He immediately withdrew.

Panicked that he might be leaving, she called, "Kane—Kane, it's me, Emily. I didn't hear you coming—you startled me, that's all. They took Lady Forester away—I saw Godfrey carrying her from the house, and there was a well-dressed man—"

"Who put you in here?"

"Godfrey."

"Damn him. What did you do?"

"Nothing. I think it was because I saw them carrying the lady away. She was unconscious. I don't know if Dr. Stoddard knows I'm here."

"Stay calm. I'll speak with my father and find out what's going on."

"But . . . doesn't he only come down at dinnertime? It can hardly be dawn yet."

"Have you forgotten? I am not a prisoner. I shall go upstairs and speak with my father."

Despite her own peril, Emily could not help but feel a glimmer of hope. No matter what else lay in store, at least Kane was at last about to leave his tomb world.

Chapter 16

• •

BRIONY WAS NO longer sure what was real and what was part of her nightmare. She drifted in and out of consciousness, racked with violent tremors and nausea. Had she been poisoned? Had Rupert accompanied Godfrey when he carried her from the doctor's house for that wild ride through the meanest streets of the city, or was she still trapped in the nightmare?

She became aware of the sound of people in distress, moaning, coughing, children wailing. She was no longer in the doctor's cellar. She was in what appeared to be a waiting room, slumped on a hard bench flanked by two shawl-wrapped women who sighed and wheezed piteously. The air was rank with fetid humanity and faint eddies of carbolic soap.

Opposite her, a row of rough-looking men clad in knitted watch caps and salt-caked jackets waited silently, their faces weatherbeaten and etched with suffering. One had a wooden stump protruding from beneath his tar's pantaloons, and another's face was ravaged with boils.

As Briony's drugged senses began to clear, she became aware of a man wearing a blood-spattered white coat sitting at a desk on a raised dais, making entries in a book, oblivious to a crowd of people who clamored for his attention.

Briony rose on unsteady legs and made her way toward the desk. She caught the eye of a woman who shrieked that the child in her arms was dying of the flux.

"Please . . . is this a hospital?"

The woman looked at her warily. "Wot did you think, you'd come to church?"

Briony pushed her way to the front of the crowd. "I am Lady Forester," she announced in as firm a tone as she could muster. "I'm not sure how I got here, but—"

"Bri! Where on earth did you spring from?"

Turning, she almost collapsed into her brother's arms.

"Edward! Oh, thank God! I've been locked up in Dr. Stoddard's cellar . . ."

His face turned white with anger. "Damn Rupert for his perfidy! Come on, let's get you out of here where we can talk. I've a little time before I start my shift and the use of a room in a boardinghouse for a few days."

Keeping his arm protectively around her, he led her outside to the gaslit street, then down an alley to the back door of a narrow three-story house. He took her up a narrow, foul-smelling staircase to a room on the top floor, and by the time they reached it, Briony's strength had left her. She sank onto a chair, gasping for breath, as Edward lit the lamp and peered at her anxiously.

"My God, Bri, what have they done to you? I thought you were in Scotland with your sister-in-law. Let's get some brandy into you, and you can tell me the whole story."

Long before she had finished relating the details of her imprisonment, Edward was beside himself with anger. When she began to tell him about the doctor's shock treatment, he groaned and clapped his hand to his forehead.

"Dear God, if I'd only known! Listen, Bri, we're going to put you to bed. I'm afraid I must go back to the hospital, as I'm on duty tonight. You see, we give rudimentary care to patients in return for our tuition and keep. I live in a dormitory with a dozen other students, but one of the doctors took a liking to me and offered me the use of this room while he's visiting his ailing mother. It's so difficult to study at the hospital, we're constantly on call and . . . anyway, you'll be safe enough here until my shift ends. Tomorrow morning I shall confront Rupert."

Briony wanted to protest, but she found she was drifting

to sleep again, and she allowed him to remove her shoes and help her into bed.

She awoke to find Edward bending over her, shaking her arm. Daylight flooded the room through soot-grimed windows, testifying to the fact that she must have slept for hours.

"Bri, wake up. Here, drink this. We must talk." His expression was even more concerned than it had been the previous evening.

She sat up and he wrapped a blanket around her shoulders and put a scalding cup of tea in her hands.

Edward regarded her gravely. "First of all, I want you to know that I will stand by you, no matter what you may decide to do."

"I don't understand—"

"The police came to the hospital last night looking for you. They searched my dormitory, questioned me. They said Ursula Markham had been shot to death, and Rupert accuses you of her murder."

The room spun dizzily out of focus. Briony felt the cup and saucer removed from her shaking hands.

Edward went on quickly, "Naturally, I feigned ignorance of your whereabouts—said I hadn't seen you. Bri, I don't for a moment believe you killed her."

"No! No, of course not! The last time I saw her was at the Christmas party when I . . . Oh, dear heaven!"

"A warrant has been issued for your arrest. We must decide what to do, and we haven't much time. Someone may tell them that I've been using this room. I hate to have to tell you this, but she was killed in Rupert's bedroom. Apparently Mrs. Winthrop heard what sounded like a pistol shot—she had left the servants' quarters for some reason; otherwise she probably wouldn't have heard anything. Anyway, she discovered the body. Rupert wasn't there. He claims you caught them together, shot her, and left. He said you'd been staying with Dr. Stoddard, getting treatment, and he first went there looking for you. Then, he claims, when he learned you'd escaped from a locked room and left the doctor's house without telling anyone, he decided he'd better report the murder to the police.''

"Lies, all lies!" Briony gasped. "I can't be absolutely sure, but I think Rupert came for me and took me from Dr. Stoddard's house to the hospital. I have a vague recollection, almost like the memory of a nightmare . . . Oh, my God, Edward, can you imagine what the police will think if I tell them this?''

"Last night the pupils of your eyes were very dilated. You were probably given a powerful sedative—laudanum perhaps. Little wonder you can't remember what happened. But you're right, this is not a story we can tell the police. Rupert is a respected lawyer with powerful friends. Dr. Stoddard will undoubtedly testify that you had a mental breakdown—you wouldn't be the first wife who tried to do away with her husband's mistress. At best, you'll be sent to an institution for the criminally insane. At worst . . .''

He didn't have to elaborate. An image of a dangling hangman's rope flashed into Briony's mind.

"Frankly, Bri, I think we'd better find a sanctuary for you. You've got to get away before the police find you.''

"But where can I go? Apart from Rupert, I have only you, Edward, and obviously I can't stay with you in a hospital dormitory. I have no money, not even coach fare to another town—nothing but the clothes on my back.''

"I'll take you to an inn I know. You can wait there until I've made plans. Don't worry, Bri, I'll think of something.''

After taking his sister across the Mersey to the Red Lion Inn, situated on the Wirral peninsula near the mouth of the river, Edward returned to Liverpool and made his way to River Court. Dark clouds were closing in, bringing the threat of a winter storm. He hoped it would bring rain rather than snow.

He stood across the street from the doctor's house, waiting for a familiar face to appear, a student or a servant who would take a message to Emily. If he could enlist her help, they might be able to prove that Briony was still a prisoner in the cellar when Mrs. Markham was murdered. But on this freezing cold morning no one left the house, and he was reluctant to ring the doorbell and face Godfrey.

A hansom cab turned the corner and proceeded down the court. He watched idly, then with interest as the cab came to a halt in front of the doctor's house. A moment later a woman alighted and walked up the steps to the front door.

From where he stood, behind an ancient elm, now winter bare but with a formidable trunk to conceal his presence, Edward could not see the woman's face, but he was struck immediately by the fact that her hair, dark as a raven's wing and without a hint of a curl or a wave, hung unfettered to her waist. Although she wore Western clothes—a fur-trimmed coat and bonnet—and carried a fur muff, that black curtain of hair proclaimed her to be Oriental. Intrigued, he stepped from his hiding place, hoping to catch a glimpse of her face.

But the front door of the doctor's house opened, and after a brief exchange Godfrey admitted her. Edward returned to his position behind the elm tree and waited.

Less than fifteen minutes later the woman reappeared. She walked down the steps to the street and looked around, apparently expecting that the hansom would have waited, but the cabbie had departed.

Edward saw now that the exotically lovely woman was Eurasian, with very fair skin, and her eyes were not the narrow slits of virtually all of the Asians he had ever seen. Almost without thinking, he started across the street toward her as though drawn by an invisible thread.

She watched him approach, and his first impression of her was to marvel at the aura of calmness she exuded, as though nothing he said or did would surprise her. He chided himself that he was allowing himself to be influenced by the Occidental myth that all Orientals were inscrutable, but he found her serenity of demeanor even more attractive than her undeniable beauty.

Reaching her side, he stammered, "I . . . Pardon my . . . Forgive me, but I saw your cab leave and wondered if I might be of service. If you'll permit me, I could walk with you to a cabstand nearby.''

Her lips curved in a smile that he had no doubt enchanted men more sophisticated than he. He felt his knees wobble slightly. When she spoke her voice was soft, well-modulated, and although her English was flawless, it was intriguingly accented, as if she had learned the language from another foreigner. ''Or you could direct me to the place where the cabs wait?''

He felt his color rise. ''Yes, of course.''

''But tell me,'' she went on before he could gather his wits, ''why were you watching this house? Oh, yes, I saw you lurking behind the tree when I arrived. Come, walk with me and explain. Perhaps our meeting here today was not random happenstance?''

''My name is Edward Darnell,'' he said, falling into step beside her. ''I was a student of the doctor's for a time, and I—well, I hoped to speak privately with one of his servants. A young lady named Emily Faraday.''

She stopped and turned to look at him. ''I think perhaps I was correct in assuming that our meeting was ordained by the fates, Mr. Darnell. Would you care to accompany me to a teahouse so that we may relate to each other all we know about Miss Faraday?''

Although he certainly had no intention of telling this exotic stranger anything about Briony, to his dismay an hour later the warmth of a tea shop's cozy fire and her calming presence had somehow extracted the whole story, except for Briony's whereabouts. Edward blinked, wondering how he had been seduced into revealing so much. ''So you see, I wanted to find out if Emily knew of Briony's presence in the house, especially at the time my brother-in-law's mistress was killed.''

Phin leaned forward and spoke softly. ''Our first task, then, is to ascertain where Emily is. You see, I was told by the doctor's assistant that she left his employ.''

''But that's impossible! She had nowhere to go.''

''Perhaps this sorry business with your sister is connected

in some way? You say your sister was locked away in the doctor's cellar. Is it possible this is where Emily is?''

"Yes, of course!" Edward said excitedly. "Emily perhaps knows about Bri!" He paused. "You haven't told me why you were also seeking Miss Faraday.''

She gave a secretive smile. "It is an old connection, through our honorable mothers. For now I am charged with reuniting Emily with her father.''

"But her father died. That's how she came to be in the doctor's service.''

"No, Fletcher Faraday is still alive. He is en route to the New World. Now, since the doctor's man insists Emily is no longer employed, and you have knowledge of the house, we must devise a way to get you into the cellar to learn if she has met the same fate as your sister.''

"I shall go back at once and demand to see Emily.''

"Not so fast, Mr. Darnell. Mr. Godfrey will simply tell you the same thing he told me. I believe we must use more covert means. Could you slip in through the tradesmen's entrance and find a way to get into the cellar?''

"With the fate of the two women I care about most in the world in jeopardy? Yes, indeed, I shall find a way." He glanced at the tea shop window as the skies turned leaden and large drops of rain spattered against the glass. "We're in for a downpour.''

Dudley had filled two pails with the kitchen leftovers, consisting mainly of moldy bread, and was about to make his way to the cellar to feed the dogs, taking his usual route through the backyard, when Cook waylaid him. "Go through the operating theater. The rain's coming down in a solid sheet—there'll be nowt left of that bread by the time you get through the yard.''

"B-but the doctor . . .'' Dudley began to shake in terror.

"There's no lecture today. The doctor had to go to the hospital. He was called out in the middle of the night, poor soul, and him only just back from London, too, and fair worn out. Now, he won't be back until late today, so you just take that bread on through the operating theater, my lad."

Dudley chewed his slack lower lip doubtfully. "B-but the door's locked."

"Mr. Godfrey's in there cleaning. You tell him I said you were to go that way."

Hanging his head to show this was not to his liking, Dudley obeyed. He made his way to the theater and paused to peer around the vestibule door. Mr. Godfrey was scrubbing the operating table, his back to the door.

Dudley chewed his lip frantically, unsure how to attract the attention of the man he feared most in the world. Should he call out? Or walk into the room? His poor befuddled brain wrestled with the problem. Godfrey had been known to box the ears of any unwary servant who got in his way, and Dudley certainly didn't want to risk his wrath.

Godfrey looked around suddenly and saw him. "What are you dithering about there for?"

"C-cook said to g-go this way. Sh-she said it's raining—"

"Come on, then, hurry up about it." Godfrey went to the cellar door and unlocked it. "Look sharp, now." He had returned to the operating table before Dudley reached the cellar door.

Stepping into the dank gloom, Dudley felt a hand clapped over his mouth. A voice whispered in his ear. "Don't make a sound, Dudley. I won't hurt you, but you must keep quiet, do you understand?"

Terrified, Dudley nodded his head.

The hand was removed. The burned features of Kane materialized in the semidarkness. Dudley had been warned not to approach Kane, or go near his quarters, and he shook with fright.

Kane carefully closed the door. "I want you to do something for me, Dudley. If you agree, in return you may ask me for anything at all. Will you agree to this exchange of favors?"

Dudley wasn't quite sure what he was being asked, but he

nodded his head vigorously. He certainly didn't want to fall afoul of this demon-faced man.

"Very good. Now, Godfrey is in there cleaning the theater. He has two wooden key rings, each with several keys on them. He used one key to open this door and left the key in the lock so he can lock up again after you've fed the dogs. The other key ring is attached to his belt. When he's finished in the theater, he will go to his room to sleep because he was out most of the night. Do you think you could slip in and get that key ring for me?"

Dudley's mouth hung open, and he stared uncomprehendingly.

Kane realized the poor lad needed simpler directions. Perhaps this wasn't such a good idea after all. Kane had been reluctant to venture into the upper reaches of the house himself, thinking he would frighten any unwary servant who stumbled into his path. He had considered demanding that Godfrey give him the key to Emily's cell, but in all probability it was Godfrey who had locked her in. From what she'd said, she had seen him carrying Lady Forester from the house. With the doctor away at the hospital, Godfrey was master of the house, and Kane feared for Emily's safety if he waited for his father's return. No, he must get her out of the cellar immediately, but clearly poor half-witted Dudley could not help.

He patted the youth's shoulder reassuringly. "Never mind, Dudley, I'll take care of it myself. You go and feed the dogs."

When Edward knocked on the doctor's door, the rain-clouds had cloaked the morning sky in gloom and the downpour continued unabated. He'd been prepared to offer the excuse that he had returned to collect some personal belongings left behind, but the door was opened by a parlor maid who simply admitted him, asking no questions. Several pieces of luggage were stacked in the hallway, and he realized he'd had the good luck to arrive at the same time as some of the students—the maid had assumed he was also a student. There was no sign of Godfrey, but it was well known that he slept during the morning after his gruesome nocturnal excursions.

Edward lingered in the hall with the other students until the maid disappeared, learning from their conversation that the doctor had been away and classes would not resume until the following day. Then he made his way to the servants' quarters.

At this time of the morning all of the servants would be at work in the kitchen or various parts of the house. Only Godfrey would be in his bed, and with Mr. Crupe's demise, only Godfrey would have the keys to the cellar. Edward prayed that Godfrey would prove to be a sound sleeper.

There were four rooms opening to a narrow landing, and these were used by the senior servants, all others being consigned to the attic. The first door he opened was obviously shared by Cook and a parlor maid. As he eased open the second door, the sound of teeth-rattling snoring confirmed that this was Godfrey's room.

For an instant the image of his sister, hiding at the inn and under possible sentence of death if she were caught, flashed into Edward's mind. What would become of Briony if he were caught breaking into the doctor's house? But then, equally urgent, Emily's sweet face implored him not to desert her. And she might well have seen or heard something while in the doctor's house that could help Briony.

He took a step into the room, and a floorboard creaked loudly. The snoring stopped. Edward held his breath. Godfrey rolled over, snorted, and resumed snoring.

Edward looked around. Godfrey's clothes lay in a crumpled heap on a chair next to the bed. He had also carelessly draped his overcoat on the back of the chair. There was a marble-topped washstand and a chest of drawers. Since Godfrey always carried the keys with him, Edward decided they were most likely on the chair with the clothes. Four swift steps took him to the chair.

A quick check showed the keys were not there. He was about to go to the chest of drawers when on an impulse he lifted the overcoat from the back of the chair. Two wooden key rings had been hooked over the chair post.

Holding the keys carefully to keep them from rattling, Edward tiptoed to the door and a moment later was on the landing.

He breathed a sigh of relief that was cut short as he felt himself seized from behind.

Chapter 17

• •

EDWARD FOUND HIMSELF being propelled along the landing by his silent adversary, and caught off guard, he offered no resistance until they reached the stairs. Then he managed to twist sideways and look over his shoulder to see who was attempting to shove him down the staircase.

Edward gasped as he looked into the pitiful remains of a face that had been hideously burned. Only one eye remained unscathed, and it bored into Edward's horrified stare, expressing a rage at the world that was frightening to behold.

"Don't make a sound," the burned man hissed between cruelly scarred lips, "or you'll wake Godfrey. Follow me. I came up through the east wing and didn't encounter any servants."

"But—"

The burned man gave Edward an impatient shove. "Don't argue if you want to save Emily."

The keys were yanked from Edward's hand, and the burned man started down the stairs. Edward had no choice but to follow.

They reached the operating theater without running into any of the household staff, and Edward noted that the burned man did not use the keys on the wooden rings to open the vestibule door, as he had his own key.

Later Edward would realize that had it not been for his fearsome guide, he might have wandered the dark chambers and corridors of the cellar for hours before finding the narrow passage lined with heavily barred doors.

A single oil lantern attached to the wall beside one of the

doors cast a faint amber glow on a small grating in the upper portion of the door. Peering inside, Edward saw Emily huddled in a corner of the tiny cell-like room.

The burned man turned a key in the lock and stepped into the cell. Emily rose to her feet, crying, "Kane! Oh, thank God you came!"

Then to Edward's amazement, she flung herself into the arms of the burned man, who held her with what appeared to be the tenderness of a lover. Edward felt his blood churn, and he was unsure if what he felt was revulsion or anger.

"Emily!" Edward said sharply. "I've come to take you away from this house."

Her startled gaze found him. "Edward! Where did you spring from?"

"I was the one who crept into Godfrey's room to get the keys," he responded, hating the irritable whine in his tone, but the burned man seemed to have stolen his moment of glory.

Emily extricated herself from Kane's embrace and took a step toward him, but before Edward could claim a similar reward, Kane said quickly, "I don't know what Godfrey is up to, but the doctor is away and Godfrey can do as he pleases. Now, listen to me, both of you. There's no time for idle conversation. I shall lead you from the cellar, and then you, Edward, will take Emily to safety. Since you are undoubtedly the student who sacrificed his cuff links to make her brooch, I assume you have no money?"

"I can take care of Emily," Edward said, his pride further wounded.

But Kane was now addressing Emily. "I have not had any need of money myself, as you know. But I want you to take this and sell it if you need to. It is a gift, given without obligation, to express my gratitude to you for treating me decently."

In the dimly lit cell Edward could not see what it was that the burned man gave her. Kane then grabbed Emily's hand and, before Edward could utter a word, led her out of the cell.

Edward followed as they hurried through the labyrinth of

corridors. At last they came to a short flight of stone steps. At the top a faint blur of daylight came through grimy windows flanking a door to the outside world.

As they climbed the steps, Edward could see that the windows offered a worm's-eye view of the flagged yard of the house. Freedom appeared to be only seconds away.

But the door to the yard was locked, and none of the keys fit.

"Can we break it down?" Edward asked.

"Our shoulders will break first," Kane responded. "We must go back. You'll have to leave through the operating theater."

They retraced their footsteps, and Kane led them past the caged animals into a chamber where he paused long enough to light a lantern. The need for this quickly became apparent when they entered a pitch-dark passageway.

For Emily, clinging to Kane's hand as he set a fast pace, her fear of again falling into Godfrey's hands outweighed her curiosity as to how her two unlikely champions had managed to join forces. Kane had given her what appeared to be a small trinket box, and the corners bit into her palm as she stumbled along between the two men.

Now they were ascending the flight of stairs leading to the theater. When they reached the cramped landing where Kane had crouched to watch her through the keyhole, he paused for a moment before unlocking the door. He looked at her, his ravaged face softened by the dim light of the lantern.

She expected him to speak, to say goodbye at least, but he silently raised his hand and with one finger gently traced the curve of her cheek. The gesture took only a split second, yet had he spent an hour telling her she had changed his life and he felt deep concern for her safety, he could not have expressed his feelings more eloquently.

Then he turned to Edward and said brusquely, "She's in your care now. Go."

He opened the door.

Emily said impulsively, "Kane, please—come with us."

Edward could not believe his ears. Kane merely gave a

short laugh that expressed more sadness than mirth and pushed them both into the theater. The door closed firmly behind them.

"Come on, Emily," Edward urged, "we must hurry before Godfrey is up and about again."

She nodded, feeling as if she were being wrenched away from a lifelong friend in leaving Kane behind. She didn't glance at the keyhole as she followed Edward through the theater.

They had just reached the vestibule door when it burst open. Godfrey stood on the threshold, a towering figure who loomed up over them like a huge bear.

Emily cried out in fear as Godfrey lashed out at Edward, sending him crashing into the wall. Edward recovered his balance and gamely raised his fists to defend himself as Godfrey uttered a bloodcurdling growl and charged him again.

It was obvious to Emily that Edward could not possibly prevail, as he was attempting to fight like a gentleman while Godfrey kicked and gouged and succeeded in knocking Edward's feet out from under him. He fell heavily to the floor, and Godfrey plunged after him, his hands fastened around Edward's throat.

In desperation Emily grabbed Godfrey's arm to try to get him to relinquish his hold, but he merely shook her off. She then jumped on his back and seized his hair, pulling with all of her might. He appeared oblivious to her.

The next second she felt someone lift her away and place her on her feet some distance away.

"Let him go, Godfrey," Kane's voice thundered.

Godfrey looked up at him. "You get yourself back where you belong. Stay out of this." His fingers tightened on Edward's throat.

"Oh, dear God! He's killing him!" Emily cried as Edward's face turned blue and he began to make gurgling sounds.

Out of the corner of her eye she saw Kane take two quick strides toward the cabinet where the doctor's knives and scalpels were laid out. She caught the glint of a blade in

Kane's hand, and then he bore down upon Godfrey. Emily covered her eyes with her hands as Kane plunged the knife into Godfrey's back.

Cowering back against the vestibule door, Emily jammed her fist against her teeth to keep from crying out. Kane rolled the now limp body of Godfrey from Edward, who looked up at his rescuer and said hoarsely, "I don't know who you are, but I'll never forget that you saved my life."

Kane helped him to his feet.

In the confusion no one had noticed the second figure standing in the vestibule. Godfrey had been accompanied by Cook, who stood in the shadows staring at his blood-soaked body. "Murder!" she screamed. "Murderers! Oh, you'll hang for this, you will!"

She turned and ran shrieking along the corridor.

Kane sighed. "Perhaps my fate was sealed the moment you came into the theater, Emily. It seems the fates always intended I should leave my safe haven and travel with you. Come on. We'd better depart before she brings the peelers."

Chapter 18

· ·

WATCHING THE RAIN drum monotonously against the windows of her room at the inn, Briony had begun to fear that Edward might not return before dark. She watched the arrivals of coaches in the courtyard below her window, anxiously scanning each emerging figure, and was unprepared for the sudden knocking on her door.

"Who . . . who's there?"

"It's me. Let me in."

Briony threw open the door. "Edward! How did you get here? I've watched the arrival of every coach."

"I hired a hansom cab and had him drop me off in an alley several blocks away, just in case I was followed."

"Goodness, you're drenched—take off your coat."

"No time. We're leaving right away."

"Where are we going?"

"To another hotel near the Liverpool docks." He gave a crooked grin. "I have a rather remarkable tale to tell you. I'll give you all the details on the way. Oh, yes, one of the people waiting for us is known to you, or so he says. His name is Kane."

Emily found it difficult not to stare at the beautiful Eurasian girl who was presently wrapping a blanket around her. The presence of Phin in the gloomy Liverpool hotel room evoked so many memories of China and such feelings of longing that it was difficult for Emily to patiently await explanations.

Kane stood at the window staring out at the rain, and Emily was certain that if he could have covered his poor burned face, he would have. Her heart ached with compassion for him, knowing what it was costing him to leave the sanctuary of his father's cellar. Although she admired his courage in saving Edward's life, she was also chillingly aware that Kane had killed a man. Edward had departed to fetch his sister, who apparently had been accused of a crime she had not committed.

"Don't worry, you'll be safe here with Phin," Edward had told her, then added with a rueful smile, "She is unconcerned that we are a band of fugitives."

Emily wondered how many women would have calmly accepted the arrival of Kane, as Phin had. She wasn't sure what the connection between Edward and Phin was, but Phin had obviously been waiting for him. Prior to his departure the two of them had conferred privately in the hallway outside the hotel room, speaking in low, urgent whispers.

The strangest aspect of the situation was that Phin had clearly also been expecting Emily. Her dark eyes had searched Emily's face in the manner of one being reunited with a long-lost friend.

Now she said gently, "I have good news for you. It is about your father."

Emily felt a stab of pain. "Perhaps you are unaware that my father passed away?"

"No," Phin said firmly. "He did not. He is very much alive and presently en route to his new post in Mexico City."

For an instant the room spun dizzily. Emily felt strong smooth hands grip hers reassuringly. "I know this is a shock to you, Miss Faraday, but it is true. You were betrayed, lied to, tricked—and so was your father. You see, your father believes *you* are dead."

Emily gasped. "Then Mr. Crupe—"

"Conspired with your father's bride."

"Tonia." Emily closed her eyes briefly as if to shut out the knowledge of her stepmother's perfidy. "I should have known." Her thoughts were racing, trying to grasp all the implications of the rapid twists and turns her life appeared to be taking. "I must go to my father at once. Dear Lord, how he must have suffered!"

"But you must beware of your stepmother. Since I myself am hoping to sail to Mexico City, perhaps you will allow me to accompany you, to offer my humble assistance?"

Emily blinked. "Forgive me, but who *are* you? You have gone to much trouble on my behalf, and yet I cannot recall that we ever met. Was it in China?"

"We have never met before today. But I wish to find your father in order to repay an old debt incurred by my mother."

"I'm sure my father will be everlastingly grateful to you for reuniting us—and Edward told me that it was you who insisted he return to the doctor's house to rescue me, so I'm sure all debts have been paid."

Emily recognized the look Phin gave her in response to this remark. It was the bland, studied, noncommittal expression of Orientals that had earned them the title of "inscrutable." "Not quite all debts, Miss Faraday," Phin murmured.

"Please, you must call me Emily, and I should be delighted to have you help me find my father, but alas, I do not have the price of a single passage to Mexico City, let alone two."

"I was not proposing to accompany you as your servant," Phin said quietly. "I will pay my own way."

Flustered, Emily said, "I'm sorry, I didn't mean to offend. I am destitute, you see, and will have to find a position in order to earn money for a passage."

At this point Kane turned to face them. "You are forgetting two things, Emily. One is the item I gave you earlier, and the second is that you, Emily, and I are all fugitives. I'm sure by now my father's cook has sent for the police and they are searching for us. Any plans we make must take that fact into consideration."

Emily's fingers tightened around the trinket box she was still holding. "But we shall explain that Godfrey was—"

She broke off before blurting out what had happened to Godfrey. There was certainly no need to involve Phin.

Phin said quietly, "I know what happened at the doctor's house, Emily, and understand that you and your friends are in grave danger. Mr. Kane, perhaps you would be so kind as to draw the curtains across the window alcove in order to give Emily privacy while she changes from her wet clothes?"

Kane immediately complied, and Phin picked up a gossamer silk robe and handed it to Emily. "Put this on for now while we find suitable clothing for you. How fortunate that you and I are the same size. We shall have no trouble outfitting you. As soon as Edward returns, I will go out and bring food for you. Later we will share all we know about Tonia and piece together the details of her plot against you."

Phin thoughtfully turned her back while Emily removed her sodden gown and donned the robe. She was shivering with cold and suddenly very tired. Sensing this, Phin said, "Why don't you lie down and rest for a little while? At least until your friend Edward returns."

The soft caress of silk against her skin and the warmth of the eiderdown quilt Phin tucked around her quickly lulled Emily's senses, and almost without realizing what was happening, she drifted off to sleep.

She awoke to the low murmur of voices in the room and lay still for a moment, observing the others from beneath half-closed lids. Kane perched awkwardly on a narrow windowsill, his head turned away from the group. Edward paced restlessly around a chair occupied by the beautiful auburn-haired woman Emily had seen in the doctor's cellar, who was surely Edward's sister, Briony, judging by the distinct family resemblance. Phin sat impassively on a wicker steamer trunk, listening to their conversation.

Edward was speaking. "I agree with Phin. No matter how justified our actions were, it will be our word against theirs. Bri, you of all people know how ruthless Rupert is. I vote for Phin's plan. We should get aboard the first vessel sailing for America. Once we're safely out of the country, Kane can emerge from hiding and tell his father it was I who killed Godfrey. The doctor will surely defend his only son and deal with any story his cook tells.''

Kane slowly swiveled his head to look at Edward. ''I cannot return to my father's house. I will go with you.''

There was an awkward silence as Edward and Briony exchanged dismayed glances. Emily silently applauded Kane's decision.

Edward cleared his throat. ''We shall need passage money for the ladies. You and I can work our way; every skipper sailing from the port leaves short-handed. I've come close to being shanghaied on more than one occasion since I began working at the hospital in the dock area. I might even be able to pass myself off as a ship's doctor and spare myself from having to climb yardarms to reef sail.''

Kane gave the derisive laugh that Emily had heard before. He said, ''You think some superstitious skipper would take me aboard? He'd as soon sign on the devil. I'd frighten his crew.''

''Your disfigurement probably seems worse to you than to others,'' Edward said with little conviction in his tone.

''Besides,'' Kane went on, ''when Emily awakens, you will see that I gave her the means to buy passage for all of us.''

Emily had placed the trinket box under the pillow, and she reached for it as she sat up.

Edward, seeing that Emily had awakened, led his sister across the room and introduced her.

''I have heard much about you, Emily,'' Briony said, a warm smile erasing some of the lines of tension from her lovely face. ''It seems we are fellow fugitives.''

''Emily doesn't know all that happened,'' Edward put in.

Briony remained silent as Edward told Emily of Rupert's plot against his wife. He finished by saying, ''I've already explained your situation to my sister, Emily, and she knows what happened before we left the doctor's house.''

Briony's fingers squeezed Emily's reassuringly. ''Courage, my dear, we will find a safe haven with Edward's help.''

The pressure of Briony's fingers caused the trinket box to press against her palm and Emily said, "When I awakened I believe Kane was talking about something he had given me, which must be in this little box."

Lifting the lid, she looked at a single diamond. She gasped at the size and brilliance of the stone.

"It belonged to my grandmother," Kane said as the others moved closer to stare at the icy beauty of the diamond. "Who passed it on to my mother. The women in my family managed to retain possession of the diamond rather than allowing their husbands to claim it under the chattel laws. They were strong women, independent, and the diamond assured this, since had they ever been abandoned by their husbands, the stone would support them. When my mother succumbed to the flux, the diamond should have gone to my sister, but I had no sister. So before my mother died, she gave it to me, her eldest son, to give to my daughter. But obviously, I shall never have a daughter, so we might as well make use of it."

Both Briony and Emily began to protest that a family heirloom could not be traded for their passage money, while Edward pointed out the difficulty of selling such a valuable stone.

Phin silently rose and went to the bedside. She took the diamond from Emily and held it up to the light, then said softly, "I will pay for everyone's passage and hold the diamond for Mr. Kane until I am repaid."

"You will not pay my way," Edward said at once. "I shall work my passage." He looked at Kane. "I already owe you my life, so please do not take offense. But if you will allow Phin to hold the diamond against repayment of Emily and Briony's passage money, I promise to repay every penny."

Kane shrugged. "The diamond was a gift to Emily, to do with as she pleases."

"I cannot possibly accept such a valuable gift!" Emily exclaimed. "When you handed me the trinket box, I had no idea what was in it, or I would have refused it. As you will recall, at the time we were in a terrible situation."

Kane scowled and turned away as Edward said, "I will repay you, Phin, I swear, and then you can return his diamond."

Phin said, "It is settled, then. I shall make the arrangements immediately."

Chapter 19

. . . .

FEARING DISCOVERY IF they remained in the hotel, the fugitives decided that Phin would rent a house and they would wait there while she purchased suitable clothes for the two women and made arrangements for their journey to America.

She found a terrace house in a slightly run-down neighborhood not far from the Pier Head. Upon alighting from a hired coach, Briony regarded the small brick house, identical to every other on the row, with some dismay.

Phin said quietly, "We will not be staying long. This was the best I could do. I tried several other landlords, who refused to speak to me. I told the owner of this house I was the maid of an ailing mistress."

Emily nodded understandingly. "I remember Father and I used to encounter people in China who treated us the same way. We're so grateful to you, Phin. I'm sure the house will suit our purpose nicely."

There were two bedrooms and a box room upstairs, and Kane immediately said he would take the tiny room intended to store luggage. Edward said he would sleep on the sitting room sofa, leaving the two bedrooms to the women. Phin whispered to Emily, "If you wouldn't mind sharing a room with me, then Lady Forester could have the other room."

Emily agreed gladly. Perhaps in the seclusion of a shared room she would learn more about the mysterious Eurasian who seemed to be in charge of everyone's destiny.

But it was Briony who proved to be most open in frankly discussing their plight. "I do hope we shan't have to remain here for long," she told Emily shortly after Phin left the house to inquire about ships' sailings. "What a triumph for the police if they were to discover us! Four fugitives in two murders!"

"Godfrey was killed in self-defense," Emily protested.

"If my brother had killed him, that would have been true. But Kane killed him, and I'm not sure that would be considered self-defense." Briony sighed. "Listen to me! I sound like the counsel for the prosecution. I suppose living with Rupert taught me the many ways the law can be twisted and manipulated. He always said that everyone went to court and lied, that the winner was simply the most eloquent and clever liar."

Emily shivered. "Please don't speak of trials! I shan't feel safe until I am on my way to Mexico City."

"I really wonder at the advisability of staying together. And what about Phin? What do any of us know about her, other than she claims her family knew your father in China? Emily, do you really think it's wise to allow her to accompany you? I am uneasy about being obligated to her for our passage money."

Emily bristled, reminded once again of the attitude of many Europeans toward Orientals. "Lady Forester, I hope you don't believe in the myth of the Yellow Peril?"

Briony flushed. "Not at all. But you must admit it's rather strange that she has taken all of us under her wing. I can't believe her reasons are completely altruistic. What does she want from us?"

"I don't know. But I do know I feel drawn to her. I trust her and have no fear of her harming us. You must understand that in China they revere their ancestors and strive to repay old debts, or even settle unfinished feuds from generations back. If Phin feels her mother owes a debt to my father, that in itself is sufficient reason for her to find him. That she stumbled upon me and my problems on the way is purely incidental."

Briony tugged at the basque of the gown Phin had loaned her, a dark green bombazine which was far too tight across the bosom. Briony was by far the most generously endowed of the women, with full breasts, rounded hips, and a tiny waist. Phin and Emily were both reed slender. "I've never worn borrowed clothing before," Briony said. "I suppose that fact alone might be coloring my thinking. That and the interminable rain. How depressing it is. I do hope Phin will bring me something comfortable to wear today."

"I wish Kane would come down from the box room," Emily said worriedly.

"I'm not sure that I do."

"Shh! He might hear you."

"Emily, while Edward is out in the coal shed, there's something else I want to ask you. I know you were not brought up here, and perhaps are not aware of certain rules of etiquette."

Echoes of Tonia, Emily thought, but she politely waited for Briony to continue.

"But I wanted to be sure you understood the implication of accepting that brooch from Edward. You see, in our society, when a woman accepts a gift of jewelry, this indicates, if not a betrothal, then the promise of one. In other words, Edward believes you'll now accept his proposal of marriage."

Emily's fingers closed protectively around the brooch she wore pinned beneath the collar of her borrowed gown. She wondered if it had occurred to Briony, as it had to her, that the brooch could be sold to provide passage money for at least one of them. Yet Emily was reluctant to suggest it, knowing how hurt Edward would be if she were to part with it.

There was no chance to respond, however, as at that point Edward came in from the coal shed carrying a copper skuttle. He placed it on the hearth, then stirred the dying embers of the fire with an iron poker. The fresh coals were wet and sputtered fitfully, almost dousing the feeble blaze.

"Don't let it go out!" Briony cried in alarm. "It's so cold in here."

"I should have covered the skuttle before I carried it across the yard," Edward said, reaching for the bellows that hung above the fireplace. "I'm beginning to realize how much we relied on servants to perform such chores."

The day passed slowly. Kane did not come downstairs. Phin had stocked the larder with bread, cheese, tea, and milk, and Emily prepared lunch. Briony seemed to expect that someone other than herself would put food on the table, and Edward was still fighting a losing battle with the living room fire.

Before eating her own sandwich, Emily took a tray up to the box room, anticipating that Kane would not join them.

She knocked on his door and called, "Kane, I've made lunch. Will you come downstairs and eat with us?"

He didn't open the door but called, "I'm not hungry."

"I thought you'd probably say that. I brought you a tray. I'll leave it outside your door. You didn't come down for breakfast. You'll have to eat sometime."

She rejoined Briony and Edward in the cramped living room. They had dragged in a gate-leg table from the dining room, as Edward had been unable to start a fire in the grate there.

"I hope Phin brings a newspaper," Edward said, crumbling his bread distractedly. "I hate not knowing what's happening."

"She's been gone a very long time," Briony observed.

"I expect she's checking with all of the shipping companies to see who has a vessel sailing first."

It was late afternoon before Phin returned, and since she carried no parcels, she had evidently not yet shopped for clothing, to Briony's obvious dismay.

Phin addressed Emily first. "There is an old Chinese curse—perhaps you've heard it?—that you be destined to live in historical times. I regret, Emily, that we might be cursed to witness history in the making. You see, I've just learned that the United States of America has proclaimed that it is its manifest destiny to expand its borders to the Pacific Ocean."

"I'm not sure I understand," Emily said.

"The Americans have declared war on Mexico," Phin

said. ''Your father and Tonia will walk right into the middle of it.''

Emily sat down abruptly. ''But my father represents England, and we are not at war with the Mexicans.''

''Wars are like whirlwinds: They sweep away everything in their path,'' Phin said, speaking with the voice of experience. ''It would be dangerous for you to go to Mexico at this time.''

''But I must go to my father! I'm afraid he might be in more danger from his new wife than from any soldiers.''

''I thought you would probably say that. May I suggest that rather than sailing to Mexico, we sail to an American port first? We can then ascertain the safest way to get in touch with your father.''

''But the Americans are also adversaries in the war.''

''I doubt there will be any battles in the United States. The Americans are invading Mexican territory, you see. Besides, you must leave England, and we'd be that much closer to your father.''

Emily turned to Edward and Briony questioningly, and Edward nodded. ''That would suit us. We'd been worrying about the language difficulty if we traveled with you to Mexico.''

''I must ask Kane how he feels about it,'' Emily remarked.

Edward frowned but made no comment.

Phin said, prophetically, ''He will agree.''

Edward was drifting off to sleep on the sitting room sofa when he heard a noise in the hall. He pushed aside the blankets and stood up, listening. There it was again. Someone was slowly easing open the front door, which creaked as it moved.

Carefully Edward felt his way around the furniture in the dark room. Was someone breaking into the house? Surely at this hour of the night no one was leaving.

He opened the sitting room door a crack and peered into the narrow hall. Silhouetted in the doorway against the glimmer of gaslight from the street was the figure of a man about to step outside.

"Kane!" Edward called in a hoarse whisper. "Where are you going?"

"Hush," Kane hissed. "Don't wake the others. I'm going back to my father's house."

Edward felt tremendously relieved. "Good idea. I'm sure your father will provide the best defense counsel for you, and as soon as Briony is safely aboard a ship, I will gladly bear witness that you had to kill Godfrey to save my life. You will be careful not to give away our hiding place, won't you?"

"You're eager to be done with me, aren't you? Sorry to disappoint you, but I'm not going to turn myself in to the law. There'll be no trial. I still intend to travel abroad. I am merely returning to collect some belongings."

"Dammit, you're liable to bring the law down on our heads! You can't come back here once you leave. The risk to the rest of us is too great."

"Go back to sleep, Edward. When you awaken I shall be back, and no one will be the wiser."

"What in God's name is worth such a risk?"

"My violin," Kane said softly and vanished into the night.

Edward stood in the chilly hall for a few minutes, wondering if he should awaken the others. He decided there was little point. Where could they go? He was about to return to the lumpy couch when a stair creaked. "Edward . . ." It was his sister's voice. "What is it? I heard voices."

"Kane is going back to River Court to collect some of his things. I tried to persuade him to stay with his father, who surely would spare no expense to defend him. I even offered to testify on his behalf—once you were safely out of the country, of course. But he insists he's going abroad with us. I fear we may have an albatross around our necks, Bri."

"I am less concerned about Kane than I am about being obligated to the Oriental woman," Briony whispered. "And I am even more worried about your infatuation with Emily.

Edward, she doesn't return your feelings, you must see that. I'm so afraid you're going to be hurt."

"I love Emily, I can't help myself. I've loved her from the moment I first saw her. I know there's no rhyme nor reason to it, but there it is. But I love you, too, and I will protect you with my life. When we arrive in America—"

"But why must we all travel to the same destination? Or even aboard the same ship? Surely we'd be safer if we split up."

"I suppose because, except for Phin, none of us have the wherewithall to pay our way, and she wants to keep us together to ensure we will eventually repay our debts. Look, Bri, you're shivering with cold. Go back to bed. Everything seems hopeless at night. Tomorrow everything will look brighter."

But his words were of little comfort as he lay awake until the first streaks of a leaden dawn crept across the sky. Edward spent the night worrying that Kane was abroad in the city and might be caught.

Just before daylight he heard the brass door knocker rapping urgently and went to open the door. Kane stood outside, his violin case under one arm and a bulging valise in his hand. Edward held open the door to admit him, averting his eyes from Kane's scarred features. One glance at that ravaged face warned that his night's expedition had produced some new terror. Even immediately after killing Godfrey, Kane had shown little emotion, but on this gray morning his expression was that of a man tortured beyond endurance.

Inside the hall Kane dropped his valise. His light amber eye glistened with tears, and when he spoke his voice was barely audible. "I killed him."

"You had no choice," Edward said quickly. "Godfrey was trying to kill me. You had to kill him."

"My father . . ." Kane said, a sob escaping from his clenched jaw. "I killed my father."

"Good God!" Edward put out a hand to steady him. "How did it happen? Did he try to prevent you from leaving?"

Kane sat on the stairs, his violin case across his knees. "I climbed into the backyard. The cellar door is locked from the outside, you see, so I was able to slip into the house that way. I considered packing my things and leaving, but . . . you must understand, although I chose to shut myself away from the world, I did not do so out of hatred of my fellow man, or even fear of ridicule. I stayed in my cellar to spare people the horror of having to look at me. All those years my only companion was my father. He cared for me, put up with my vile moods, and spent his every waking moment searching for a way to restore my features. Never once did he blame me for killing his other son."

"What happened to your father—did he catch you in the cellar?"

Kane shook his head. "I didn't want to leave without a word, nor did I want to awaken him, for I knew he would persuade me to stay and plead that there were extenuating circumstances connected with Godfrey's death. So I decided to slip up to his study next to the theater and leave a note in his journal, where no one else would see it."

"What happened to the note?" Edward asked anxiously. "You didn't give away our plans, did you? You didn't leave it?"

"I went into the theater," Kane whispered. "There was a coffin, lying on the operating table. I couldn't understand why a coffin would be there. The cadavers my father used never arrived in coffins. I don't know what propelled me toward it, but I found myself walking through the darkened theater. . . . The rain had stopped and the clouds parted briefly. . . . The skylight gave only a faint gleam of starlight. . . . I stopped at the first cabinet and lit a candle. The coffin lid was down, and a death certificate lay atop it. I saw at once the certificate was signed by another doctor. I stared uncomprehendingly at the signature, and the cause of death—heart failure. Then I looked at the name of the deceased. . . . It was my father." Kane buried his face in his hands and wept.

Edward awkwardly placed a hand on his shoulder. "But

he died from natural causes. Why do you say you killed him?''

Kane raised his face, and his tears streamed through granulated flesh like rivers wending through rugged terrain. ''You're a medical student. You know as well as I that a shock such as my father suffered when he learned what I'd done would be enough in a man of his age to bring on heart failure. I killed him just as surely as I killed my brother, and just as surely as I plunged that knife into Godfrey's black heart.''

''But you couldn't help any of it.''

''I should have sent you and Emily on your way and stayed to face my father. If I'd told him what really happened, perhaps he'd still be alive. Instead I ran like a frightened rabbit.'' Kane stopped short. ''No, it wasn't fear that drove me.'' He stood up so suddenly that Edward stepped backward in alarm.

Kane gave him a travesty of a smile that was terrible to behold. ''Shall I tell you why I wanted to accompany you to America? Shall I complete the nightmare for you?''

''You're distraught, understandably so,'' Edward said carefully, recognizing the other man's fragile emotional state and fearing what it might precipitate. ''Look, I brought a sedative from the hospital in case Briony needed it. Let me give you something to calm you down.''

''A dose of laudanum, Doctor? No, thank you. I'd rather burden you with my vile thoughts so that you can worry about them—and intercede if I attempt to act upon them.''

''You're irrational with grief. If you won't let me help you, then please, stay away from the women until you've calmed down.''

Kane stood still for a moment, obviously doing battle with himself as to whether he should reveal some ghastly secret to a man who might use it against him. Evidently prudence prevailed as instead he opened the valise and withdrew a second similar bag from inside it. Edward saw that it was a doctor's black bag.

For a moment Kane held the bag lovingly, then handed it to Edward. ''This was my father's. You said you might try to pass yourself off as a ship's doctor. Here's the prop you need.''

He turned and started up the stairs, then stopped and looked back. "And by the way, if some unsuspecting skipper signs you on, I can probably help you with most of the injuries and sicknesses seamen suffer. You see, other than my music, there was little to do in my cellar, so I spent most of my time at the operating theater keyhole, observing my father at work, listening to his lectures to the students.'' He paused, then added, "Which, of course, was my undoing.''

Looking into the raw yearning in Kane's eyes, Edward understood. Emily had gone into the theater, and like himself, Kane had been moved by her delicate beauty, her innocence and vulnerability. Good God, Edward thought, horrified, the man is in love with her!

Edward stood at the foot of the stairs for several minutes, gripping Dr. Stoddard's bag, now more than ever convinced that the sooner he separated Emily and Briony from Kane and Phin, the better.

When the three women came down for breakfast, Edward had managed to light the fire and was gingerly placing damp coal on the blazing kindling. He told them briefly of Kane's nocturnal quest and of the doctor's demise. Their reactions, he thought, were significant.

Emily expressed genuine sympathy for Kane, and Edward had to persuade her not to go running upstairs to him. "He asks that we leave him alone, Emily. Let's respect his wishes.''

"But how he must be suffering! Oh, the poor man.''

Briony said, "Well, I for one, shan't shed any tears for the deceased doctor. It does seem a judgment on him.''

Phin murmured thoughtfully, "We must leave at once. I believe this news makes our departure even more imperative.''

"I agree," Edward said. "Please book passage for Emily and Briony and yourself at once. I believe Kane and I should work our way, not necessarily aboard the same ship. A hue and cry has surely been raised for him, and he'd be less likely to be caught if he boarded a ship as a seaman rather than as a passenger. There's a tavern I know near Princes' Dock where the crimps hang about waiting to drag unwary drunks into a longboat and put them aboard a ship to sail with the next tide. They aren't too particular about a man's looks.''

''Shanghaiied? Oh, Edward, no!'' Briony exclaimed. ''Apart from any other consideration, you'd have no control over your destination.''

''Oh, I shan't let the crimps take us against our will. I meant we could offer ourselves willingly, provided they get us aboard a ship bound for the Americas. Kane brought his father's medical bag. I shall try to pass myself off as a ship's doctor.''

''And Kane? What will he do?'' Emily inquired.

''He'll be an able-bodied seaman,'' Edward answered. ''He *is* able-bodied, after all.'' He felt a momentary pang of guilt, since obviously it should have been Kane who carried the doctor's bag aboard a ship. All those years of observing the theater surely qualified him far more than Edward's scant weeks at the profession. But even an ignorant seaman might balk at being treated by a doctor with a caricature of a face, and they both knew it.

''No,'' Emily said sharply. ''Kane cannot be exposed to the brutalities of the life of an ordinary seaman in the fo'c'sle. He has spent years sheltered from the outside world; he could not survive such a voyage. Why do you suggest such a thing, Edward?''

''I am prepared to endure the hardship of a seaman's life myself, am I not? There is no guarantee I shall be signed on as a doctor. I may end up in the fo'c'sle myself.''

''Because of false pride, Edward,'' Briony reminded him. ''There is no need for you to work your way. Besides, Kane has the means to pay for his passage. Why should he work?''

The discussion had become heated, and no one had heard the door open, or knew how long Kane had stood there, until his voice sliced into the conversation. ''Thank you for your concern, Emily, but rest assured I have no intention of wrestling with wet canvas high above pitching decks. My hands are too important to me to risk injuring them. I shall take my chances and travel as a passenger, but not in your party. There is no need for any of the other passengers or crew to know we are acquainted. If Edward insists upon working his passage, so be it, although as his sister points out, there is no need.''

Phin, who had listened without comment, now said, ''There are cabins available aboard an American packet sailing for New York in five days. I think it would be safer to take an American ship, as you may still be under British jurisdiction on an English vessel. Even so, we shall have to be careful, use false names, and keep to ourselves, in view of the nature of the crimes of which you are accused.''

''Book cabins for the others, Phin,'' Edward said. ''I'll work my passage and meet you in New York.''

Edward left the following day aboard a merchantman bound for New York, after ascertaining the name of the vessel the others were booked aboard. He promised to meet them in New York.

The night before they sailed, Phin burned joss sticks to Tai Kung, her founding ancestor, which Emily understood but which endeared Phin to Briony not at all.

A closed coach was hired to take the three women to the docks after dark, and Kane's plan was to slip aboard just before the ship sailed. They boarded the Black Ball Line packet *Pacific*, and Phin said the name of the ship was a good omen, as the vessel was carrying them across the Atlantic, but their eventual destination would be to the shores of the Pacific ocean.

Emily worried that Kane would be caught, but since they were not supposed to know him, she daren't ask if he was among the passengers. She was not a good sailor but wished the ship would leave the sanctuary of the river and head out into the open sea so that she might assure herself that Kane had also escaped.

Chapter 20

··

THE *LIVERPOOL COURIER*'s shipping correspondent had described the *Pacific*'s accommodations in awed terms, stating that her dining room was forty feet by fourteen, with an elliptical arch supported by handsome pillars of Egyptian porphyry . . .

Unfortunately the dining room and the fourteen first-class cabins that led off it had been deducted from the ship's cubic capacity, leaving the bulk of the emigrants virtually stowed in the 'tween decks. Conditions were primitive, emigrants carried their own food and fought for a place at the stoves to cook it, then spent miserable nights on wooden shelves in a battened-down, heaving and pitching ship.

Since only two cabins had been available so close to the departure date, Kane had been booked into one and the three women had to share the other. When Briony expressed dismay at their cramped quarters, Phin sharply reminded her of the wretched conditions of emigrants unable to pay for first-class accommodations.

"Perhaps Kane did not get aboard in time," Briony remarked. "I shall ask the purser if there is an empty cabin."

Emily waited in an agony of suspense until Briony returned with the news that the last passenger had rushed aboard almost as the crew were casting off.

Emily suffered a severe case of *mal de mer* the moment the ship left the river and began to plow the heaving waters of the Irish Sea, which was not helped by finding herself cast in the role of peacemaker between two sharply opinionated women. She quickly realized that for all Phin's soft

and gentle facade, beneath her practiced charm lay a woman
of steel will who regarded Briony as a representative of that
class of Englishwoman whose pampered existence had
prepared her for little beyond presiding over a dinner party
or issuing orders to a household staff. But Emily recognized
that Briony was no ordinary upper-class Englishwoman.
She had been ill-used by a husband and the society to which
she belonged and had emerged from the ordeal determined
never to find herself in such dire straits again. In addition,
she had always been a firebrand, headstrong and impulsive,
with ideas Emily had heard few women express. Ironically,
Emily soon realized that Phin and Briony, while on the
surface appearing to be poles apart, actually had more in
common than they realized.

Kane never left his cabin, or at least they did not see him
in the dining room or on deck.

Three days out Emily at last felt well enough to accompany Briony to the dining room, but Phin declined to join
them. "I shall have my meals brought to the cabin."

"Surely not for the duration of the voyage?" Briony
asked.

"Yes. I prefer to eat alone."

Leaving the cabin, Briony and Emily moved cautiously,
as the ship was encountering heavy swells. Briony said,
"Phin is acting rather snobbishly, don't you think?"

Emily hastened to defend her. "I think she probably feels
uncomfortable with the other passengers. You know how
most Europeans regard Asians—with suspicion and dis-
trust."

"I doubt Phin feels uncomfortable—perhaps you do, on
her behalf. You're such a sensitive soul," Briony replied. "I
believe what Phin feels for most Europeans is contempt."

"Oh, no, I'm sure you're wrong. Besides, apart from any
other consideration, I think Phin avoids the dining room so
that we won't be obligated to have her sit at our table,
calling attention to us. After all, we did decide not to
become too friendly with any of the other passengers, for
fear of giving away our identities, didn't we? Please don't
think ill of her. She's done so much for us."

Briony shrugged. "I don't think ill of her. I think perhaps I envy her. I've never before met a woman so completely independent. It is a state I've vowed to acquire for myself."

As they were about to enter the dining room, the ship was struck by a strong swell and lurched suddenly.

Emily clutched one of the arches and kept her balance, but Briony was flung across the sloping deck. She would have fallen had it not been for a tall, silver-haired man who quickly stepped forward and caught her in his arms.

He steadied her until the ship finished rolling, then offered an arm to both women. "May I escort you ladies to your table? I'm one of those fortunate individuals who was born with sea legs."

Briony blushed prettily and took the offered arm, and Emily followed suit, since there seemed no gracious way to refuse. They had noticed this particular passenger before; indeed, it would have been difficult not to, as he strode about the ship with even more authority than the captain, and despite his silver hair, there was a restless, youthful energy to his rangy body, and his tanned, craggy features were dominated by piercingly blue eyes that reflected none of the weariness of age. He was traveling alone, and his accent proclaimed him to be an American.

When they reached their table, he pulled out chairs for them, then smiled and bowed. "May I introduce myself? My name is Max Seadon."

Briony hesitated for a moment, then introduced Emily and herself by the names they were using. Mrs. Forest and Miss Day. Edward had worried they were too close to their real names, but Briony insisted that was all to the good; they would be less likely to forget to use them. After considering the wisdom of this plan, Edward decided to change his name from Darnell to Dale. Kane could continue to call himself that, since no one outside their group had heard the pseudonym.

Emily felt the impact of the look Seadon gave Briony, noted the way his hand lingered on the back of her chair, and thought, why, Briony has made a conquest!

Max Seadon stood beside their table for so long that it

became an embarrassment, and Briony was forced to invite him to join them. He accepted with alacrity, and upon learning this was their first visit to his homeland, regaled them with descriptions of the vast and sparsely populated land to which they journeyed. He spoke with equal knowledge of the bustling ports of the Atlantic seaboard, the gracious cities of the south, and the great empty spaces to the West—the prairies, mountains, sweeping valleys, and vast deserts.

Spellbound, Emily listened attentively. When he paused to ask if New York was their final destination, she glanced questioningly in Briony's direction and was surprised to see that she had narrowed her eyes and was quivering in anticipation of responding to Seadon's glowing description of his country.

Briony leaned forward, and her sweet tone belied her query, "And since you already have this vast, beautiful country, Mr. Seadon, perhaps you can explain to me why you Americans have decided to invade Mexican territory?"

When Briony felt strongly about something, Emily had noted that her blue eyes changed color, emitting green sparks, and at the moment they were a veritable explosion of sparks. Seadon's vivid blue gaze returned Briony's stare with a hint of amused condescension that Emily knew would infuriate Briony.

Seadon said, "I could give you a summary of Mexican-American relations and tell you of a friend who died in Texas at the Alamo, but I'm not sure any argument justifies war."

"How fortunate it is, then, that you are not of an age that will require you to fight," Briony said sweetly, and Emily gasped at her rudeness. But Seadon merely chuckled and agreed that his advanced age certainly would preclude joining the army.

The ship was now pitching even more noticeably, and Emily's stomach felt queasy. She rose unsteadily to her feet and said, "If you will excuse me, I think I'd better return to our cabin. Please don't let me interrupt your dinner."

"I'll walk you back to your cabin," Seadon said.

"No! I mean, no, thank you. I'd much rather you stayed and finished your meal."

But he insisted on taking her arm and leading her back to her cabin. Emily was quite certain he then rejoined Briony.

For four days the ship battled late winter squalls, and Emily clung in abject misery to her bunk. She had been troubled to a much lesser degree with seasickness on the long voyages to and from the Far East, but it seemed the Atlantic was the most capricious sea of all.

Phin took care of her, coaxing her to take a little dry bread and weak tea and bundling blankets over her when she shook with chills. Briony offered her sympathy, but seeing that Phin was in charge, quickly escaped from the cramped cabin.

At last the storm abated, and Emily was again able to venture into the dining room. To her surprise, Max Seadon came to their table as a matter of course, and it was clear he had been in the habit of taking all of his meals with Briony.

"Glad to see you're feeling better, Miss Day," Seadon said. "Have a brisk walk around the deck later; some fresh air will do wonders for your appetite."

Emily nodded and unfolded her napkin.

Briony said, "Perhaps you should give up your walks, Max, or we'll surely run out of food before we reach America. Emily, he has the appetite of an elephant."

Emily blinked. *Max?* Had the two of them become close enough friends that she felt she could tease him about his appetite? What else had she told him? Emily felt apprehensive.

But it soon became clear that neither Briony nor Max confided anything about their personal lives. They had a lively discussion about recent events in the world in general and their particular countries in particular; they spoke of books and the theater and food and the law. They acted like old friends who shared a number of mutual interests.

In the following days Emily was aware of only one awkward moment, when Max Seadon suddenly said, "Have either of you seen the mysterious passenger in cabin number nine? Apparently he leaves the cabin only after dark, and no one has seen his face.''

''No,'' Emily responded quickly. ''We haven't seen him, but since he apparently values his privacy, I think everyone should leave him alone.''

In fact, she had stopped by Kane's cabin several times, tapped on the door, and inquired softly if he was all right. His muffled response had been in the affirmative. She didn't expect him to invite her in, which would have been akin to a single girl entering a gentleman's bedroom, but she did wish he'd come out for a moment and talk to her.

As they had finished dinner when Max mentioned Kane, Emily excused herself and made her way to cabin number nine. With most of the other passengers still at dinner, the companionway was deserted.

She tapped on Kane's door and called, ''It's me, Emily. I need to talk to you. Could you come for a walk around the deck with me? It's a fine clear evening, and the sea is calm. There's nobody about—they're all at dinner. Please, Kane.''

There was such a long pause that she was afraid he was asleep, but then the door opened and Kane emerged from the darkness. He wore a heavy coat and a black hat pulled low over his forehead.

Emily pulled her cape close to her body as they went out onto the deck. Although the seas were calm, with a silver ribbon of moonlight shimmering from ship to horizon, a bitingly cold breeze took her breath away. She clutched the wooden rail, which was wet with spray, and was grateful that Kane positioned himself to the windward, protecting her from the icy gusts of air.

''You'll find it easier to ride the waves if you stand with your feet apart,'' Kane said. ''Save your ladylike pose of feet together, ankles together, for dry land.''

''For one who has spent the entire voyage in his cabin, you seem quite at home on a swaying deck,'' Emily answered.

''Ah, but I have walked this deck almost every midnight since we embarked. I have frightened more than one unwary sailor out of his wits when he stumbled across my path.''

"Oh," Emily said, somewhat deflated. "I was afraid you'd exchanged one prison for another. I didn't know you'd been in the habit of taking midnight strolls. I was worried about you, but I see now I didn't need to be. So in future I will worry only about poor Edward and how he is faring."

"Poor Edward didn't have to martyr himself; he could have shared my cabin."

"I've heard such terrible stories about a seaman's lot aboard merchantmen. Are they true? I haven't really seen much of the crew of this ship except for the cabin and dining room stewards. It must be terrifying to climb aloft in a storm."

"Few men willingly go to sea, and Edward knew what to expect. Aboard most merchantmen the seamen are subjected to brutal beatings by sadistic first mates, fight flapping canvas high above pitching decks, and live in conditions in the fo'c'sle that make the *Pacific*'s 'tween-decks emigrant accommodations seem luxurious by comparison. Your Edward will probably be forever changed by his experiences at sea, so prepare yourself."

Emily shivered.

"Come on, tuck your arm through mine, and we'll walk. It's too cold to stand still." When she hesitated, he added sharply, "If you're afraid someone will see you with me, then go back to your cabin."

Emily silently slipped her arm through his, and they began to pace the moonlit deck.

She did feel exhilarated by the stroll and knew she would sleep better that night. When at length she said she wished to return to her cabin, he led her back without argument.

Later she realized that it was the worst possible time to go back to the cabins, as they were adjacent to the dining room and many of the passengers had finished their meal and were leaving.

The instant Emily and Kane stepped into the lighted companionway, they were confronted by two dowagers who stopped dead in their tracks. Upon catching sight of Kane, one woman clutched her throat and gave a strangled gasp while the other shrieked in terror.

"Good night, Miss Day," Kane said shortly and pushed past the two women to rush back to the sanctuary of his cabin.

"Oh, no," Emily whispered, tears springing to her eyes. "No, no, *no*!"

She returned to her own cabin and, finding Phin there, related the incident to her.

"He must learn not to care," Phin said. "It is a choice he can make. There is nothing you can do to make it easy for him."

"But if it had not been for me insisting he leave his cabin—"

"Emily, sooner or later he has to face the world. We all do. Now, tell me about the man who has been dining with Briony. I think perhaps he should concern us more than Kane. He and Briony seem to have become inseparable."

"She teases him unmercifully about his age. I think she regards him as a sort of favorite uncle."

"But how does *he* regard *her*, that's the question," Phin responded thoughtfully.

"He said the voyage will take about thirty-three days, perhaps longer because of the storms, and we've been en route for a month, so I suppose their friendship will soon be coming to an end anyway."

As the *Pacific* drew close to America, Seadon's enormous appetite apparently deserted him, and he picked moodily at his food during their last dinner at sea. At length he put down his fork and asked Briony if she would stroll around the deck with him.

Briony hesitated, then said, "I'll get my wrap."

Seeing the proprietary way Max held Briony's arm as they left the dining room, Emily felt both a thrill of excitement and a stab of alarm. Briony was, after all, a married woman. What would she say to him—what *could* she say? She certainly couldn't divulge her past. It was a moment before Emily realized that they knew virtually nothing about Seadon's past, either.

These thoughts were also very much on Briony's mind as she and Max walked to the bow to search the darkness for the first glimpse of land.

She had hoped to avoid any declaration of feelings, to part company on the same lighthearted, slightly adversarial note that had brought them together.

"I've enjoyed your companionship during the voyage, Max," Briony said, her tone more stilted than she would have liked. "Tomorrow there will be so much confusion, with the bustle of disembarkation and so on, and my brother will be meeting the ship, and well . . . I thought perhaps we should say goodbye tonight."

"Oh, you did, did you? Is that why you agreed to come up on deck with me? In order to dismiss me?"

"That's an odd way of putting it, but, well, yes—we shan't see each other again after tomorrow anyway."

"Briony, neither of us have talked much about our past—or our future—but I have the distinct impression that you have not yet decided what you will do after you arrive in New York. Yes, I know your brother will be meeting you, but Emily let slip that he had sailed as either a ship's doctor or a seaman. That fact, and your obvious breeding, leads me to certain conclusions. First, aristocrats—members of the upper classes of European countries—don't emigrate. Yet you make no mention of this being a visit or that you ever intend to return to England. Therefore, I believe you intend to remain permanently in my country."

"I don't see that our plans are any of your concern."

"Perhaps not. But hear me out. What if I were to tell you that every other woman who passed through my life—and there have been many—prepared me for you? That I never expected to find in my maturity what passed me by in my youth—a woman I could love with my whole heart and mind and body and soul. That I could offer you an unselfish love on any terms you require, asking nothing in return, only that you let me take care of you, be with you."

She didn't look at him. "I would say that—forgive me—there's no fool like an old fool. You don't know me. You think the past month aboard this ship bears any resemblance to life on dry land? This is a dreamworld, unconnected to reality. The woman you've known on this voyage is not the one who existed before we sailed. I doubt you could have even tolerated that woman. And make no mistake, she's still there.''

Feeling a stab of guilt at her bluntness, she turned then and laid her hand on his arm. ''Max, you're a nice man and I've enjoyed your companionship. But I doubt very much I shall ever allow myself to become any man's chattel again, no matter how strong his protestations of love are. Besides, I think perhaps the moonlight on the ocean bewitched you, and later on you'll be grateful to me that I didn't take the little speech you just made seriously.''

A slow grin spread over his rugged features. ''Good, I'm glad. I didn't want you to take it seriously. I wanted to be sure you didn't harbor any female fantasies about my taking care of you for the rest of your life. I've been a bachelor too long to have my wings clipped now. However, I do have a different kind of proposal to make to you.''

When Briony gasped in outrage, he went on quickly. ''No, I'm not going to ask you to be my mistress, either—I have far too much respect for you. What I'd like to offer you is a different kind of position. Let me explain. I'm what you might call a jack-of-all-trades—done a little of everything in my day. I was in Europe to buy various goods. Now, you took me to task about the Mexican War, and it does have a bearing on my future plans. I've traveled the western half of the country, Briony, and I believe it's inevitable that it will become part of the United States. The Mexicans can't hold it. We had to consider the British settlement in Oregon and the Russian presence in Alta California. If we hadn't moved in, they might have attempted to take over.''

''There's really no need to explain this to me. Max, now that we're so close to getting off this ship, I can tell you that my traveling companion—Emily—is en route to join her father, who sailed to a diplomatic post in Mexico City just before the war started. If we exhibited any interest in the Mexican territory, that is the only reason.''

''Bear with me, Briony. I will explain my own interest in

the Mexican territory in a moment. But first, let me ask you a blunt question. Do you and your brother have any prospects, or income, with which to support yourselves in America?''

''That's none of your business.''

''It is if you're going to be looking for a position, because I have one I'd like to offer you.''

''How could you possibly know what type of position I'm qualified for? If you want a governess for your children, I'm not interested.''

''I don't have any children—at least, none that I know of. What I need is somebody who has experience running a large house, supervising a staff of servants, and providing all the touches of refinement the great homes of England are famous for. I need someone with the presence of a superior hostess, ladylike in demeanor, yet with a certain tensile strength I see in you, because I'm going to turn her into a hardheaded businesswoman.''

''Tell me more,'' Briony said, intrigued in spite of herself.

''The Mexicans have a *presidio* in Monterey and make a pretense of running their Alta California territory from there, but I believe the territory is actually governed from Mexico City. Now, farther north there's a small settlement at a place called Yerba Buena, on a beautiful bay that is a natural harbor. Once the war ends, I'm convinced that's where the growth will be. Ships will bring goods to that port, and where there's seagoing commerce, there'll be a need for hotels. I aim to open the first hotel in Yerba Buena, and it's going to be the finest in the West because I'm going to hire a woman with experience running a fine house in England to manage my hotel. Do you want the job?''

Briony drew a deep breath and answered unhesitatingly, ''Yes. Providing my brother can accompany me.''

Even in the darkness Briony was aware that he frowned. ''I don't hire men I've never met.''

''You wouldn't have to hire him. I'm sure Edward will find his own position.''

''In that case he can tag along. I own a hotel in Texas, and that's where we'll head first. Later, when the war's over, we'll scout Yerba Buena.''

"I might not be able to go with you right away."

"Why not?"

"I borrowed my transatlantic fare and must repay it."

"From whom?"

She hesitated, thinking of the complicated pact they had made with Kane and Phin.

"I'd rather not say. Perhaps after I've talked to my brother, we can discuss how and when I will take you up on your offer of employment.''

"You're hoping your brother will be able to repay your debt? Don't count on it if he worked his passage. How about my advancing you the money, then deducting it later from your salary?"

"That might be acceptable," Briony said carefully. She hated to be obligated, but she hadn't much faith that Edward would have earned enough to pay Phin, and the sooner she was out of debt the better.

"Good," Max said, taking her hand in his to seal a bargain he apparently considered already made.

Chapter 21

••

PHIN CAME INSTANTLY awake as someone gently touched her cheek. The ship had docked at New York late in the evening, and passengers would not begin disembarking until daylight.

Emily's voice whispered urgently in her ear, "Phin, can you come quickly? I think Kane is ill. Don't wake Briony; she was up awfully late with Mr. Seadon."

Silently Phin rose and donned her silk kimono, and the two women made their way to Kane's cabin. The ship was now at anchor, and it felt strange not to battle the heaving deck.

"What happened?" Phin asked.

"I went to see if he was ready to disembark tomorrow morning. I knocked on his door, but he didn't answer. I could hear him moaning, so I went inside, and he was lying facedown on his bunk. He was very angry and told me to get out and leave him alone and that if I fetched a steward, he would toss him overboard. Oh, Phin, he sounded so anguished I didn't know what to do."

"I do hope he will not toss me overboard," Phin murmured.

Emily knocked on the cabin door and called softly, "Kane, it's just me and Phin. Please, just let us talk for a moment."

"Go away, both of you. Leave me alone." His voice was a low growl.

Phin laid her hand on Emily's arm. "Wait here. I'll go inside and talk to him."

Before Emily could protest, Phin pushed open the door

and went inside. It occurred to Emily that he must have hoped someone would go to him, since he'd left his door unlocked.

Phin was gone for about a quarter of an hour and Emily waited, straining to hear what was happening inside the cabin, but there was no discernible sound. If they were conversing, it was in low tones.

At length the door opened and Phin emerged. She motioned for Emily to follow her.

"He is not physically ill," she said. "His malaise is one of the mind. He doesn't want to go ashore and face people tomorrow. I have something in my trunk that will help him."

Emily wrung her hands. "Phin, I owe Kane my life. I don't know what will happen to any of us in America, but no matter what, I must see that Kane is all right. We must persuade him to travel with us. He needs someone to take care of him, or I fear he will simply give up the struggle to exist."

"How strange that you feel so. I never cease to marvel at the backward beliefs of Europeans. In my culture it would be the obligation of the one who saves a life to be responsible for the rescued, not the other way around. However, little sister, if the welfare of the man Kane is so important to you, then we will take care of him."

Emily smiled and squeezed Phin's arm gratefully. She assumed the Eurasian girl's calling her "little sister" was a term of endearment for a friend, and it was good to know Phin considered her so, as Emily liked and admired Phin very much.

"Besides, I believe some people enter our lives for a reason, that some purpose will be served," Phin continued, almost to herself, her eyes glazing as she perhaps made a connection to someone in her own life, "and that our paths are bound to cross until that purpose is revealed to us and served."

"Destiny," Emily responded.

"Yes," Phin said. "Now I must take my magic potion to Kane."

Emily lay in her bunk for a long time that night, unable to sleep. Apart from the unaccustomed lack of movement of the ship, she felt daunted by the enormous task that lay ahead. She was less than halfway toward her destination of Mexico City. It would take months to send word to her father that she was alive, if indeed such communication was possible, since the United States and Mexico were at war. How would she survive in the meantime? She couldn't continue to take from Phin. An old solution to her dilemma tugged at her consciousness, and because of it, sleep continued to elude her.

A new and different Edward met their ship. He seemed much older, and a hard gleam in his eyes hinted that he had seen sights aboard the merchantman on which he'd sailed that had forever changed him. He was thinner, more restless, more abrupt in his speech, more wary of those around him.

They were reunited on the quay, and he was clearly suspicious of Max Seadon, who had disembarked with them and who stayed close by Briony's side.

After embracing both his sister and Emily, Edward bowed to Phin, then shook Kane's hand. Kane's hat was pulled low over his forehead and his coat collar was turned up, but the morning sunlight found his scars, and people passing by turned away. Oddly, he seemed oblivious of the horrified stares, curiously detached in the manner of a sleepwalker. Emily decided that Phin's "magic potion" must have produced this state, and she found this vaguely disturbing.

Briony introduced Max, and Edward said shortly, "How do you do. If you'll excuse us, Mr. Seadon, I have a hired carriage waiting."

"Edward—Mr. Seadon has a friend who owns a hotel here," Briony said quickly as Edward attempted to lead her away.

"I've taken rooms in a boardinghouse," Edward said.

"Oh, let's all at least have lunch and talk about it," Max said easily.

"I think not," Edward answered.

"Edward, please don't be rude," Briony said. "Mr. Seadon has something to discuss with us that is to our advantage."

"Briony, I don't think it's a good idea—" Edward began.

Seadon leaned close to Edward's ear. "Let's not have a scene here. *I know what happened in England.* I still would like to offer you and your sister gainful employment. Rest assured, I'm not going to sell any of these women into white slavery."

Clearly taken aback at the apparent disclosure that this man knew they were wanted felons, Edward did not argue further. Then, as he took Emily's hand, his expression softened, the look of love in his eyes needing no words.

During the journey from the docks to Seadon's friend's hotel in Manhattan, everyone in the hired coach was too excited by their first sight of the bustling city to notice that Briony was silent and withdrawn.

When they reached the hotel, they were conducted to a banquet room, where several tables were set for lunch. Seadon indicated that Briony and Edward were to join him at a table set apart from the others. Wordlessly Briony went straight to the table and was followed by her brother. Max took a moment to indicate to the others the adjacent powder rooms and cloakroom.

As Edward pulled out a chair for Briony, he muttered, "Good God, Bri, what were you thinking of? How could you possibly have been so foolish as to confide in that man? Don't you know how he will use that information against you? Does he know everything?"

"I told him *nothing* about any of us," Briony whispered angrily. "I don't *know* what he knows, or how he could have found out. He wants me to run a hotel he intends to build in the Mexican territory once the war is won. Until then I am to train for the position in a hotel he owns in Texas."

"Are you sure that's all he wants from you? Bri, you're a beautiful woman, and I saw the way he looks at you."

"He assures me he wants only a business relationship. In

fact, he was concerned that I might have designs on him.''

''I find this hard to believe—'' Edward broke off as Max approached their table.

Taking his seat, Max looked at Briony. ''From the sparks emitting from your eyes, I assume you are offended by the means I used to get your brother to come and talk about our future plans.''

''What exactly did you mean by the remark that you knew what happened in England?'' Briony demanded.

Seadon smiled, but he gave Edward a hard look as he spoke. ''I have no idea what happened in England, but it wasn't difficult to imagine that something drove you and your brother to leave.''

''Explain yourself, sir,'' Edward said.

''You and your sister are not our typical immigrants. The only aristocrats who ordinarily come to our shores are the ones we call remittance men. In other words, their families pay them to stay away. But here we have a brother and a sister—he working his passage, and she wearing a wedding ring but making no mention of either a husband or widow-hood. The whole situation smacks of a hasty departure. But let me assure you that I don't care what happened back in England to drive you here. It's how you both acquit yourselves in the future that counts. Now—shall I have lunch served, and we'll talk about the hotel business?''

''I'll listen to what you have to say,'' Edward replied slowly. ''But I want you both to understand that my plans will include Emily, whom I intend to ask to be my wife.''

''Good. I was concerned about her and am happy to hear you intend to take care of her. She can certainly accompany us.'' Max signaled the waiters who hovered discreetly in the background to begin serving. ''But what about the other two? I must admit to being surprised when the unfortunate Mr. Kane joined our party—and I'm more than a little uneasy about the Eurasian. In the hotel business, despite our personal feelings, of necessity we must cater to our guests' sensitivities—and prejudices.''

''Max is right, Edward,'' Briony said. ''You should make it clear to Emily that it is time to bid both of them farewell.

Max has generously offered to repay our debt to Phin, so we will be relieved of that obligation.''

Before the luncheon ended, Edward promised to consider Max's offer of employment and to give him a decision after he'd spoken to Emily.

Emily was sitting at her dressing table in her hotel room shortly after dinner on her first day in America when Phin knocked and entered the room.

"May I speak frankly with you, little sister?" Phin asked, taking the hairbrush from Emily's hand and running it through her long tresses.

"Yes, of course, Phin."

"I heard Edward ask you to go for a walk with him. You know, of course, that he is about to ask you to marry him?"

Emily sighed deeply. "I thought it best to tell him privately that I cannot think of devoting myself to another man until I have found my father. Perhaps I can make him understand."

"Do you care for Edward?"

"I like and admire him very much, and he has been so kind to me. Yes, I suppose I do care for him, in a way."

"Then you should marry him."

Emily gasped, but before she could protest, Phin went on, "Listen to what I have to say. I believe I am in some ways wiser, more experienced in the ways of the world, than you are. You are a young, single woman in a foreign country. You need the protection, and the respectability, of a husband at your side. If Edward intended to remain on the East Coast, I would not suggest this. But he and his sister have received an offer of employment with Max Seadon, who plans to build a hotel in the Mexican territory of Alta California. Mr. Seadon intends to leave shortly for the Republic of Texas, which I understand was also wrested from Mexican control by the Americans. I believe we should journey with them. It will place us that much closer to your father. At the moment, with the upheaval of the war, we have little hope of sending word to him—or, if we did, that his new wife wouldn't intercept it. We must keep in mind that she conspired against you."

Emily was silent, considering. She was fond of Edward, owed him a great deal. Most women chose their husbands—or had husbands chosen for them—with fewer reasons than she could enumerate for accepting Edward's proposal. Everything Phin said about reaching her father was true. Still, she hesitated. Was she foolish to hope for more from a lifetime union?

"There is something else we must discuss before you go to Edward," Phin added. "I wish to travel with you as your personal maid and companion."

"Oh, no! You are far more to me—"

Phin cut her short. "Yes, of course, you and I understand that. But for appearances' sake, it would be better for me to adopt the role of servant. Also, this would give them no excuse to separate us, as indeed they will try. Trust my judgment in this matter, Emily."

She gently pulled Emily's hair up on top of her head and secured it with hairpins. "You look very pretty, little sister. Edward will refuse you nothing."

"Alas, I fear there is one condition he will not meet," Emily said sadly. "I cannot leave Kane behind."

Wrapped warmly in one of Phin's fur-trimmed cloaks, Emily walked beside Edward in the park that evening, the clean cold bite of the late-winter air almost taking her breath away. She waited for Edward to speak, still troubled by the advice Phin had given but unable to think of any alternatives.

Edward stopped beside a bench and said, "Let's sit here for a moment." He sat close to her and picked up her hand, cradling it in his.

She asked, "Was the voyage horrible? You seem so—different."

"It was the most brutal, humiliating experience of my life. But I endured, and, I feel, ultimately triumphed. I shall have no fear of anything else life throws my way. But let's not speak of the past; I want to talk about our future, Emily.

You must know how much I love you. There is nothing I would not do for you. Max Seadon has invited both Briony and myself to go with him to the Republic of Texas, then later to the Mexican territory. Knowing that you hope to find your father in Mexico, these plans of Seadon and my sister's interested me.''

Edward pushed and raised her hand to his lips. Although she wore gloves, he kissed her fingers reverently and asked, "If I agree to go with them, will you come, too, as my wife?"

Until that moment Emily hadn't been sure exactly how she would respond. But suddenly the way became clear. "Edward, I am very fond of you. But I can't marry you. I must find my father. I don't know how, or by what means, but it would be so unfair to you if I were to become your wife before my search is over. How could I devote myself to you properly?"

He was silent for an interminably long minute, then said heavily, "Emily, you are young and without means. Mexico is a continent away and at war. How can you travel there—indeed, how can you support yourself? You need a husband's protection. You say you are fond of me; that's enough for me. You'll learn to care for me in time, I know you will, for I shall devote my every waking minute to bringing that about."

"Edward, I'm sorry. I *do* care about you, far too much to allow you to take a second place in my life."

He slipped his arm around her shoulder. "I suppose I expected this to be your response. Ever since I met your ship this morning and was confronted by the formidable Max Seadon and my sister's determination to work for him, I've been thinking about what I would do if you refused me. Emily, I decided I would still want to take care of you—I don't want you to be adrift on this great continent. Would you reconsider and marry me if I were to leave you immediately after the ceremony?"

"What on earth do you mean?"

"I intend to join the army and fight the Mexicans. Please don't interpret this as a plea for sympathy for a departing soldier, but if I knew you were waiting for me, it would be an incentive to stay alive—I would be able to look forward to being with you again. I don't know how long this war will last, Emily, but surely by the time it ends, you will have found your father. Allow me to be a husband—albeit an absent husband—until then. I would send my army pay to you, and at least you would not be destitute. I swear that if I survive the war and after we are reunited you no longer wish to be my wife, I will give you an annulment.''

"Oh, Edward!" Emily said, her eyes misting. "How can I possibly refuse such a sweet and generous offer? But it is so unfair to you—how can I accept it?''

"It would be the greatest favor you could bestow upon me, Emily. Please believe me. I love you to distraction. I am willing to accept the merest crumbs of affection. If you could write to me occasionally—I'm not sure where I shall be or even if your letters would reach me—but just to anticipate a letter from a dear wife . . . to dream of you, think of you waiting for my return, ah, Emily, don't you see, you would be doing far more for me than I would be for you?''

Emily felt overwhelmed by the magnitude of his love, swept away by the romantic ideal of chaste love, of marriage to a departing soldier who needed a wife to be waiting for his return. She was scarcely aware of her whispered acquiescence until Edward wrapped her in his arms and kissed her lips to seal their bond.

When he released her, he said breathlessly, "I've made inquiries. We can be married by a justice of the peace tomorrow. I shall be leaving at midnight tomorrow night.''

Chapter 22

• •

UPON THEIR RETURN to the hotel, they found that Phin and Kane had retired to their rooms and Briony had left word for them to join her in Max's private suite. There they found Max and Briony sipping hot toddies before a marble fireplace with a blazing fire.

"Come and warm yourselves, you two," Briony called as they entered. "Max and I are discussing our travel plans."

Taking Emily's hand in his and smiling broadly, Edward announced, "Emily has consented to be my wife. We'll be married tomorrow."

Emily noted that he said nothing about having already enlisted in the army, or that he would be leaving within hours of the wedding.

Briony instantly rose to her feet and embraced Emily. "Now I shall have a sister. I'm so happy for both of you." Then she turned to her brother and protested, "But, Edward, we can't possibly find a wedding dress and make arrangements overnight! Is such haste really necessary?"

"Yes, it is. I've arranged for a civil ceremony, and it must be tomorrow," Edward said. "Emily understands and agrees. She will look beautiful no matter what she wears."

Briony must have recognized some unspoken message in her brother's tone, for she did not argue with him. Instead she slipped her arm through Emily's and said, "Then let's go to our rooms and ransack our luggage for suitable gowns."

Edward turned to Max and said, "If you'll excuse me, sir, I'd like to turn in, too."

"Of course," Max said. "Good night."

"I must tell Phin the news," Emily said as they left Max's suite.

Briony glanced sideways, her eyes narrowed slightly. "I suppose you will want her to attend the ceremony."

"Yes, of course," Emily answered, surprised by the question.

"Edward did explain that Max is going to repay our debt to her—as an advance against future salaries—so you're no longer going to be under any obligation to Phin?"

"No, I didn't know that." Emily wasn't sure why this was brought up now, but they had reached Phin's door, so she knocked and, when she heard Phin's soft response, went inside.

"Edward and I will be married tomorrow," Emily said, and Phin nodded but did not embrace her, as though a business arrangement had been agreed upon, and murmured, "We must prepare."

"We were on our way to look through our rather pitifully small wardrobes to decide what to wear," Briony said.

Phin walked over to her open trunk and removed a beautiful silk gown of palest lemon-yellow, the bodice embroidered with rich purples, blues, and greens. "This might fit you, Emily."

"Oh, Phin, it's lovely!" Emily exclaimed.

Briony said stiffly, "Emily, the dress *is* lovely, but . . . it's really too exotic and foreign-looking for a civil ceremony in the afternoon. The gown you're wearing would be more suitable if we can't find anything else."

She was wearing a plain blue bombazine, which had been hastily purchased before leaving England, and this was the dress she wore the following day when she became Mrs. Edward Dale, who had once been Sir Edward Darnell.

Their vows were exchanged in the dismal parlor of an elderly justice of the peace in the presence of Briony, Max Seadon, and Phin. Kane had declined to attend and did not put in an appearance at their wedding breakfast, as the first meal a married couple had together was called, although of course, it was actually lunch and took place at the hotel of Max's friend.

Max had provided a bottle of champagne and an array of delicacies, but Emily was too nervous to eat. Max also announced that his wedding present would be to provide the bridal suite, to which they repaired late that afternoon.

After the breathless pace of the previous hours, Emily found the bridal suite silent and vaguely oppressive. Alone with her bridegroom she felt shy and apprehensive. Would he expect to consummate the union? Surely not in the broad daylight of the afternoon, or with the possibility of a promised annulment at some future time?

Edward gently folded her into his arms and kissed her tenderly. "My dear wife, you're trembling. There's no need to be afraid. In the eyes of the world we are now man and wife, but we will only become one in God's eyes when you are ready to give yourself to me willingly and freely. Pray that this war will end soon so that we may be together. Remember that I will love you always."

She offered her lips again, liking the way his mouth tasted, feeling safe in the circle of his arms.

But his kiss was brief. He took her hand and led her to a sofa. "We haven't much time, Emily. I must be on a train in less than an hour. Don't tell the others until I am on my way. I've written a letter to my sister."

He withdrew an envelope from his inside pocket and handed it to her. "Give this to Bri after I've left."

A tear formed at the corner of Emily's eye and slipped down her cheek. "I feel so afraid for you, Edward," she whispered.

"Don't worry about me. I have volunteered for medical duties, so shall be quite safe. It is you I'm worried about. Promise me you'll stay with Briony. She will take care of you." His finger traced the curve of her cheek, and his eyes fixed so intently upon her face that he seemed to be burning her image into his memory. "And it would be good to know that my two ladies are together."

"But Phin and I must try to find my father," Emily said. "I'm not sure—" She broke off as his expression changed.

He stared at her for a moment. "You're very fond of Phin, I know, and we are all deeply indebted to her. But we have to face facts. She is not . . ." He flushed uncomfortably. "I suppose the kindest thing I could say about her is that she is an adventuress and not a suitable companion for a respectable married woman."

Emily was aghast. "She was more than suitable when we were fugitives—when we desperately needed help and a way to escape the hangman's rope. How unkind to call her an adventuress! Surely you are not suggesting that I part company with Phin. That's out of the question! Apart from the fact that I am eternally grateful to her, and value her friendship greatly, she and I have made a pact—our quest is to find my father."

He sighed deeply. "Then I can only caution you that we are judged by the people with whom we associate. I can only hope that she will do nothing to bring shame to you. Emily, you lived in China; surely you realize what type of woman Phin is."

Emily jumped to her feet, her eyes blazing. "I will not hear another word spoken against Phin! She is my dear friend."

He rose to his feet and offered his hand to help her up. "Then I'll say no more. Kiss me, dear wife, for I must leave now."

The night was long and lonely, filled with doubts and apprehensions. Emily was glad when the dawn broke. She dressed and went down to the deserted dining room, then spent another two hours pacing restlessly until first Max and then Briony came down to breakfast.

"Edward has joined the army and gone to fight the Mexicans," she said, handing his letter to Briony. "He left this for you."

Briony's hand flew to her throat, and she turned pale. She clutched the envelope to her heart. "Now the reason for the hasty wedding becomes clear. Oh, Emily, why didn't you tell us yesterday? I might never see my brother again and did not have a chance to bid him a proper goodbye."

"Edward asked me to not tell anyone until after he was gone."

Max said, "He didn't want any tearful goodbyes, Briony. Nor did he want to be beholden to anyone—least of all me, I suspect. Frankly, I admire his courage and initiative."

"Of course I am proud of my brother," Briony said. "If you will both excuse me, I'll return to my room to read my letter."

"I'll have a tray sent up to you," Max said.

Briony passed Phin on her way from the dining room, and Emily quickly relayed the news. Phin made no comment, but Emily thought she might have uttered a faint sigh of dismay.

"Do you think Kane will come down to breakfast?" Emily asked

"I can answer that," Max responded. "He asked for tea and toast to be sent to his room."

"I must go and talk to him later. Will you come with me, Phin?"

Phin nodded. She filled two dishes with stewed dried fruits from the buffet sideboard and took them to the table. "First we must have breakfast."

"I'm not very hungry," Emily said, for the first time feeling responsible that Edward had placed himself in danger.

Max was piling eggs, ham, fried potatoes, and biscuits onto his plate and, as if reading her thoughts, commented, "Edward is a lucky young man to have such a charming wife waiting for him. He is also smart enough to realize that the army is the perfect place for a fugitive to erase any trail he's left behind him."

"Edward is not a fugitive." Emily declared. "Why do you say he is?" She believed this, since she didn't consider anything her new husband had done was a crime, no matter what the law said.

Max smiled. "Ah, he's doubly lucky. His wife is not only lovely but loyal."

They ate a rather strained breakfast, and then Emily and Phin went up to Kane's room.

He opened the door only a crack in response to Emily's

knock, and standing out in the hallway, she told him she had married Edward and that he had joined the army.

"He played on your sympathy," Kane said at once. "Would you have married him if he had not been off to the war to fight and possibly die?"

"Yes, of course I would. How can you suggest such a thing? You're impossible, Kane, I don't know why I bother with you." She turned and walked away and was surprised when Phin did not follow. She assumed the two of them talked about her hasty marriage and departed bridegroom. At the back of Emily's mind the thought hovered that Phin remaining alone in a man's room was surely the stuff of lost reputations. Was there a way to point out the folly of such improprieties without offending Phin?

Events crowded one upon the other all day long, leaving little time to brood. Max Seadon repaid Phin, who returned Kane's diamond. After reading Edward's letter, Briony suggested that Emily should travel with them to Texas to await the end of the war and her husband's return.

Since there was no mention of either Phin or Kane in the invitation, Emily politely declined on the grounds that she wanted to send word to her father.

"But where will you go, what will you do?" Briony asked.

"We'll stay here in New York. Phin has devised a plan. She hasn't told me all the details yet. She is going to find a place for us."

Briony seemed about to make a comment, then changed her mind. "Will you promise to keep in touch with me and consider joining us as soon as you hear from your father? After all, Texas is much closer to Mexico than New York."

"Oh, yes, of course I will."

Max whirled Briony away to a veritable orgy of shopping for clothes and for various items for his hotel that would not be available in Texas, and during the following days Emily saw little of them. Kane kept to himself, refusing to speak to Emily, but Phin reported that Kane had paid his own hotel bill and that on at least one occasion she had seen Max leaving Kane's room.

This worried Emily, as Max was such a forceful individual and was already suspicious about their sudden departure from England. She didn't want him badgering Kane, who might very well get angry and give away the fact that they were fugitives. She decided to warn Kane of Max's suspicions and so went to Kane's room, determined that this time he would talk to her. She knocked on the door.

There was no response. She pounded on the door and called to him until a passing porter stopped her. "Pardon me, miss, but the gentleman who was in that room has gone."

"Gone?" Emily repeated. "What do you mean?"

"Checked out last night, miss. Paid his bill and checked out. I took his bags to a hackney myself."

Emily flew down to the lobby, and the desk clerk confirmed what the porter had told her.

"Did he leave a message for Mrs. Edward Dale?"

"No, ma'am. Mr. Kane didn't leave any messages."

Emily was distraught when she confronted Max. "You spoke with him. Did you know he intended to leave?"

"No," Max said. "Why are you so interested in him?"

"He is a friend. Did he say where he was going?"

"No."

"Oh, dear heaven, where will he go? What will he do? We must find him."

"He's a free agent, Emily."

"You don't understand—he isn't used to being out on his own. Please, can you help me find him?"

"I'll make some inquiries. But you must realize it will be like looking for a needle in a haystack in a city of this size. Still, I'll contact some friends. If he's checked into another hotel, we might find him. I doubt anyone will forget his face."

But Kane had vanished without a trace. He might just as well have dropped off the earth.

Chapter 23

....

PHIN ACCOMPANIED EMILY to the offices of the British Consulate but left her at the door. "I'll wait for you here. Be careful—say as little as possible."

Emily nodded. They had decided they could not divulge Emily's relationship to Fletcher Faraday for fear of alerting the British authorities that his daughter was a fugitive from justice. Phin suggested that she use her married name and claim he was a favorite uncle whom she hoped to visit after her tour of the United States but was unsure how to proceed because of the war. She would ask that they contact him on her behalf.

The clerk to whom Emily addressed this question smiled apologetically. "Mrs. Dale, I'm afraid our contacts with Mexico City must be made via England, who routes our diplomatic pouches through the Caribbean to Mexico, then back to England, then to us. As you can imagine, this takes months. All of us hope this unfortunate state of hostilities will end soon. However . . ." He spread his hands help-lessly.

"Will you please send a letter from me to my . . . uncle, nevertheless? I shall remain here until I receive his response, no matter how long it takes."

"We can inform him that his niece wishes to hear from him, and he can send word to you. If you will give me your address?"

"I am staying at a hotel—but I'm unsure where I may be by the time his reply arrives. Perhaps you could have him send a letter to me in care of the consulate?"

Relaying this information to Phin, Emily said with a

worried frown, "What on earth will my father think when he hears a niece named Mrs. Edward Dale is in New York? We have no other relatives."

For an instant a strange look appeared on Phin's delicate features, but then she smiled reassuringly and replied, "When you return to give the consulate your address, you will be sure to include the information that your father is unaware of your marriage and that he will know you by your maiden name of Emily—What was your mother's maiden name?"

"Lowery."

"We'll hope he'll be curious enough to write to Emily Lowery. We must be patient, little sister."

Phin and Emily moved into a small apartment on the Lower East Side and filled those first days with excursions to all the places of interest the fascinating city had to offer. She wrote to Edward faithfully, and occasionally to Briony in Texas, but did not hear from her husband or his sister. Phin would disappear some evenings, offering no explanation as to where she was going, and Emily was too polite to question her.

Although she knew it was probably still too early to receive word from Mexico City, Emily got into the habit of calling at the consulate every day to see if they had heard from her "uncle" and to ask for any news of the war they had. She was assured that Mexico City was far from the battlegrounds.

Then her first letter from Edward arrived, creating a vivid picture of the distant war.

He had written:

My Dear Wife,

    At long last I have received three letters from you. How can I express my gratitude and joy—how can I tell you how much your words of encouragement and concern for my safety mean to me? I wrote to you at the hotel where I left you, as Briony wrote that you had not accompanied her to Texas. Perhaps by now you have received those letters. [She had not.]

I am a medical officer and so far have dealt with more sick and ailing soldiers than wounded warriors. We are in a place called Matamoros, which is in American hands, and it seems every man in the United States wants to fight Mexicans. Volunteers pour into this dusty, flea-ridden town in ever-increasing numbers. "The Halls of Montezuma" is a phrase on everyone's lips, and men can't wait to see for themselves the exotic señoritas, the volcanoes and desert (not to mention the silver mines and other riches that glitter beckoningly in their imaginations).

Today I heard that Congress limited enlistments, and state after state is turning applicants away from recruiting offices. Some of these would-be warriors simply head in the general direction of the Rio Grande, and most of them end up here in Matamoros. Someone should warn them what awaits them.

Searingly hot days made more miserable by black clouds of flies, desert-cool nights filled with mosquitoes so enormous the men call them "nighthawks." Sickness is rampant among the "seven-dollar targets," as the recruits call themselves (that being the amount of their monthly pay). Our tent hospitals are filled to overflowing with men in the throes of fever or wasting away from dysentery. I estimate that for every man killed in battle, we lose ten to disease.

The new arrivals come filled with bravado, however, and the town is booming. Hotels, bars, lunchrooms have sprung up—even a bowling alley and a theater. There's a fountain selling "soda with syrups" along with a daguerreotypist and a dentist.

I am convinced that the Americans will win this war, and if what is happening here in Matamoros is an indication for what will happen to the Mexican territory of Alta California after it becomes part of the union, then Max Seadon's prophecy about business opportunities there is well founded.

Have you heard from my sister? I received a couple of brief notes. Apparently she is busy learning the hotel business in Texas and enjoying quite a social whirl in San

Antonio. If I am ever granted leave, I may try to visit her but am unsure how much time I would need. This continent is so vast, and distances so great. I must confess I worry about Bri's association with Seadon, but no one, least of all her younger brother, has ever been able to dictate to Bri, so I can only hope Seadon treats her honorably.

I worry even more about you, my dearest Emily. Are you managing? Are you lonely? Have you received the allotment I made to you—above all, is it enough to live on? I spent such a limited time as a civilian in New York that I really have no idea of the cost of living there. Indeed, I still can't reconcile the value of dollars and cents against pounds, shillings, and pence.

Is Phin Tsu still with you? I was glad to hear you have a companion, but please remember what I said to you before I left.

If there is any way for me to get in touch with the British Embassy in Mexico, I will do so. But Mexico City is a long way from Matamoros, and my chances of doing so are not good.

I must return to duty now, my dearest. I will write again soon. Please take care of yourself. You are constantly in my thoughts, always in my heart. I love you so much and count the days until we can be together again.

Your devoted husband,
Edward.

As the weeks drifted into months, Emily's daily visits to the British Consulate became routine. The consular officials and clerks got to know her and remarked they could set their watches by the regularity of her arrivals. If they wondered why she doggedly waited to hear from an uncle in distant Mexico, no one questioned her. The response to her query was always the same: "No word from your uncle yet."

The war dragged on. Emily left financial matters to Phin, who seemed to have a head for them. Phin assured her that Edward's army allotment paid Emily's way.

Then, on a sweltering midsummer day when Emily

arrived at the consulate, she was met by a senior clerk named Mr. Blakely.

"Mrs. Dale, will you accompany me into my private office?" He was a tall, silver-haired man who reminded her, unnervingly, of Max Seadon, except that Blakely wore a sympathetic expression rather than the slightly sardonic one with which Seadon faced the world.

Emily followed him into his office, knowing instinctively that his news could only be bad. Horrible possibilities flashed into her mind. Had they learned her true identity and intended to deport her back to England to stand trial as an accessory to murder? Was her father ill? Had he returned to England? Had he disclaimed all knowledge of a niece named Mrs. Dale and refused to contact her?

"Please sit down, Mrs. Dale," Blakely said.

She perched on the edge of a straight-back chair facing the shining expanse of a well-polished desk, held her breath, and waited for him to speak.

"I regret I have some very distressing news for you," he said in a voice that sounded like the hollow grinding of tumbrel wheels. "Your uncle Fletcher Faraday and aunt—"

"She isn't my aunt," Emily blurted out without thinking. He raised an eyebrow. She added, "I mean, she is my uncle's second wife."

"I see. Well . . . the unfortunate fact of the matter is . . . they never reached Mexico City."

Emily blinked uncomprehendingly. "But I know they left England bound for Mexico."

"Fletcher Faraday never arrived to take up his post, and the embassy in Mexico City never heard from him. He and his bride simply disappeared after disembarking from the ship that brought them from England. We can only assume that they were either caught in a skirmish between American and Mexican troops or were set upon by bandits or perhaps hostile Indians. I'm very sorry to have to give you this sad news, Mrs. Dale, but it seems very likely that both your uncle and his wife died, or were killed, some months ago. There is no other explanation for their disappearance and subsequent prolonged silence. If they were still alive, someone would have heard from them.''

The walls seemed to close in on Emily. She gripped the edge of Blakely's desk, feeling if she let go she might fall.

Then somehow he was helping her to her feet, inquiring if she would like a glass of water, asking if he could be of any further assistance to her.

She shook her head, her mouth dry.

"May I express my deepest sympathy, Mrs. Dale? And please, do not hesitate . . .''

Emily wasn't listening. She stumbled from the room and out into the street. The summer heat rose from the baked sidewalk in searing eddies, wafting beneath her skirts and burning the soles of her shoes. She thought, irrelevantly, that she must ask Phin if their budget would stretch to taking her shoes to the cobbler.

Ignoring an approaching horse car, Emily kept walking. She felt numb, unable to either accept or even deny that her father could be dead. Rather her mind dismissed the fact that she had visited the consulate that day.

Eventually the rising heat, a terrible thirst, and aching feet drove her back to the apartment. By then something akin to acceptance of the message from Mexico had set in.

Phin wasn't home. She arrived an hour later to find Emily folding and packing clothes into a trunk.

"You heard from your father? We are going to him at last?'' Phin's excited smile faded when Emily raised her head and looked at her. Emily related Mr. Blakely's news in a tearful voice.

Phin glanced at the half-filled trunk questioningly. "You wish to join your sister-in-law in San Antonio?''

Emily looked at her blankly. She appeared to be dazed. "I don't know—I hadn't thought—I . . . just felt I must leave New York. Perhaps I should go to Edward in Matamoros.''

Phin said gently, "You know that is out of the question. Listen to me, Emily. There are many reasons why your father might not have reached Mexico City, especially in such perilous times as these. There are also many reasons why he would choose not to get in touch with anyone to explain where he is. Remember, he believes his only daughter is dead.''

Emily seemed to be struggling to emerge from some paralyzing cocoon. ''He might be still alive? Is that what you're saying? Oh, could it be possible?''

''I'm saying only that we have no proof he is *not* still alive. When the war ends, I believe we should attempt to retrace his steps to the point where he dropped from sight.''

Emily looked at her with drowning eyes. ''Do I dare hope? Wouldn't the disappointment be too cruel?''

''There is always hope.''

''Do *you* believe there's hope?''

''Emily, I am going to tell you something now, but before I do, I want you to promise that this will be our secret for as long as I deem necessary. Will you give me your most solemn word?''

''Yes, of course I will. But you didn't answer my question about my father.''

''*Our* father, Emily. He is father to both of us.''

For a moment Emily didn't comprehend. She stared at Phin, wondering if her friend had taken leave of her senses or was speaking metaphorically in some attempt to share her grief.

''I am going to make a pot of tea,'' Phin said. ''And then I am going to tell you about my mother, and myself, and explain to you why I must know for certain whether Father is alive or dead. Come, little sister, leave the packing for now.''

They sat up most of the night, talking. There were questions to be asked and answers to be given. Emily tried to conceal her shock that her father had loved and abandoned a Chinese woman, but Phin seemed to understand what she was feeling.

''Do not judge him, Emily,'' she said. ''He and my mother both knew their liaison was doomed from the start, and when he left her, Father did not know that she was carrying me. You are inexperienced in the ways of men and women, little sister. Your father is still the same man you always believed him to be.''

"But he never told me there had been anyone in his life before Mother.''

"Few men speak of their former loves, and never to the daughters of their wives. It is not surprising that he did not wish you to know about my mother. She suffered revilement from her own people because she loved a foreigner and could not conceal it, for she had me. In your father's case it would have been even more detrimental—his diplomatic career might have been ruined.''

Emily saw the wisdom of Phin's words and, sighing, nodded. "It's all so sad.'' She saw then that Phin was watching her with a mixture of hope and trepidation on her exquisite features. Emily said, "But we mustn't be sad. We have the gift of each other. I always wanted a sister, Phin.'' Her brow knitted slightly. "Someone else said that recently. Who? Oh, yes, Briony. How wonderful that I now have two sisters.'' She tried to imbue her words with an enthusiasm she didn't feel.

Phin made no comment, and Emily recalled that she and Briony had not exactly been compatible. She said quickly, "Oh, Father *must* be still alive. I couldn't bear it if you never knew him. He's so kind, so patient, a gentleman in every sense of the word. You'll like him, Phin, I know you will.''

"Emily, before I told you that I am your half sister, you gave me your word that you would keep this a secret. Promise me now that no one else will learn what I have told you tonight. *We* know we are sisters, and that's all that matters. If we find Father alive, then he must have time to get to know me, and I him, before we decide whether or not to break the news to him that he has another daughter, which will be a severe shock to him. If he is dead, then there is no need to tell anyone else.''

"But I don't understand why—''

"You gave your solemn promise,'' Phin reminded her. "Only we two will know the truth of our blood tie until I receive a sign that the time is right to confide in others. Now

I will light the joss sticks and pray to Kwan Yin for guidance."

"I shall write to Briony in San Antonio," Emily said the following morning as they lingered over their breakfast tea. "I'll tell her of the disappointing news from Mexico City but stress that I'm not giving up hope that Father is still alive. Then I'll ask her if her invitation to join her is still in effect. Texas is, after all, much closer to Mexico."

A veil seemed to descend over Phin's dark eyes. "We do not need to go to Briony. We can go anywhere we choose. I do not wish to be obligated to her."

"But she's helping Max Seadon run his hotel there, and it would be reassuring to have a destination and someone waiting for us at the end of a very long journey. We can pay for our board and lodging, and besides . . . well, I *am* married to her brother, and it was Edward's wish that she and I be together."

A hint of a smile curved Phin's lips. "Are you? Are you really a married woman, Emily?"

Emily flushed. "What do you mean?"

"Your marriage was not consummated, was it?"

"How did you know?"

"You told me your groom left that afternoon. Besides, you did not wear the expression of a woman who had been introduced to the pleasures of the flesh."

"Phin! For heaven's sake, women do not enjoy the marital bed! That part of marriage is for men's pleasure. For us it is only a duty to be performed so that we may bear children."

"Who told you that?"

"Doris did. I shared a room with her in the doctor's house."

"I see. Did you speak of this with your husband?"

"Of course not! But Edward was considerate enough to postpone his conjugal rights until the war ends. I'm sure he didn't want me to bear a child alone."

Emily lowered her eyes, knowing there was more to the lack of consummation than that but not wishing to diminish herself in Phin's eyes. She had married Edward because she didn't know how she could survive alone. If only Phin had confided of their blood tie before she took that rash step!

"It is not necessary to bear a child if one does not wish to," Phin said. "There are ways to prevent conception. Your Edward has studied medicine; he surely knew that."

Growing increasingly uncomfortable with the conversation, Emily murmured, "Please, let's change the subject?"

"Did you refuse him?" Phin persisted. "We are sisters, Emily, you can tell me. Perhaps I can help you."

"I told him I didn't love him, and he said I didn't have to give myself until I was ready, and if I didn't want to be married to him when he comes back from the war, we could get an annulment. There! Are you satisfied? Now please leave me alone."

She ran from the room, hastily donned her bonnet, and went for a walk. Phin didn't follow, and for this Emily was grateful. She needed time alone to think about the two equilibrium-shattering pieces of news she had received in the last twenty-four hours.

The morning sunlight was warm but not yet hot, and their street of brownstones was lined with trees to provide intervals of shade. In the evening the stoops would be crowded with people seeking escape from the stifling heat indoors, but this time of day everyone was working. After her own ordeal of working long hard hours in the doctor's household, Emily felt guilty about her present idleness. The small flat she shared with Phin was quickly cleaned, and Phin was such an excellent cook that most of the meal preparation fell to her. Phin had found Chinatown and shopped for their food there, and Emily was happy to again be eating the tasty dishes she had enjoyed in China. There was little for Emily to do. She had no books to read, no embroidery to work on, and was quite sure Edward's small allotment would not cover the purchases of either books or embroidery silks. After her conversation with Phin about her marriage, she felt even guiltier about taking Edward's money. Perhaps she should try to find a position of some sort. She shivered, remembering the doctor's house. Not in service, never again. Besides, married women did not work; who would hire her?

As she walked the city streets that morning, Emily was lost in thought, striving to accept the possible loss of her father and the knowledge that she had a half sister. Despite what she'd told Phin, Emily wasn't sure whether to be happy or dismayed to find she had a Eurasian half sister, especially one her husband had called an adventuress. Would their father have the same reaction to Phin? Emily didn't even want to think about her father's bride. Tonia would have a fit if she were presented with a Eurasian stepdaughter. That particular thought gave Emily a moment's guilty pleasure.

She had been walking for some time and found herself on an unfamiliar street, dodging a great many more pedestrians. Horse-drawn wagons rumbled by loaded with goods. Men pushed handcarts of fruits and vegetables. A dripping ice wagon went by followed by a hoard of laughing, shouting children. A shopkeeper swept the pavement in front of his store and smiled at her as she passed.

Suddenly, above the sound of grinding wagon wheels and shouted conversations, some in foreign tongues, most in the accented English she had come to associate with the city, she distinctly heard the unmistakable drawl of Oxford accents.

"Well, you do as you please, old boy, but I'm going to let her have my Chaucer."

"For a wager on a nag that can't possibly win? You're a fool, Reggie. You may need the price of a meal before your next allowance arrives."

Two young men caught up with her and walked on by. They were well dressed, and one of them carried a portmanteau. They entered an establishment halfway down the next block. Curious, Emily followed.

She found herself in front of a shop window filled with books. Catching her breath in delight at the sight of some familiar titles and many new ones, she read the sign painted in gilt letters on the window: MRS. FITZWORTHY'S LENDING LIBRARY.

Emily had seen subscription libraries in England and thought what a wonderful idea they were. This was evidently a similar endeavor. She pushed open the door and went inside.

Phin made her way down the cellar steps, picking up her skirts to step over two Chinese men sprawled halfway down. The glassy eyes and lolling heads, the ungainly position of limbs, and complete disinterest in her or their surroundings told their own story.

In the cellar the yellow lamplight fought a losing battle with spirals of smoke rising from a dozen pipes, and the smell of burning incense did little to alleviate the sickly sweet odor of opium.

The cribs along the walls were occupied by sleeping men and a few women, although most of the latter were no longer recognizable as being females.

Phin made as rapid a tour of the cellar as was possible, given the closely packed bodies and dim light. Then she bent over an old man seated alone in a corner. "Where is he, Uncle? Was he here last night? Have you seen him?"

The old man stared right through her. She seized his scrawny shoulder and gave him a slight shake. "When did you see him last?"

He blinked through the haze, attempting to focus narrow slits of eyes that seemed too tiny to accommodate their dilated pupils, and, recognizing her, shook his head, his wisps of white beard moving like fragile cobwebs on his leathery chin. "No see him, two, maybe three days."

Phin let go of his shoulder and made her way back up the cellar steps. It was a relief to be in the open air again. She drew a deep breath. There was no time now to make a search. Besides, he was probably sleeping in an alley somewhere. If he hadn't been to the cellar for two or three days, he would surely be back tonight. She would return after dark.

She hurried back to their apartment, but Emily had not returned. Phin began to worry about her. She was such an innocent. Had the news about her father, then her own bombshell, been too much for her?

Just as she was about to begin a frantic search, Emily, smiling happily, returned.

"Oh, Phin, you'll never guess what I found! A lending library! For a small fee one can take a book home for a week or so and read it. But that isn't all! The lady who runs the library fell from a ladder—she was reaching for a book on the top shelf—she's quite old and not too spry—and she broke her arm. I started chatting with her, and she was quite impressed with my knowledge of books. She told me she hadn't been able to put away the returned books on the upper shelves for days, and she offered me a job! Just a few hours a day, and it's only for a month or so until her arm heals, but she will pay me a small salary, and I can read all the books I want to without charge!"

Phin smiled. "That is indeed good news. Now I shan't worry about leaving you alone in the evenings when I go out."

Emily's smile faded. "Now that we're sisters, Phin, would you like to tell me where you go in the evening?"

Phin's reply was accompanied by that veiled look that warned not to pry. "I go to be with my own people."

"Oriental or Caucasian? Both are your people, Phin," Emily said, hurt. She sat down and opened the book Mrs. Fitzworthy had loaned her, thinking that there was much Phin had not confided, considering they were sisters.

As soon as the summer dusk fell, Phin dressed in a simple dark gown and slipped a black silk shawl over her shoulders. Emily glanced at her and felt a faint stirring of apprehension. Phin usually dressed much more elaborately in the evening.

"Don't wait up for me," Phin said, as she always did.

"Phin, where are you going dressed like that? Surely not to meet a gentleman."

"Don't worry about me."

"Phin, is there someone you're seeing? Why don't you ever bring him here?"

"There is no one of importance."

"Has there ever been? Have you ever loved a man, Phin?"

"Yes."

"How did it feel? How did you know it was true love?"

"It was like no other feeling on earth. When it happens, you will know."

"Why did you not marry him?"

Phin gave a small, sad smile. "Marriage was not possible, nor would he keep me as a concubine, although I humbled myself to beg that he do so. He was a foreign devil who burst into my life and forever changed it. His name was Brent Carlisle. He was an American, a soldier of fortune. No more questions. I must go now. Good night, little sister."

Phin made her way through the dark streets, moving like a shadow in her black clothes. She reached the cellar as the night's customers began to arrive, and she settled down to wait.

As midnight approached she knew her visit had again been fruitless. She left to search all of the adjacent alleys.

She was accosted several times by men inquiring as to her price. A sharp response sent them staggering away into the night. Then one Chinese man, more persistent than the rest, attempted to drag her into a doorway.

The knife appeared in her hand faster than he could blink, the blade glinting in the streetlight. He leapt backward in alarm, then turned and ran. Phin slipped the knife back under her shawl and continued her search.

She found him lying in a litter-strewn alley only a block away from the cellar where he had undoubtedly been heading. He was semiconscious, his shirt caked with dried blood. He had been stripped of his shoes and any money or possessions he had carried.

"How could anyone do this to him?" Emily wept over Kane's battered body as Phin prepared to clean his wounds.

Ignoring the question, Phin said calmly, "He was stabbed in the back, here near his shoulder, and again in the upper arm. He's lost a lot of blood, but I believe if we can keep the wounds from becoming infected, he may recover."

"May recover? He *must* recover! Phin, it will be all my fault if he dies."

"Don't even think that, Emily. Any fault lies with him alone."

"We need a doctor right away. Shall I go?"

"I will go to the herb doctor first thing in the morning and get poultices for the wounds and advice as to how to treat him."

"A Chinese doctor? Don't you think we should fetch an American doctor?"

Phin applied a clean dressing to one of the wounds as Emily mopped Kane's fevered brow. Despite his semiconscious state, he writhed and twisted in the bed, making ministering to him difficult.

"Emily, we need a Chinese doctor. Kane has a more serious malady than the wounds you see. I want you to take some sheets and tear them into strips. We may have to bind him to the bed."

Emily gasped. "Surely that would hurt him. Why would you want to tie him down?"

As Phin began to clean the second wound, Kane thrashed even more wildly, and Emily was forced to hold him. When the dressing was in place, they sat on either side of the bed, exhausted, still holding his arms to his sides.

"Do you remember the last night we were on the ship?" Phin asked at length as Kane's struggles grew feebler. "You asked me to go to his cabin because he was moaning and you thought he was ill. His sickness was of the mind. He didn't want to disembark, or to face a new life, new people here. He spoke of jumping into the water, of ending his life. He was in such a state that I feared he might bring the law down on all of our heads. I couldn't risk that. So I gave him something to calm him down."

"Yes, I remember. Can you give it to him again? I'll hold him while—"

"No," Phin interrupted. "He must never touch that particular remedy again. You see, some people can take it only once, or use it occasionally, without ill effect. Others become completely dependent upon it, cannot live without it, and will sacrifice everything to get it.''

Emily's memories of China stirred and comprehension dawned. ''Oh, dear God in heaven! You gave him opium. You have destroyed him. He is lost!''

''No,'' Phin said sharply. ''Not if we can keep him away from it long enough for his cravings to subside. He will go through the tortures of the damned, but I believe the fact that he is weak and wounded is to our advantage. We will keep him here and watch over him night and day. I know of a Chinese herbalist and acupuncturist who will help us.''

''Phin,'' Emily said suddenly. ''How did you know where Kane was living? Have you known of his whereabouts all along and yet let me worry myself to death about him?''

''I did not know where he'd gone until a few days ago. He left us at the hotel because I refused to obtain more opium for him. I could see that he was one of those who would let it rule his life. He went in search of the oblivion he believed would end his pain. A few days ago an acquaintance told me of a disfigured Caucasian who had asked several merchants if they would purchase a violin.''

Emily felt faint. ''Not his Stradivari! I can't believe he would part with it.''

''I've seen men sell their own mothers for an hour's oblivion. Don't worry, the violin is safe. I had my friend buy it and hold it for me. I'll get it back. However, Kane's diamond and other valuables are gone forever.''

Emily wrung out a cloth in a basin of cool water on the bedside table and gently mopped Kane's brow again, using her fingers to stroke back his hair. At her touch he stirred and suddenly opened his eyes and looked at her.

For an instant the pain and torment left that golden eye, and it locked onto hers with such intensity and longing that her breath stopped somewhere between her heart and her throat. His cruelly twisted lips moved, and although no sound escaped, she knew he was attempting to say her name.

She picked up his hand and squeezed his fingers reassuringly. "It's all right. You're safe with Phin and me. We're going to take care of you."

Phin picked up a glass of water and said, "Hold his head."

Emily cradled his head in her arms, and he took a sip of water. It was his last rational moment.

She laid his head back on the pillow as a tremor passed through his body. Moments later he was again writhing in agony, and they had to fight to keep him in the bed.

It was a very long night. Emily cringed in horror as Kane in his delirium cursed them and the God who made him and wished for death. She did not know that his ordeal—and theirs—was only just beginning.

Part II

Chapter 24

· ·

San Francisco, California, 1849

EMILY LEANED PERILOUSLY far out over the ship's rail to catch her first glimpse of San Francisco, which was the name the Americans had given the former Mexican settlement of Yerba Buena. The booming city sprawled untidily around the beautiful bay, and ships of every size and shape jostled for space to unload the cargoes of goods and gold seekers of every nationality.

The end of the war had caused a deep financial depression on the Eastern Seaboard, and the discovery of gold at Sutter's Mill had precipitated a stampede west. She and Phin had waited for months for a place aboard a ship, and then endured the hazards of sailing around Cape Horn, which Phin felt was the safest route to take to California. Their alternatives had been an overland journey through hostile Indian territory, facing starvation and the challenge of the High Sierras, or the overcrowded Panama route, which felled many with deadly diseases. The voyage around the Horn and then up the coasts of South and North America had been long and trying, and Emily had been convinced they would all perish as their vessel was lashed unmercifully by the gales of the Strait of Magellan. She had been seasick most of the voyage, and her clothes now hung loosely on her thin body. She felt euphoric that it was at last over.

Phin placed a restraining hand over Emily's. "Be careful. Don't fall into the sea now that we have almost reached land. We've come too far and endured too many storms to risk drowning you now. Your husband would never forgive us.''

Some of Emily's excitement waned at the mention of Edward. She could hardly recall what he looked like, and the memory of the brief civil ceremony that had made them man and wife seemed no more real than a half-forgotten dream. Now here she was, three years later, about to be reunited with a man she barely remembered.

She said abruptly, ''I'm going to see if Kane will come up on deck. He shouldn't miss this sight.''

Phin's hand tightened on hers. ''Leave him in his cabin. Edward and his sister are probably waiting for you on the quay. Don't thrust Kane upon them without warning. You must break the news of his presence carefully.''

Emily bit her lip. ''I should have written and told them. I just didn't think . . .''

''That he would still be with you after three years?'' Phin finished for her.

They regarded each other silently for a moment, recalling the grim days when Kane had hovered between life and death, fighting demons too terrible to imagine. At some time during his long convalescence Emily had given up on the idea of traveling to Briony in San Antonio and decided instead to stay in New York until the war ended.

The three of them had become a family of sorts. Although Emily had been forced to give up her part-time work at the lending library in order to care for Kane, when he was well enough to leave in Phin's care, she returned to find Mrs. Fitzworthy had had another setback with her broken arm and had decided to retire. She hired Emily to run the library for her. A few months later the proprietor of a nearby music shop asked if she knew anyone capable of copying sheet music for him. The job was perfect for Kane, who readily agreed to do it, and it seemed the small amount of money he earned helped him feel less dependent upon the two women. His recovery proceeded rapidly after that, and the best day of all was when Phin returned his beloved violin to him and he took it lovingly in his arms and played for them.

Now with their ship about to drop anchor, Emily felt a

moment's regret that their sojourn in New York had come to an end. But Edward was out of the army and waiting for her in San Francisco, and somewhere her father either lay in an unmarked grave or was living a new life. She and Phin had to know the fate that had befallen the man who had given them life.

Briony crossed Portsmouth Square, which had once been a potato patch and was now the hub of a lusty whirl of life in a brawling infant of a city growing at a dizzying rate. Well-dressed citizens moved about the town impervious to the muddy streets and the occasional presence of an itinerant mule or donkey strolling the thoroughfare.

Surrounding the square, on Washington, Kearny, Dupont, and Clay streets, stood hotels, restaurants, plush saloons, and gambling halls. Lifting her skirts above the mud, Briony hurried to the grandest hotel of all, the Rosebriar, which occupied a prominent corner of the square and sprawled down the adjacent street.

Snapping open her pendant watch, Briony realized that Emily's ship must be nearing port, as it had been sighted off the coast early that morning. She debated whether to go straight to the wharf, then decided against it. Edward was probably already there waiting to meet his wife. There would be time enough for her own reunion with her sister-in-law after she had dealt with Max.

The doorman at the Rosebriar, resplendent in a burgundy frock coat, tipped his hat and held the door for her. She stepped into the marble-floored lobby, and some of her irritation dissipated as she beheld her handiwork. Max had given her free rein with the design, building, and decoration of the hotel, sparing no expense, and she had created an atmosphere of tranquillity and beauty that quite literally took the breath away from travelers seeing it for the first time. The overall impression was of soft shades of rose, extremely flattering to female complexions, and soothing to men recently arrived from brutal voyages or taking a break from the rough-and-tumble goldfields. The marble of the floor and brocaded walls ranged from the most delicate shade of shell pink to deepest rose, with hints of tearose and plum, in shadings and patterns so subtle that the effect was of being surrounded by a filtered and magically rosy aura.

As she ascended the magnificent twice-turning staircase, her gaze lingered lovingly on the twin chandeliers that dominated the lobby, then searched the intricately carved balustrade for any speck of dust or slight chip in the gilt paint, a habit that was unnecessary, for every member of the staff took pride in the hotel and needed little supervision.

Briony had originally planned to model the Rosebriar after Hampton Court Palace in London, which she had visited and fallen in love with as a young girl before her marriage to Rupert. She had discovered that the royal architect had drawn up plans to replace an old Tudor palace at Hampton Court with a model of Versailles, but Sir Christopher Wren had to settle for remodeling two sides and one courtyard of the old palace. The resulting Tudor and Stuart mixture made Hampton Court Palace too unique to copy. Still, beginning with that premise, Briony's hotel had captured the mellow, rambling and romantic aspects of the Tudor style, blending them perfectly with the trim, neat, and orderly Stuart touches, combined with her own unique sense of style. Rooms at the Rosebriar were never empty, the dining rooms and banquet rooms booked months in advance. Every afternoon she presided over afternoon tea served at four o'clock in the mezzanine, and the wealthy matrons of the town, already separating themselves into a privileged class, clustered about the elegantly set tables nibbling tiny cucumber sandwiches and selected petits fours from gleaming silver three-tier serving plates, while Briony poured tea from a silver pot that had once belonged to Louis XIV.

Only Max Seadon's office resisted her efforts of harmony and serenity. She opened the door without knocking and walked into a room spartan in its appointments, with bare parquet floor and undraped floor-to-ceiling windows overlooking the bay. A desk of massive proportions, hewn from local pine, dominated the room. Max had rejected the desk Briony purchased for him with the remark, ''I was here once when the ground shook and some of the adobe houses the *Californios* lived in barely remained standing. If I'm to be relegated to the third floor, I'm going to have a sturdy piece of furniture to ride down to the ground if there's another earthquake."

"My hotel is built to withstand anything man or nature can devise," Briony said confidently, and Max laughed. "*Your* hotel, huh?"

There were occasional earth tremors, but after a while most people hardly noticed them. Besides, the architect who had designed the Rosebriar assured her that the worst that would happen in a strong quake would be the loss of a little plaster from the ceilings and possibly broken windows, that the basic structure would stand because of a clever arrangement of support beams and arches.

Briony gave the pine desk a baleful glance as she entered Max's office. He was standing at the window, watching a ship sail into the bay.

Hearing her footsteps, he turned and smiled. Briony wasn't sure whether to be pleased or resentful that in three years he had apparently not aged a single day. In fact, despite his silver hair, he seemed younger, more vigorous than ever. And despite her best efforts to smooth his rough edges, he was no closer to acquiring the attributes of a gentleman.

He said, "Look at that, Bri, if that isn't the most beautiful sight I've ever seen—except for you, of course."

"I don't have time to admire a ship, Max—"

"Not just a ship, my dear, a clipper. Fastest ship on the ocean. Look at those trim lines. She's built for speed, just like you."

"A clipper? Is that the new Bardine ship—the *Antonia?*" Briony's lips curved into a grimace. "I'm surprised you would compare her to me; why not for that low-class female for whom the ship's named? You seem to admire her greatly."

He turned to look at her, one sun-bleached eyebrow raised, his expression amused. "Ah, I see."

"Damn you, you don't see at all. In the unlikely event the

paths of Tonia Bardine and I had crossed in England, I would never have dreamed of adding her to a guest list. Why should I associate with someone here with whom I wouldn't dream of socializing at home? And as for Henry Bardine, he's an uncouth sea captain—a pirate probably—made his money swindling miners and immigrants and exploiting—''

Max held up his hands in mock surrender. "I'll grant that the Bardines are not the crème de la crème—is that how you say it?—of Nob Hill society. However, they're richer than Croesus, and social standing notwithstanding, you can't ignore a man who owns half the town. Besides, they wanted to book the dining room to celebrate the arrival of the *Antonia* for the same night as your party. It seemed to me only good business to invite them."

"My party is a private one to introduce Edward and Emily to a select group of friends. You had no right to include Tonia and Henry Bardine."

"*Our* party, remember? Who's footing the bill, and whose hotel banquet room is being used? If I want the Bardines, then by God, they'll be here. I've indulged your every whim, Briony, but you're not my wife, so don't choose my friends."

Briony placed her hand on his desk and leaned forward, almost feeling the angry sparks fly from her eyes. "And you are not my master. Have your damn party in your damn banquet room and invite all the scum of the bay for all I care. As for my brother and his wife and myself, we will have our own private party."

"In Edward's unfinished house, I presume?"

"The house *is* finished. It's just not furnished yet. Not that it's any of your business."

Max gave her the crooked grin that usually disarmed her, but today it only added to her anger. "Come on, Bri," he said, "let's not quarrel over this. It isn't worth it. You've invited everybody in San Francisco to the party. The Bardines will be lost in the crowd."

"Find another hostess, Max," Briony hissed. "Because I shall be entertaining my brother and sister-in-law that night." She turned and strode from the room, slamming the door behind her.

Emily knocked on Kane's cabin door, and he called, "Come."

He was sitting on his bunk, his packed bags awaiting collection by the steward, his violin case across his lap.

"I see you're all ready," Emily said. She went to his porthole. "Were you able to see the town as we came in? What a beautiful bay this is. In fact, the coast all the way from Mexico is breathtaking, isn't it? I think we're going to be happy here."

"I shouldn't have come," Kane said. "I can't believe I did. Perhaps I thought we'd be shipwrecked somewhere along the way and would spend the rest of our lives on some idyllic island."

She turned to face him. "You felt like that about New York at first."

"We were happy in New York, weren't we, the three of us? We had our work and each other for companionship. How quickly the days slipped away from us. Why didn't we realize that time was passing and savor it more?"

Emily's heart sank at the sadness in his voice. She said quickly, "You'll get used to it here. Edward wrote that the climate is very mild, and with immigrants arriving from all over the world, it's the perfect place for us to begin a new life."

"I shall never see you again after we land. Your husband will not permit it."

"What nonsense! Edward owes you his life. He will not have forgotten that."

"The man would have to be a saint to allow you to saddle him with a worthless monster like me who cannot make a living and who would surely frighten to death any children you may have."

"Kane, we've been over this a dozen times. You can make a living if you choose to. Fortunes are being made in the goldfields"—she held up her hand as he started to protest—"I'm not suggesting you become a miner, but there must be many other opportunities due to the sheer numbers of new arrivals. Until you find a place of your own, you will be our guest. Edward has built a fine house, and you and Phin will stay with us for as long as you wish.''

''Have you told Edward this? Does he know Phin and I are accompanying you?''

Emily felt herself flush. ''I didn't write and tell him for the simple reason I didn't know, not until the last minute, whether or not you would really come.''

Phin's soft voice spoke from the open cabin door, ''The captain has dropped anchor, and boats are being lowered to take passengers ashore. Emily, why don't you go first? Kane and I will come later. We will find a hotel. Perhaps after we're all settled, you'll visit us. This is not the time to confront your husband.''

Emily felt both relief and guilt that she would not have to explain their presence to anyone for a while, but another worry surfaced. ''Will you go to Max Seadon's hotel? The Rosebriar?''

''No. There are other hotels. We'll send word to you where we are staying.''

Emily embraced Phin and then turned to Kane and offered her hand. He took it in his and held it for a moment.

She started to leave, then turned and said, ''I shall feel strange being away from you and Phin. I shall miss you both. But it will only be for a few days, I promise.''

Heart thumping nervously, Emily made her way back to her own cabin and prepared to meet her husband.

Chapter 25

······························

EDWARD HAD CHANGED far more than Emily expected. There was no hesitation or tentativeness in the way he swept her into his arms and kissed her full on the mouth, on the quay, in full view of everyone.

He seemed taller, broader, his fair skin tanned a golden bronze by the southern sun, which had also bleached strands of his red-gold hair. He had lost the innocent look of youth and acquired a flinty aplomb. He had the look of a man accustomed to giving orders and having them obeyed and who would not flinch from adversity, yet there was also deep compassion in his eyes. Emily had expected him to be a stranger to her, but not that she would feel a rush of emotion that seemed equally made of excitement and trepidation.

"Please, Edward," Emily said as he swung her off her feet. "Everyone is watching us."

Laughing, he set her down on the rough boards of the quay. "They're watching the arrival of Henry Bardine's clipper ship. He hopes it will beat the speed record of the *Flying Cloud*."

Emily turned to look at the ship, and for the first time saw the name painted on the hull. Her heart skipped. The *Antonia*. A coincidence, she thought, nothing more. But if her father and Tonia had survived the war, it would not be beyond the reaches of imagination that they were living in what had formerly been Mexican territory. This did not explain how Tonia's name came to appear on a ship, however, and Emily regretfully concluded that the vessel had been named for some other Antonia.

"Come on, let's get your bags into the carriage. I'll send someone for your trunks later," Edward said, taking her arm. "I can't wait for you to see our house. I've been waiting for you to arrive before I buy furniture—I just have the bare necessities so far. Bri will help you. You should see what she's done to the Rosebriar—it's a veritable palace."

He lifted her over the mud bordering the quay and placed her in a handsomely appointed carriage, drawn by a pair of fine horses. Emily knew that he, in common with every other man in town, had spent most of the previous year in the goldfields. Evidently he had done well.

"How is your sister?" Emily asked as Edward climbed in beside her and jerked the reins to urge the horses forward.

"She's absolutely marvelous. The Grand Dame of San Francisco, queen of Nob Hill, leader of society. It's amazing, really, how Bri's managed to forge such a position for herself, as she works like a Trojan. Nobody here seems to care that she works for a living, though, or that she chooses to remain a widow rather than become a wife. Since we don't discuss our past, rumors abound—that Bri was married to a duke, or even a prince! She receives at least two proposals of marriage a week, from the richest and most eligible men in town. Since she refuses them all, another rumor has it that she and Max Seadon have an arrangement."

"And do they?"

"I doubt it. He's everything Bri dislikes in a man—a lifelong bachelor, a gambler, an opportunist, a bit of a diamond in the rough, certainly not a gentleman."

"Perhaps, after being married to a gentleman who mistreated her so, she's able to overlook some of Max's shortcomings," Emily suggested.

"No, I'm sure they have only a business arrangement. Besides, she's not free to marry anyone else, is she? Not while Rupert lives." Edward glanced sideways at her. "My dearest wife, I can't believe you're here beside me at last. You look lovely, but I can see the voyage took its toll. Never mind, we'll soon put some flesh back on your bones. You're going to love it here, Emily, there's such a sense of vitality, energy. You can't believe how fast the town is growing.''

He began to tell her that not only had fortunes been made in the goldfields, but those traders and businessmen who remained in San Francisco were also prospering. ''Be prepared for potatoes and onions to cost a dollar each,'' he warned. ''But don't worry about it. You see, those who were here first had the biggest strikes. When I arrived at the end of the war, it wasn't unusual for a man to dig twenty or thirty thousand dollars' worth of gold out of a claim in a single week. The gold was practically on the surface of the ground. Max told me he actually scraped gold from around the roots of a tree with his pocketknife. But those rich pockets were soon worked out. Now a man stands waist-deep in icy water washing buckets of pay dirt. In the summer the sun bakes their heads and addles their brains, and for all that misery the most they can hope for is a living wage from their claims.''

''So you are no longer prospecting for gold?'' Emily asked.

''No. I sold my various claims and invested in several businesses. A bank, a lumber mill, and an emporium. I also have an interest in a second hotel Max is building.''

''From the way you wrote about treating the sick and wounded soldiers, I thought perhaps you might continue—''

''My doctoring days are over, thank God. Although I must admit this town could use a few good doctors. By the way, other than Briony and Max, no one knows I have any medical skills whatsoever, and I'd prefer to keep it that way. Now, let me tell you of some of the plans I've made for us.''

Emily listened for a hint that Edward remembered his promise to release her from their marriage vows if she requested it, but no such hint was given. Had he forgotten? Did he expect they would begin their married life without any preliminaries? Wasn't she as much a stranger to him as he was to her? But as she listened to him speak with such enthusiasm about his new home and watched the animation of his features, she felt a stirring of admiration and affection. He might be a stranger to her, but he was a beguiling stranger.

They were climbing a steep hill, and he gave the horses their heads, not using the whip or urging them to go faster than they chose. He then perhaps unwittingly answered her unspoken question by saying, "At last more women are arriving. When I first came here, women were so scarce that men would dance with each other at the weekly dances, and woebetide any man seen with a patch on his trousers—that indicated sewing skills! You'll still find yourself vastly outnumbered, but Briony knows every respectable woman in town, so put yourself in her hands. She has an afternoon tea every day at the Rosebriar and will introduce you to her friends there. She's planning a welcome party for us, too. I'm so glad you didn't bring Phin with you; that could have caused a problem."

Emily's head snapped in his direction. "But Phin *is* here. I wrote you that she would be coming."

He tried to hide his dismay. "Yes, I know you did. I suppose I hoped she'd changed her mind as she didn't come ashore with you."

"She didn't want to intrude upon our reunion, so she stayed on the ship. She's going to take a hotel room. Don't worry, she isn't going to the Rosebriar," Emily replied stiffly.

His expression, as far as she could tell by his profile, was carefully blank. "Emily, there *are* some Oriental women in town. Most of them in the bordellos. It will be assumed that Phin is one of them. You can't continue to associate with her. We are leaving behind a past we'd all prefer to forget, and so must be careful not to tarnish our reputations here. Max and I are prominent businessmen. Briony is the reigning queen of society. You have to put any selfish reasons for your friendship with Phin aside for the good of all of us. We'd lose some very important clients and customers if you were to be seen with her."

Emily was dumbfounded. She was trying to gather her wits to respond when he reined the horses in front of a handsome brick house at the crest of the hill. The moment the carriage came to a halt, the front doors opened and Briony came running down the steps, her arms wide in welcome. She wore a jade-green gown that set off her elaborately styled auburn hair to perfection. Beside her sister-in-law's womanly curves, Emily felt like a gangly schoolgirl in her creased travel costume consisting of a navy blue skirt and jacket.

"Welcome home, Emily, it's so good to see you again! Forgive me for not meeting your ship, but I thought it better to come here and be sure your housekeeper had everything ready."

Like her brother, Briony had changed. She was still so beautiful that it was a pleasure to simply look at her, but like Edward she had acquired a certain steely facade, and her gaze was unflinching. Emily had seen that same look in the eyes of the skipper of their ship when the worst of the gales of the Strait of Magellan had tossed the vessel like a cork upon mountainous waves. It was a look that said damn you, you won't beat me.

Emily suddenly felt more than a little awed and quite a bit intimidated by her husband and sister-in-law.

They ushered her into a circular hall with a graceful spiral staircase leading to the upper floors. Open doors revealed an almost complete absence of furniture until they entered a sitting room containing a pair of Queen Anne sofas, a Persian rug, and a marble-topped occasional table. Briony had compensated for the few pieces by filling blank walls and empty window alcoves with a profusion of potted plants and heaps of silk and tapestry cushions. She gestured laughingly at the latter and said, "I hope this doesn't look too much like a bordello—it's just temporary until you select your own furnishings."

"Bri!" Edward protested. "Emily will think you're familiar with the interior of a bordello!"

Briony laughed. "Emily is going to find out soon enough that we have almost as many bordellos as we do hotels. And although I've never actually been inside a bordello, well, every nice woman wonders not only about what they look like, but also about the women who—"

She broke off as she realized Emily was blushing to the roots of her hair. "Come on, Emily, I'll take you upstairs now so you can see your bedroom. Other than the kitchen, we haven't touched the other rooms.''

"I'll bring in the bags," Edward said.

Feeling a flutter of apprehension, Emily followed Briony up the stairs. "We just bought beds," Briony said. "There's a dressing room where you can hang your clothes, and I thought tomorrow we'd see about some chests of drawers and dressers.''

The first door she opened revealed a sunny, spacious room. A four-poster bed stood on a small dais in the center of the room. A patchwork quilt of pieces of dark velvet covered the bed. Briony didn't enter the room; she merely waved her hand and said, "This one is for Edward. Yours is next door—they're connected through the dressing room.''

Emily let out her breath slowly. Of course, the English upper classes occupied separate bedrooms. Only the lower classes slept in the same room. Her relief was so great that she exclaimed in pleasure at the sight of the pretty broderie anglaise curtains at the window of her room, which matched the canopy over her bed and trimmed the pink velvet quilt.

Briony watched as Emily ran to the window to admire the sweeping view of the bay, then turned to touch the soft luxury of the velvet quilt. Emily said sincerely, "It's lovely. Thank you.''

"I hope you'll be happy here, Emily." Briony paused. "I hope you'll make Edward happy. He endured so much in the war. He deserves peace and contentment—and a loving wife now.''

Was there a veiled warning in Briony's voice? Emily wondered. Not knowing how to reply, she attempted a reassuring smile.

"When you're ready, I'll take you down to the kitchen and introduce you to Josefa, your housekeeper. Her English is quite limited, but she's a hard worker. I employed her at the Rosebriar for a time, and she worked at one of the largest haciendas in the territory before the war.''

Josefa proved to be young and quite lovely, with raven hair and large dark eyes. She had prepared a meal that Emily found quite exotic, and which she learned consisted of a delicious shellfish called abalone, followed by spicy beef and red beans. Emily felt so tired by the end of dinner, she could scarcely keep her eyes open.

Grateful to be again on dry land, Emily slept soundly her first night in San Francisco. Her first thought upon awakening was to remember the pulsing hunger of her husband's kiss as he left her at her bedroom door the previous night, and the second was to wonder how Phin and Kane were faring.

Last night Edward had said, "Good night, my love."

He'd hesitated for a moment, and she lowered her eyes, knowing he hoped she would invite him to her bed.

At length he said quietly, "Sleep well, Emily. I know you're exhausted from the voyage. I'll see you at breakfast."

His eyes lit up when she entered the morning room the following day, and she felt an answering smile pluck at her lips. How handsome he was, how kind and considerate. "Good morning," she murmured.

"Did you sleep well? You look rested." He rose to pull out a chair for her.

The morning room was built at the corner of the house, which formed a semicircular tower, and he'd placed a wooden table and chairs in the alcove to create a breakfast nook. This morning fog hung over the ocean, and ghostly tendrils crept up the hill. The room was filled with the aromas of freshly baked tortillas and omelets filled with onions and peppers. An archway opened the room to the kitchen, where Josefa stood at a woodburning stove cooking eggs. She flashed a shy smile and said, "*Buenos días, señora.*"

Emily thought, in delight, how foreign it all is! For a moment she was a little girl again, setting forth with her father on another glorious adventure abroad.

"If you're up to it," Edward was saying, "we'll go to the emporium after breakfast, and you can look at the furniture we have in stock. When the *Antonia*'s cargo is unloaded, there'll be several crates of new pieces from the East Coast, and you might want to wait for the drawing room furniture until then.''

There it was again: the *Antonia*.

"Are you acquainted with the owner of the clipper ship?" she asked. "A Mr. Henry Bardine, I believe you said?"

Edward gave a wry smile. "Oh, yes, indeed. But not on good enough terms to get any preferential treatment of my cargo. He's a rather rough fellow—a former sea captain who makes Max Seadon look like a gentleman by comparison."

Josefa placed a steaming plate in front of Emily, and she picked up her fork. "And Mrs. Bardine? What is she like?"

Edward frowned. "She's English, as a matter of fact, although she has a vaguely foreign look—almost Oriental, yet not really—difficult to explain. I mean, she has none of Phin's Asiatic features, yet there's something about her eyes—and a faint olive cast to her skin. Not only that, but she speaks in a way that makes you think she either learned another language first or is an actress. Bri says it's simply that Tonia Bardine was born into the lower classes and taught herself to speak like a lady. I don't know. I do know that hardly any of the women in town, including Bri, can stand Tonia, and this infuriates both her and her husband. Max is the only man in town who gives them the time of day."

"Tonia . . . she calls herself Tonia, then? And her hair is raven dark, almost as dark as Phin's, and she has been married to her present husband for three years or less?"

"Why . . . yes, I believe so." He looked at her in surprise. "Do you know her?"

"Edward, I'm beginning to think that Mrs. Bardine might be the same woman who married my father."

He considered this for a moment. "They disappeared while en route to Mexico City. . . . It's certainly possible they could have come here. But what became of your father? You don't think . . . my God, that your father might have met with foul play?"

Emily shivered. "Oh, I pray not! But I must meet this woman and learn for certain if it is she."

"Well, as a matter of fact, Max took it upon himself to invite the Bardines to a welcoming party Bri planned for you at the Rosebriar. Bri was furious and informed him that neither she nor we would attend. Max, being the stubborn chap he is, didn't cancel the party at the hotel. If we explain our fears to Briony, perhaps we could still go to the Rosebriar. If Mrs. Bardine is in fact your father's wife, or God forbid, his widow, you'll be meeting her again on neutral ground. We can't very well turn up on her doorstep with some story about a missing stepmother, in case it isn't the same woman."

"Yes, that's true. When is the party to be held?"

"Saturday night. Just two days away. We'll call on Briony this afternoon and explain the situation to her."

They finished breakfast, and Edward suggested he take her for a drive around the city, stop at the emporium and perhaps the dressmaker's shop, and then have lunch at the Rosebriar.

As Emily dressed to go out, she wondered when she would hear from Phin and Kane, and how she might slip away to see them.

Chapter 26

● ●

PHIN AND KANE had been turned away from every hotel in San Francisco and came at last to an address on the edge of town, which, they had been told, was a boardinghouse run by an old Chinese woman.

Exhausted and dispirited, Kane dropped their bags in the mud in front of a ramshackle wooden building that looked more like a barn than a house. The surrounding area was crowded with a hodgepodge of scruffy tents, lean-tos, and all sorts of makeshift houses, above which hung the sounds and smells of too many people to be sheltered either comfortably or hygienically.

Surveying the ugly two-story house with its sagging front porch, Kane said gloomily, "Even if this Mrs. Ling is willing to take us in as boarders, I for one would rather sleep in the street."

"And fall prey to robbers—or worse? Wait here. I'll go and talk to her."

"I'll turn my back," Kane said sarcastically. "It's getting dark; maybe she won't see my face."

"Self-pity is the most unattractive of human traits," Phin said sharply. "Don't ever indulge in it in my presence again. Emily is no longer with us to shield you, and I will offer you no sympathy, because that is not what you need. If you believe the hotels all turned us away because of your scars, you are a fool. They sent us away because of my race."

She walked up a short flight of rickety steps and knocked on the door. Kane drew back into the shadows. A moment later the door opened, and Phin murmured a few words he didn't hear. She disappeared into the house.

Five minutes later she came to the door and called to him through the misty twilight. "Kane—bring the bags. Mrs. Ling has rooms for us."

He was surprised to find that the interior of the house was spotlessly clean and neat, if sparsely furnished. The room to which he was shown, on the ground floor, contained only a chest of drawers and a single chair. Mrs. Ling, as ancient and wrinkled and brown as an autumn leaf, pointed to a closet door and said something in Chinese to Phin, who translated: "The bed is in the closet. You will roll it up in the daytime, as Mrs. Ling cleans the rooms every day. All of your possessions must be kept in the closet or in the drawers."

"She speaks only Chinese, then?"

"Her dialect is Mandarin. I have not yet ascertained what other languages or dialects she speaks."

"She has another room—for you?"

"Upstairs. Directly above this one. If you need me, you can find a stick to knock on your ceiling. We are too late for the evening meal, but Mrs. Ling will bring you a tray of fruit and rice cakes and a pot of tea."

The old woman had departed as silently as a shadow.

Kane said, "We should send a message to Emily, to let her know where we're staying."

"No," Phin said shortly. "Not yet, anyway. Let's give her time to settle in with her husband. We shall manage very well on our own for a while."

"But I want—" Kane began angrily.

"I know what you want," Phin interrupted. "You want Emily. But you can't have her. Accept it."

"Damn you, Phin, Emily is my friend, and as for me, I'd do anything in the world for her."

"Good. Then leave her alone for a while."

Throughout the morning Emily felt as if she were living at an accelerated pace with no time to savor all of the sights and sounds and smells of her new home, or to observe her husband, or to examine her own feelings toward either of them.

By the time they reached the Rosebriar, however, she realized she was more than a little enchanted by San Francisco and even more bewitched by Edward.

How could she not have noticed three years ago how handsome he was, how kind and solicitous, or how other people reacted to him with such warmth and respect? She felt giddy as a schoolgirl in the throes of her first crush and reveled in the sensation. How many married matrons nearing twenty, as she was, fell madly in love with their husbands? She suddenly felt shy in his presence, unsure what to say or do about the rush of feeling that overwhelmed her with its intensity.

In the beautifully appointed dining room of the Rosebriar, Briony, wearing a stunning deep rose gown with a bodice decorated with jet beads, showed them to their table. Emily expressed her admiration of the fine linen cloth and engraved silverware, the fresh rosebuds in silver vases, and the soothing sound of pianoforte music that was an unintrusive background to conversation.

Briony smiled with pleasure at the compliment. "We're all very proud of the Rosebriar. There's no finer hotel in the city."

Max Seadon joined them the moment they were seated. He looked, Emily thought, exactly the same as he had on the transatlantic crossing, except that his clothes were perhaps a little more flamboyant. He said, "Welcome to San Francisco. Glad you finally decided to join us, Emily. Briony was hoping you'd come to San Antonio, but I guess you had better things to do in New York?"

Was there a hint of censure in his tone? Emily felt herself flush, but before she could respond, Edward said, "Emily did, indeed, have better things to do in New York. My wife ran a lending library there. I'm very proud of her. I doubt such a pursuit would have been possible in San Antonio."

"Oh, we had a couple of people in San Antone who could read," Max replied dryly. He seemed to deliberately slow his speech to a drawl, dropping syllables from *Antonio*.

"Now, now, you two!" Briony exclaimed. "Let's not spoil this happy occasion by bickering." She turned to Emily. "Max and Edward seem to clash constantly, usually about the most trivial of matters."

"The spell of homesickness you suffered in Texas wasn't exactly trivial," Max commented. "You said yourself you wished your sister-in-law would come so you could commiserate with each other about all of the barbarians you had to deal with."

Emily, who had not felt homesick for a country she scarcely knew, murmured, "Briony, I'm sorry, I had no idea. You should have written and told me."

"Max is exaggerating. Are you joining us for lunch, Max?" Briony asked pointedly. "Or do you have other things to do?"

He grinned. "I guess I have other things to do. If you'll excuse me." He made his way through the rapidly filling dining room, stopping at several tables to greet patrons. Briony watched him go, a slight frown creasing her lovely face.

Emily observed this in surprise. She remembered the easy camaraderie Briony and Max had enjoyed aboard the ship and wondered what had transpired to cause the present tension between them, which was as palpable as the rich aroma of roast meat that preceded a waiter bearing a tray of covered dishes.

Briony motioned for him to come to their table. "You may serve us now." She turned to Emily. "I ordered a special luncheon for you. I do hope you enjoy it."

The meal came as close to being English fare as Briony could devise, with a joint of beef, Yorkshire pudding, and some rather small roast potatoes. For dessert there was both rice pudding and bread pudding, swimming in a rich custard sauce. After spending so long at sea suffering from *mal de mer*, Emily couldn't do justice to the rich food and apologized for her small appetite.

"You did very well," Edward assured her. "Now, before Briony escapes, we must tell her your suspicions about Tonia Bardine."

They explained the situation and then asked if Briony would mind if they attended the party at the Rosebriar in order to determine if Tonia Bardine and Tonia Faraday were one and the same.

"No, of course not," Briony said. "I'll tell Max that you'll be there. But I shan't be there myself. You do understand? Whoever that woman is, she is not a person with whom I intend to associate, and since I've already made this clear to Max, I can't capitulate now."

Emily shivered. If Mrs. Bardine proved to be her step-mother, she would have to keep in mind that the woman had tried to have her killed—and most likely believed she had succeeded.

"Whatever happens," Briony added, "don't tell Max about her. And if she is, indeed, your stepmother, let's hope she isn't in touch with anyone in England. Or we could all be in trouble."

A messenger delivered to the Rosebriar a brief note from Phin, saying only that she and Kane had found a comfortable boardinghouse and were settling in. Unfortunately she had neglected to include the address, so Emily could not respond. However, she was so busy settling in to her own new home and attempting to find a suitable dress for the forthcoming party that she didn't have time to dwell on this.

Briony took her to a dressmaker who had several dresses for sale in her shop, and they found one that required only minor alterations. It was a beautiful watered silk, in shimmering shades of blue and lavender, but the low décolletage was dismaying. Emily had lost so much weight she bemoaned her lack of bosom to show off the dress to its best advantage.

"We'll have the seamstress put some lace around the neckline," Briony said, "and a little ruching of the bodice should disguise the looseness there."

The dress was ordered, along with curtains and draperies for the house. Emily also found several pieces of furniture that had been shipped from the East Coast aboard the *Antonia*. During the two and a half days that passed between her arrival in San Francisco and the day of the party at the Rosebriar, she was too busy to worry about the possible consequences of her meeting with the infamous Mrs. Bardine.

But at night, after Edward had kissed Emily at her bedroom door and then left her, she wished she could find the courage to ask him to come into her room.

She almost uttered the words the night before the party but became so tongue-tied she began to stammer. "Edward . . . I-I—wh-when we were married . . . I—"

He placed his finger against her lips to silence her. "It's all right, Emily, I understand, you don't have to remind me of my promise to you. Although I want you desperately, I will abide by that promise. I know I'm a stranger to you and you need time to get to know me before you give me your answer. Please—allow me to court you for a time, until you feel at ease with me in daily living, before you decide whether you wish to be my wife."

Alone in her room, Emily chided herself for not giving voice to her growing feelings of love for her husband. But what could she say in view of his request that she wait before discussing whether or not their wedding vows were to be permanent?

She glanced at the dressing room separating her room from his. Perhaps it would be better to say nothing at all—to simply show him by her actions that she wished to consummate their union. What if she were to slip into his room? Perhaps wait until he was in bed and then . . . simply join him?

This thought tantalized her as she let down her hair and brushed it, washed herself at her newly purchased marble-topped washstand with its china bowl and pitcher, then donned a fine lawn nightgown. She dabbed a little eau de cologne on her wrists and behind her ears, sprinkled rosewater on a piece of silk and polished her hair with it.

Her eyes kept darting to the china clock on her dressing table. How long would it take Edward to prepare for bed? After half an hour had passed, she walked slowly into the dressing room and pressed her ear to the adjoining door.

There was no sound from within her husband's room.

Slowly she turned the doorknob and pushed open the door. Moonlight flooded the room from the uncurtained window, clearly illuminating the bed. The counterpane had been turned back, but the bed, indeed the entire room, was empty. Edward must have gone back downstairs.

Disappointed, Emily returned to her own room.

She lay awake for a long time. Tomorrow was the day of the party. Perhaps after they returned from the Rosebriar, there would be an opportunity for her to tell Edward of her feelings for him.

A little after midnight she heard the muffled sound of carriage wheels in the street below. Emily slipped out of bed, went to the window, and looked down. Edward was unharnessing the horses.

He had been out somewhere. Where, at this time of night?

She went back to bed, feeling puzzled and disturbed.

They had been apart for three years. What did she know of his life during that time? He had been an army medical officer, spent time prospecting for gold, became a business-man. *What else had he become*? Did anyone ever truly *know* another human being?

That night her dreams were filled with vague and frightening images that she could not recall when she awakened the next morning.

Edward was late coming down to breakfast. He was red-eyed and seemed distracted. Halfway through the meal he said, "I have to go out for a while, Emily. I'll be back in plenty of time for the party tonight, but I may be gone most of the day. A friend needs my help."

Without further explanation, he rose from the table and departed, leaving her feeling shut out and uneasy.

Briony arrived a little while later, bringing Emily's party dress, which immediately lifted her spirits. "I'll send my maid over to help you wash your hair," Briony offered. "And you must be sure to take a nap this afternoon. Our parties last all night long. San Franciscans play as hard as they work."

"Are you sure you won't come?" Emily asked. "I shan't

know a soul except Edward and Max if you're not there."

Briony's eyes glittered, but her tone remained light. "No, I can't come. Apart from my dislike of Tonia Bardine, it would be a victory for Max. You'll be in good hands. Edward will introduce you to some charming people, who are going to like you immediately, I do assure you."

"Does Edward still like me, do you think?" Emily asked shyly.

Briony laughed. "What an extraordinary thing to ask! He counted the minutes until you arrived."

"But . . . well, we haven't seen each other for three years. People change. Perhaps I am not the girl he remembers."

"And he is surely not the man you remember," Briony said gently. "You have both matured. Trust that your love for each other has also matured. Give yourselves time to get reacquainted."

Emily tried to hide her sigh. After all, Briony was unaware of the bargain she had struck with Edward when she married him. "Briony . . . Edward's bank and lumber mill and the emporium . . . aren't open late at night, are they?"

"No, of course not. Why do you ask?"

Thinking quickly, Emily decided not to confide that her husband had left the house late at night. "Oh . . . I just wondered if any of the people who work for Edward would be coming to the party."

"Indeed yes. You'll meet all of them. I must go now, Emily. Do you have everything you need for tonight? If not I could have my maid pick it up on her way over."

"No, thank you. I have everything. Thank you again, Briony, for all your help."

After seeing her sister-in-law to the door, Emily went upstairs. She stood for a moment staring at her husband's bedroom door, sorely tempted to go inside the room and see if she could find a hint as to where he went late at night. Integrity prevailed over curiosity, however, and instead she went into her own room to hang her beautiful new gown in the dressing room.

* * *

Following Briony's advice, Emily took an afternoon nap
and was awakened by Briony's maid, a handsome dusky-
skinned woman in whose face the best features of both the
African and Indian races were combined. She was called
Topaz, a name Emily thought surely must have been
bestowed upon her by her mistress.

"Time to dress, Miz Dale," Topaz said, "I got us some
fresh flowers for your hair."

Unaccustomed to daytime sleep, Emily sat up, rubbing
her eyes. "Did my husband return?"

"Oh, yes, ma'am. He done come home 'bout two hours
ago. Then some li'l Indian boy come for him, and off he
went again."

"Oh, no!" Emily was wide awake now. "You mean he
isn't here now?"

"He got plenty of time to dress. It don't take a man no
time at all. Don't you fret none, Miz Dale."

But Emily fretted throughout her toilette. What if he
didn't return in time to take her to the Rosebriar? What
could he possibly be doing, and who was the "little Indian
boy" who came for him?

With only minutes left before they were supposed to
leave for the hotel in order to stand in the receiving line,
Emily heard sounds in her husband's bedroom. She let out
her breath in relief.

Topaz accompanied them to the hotel, where Briony had
a suite of rooms, so there was no opportunity for Emily to
question Edward in the carriage. He looked tired and
strained but was impeccably dressed and freshly shaved.

The hotel was ablaze with lights and the banquet room
filled with flowers. An orchestra was tuning up, and a buffet
table groaned under the weight of an array of dishes.
Waiters hurried about, putting the finishing touches to the
room.

Max Seadon greeted them at the doors. "The first of the
guests are already here. I've got them corralled in the back
room. I was expecting you half an hour ago."

"Sorry. I had to go out," Edward said.

"You look lovely, Emily," Max said.

"Thank you."

Max beckoned to someone standing behind them, and Emily turned to see a tall, generously endowed woman approach. She was dark-haired and dressed in a garnet-red ball gown. "May I present my hostess for the evening, Mrs. Annabelle Clark?"

Edward greeted the woman politely, and Emily knew he must be smarting because Max had invited another woman to replace Briony.

Since guests were now arriving in groups, they quickly formed a receiving line, and a waiter was dispatched to bring the early arrivals from the back room.

Faces and names whirled by. These were like no people Emily had ever seen. There was a certain boldness in their eyes, a hint of a swagger in their step, and why not? Emily thought. They had all endured incredible hardships just to reach California. Their accents proclaimed them to be from all over the world, and Emily recalled Edward writing her of his first impressions of the motley array of individuals who had settled Yerba Buena: soldiers of fortune and gold seekers of many nationalities, Russian fur traders, Spanish adventurers, Mexican bandits. As the former Mexican territory struggled for autonomy, a state different in every way from the Calvinist-dominated eastern settlements was emerging.

As the flow of guests slowed to an occasional late arrival, Max suggested they sit at one of the tables bordering the dance floor, and he would open a bottle of champagne. It was only then that Emily realized the Bardines had not arrived. When they were seated at their table, she mentioned this to Max.

"Oh, Tonia always arrives later, to make an entrance. She'll be here. She wouldn't miss a chance to hobnob with San Francisco's upper crust. She's tried too hard to break into society to pass up an opportunity like this. Especially since she's no doubt heard that Briony isn't going to be here."

Annabelle Clark, who was apparently a widow, as no

husband put in an appearance, now leaned closer to Emily
and said in a stage whisper, "You'll know the minute the
Bardines arrive. Henry has a very loud voice, reeks of cigar
smoke, and treats the help as if they had no feelings at all.
Now, much as I love Max, and much as I love being his
hostess for the evening, I do wish the Bardines weren't
coming—even though, in that case, I wouldn't be here,
Briony would. Emily—may I call you that?—you must tell
me what the women on the East Coast were wearing when
you left. You see, I came here from San Antonio, and so I'm
really out of touch with the current fashions. Why, in Texas
they were wearing . . ."

Whatever they had been wearing in Texas would remain
undisclosed, as at that moment a booming laugh rang out,
drowning most of the low murmur of conversation in the
room. A very large, heavyset man wearing an ominous
black patch over one eye had entered the room.

Emily gave him only a fleeting glance before her gaze
fastened on the woman at his side. Dressed in white satin,
which showed off her dark hair to perfection, diamonds
glittering at her throat and wrists, the green-gold eyes of the
woman who now called herself Mrs. Henry Bardine swept
the room.

A drum seemed to be pounding in Emily's head. She was
staring at Tonia Faraday, her father's bride.

. . . .

Chapter 27

EMILY SAT FROZEN in her chair, staring at Tonia Bardine. She was vaguely aware of Edward's hand finding hers under the table and his barely audible question, "Is it she?"

Emily nodded.

At that moment an extraordinary thing happened. Tonia looked directly at Emily, and then, after not a flicker of recognition, her glance moved to Max, and she gave him a seductive smile.

"I need some air," Emily whispered. "Could we step outside for a few minutes?"

"You'll excuse us, won't you?" Edward said, rising instantly to take her arm. "My wife is still recovering from the long voyage. We'll be back in a moment."

The Bardines were headed directly toward them, and Tonia's gown brushed against Emily as they passed by. Tonia's gaze connected briefly with Emily's, flickered appraisingly over her face and gown, then turned her full attention to Max. She called out to him, in the voice Emily remembered so well, "Max Seadon, you handsome devil, I'm bringing you my dance card, and I expect you to put your name on at least three dances."

Emily walked with shaking knees to the nearest door, and as soon as they were out of the room, she swayed against Edward. He helped her to the closest of a series of small courtyards within the hotel and led her to a bench flanked by clay pots of ferns. She sat down, feeling as breathless as if she had been running. "She didn't recognize me. She looked right at me, twice, and didn't know me!"

"It's been almost four years since she saw you, Emily. You were little more than a child then. You're a woman now. Besides, she believes you are dead—she had no reason to look for you."

"I wanted to speak to her the moment I recognized her, but then, when she looked right through me, I remembered what Briony had said—that we must be careful in case she finds out what happened in England. Knowing Tonia, she would use such information to her own advantage."

"But you must find out what became of your father. Perhaps we can do that without your identifying yourself to her. What if I were to tell her I know she was married to Fletcher Faraday and ask what became of him?"

"Wouldn't she wonder why you haven't brought this up before now?"

"Not really. I've never been in a social setting with her before, or even had a private conversation with her. I've only seen her about town. Her husband uses my bank, and she's shopped in my emporium. I could say that I knew your father in England and perhaps had seen her shortly after their wedding."

"Oh, yes, Edward, that would be a good idea."

"I'll ask her to dance with me, so no one else will hear."

"Don't let her bewitch you, as she did my father."

Edward smiled at her, his eyes alight with love. "Never fear, I'm too wildly, wonderfully in love with my wife."

By the time they returned, Tonia was dancing with Max, who whirled her around the floor in a Viennese waltz. Henry Bardine sat at Max's table, wolfing down hors d'oeuvres and drinking a large glass of whiskey.

"Come on," Edward said, taking Emily's hand. "Let's finish the dance."

He was an excellent dancer, his lead strong and sure, and as she fitted her steps to his, Emily immediately felt better, the music and graceful movement helping to dispel her tension.

When the music ended, Edward led her back to Max's table and Max said, "You know Edward, don't you, Henry? May I present his wife, Mrs. Emily Dale? Emily, this is Mr.

and Mrs. Henry Bardine. The clipper that arrived at the same time as your ship was built by Henry—in Burma, wasn't it?—and named for Antonia.''

For a breath-stopping moment Emily felt Tonia's scrutiny. She offered her gloved hand, and Tonia held it for a second longer than necessary.

Surely at such close range she must recognize me, Emily thought. But Tonia merely murmured, ''How do you do.'' Then she turned to her husband and said, ''Henry, come on, Max is going to introduce us to his friends.''

The three of them left the table to begin circulating the room, and Annabelle Clark muttered, ''Just look at the way that hussy is flirting with Max. Right under her husband's nose, too.''

At that moment one of the unattached male guests approached and greeted Edward, was introduced to Emily, and promptly asked if he might have the next dance with her.

Her partner was an exuberant, but inexpert, dancer and as she was spun in dizzying turns, Emily tried to keep an eye on Tonia, but did not see her again until near the end of the waltz. She was dancing with Edward. Emily tried to read their expressions, but her partner danced her out of view.

For the next hour she and Edward were introduced to far too many people to remember and danced, it seemed, with everyone but each other. They were relieved when at last the music stopped, and Max announced that dinner was being served in the adjoining dining room. Emily realized now that the laden buffet table had contained only hors d'oeuvres and snacks. She gazed with dismay at a long line of waiters carrying trays to the tables set up in the dining room. San Franciscans had such appetites!

Max took Emily's arm, and Edward accompanied Annabelle. They were seated at the head table, and Emily wasn't sure whether to be relieved or disappointed that the Bardines had been relegated to a table on the far side of the room. There was no opportunity for Emily to speak privately with Edward, who regarded her from the opposite side of the table with a worried expression.

The seven-course dinner dragged on interminably. The other four guests at their table were Texans Max had known in San Antonio, and apart from addressing an occasional polite remark in the general direction of Edward or Emily, they regaled one another with reminiscences of wild times in Texas. One of the men, as lean and rangy as Max, but with coal-black hair and mustache, began to speak about "the Rangers" but was immediately cut short by Max, who promptly changed the subject. Several drinks later she heard the same man mention the name Joaquin Murrieta and mutter something about forming a Vigilance Committee.

At this point Max rose and said, "This isn't the time or the place to discuss such matters. Why don't we take the ladies back into the ballroom and then adjourn to the smoking room for our brandy and cigars?"

Emily gave Edward a stricken glance, not wanting him to be dragged off before she had a chance to speak with him. He said, "If you gentlemen will excuse me, I'll stay with my wife. We've been apart for three years, you know."

The men exchanged knowing glances and slapped him on the back before escorting their partners to the ballroom and then departing to the smoking room. The orchestra was playing again, and Edward bowed to Emily. "May I?"

The moment they were on the dance floor, Emily said, "Did you ask her about my father?"

He nodded but didn't answer. Emily found herself being led in the direction of the doors, and moments later they were in the lobby. She looked at her husband in bewilderment.

Edward said quietly, "I thought perhaps you'd want me to take you home. Emily . . . I'm so sorry. Your father is dead."

In the carriage on their way home Edward related his conversation with Tonia. "Apparently Tonia and your father disembarked from their ship at Veracruz to find the war in progress and the country in the throes of upheaval and confusion. They boarded a stagecoach for the overland journey to Mexico City, and somewhere between Veracruz and their destination they were set upon by bandits, who killed all of the men and kidnapped her.''

Emily gripped his arm tightly. "Did he suffer? Was it quick? Did she say?''

"She couldn't go into detail, Emily, not out on the dance floor with other couples nearby. But I'm sure the men must have fallen in a hail of gunshot. She said there were no other women on the coach. Tonia said she was fortunate that she spent only a couple of days with the bandits before being rescued by American soldiers—''

He broke off, and when he did not continue for a moment, Emily asked, "What is it?''

"I don't know. Perhaps I didn't hear her clearly, or misunderstood, what with the music and conversation of other dancers. But I don't believe American troops had reached the state of Veracruz at the time your father arrived. Perhaps she said she was rescued by Mexican soldiers.''

"What did Tonia say happened next? Where has she been for the past three years?''

"She said she found a protector—an elderly gentleman who had been visiting his family in Mexico City and was returning to his home, a hacienda in Alta California near the Pacific Coast. She accompanied him to a settlement of *Californios* and lived at the hacienda for a time. Then Henry Bardine's ship dropped anchor to pick up a cargo of hides to take north to Yerba Buena, and he and his officers were invited to a fiesta, where she met him.''

"So she married him, without a second thought, just as fast as she married my father.''

"It would seem so.''

The bubble that had been trapped in Emily's throat since Edward gave her the news of her father's death now burst in a flood of tears and choking sobs. She had never known such anguish, and the most desolate thought of all was that her grief would be permanent; it would never leave her.

She laid her head on Edward's shoulder as he kept his arm tightly around her, holding the reins with his other hand. When she was at last able to speak, she said, "I must find Phin. I have to tell her. . . . Can you find out where she's staying?''

"There's an old woman who lives on the outskirts of town, a Mrs. Ling. She seems to keep track of all the Asians. If Phin isn't staying with her, she'll know where she is. I'll go and get her and bring her to you.''

Phin knelt on a reed mat in the center of a starkly bare room. She wore a peacock-blue robe with a golden dragon, ferocious, rearing, embroidered on the back, and in the flickering candlelight the silk threads of the mythic beast seemed to move, giving it life.

Her midnight-black hair had fallen forward as she bent her head, her fingers busy with the joss ornaments or sticks he knew would be on the floor in front of her.

So engrossed in her private ritual was she that she had not heard him open her door. Then she stiffened, instinct telling her what her ears had missed.

She only half turned, and in profile she appeared to him to be wholly Oriental, her calm, watchful attitude, her worshipful pose, her infinite patience—she was undoubtedly appealing to her gods or to her ancestors for guidance—no vestige of her Caucasian blood seemed evident. In the amber glow of the candles her skin appeared more yellow than in clearer light, adding to the illusion. Her voice, when she spoke, seemed labored, thick, as if she were drowning in a pool of some viscous fluid. "Go away. I cannot talk to you now.''

"You haven't talked to me for days,'' Kane said. "I need to know if you've heard from Emily.''

"Her husband came for me and took me to their home. I spoke with her at length.''

"Yes?''

"Her father is dead.''

"Ah, dear God, how she must be suffering. I must go to her.''

Phin's head snapped upright, and she tossed her long black hair back over her shoulder. "She has a husband to comfort her in her grief. She does not need you.''

He recognized then what he was hearing in Phin's voice. She, too, was immersed in grief.

"You must be saddened that you were too late to repay your mother's debt to the late Mr. Fletcher Faraday. What will you do now? Will you return to China?"

"Not yet. There is more for me to do here. Leave me now."

He stepped back, closing the door, and went back upstairs to his room. He picked up his violin and began to play. As his music enveloped him, he lost himself in the sound, allowed it to drive away all thoughts of rushing to Emily's side, all fears that soon Phin, too, might desert him.

Kane was wide awake at midnight when Phin came to his room. She was still wearing the peacock-blue robe, but now she had dusted her face with white powder, ringed her eyes with kohl, emphasizing their slanted aspect, and painted her lips with cochineal. Two spots of artificial blush dotted her cheekbones. She had created a mask behind which to hide, and he understood this need she had to disguise herself and the reason for it.

He removed his violin from his shoulder and laid it back in its case, sighing as he did so. "I wondered how long it would be before you—"

"This is not like before," she said with a savagery that struck him like a whip. "This time I will avenge the death of Emily's father."

"You believe someone is responsible for his death?"

"Edward came for me in a pony trap and took me to his house to be with Emily." Phin paced the room restlessly as she spoke. "Naturally he came after dark, so no one would see me. I spent several hours with her and heard the details, or as much as they knew, of her father's death."

She told him all she had learned, and as she moved about his small room, he saw now that she was naked beneath the silk robe. He felt a stirring in his groin and looked away, the memories of certain afternoons in New York, when Emily had been at the lending library, returning to haunt him.

Phin concluded, "That woman—Antonia—tried to do away with Emily. I believe she murdered Emily's father, or had someone else kill him. In either case, she must pay for her crimes.''

"I've wondered many times about your quest to find Emily's father, Phin. This vow to avenge his death confirms a suspicion I've had from the beginning. You spoke of your mother's connection to the Faradays, of old debts, of your father being a Caucasian. You are Emily's half sister, are you not?''

"There is little point in denying it, at least to you.''

"Perhaps you are wrong to blame your father's wife for his death?''

"I have dreamed of it three times now. In my dream he is lying in the desert, his blood soaking into the sand, and she stands over him, watching him die, offering no succor. She shows no pity, no feelings at all, and he stares at her beseechingly as she turns and walks away from him.''

"But that dream does not tell you she killed him.''

"She left him to die, and that is the same as killing him.''

"You said she was taken by bandits. Were they in your dream? They would have dragged her away, rendering her incapable of helping her husband. Understand that I am merely attempting to play devil's advocate.''

"I do not wish to argue with you. I have to go. I may not be back for several days. Is there anything you need? Mrs. Ling will give you all of your meals.''

"Where are you going? At least tell me that.''

"I have learned a great deal more about Tonia Bardine than even Emily knows. Mrs. Ling told me that when Henry Bardine first brought Tonia here, he left her ashore and sailed back to the Eastern Seaboard of the United States—he was, of course, gone for months, leaving her to fend for herself.''

Phin stopped pacing and stood in front of him. Her robe had slipped to one side, revealing a small, perfectly shaped breast. She saw the direction of his glance and said impatiently, "I have time to take care of you if you need—''

"No," he said sharply. "I've told you, I don't want that. Tell me where you're going. Which house of sin has hired you?''

"As I was saying, Tonia was left to her own devices in a town bursting at the seams with lonely men. She brought in Mexican girls at first; later she brought women from the East. By the time Henry Bardine returned, she had a fine house and servants and pretended her late husband's family had sent her a handsome settlement. Only a few people in town know that a certain house near the waterfront catering mainly to seamen and offering girls of different colors and cultures, and a second, more exclusive one called Lantern House that is filled with Asian girls, are still owned by Tonia Bardine and provide a considerable private income for her. Not even her husband is aware of her secret business. Mrs. Ling knows because she has provided several Chinese girls for the Lantern House." Phin paused and then added, "She is about to provide a Eurasian."

Before he could stop himself, Kane's hand shot out and caught hers. "Don't go there. Don't do it. Please."

Her long fingers squirmed inside the prison of his hand, seeking freedom. "I will find a way to destroy Tonia Bardine, just as she destroyed my father and caused my little sister pain. The best way to find my enemy's vulnerability is to work for her."

"Phin, it's wrong, sinful—can't you understand? You're condemning your soul to everlasting purgatory."

"When I came to you, when you screamed you wanted to die, you did not think it was wrong and sinful then. What hypocrites you barbarians are! You castigate others for doing what you yourselves do in secret at every opportunity."

She freed her hand and ran from the room.

Kane sank into his chair and buried his face in his hands, rubbing his fingers over his granulated flesh, tracing the jagged path of his scars, feeling his ugliness. His soul raged that if he were half a man, he would stop her. Dear lord, if he were half a man he would not allow a woman to support him, and yet wasn't that what he was doing? At least in New York he had earned a small wage.

New York . . . Unbidden, the memories came back.

He remembered little of those first days after Phin and

Emily rescued him. The twisting, writhing torments of his body, the bones that felt as if they were being prodded with red-hot knives, the shrieking pain in his head, the fluttering of his heart—oh, he remembered that, along with Emily's gentle ministrations. He remembered begging Phin for relief-giving opium and then threatening to kill her if she refused. These memories were fragmented, tossed about in his mind like the particles in a kaleidoscope.

Emily's concern and her distress over his physical miseries, and the least of these were his wounds, tormented him almost as much as his body's agony. The two women kept him tied to the bed, or surely he would have escaped and jumped into the river to end his suffering.

Then one night Phin came to relieve Emily of her watch over him, and the curses and moans he had subdued in Emily's presence were vented on Phin. She stood over him for a while, listening to his ranting, and then calmly disrobed.

He recalled, even now, how the sight of her nakedness had stayed his madness, distracting him from the sorry condition of his own body as he gazed with wonder upon hers. She looked like a golden statue cast by a master sculptor.

She said softly, "There is another opiate for your senses, Kane. I am going to lie with you, and then you will sleep."

She did not untie his bonds. She lifted his nightshirt, and he held his breath as her cool efficient fingers coaxed his manhood to her bidding. After a time all of his feelings were concentrated in that one part of him, and his writhing limbs ceased to be a cacophony of pain and became instead an accompanying symphony for the pulsing melody of his loins as she mounted him.

He had never lain with a woman before and could not have imagined the magic Phin created. Nor could he have foreseen that dependence upon the release she gave would be just as addicting as the opium.

When he tried, in stumbling schoolboy phrases, to thank her, she dismissed his gratitude. "It is nothing to me. I have been taught to give pleasure to a man. It is my profession, and I am very good at it. Sleep now, Kane, and dream of me so that there will be no demons to pursue you this night.''

He did sleep, and the following night Phin repeated her miracle cure. A few days later Mrs. Fitzworthy asked Emily to run her lending library, leaving Phin and Kane alone during the day.

She came to him almost every afternoon, bringing different delights. He wondered how he could love Emily chastely, yet be a slave to his passion for Phin, but her spell was so binding that somehow he was able to separate his spiritual love from his earthly desire. After a while it was no longer necessary for him to be a prisoner. His bonds removed, Phin then taught him how to be an active participant in the act of love.

He thought of it as lovemaking, never anything else. Not until the day Phin came to him with her face powdered and painted and said she would be gone overnight. ''I have hired a housekeeper—a Chinese woman who speaks little English, but Emily must have a chaperone, since I expect to be away from time to time.''

''You're going to a man,'' he said raggedly. ''Don't spend the night with a stranger. Don't live a life of sin.''

She turned on him like an angry tiger. ''Do not speak to me of sin! I do not subscribe to your God, or to your God's laws or your barbarian's rules for living. The only sins I recognize are willful cruelty and lack of respect for one's ancestors.''

Then she left and he did not see her again for a week.

Fortunately Emily brought him the sheet music to copy the next day, and he filled his empty hours copying ballads. The Chinese housekeeper, Mrs. Hsiang, slept on a pallet in the small kitchen and seemed to fade into the cabbage roses of the wallpaper when she was not serving them delectable dishes of food or fragrant pots of tea.

When Phin returned early one evening, she offered no explanation of her absence to either Emily or Kane, and he had to resist the urge to seize her and shake her and demand to know where she had been and with whom.

He waited impatiently for Emily to depart for the lending

library the following morning so that he could speak privately to Phin, but she stayed in her bed until noon. When she finally emerged from her room, his heart sank. Her face was again painted, her hair elaborately coiffed and dressed with golden tassels and seed pearls. She was dressed in the Chinese style, black silk trousers and a brilliantly red silk mandarin jacket embroidered with black and gold.

Kane grabbed her wrist and pulled her into his room, away from the presence of Mrs. Hsiang.

Phin gave him a knowing glance and ignored his angry torrent of questions and accusations. Her attitude was businesslike, and she remained fully clothed as she unbuttoned his britches and, with a few expert strokes, brought him to climax.

He was mortified, ashamed. Afterward he rationalized that he had not stopped her because he wanted to believe what she was doing was only a preliminary to lovemaking. But she immediately turned to leave.

"Why? Phin, for God's sake, why?" he called after her.

"I am in a hurry. I do not have time for more."

"*I do not want less*! This is . . . disgusting, obscene. I want to make love to you."

She regarded him over her shoulders, the tassels and pearls dangling from her blue-black hair almost, but not quite, concealing her expression of contempt. "You want to make love to Emily. You use me as a substitute for her. But you cannot ever possess either of us. If you are now recovered from the hold the opium has had over you, then find yourself a woman who will let you make love to her. I am not that woman. My services have nothing to do with lovemaking, as you have just pointed out."

"No woman would have me."

"If you believe that, then it is true."

Phin never came to him again. Frequently she was gone for an evening. Sometimes she would leave for a few days, and occasionally for as long as a month.

With Phin gone, so, too, was the sexual tension she generated. He enjoyed the quiet warmth of Emily's companionship. They would read the books she borrowed from the library, or he would play his violin for her. They talked. They became closer than friends, perhaps closer than many brothers and sisters. Never by word or deed did he let her know he loved her, not as a sister or a friend, but as a woman. Yet he felt tainted by his affair with Phin; in some obscure way it had been an infidelity, a betrayal of Emily.

One evening when they were alone he asked her, "Do you ever wonder where Phin goes, what she does?"

Emily blushed, and he realized she had guessed the true nature of Phin's association with men. But she answered, "Phin is an escort, paid to be a companion or a hostess to a gentleman who has no wife to perform such duties for him. Occasionally she stays with one gentleman for weeks, or even months. Other times for only an evening."

Kane made no comment, nor did either of them ever discuss Phin's other life again.

Now here they were on the far side of the world in this uncut gem of a city, and Phin was again about to embark on a way of life that was abhorrent to him.

Kane aroused himself from his reverie. Had she left the boardinghouse yet? He made his way quickly downstairs and went to her room. She was packing a valise with toilet articles and other items. He hastily averted his gaze, recognizing some of those items for what they were.

"What do you want?" Phin asked curtly.

"I have never visited a house of ill repute," he began.

"In my country we called them houses of delights. Shall we compromise and say bordello?"

He was at her side in two strides. He placed his hands on her head, his thumbs pressing lightly against her fine sculpted cheekbones, his fingers caressing her hair just behind her ears, then moving aside the long straight strands to find the scalp beneath.

"What's in here, Phin?" he asked softly. "Oh, I don't mean bone and sinew and gray matter. What thoughts? What memories? What hopes and dreams?"

"No hopes and dreams, Kane. Not in the sense you mean."

"This living skull, this beautiful face. I cannot comprehend the stream of thought that accepts the life you lead. Surely only images as fair as yourself should fill your mind.''

She pushed his hands away. ''I do not have time for your false perceptions, Kane.''

''Very well. Let me say what I came to say. I remember reading that many musicians started their careers in houses of . . . in bordellos. That the music helped drown out the . . . other sounds.''

Phin dropped a bottle of perfumed oil into her valise and looked up, studying his face thoughtfully.

He didn't flinch from her scrutiny. ''Perhaps I could be hidden in some curtained recess and play my violin out of sight?''

She considered for a moment and then said, ''I will see what can be done. But not in the house to which I am going.''

''I *must* be where you are going,'' he said firmly. ''You are embarking upon a dangerous quest, and I fear for your safety. I want to be close by, in case you need me.''

Phin gave him an odd little smile. ''Very well, I will see if the mama-san at the Lantern House will employ the two of us.''

Chapter 28

• •

Arizona, 1849

THE CHATTERING OF wrens in the desert chaparral awakened him. He was lying in a sandy arroyo, sheltered by a wickiup. Directly in front of him an Apache squaw crouched over her cooking pot, which was suspended over a fire of twigs that burned aromatically in the cool morning air.

In his sleep he had squirmed toward the open end of the wickiup, and by turning his head he could see the entrance to the arroyo was guarded by two braves whose buckskins made them almost invisible against the dun-colored rocks.

For a moment he lay still, savoring the bare bones beauty of purple mountains against the pale dawn sky.

Some of the old men and children were arising, stretching and yawning and finding their way to the women at the cooking fires. The raiding party had returned from their foray across the border, bringing a fine string of Mexican horses.

As he hovered in the mystical instant between sleep and wakefulness, still in that state of limbo, of unawareness of his being or purpose, the sun slipped over the rim of the earth. He was blinded by the pure silver light, and the landscape before him dissolved, blurred, and vanished.

He was not sure what happened next. A sharp pain in his temple, a flash of light that came from inside his head, a peeling away of a layer of the darkness that had shrouded his mind for . . . how long?

Blinking, he struggled to hold on to the sensation. There

had been other such moments, but they'd slipped away before he could capture them. He concentrated, trying desperately to grope toward the knowledge that lay tantalizingly just out of reach.

An image formed in his mind, vividly clear. He was seated next to the window of a coach traveling through rolling brown hills. He could see the other passengers and noted that he was dressed as they were.

Beyond the window the countryside appeared empty, devoid of human life, and he idly watched the endless vistas pass by. Then suddenly horsemen appeared along the ridge, the sun at their backs. He remembered feeling no fear at first, only a heart-stopping awe at the magnificence of the braves.

There were about twenty in the war party. They were stripped to the waist, their flesh smooth as burnished copper, faces daubed with war paint, eagle feathers adorning scalp locks.

A bloodcurdling yell rent the air, and then they were galloping toward the stagecoach, the sunlight glinting on their lances.

The driver whipped his team forward, yelling, "Comanches—don't see any guns—maybe we can outrun them."

A hail of arrows had flown toward them, and somebody had pushed a gun into his hand.

Comanche. The word echoed in his head. He struggled into a sitting position, pushing aside the soft hides that had warmed him in the cool desert night. He pressed his fist to his forehead in a protective gesture, as if to contain the memories before they returned to that void in his mind he had tried so vainly to plumb.

They had been attacked by Comanche. Yet he knew the tribe he was with now were Chiricahua Apache. They were the *Tin-ne-ah*, the People. He decided not to concern himself about that now but to stay with the long-ago pictures reforming in his mind.

He closed his eyes, recalled the rocking of the stagecoach as they raced along the rocky trail, the sound of gunfire, sudden brief silences broken by the swish of arrows as the war party gained on them. Their guard was hit, and he fell beneath the churning hooves of the team.

They had almost reached the shelter of a canyon when the coach rocked more violently than ever and one of the horses screamed. A wheel struck a boulder and went careening away. The stagecoach teetered precariously for a heart-stopping second, then crashed over onto its side.

Tumbling in space, objects crashing into him, his breath knocked out of him, coming to rest beneath the bulk of another passenger. A hissing sound, then a grunt of pain. The body above him jerked convulsively, and he was sprayed with blood.

Shivering now, caught up in the flood of returning memories, he saw himself lying behind the overturned coach, reloading and firing a pistol until it was red hot, snatching a rifle from dead hands nearby.

The Comanche circled, swinging their bodies behind their horses as they closed in, so that only a foot showing above the back or a hand grasping the horse's withers was visible. Then they would rear up, shooting arrows faster than the eye could follow, with deadly accuracy.

The fleeting twilight followed by the abrupt nightfall of the Southwest brought respite. The stagecoach driver, gallantly fighting on despite an arrow imbedded in his shoulder, said, "Save your ammo. They don't like to attack at night."

One of the remaining passengers said, "We can make a run for it on foot—"

"Don't like to fight in the dark, but they'll keep watch and cut us down if we move," the driver responded.

"One of us might make it," the terrified passenger insisted.

"Feel free to try, but you've got a better chance here."

"We're all going to die!"

"Maybe so. But you knew the risks. No stage stations for miles, no settlements, no forts, and hostiles behind every rock. You all had a damn good reason for risking crossing the Arizona Territory."

The echo of that distant voice reverberated through his brain. *A damn good reason.* What was his? Where had he been going, where had he come from? The other passengers had all been strangers to him, of that he was convinced. He was certain he had been traveling alone.

He remembered the long night passing, the last star fading into the sunrise, then the horde of red warriors, their ponies leaping over the fallen horses as they came in for the kill.

His gun was empty and there was no more ammunition. He grasped the searingly hot barrel of his rifle and swung it aloft. A red haze enclosed him, filled with blurred shadows, war cries, shrieks of agony, grunts, death rattles, and his own voice, mad with fear and a blood lust he had not known he possessed. "Come on, you red bastards, finish me if you can, but I'll take some of you with me."

Swinging the rifle butt, he felt an unholy satisfaction as he heard wood crack against skull and bone. The memory of his moments of glory made his blood race and his heart pound. How many bronze men had gone down to his blows? How long had he remained on his feet? *Until he was the last White-eyes alive.*

White-eyes. A Chiricahua Apache description for blue-eyed people, the only name they had ever addressed him by. How long had he been with the Chiricahua? What became of the Comanche war party?

His fingers dug into his forehead as if to force open the door of his memory. A veil lifted briefly, and he had a terrifying glimpse of the horrors that had shut down his knowledge of his past life before he came to the Apache. He remembered two summers in the rancherias, which were camps where the nomadic Apache spent their summers. Since the winters of the Southwest differed little in climate from the summers, except for longer nights and brief rains, it was difficult to remember if there had been two or three winters.

No—don't dwell on recent memory—reach back into that distant darkness, for the horror . . .

He groaned, wanting revelation yet fearing it.

Drawing a deep breath, he closed his eyes and forced himself to recapture the image of the attacking Comanche, of defending himself against a dozen braves.

The memory of pain came then. Sharply defined, startling in its intensity. Something had struck his head an excruciating blow that caused an explosion of white-hot flame in his brain and then . . . merciful oblivion.

When he came to his senses, he was lying on the ground, his arms and legs bound with strips of rawhide that were already drying in the rising sun, tightening and biting into his flesh. Flies buzzed in a hungry swarm about his face, crawling on eyelids he blinked furiously in order to see his captors.

Vague shapes materialized in the yellow dust, making sounds that sickened him. The Comanche were mutilating the corpses.

He tried to turn his head away from the butchery, but the movement brought pain in hot waves, along with the numbing realization that he had been spared only temporarily, in order to endure a slower death.

His present self cringed from the memory, and he cried out and struggled to his feet, wanting to run, unwilling to remember the torture. He burst out of the wickiup and into the restraining arms of Sings Softly. For an instant he stared at her, wild-eyed, and gradually his labored breathing subsided. He wrenched her arms away from him and stumbled off into the desert.

Dwelling on the memory of his time with the *Tin-ne-ah* was safer than trying to go back to find the man he had been before.

In the beginning he had been a slave. During the summer sojourns in the rancherias the Apache used slaves to build their wickiups, which were oval-shaped lodges made of branches and hides, and a ramada called a squaw cooler used for outdoor cooking and dining. The slaves also harvested fruits and nuts, tended the ponies, and made the mescal the Apache liked to drink.

But he was unique among the Apache's male slaves, who

were mainly Mexican farmers and Indians from other tribes, as he had knowledge of the white-eyes' firearms. A war party had brought in a wagon filled with guns and ammunition, captured from Mexican soldiers who were engaged in a great battle with the white-eyes. Some of the captured rifles were new to the Apache. Furthermore, the flintlocks, with which they were familiar, had been modified, and the men were apprehensive about using them. He demonstrated his knowledge of the new method of ignition and use of a hammer instead of a flint by killing an antelope with a single shot at a range of more than three hundred yards. He was told he would be trained in the ways of the *Tin-ne-ah*, and if he proved worthy, he might one day even become a Chiricahua brave, with all of the rights and privileges of a warrior.

He learned their language and their Life-way, filling the empty void of his mind with new skills, new knowledge. He was taught the Apache legends of how the earth was born, of the myths of Raven, Coyote, Mink. He learned about the gods of the wind, the rain, the dawn, the sun; about the sacred plants used in ceremonies to cure sickness, both physical and mental, and to protect those sent on dangerous missions, rather than to inspire any sense of worship. He learned that when the nomads moved on, no sign that their moccasins had touched the earth was to remain. He learned the ceremonial dances, to bring rain, to stimulate and protect the harvest, to promote the general welfare of the tribe. He learned to use bow and arrow, lance and knife, as efficiently as he used a rifle or a pistol. He wore comfortable buckskin leggings and a shirt decorated with turquoise beads, and he rode with only a blanket on the back of his horse.

In the early days, as his body slowly healed, he was struck most by the absolute fearlessness of the Apache braves. Their reputation for being the most fierce of all the tribes was well deserved. But soon he came to realize that they cared for their children, treated their sick and wounded with surprising compassion, and took from the land and from others only what they needed to survive.

Now he was ready to be initiated into the tribe. The chief

had promised his daughter would become his squaw. She was beautiful, with quick laughter and lively ways, such a favorite with the old chief that in a culture that did not bother to name squaws, she had been given a name. In their language her name sounded to him like Sings Softly, and he preferred that name to the sound of the Apache words, because she often sang while she worked. When there was no Apache word for what he wanted to express, he used his own tongue, which he supposed was that of the Americans. He had not spoken to an American since he came to the *Tin-ne-ah,* so couldn't be sure.

The sun was warm on his back. His heartbeat had slowed to normal. He was losing the moment of revelation when the mind pictures of being captured by the Comanche returned. He shivered, despite the warmth of the rising sun, and forced himself back to that moment when he lay bound by rawhide as the Comanche violated the corpses of his companions.

Crouching on his haunches, he began to pant, then to sweat as he plunged back into the memories of what the Comanche had done to him.

The days and nights he was a captive of the Comanche were an unending stream of horror. He'd been humiliated by the squaws. He had run a gauntlet where he was beaten with sticks. He had been used for target practice, with arrows piercing nonvital parts of his body. He had been staked out on an ant hill. With each new torture he prayed for death but was snatched from the jaws of oblivion at the last minute in order to endure further agonies.

Eventually the Comanche tired of their sport, and he was tied to a stake, branches and twigs heaped around him.

He prayed to his God for final deliverance as his funeral pyre was lit. He heard the crackle of the flames, inhaled deeply the acrid smoke, hoping the end would come swiftly.

Then suddenly a medicine man pushed through the circle of Comanche, leapt over the burning branches, cut him free, and dragged him clear of the flames.

He remembered a feeble sound emitting from his scorched

throat, a cry of frustration that he was to be cheated of the release of death once again.

But this time he was carried to a wickiup, and a soothing liniment made of aloe pulp and other herbs was applied to his burned and tortured skin, and leaves were wrapped over his wounds. Much later he was amazed to find his flesh had healed without scars.

The medicine man proved to be an Apache shaman, member of a Chiricahua clan who had a stronghold in the nearby mountains, although they roamed freely across Arizona and Mexico. They traded goods and captives with the Comanche. The Apache did not usually spare white-eyes males, who were considered too much trouble, but the shaman had witnessed the courage of this particular white-eyes during his ordeal by torture and had been impressed by the dignity with which he faced death. The shaman decided this was an omen that the white-eyes might be of value to the Chiricahua. Did not their chief wish to find a white-eyes who could explain the working of the new rifles? Not only to shoot with them but also to maintain them. The tribe had had some disastrous experiences with captured guns. Perhaps this one could even be trained in the Life-way. Certainly his display of courage suggested he was worth saving, at least temporarily. After much haggling back and forth, the Comanche traded him to the Apache.

Now two—or could it be three years later?—he trembled violently after reliving his suffering. His torture at the hands of the Comanche had been like a terrible punctuation mark in his life. A black curtain had descended upon those days of agony and everything that went before. He had no memory of anything but his life with the Chiricahua Apache.

Until today.

Now the memory of the Comanche attack on the stagecoach had returned, and windows into his past began to open, giving glimpses of another life. Fleeting images of a gentle golden-haired child flashed into his mind, instantly obliterated by another face, that of a beautiful black-haired woman, and as soon as he saw the woman's face, he felt overwhelming rage. Who was she? What had she done to cause him to hate her?

The windows in his memory revealed other images. The splendor and decadence of Cathay, a fog-shrouded cemetery, long sea voyages . . . Was he a sailor? No, he did not believe so. The pictures formed but faded too swiftly to study and analyze.

Then all at once a single thought crystallized, and he knew for a certainty that the long night of seeking his identity was over. The light of dawn might creep more slowly than he would wish, but soon he would remember everything.

He spoke aloud, needing to give the thought proper weight. "My name is Fletcher Faraday. I am an Englishman. When I was captured by the Comanche, I was pursuing my wife, who betrayed me."

Chapter 29

• •

EMILY ROSE EARLY and performed her ablutions with care. She washed her face, cleaned her teeth with baking soda, brushed her hair until it shone, then donned her prettiest day dress, a silver- and gray-striped muslin with a little lace collar that was a perfect foil for the brooch Edward had given her and which was still her favorite piece of jewelry. He had sacrificed his cuff links for the brooch, and when she wore it she felt cared for and loved. He was her hero, her husband, and her love for him filled her with a joy that not even her grief over the news of her father's death could diminish.

How kind Edward had been, scarcely leaving her side these past days, making sure her every minute was filled with activities to take her mind off her loss. But still he left her at her bedroom door each night. She had decided that perhaps the time to discuss this was not at the moment of his good-night kiss but in the first light of day with bedtime still hours away.

She buttoned her shoes, gave herself a last quick appraisal in her dressing table mirror, and ran downstairs to the morning room.

Josefa was setting the table. A single place setting. Emily's heart sank. "Has my husband breakfasted already? Has he gone to the bank? The lumber mill?" She knew he left the running of the emporium solely to a capable store manager.

The dark eyes of the housekeeper regarded her sympathetically, and Emily was sure the Mexican girl was aware that Edward's sleeping arrangements were not those of an ardent bridegroom. In her halting English Josefa replied, "The señor . . . him not come home."

"Not come home? You mean he left the house last night?"

Josefa nodded and spread her hands in a helpless gesture.

Emily hung her head in shame. She stumbled from the morning room, ignoring the housekeeper's plea to please stay and eat something, and went into the front parlor, which afforded a view of the street leading up the hill.

For two hours she watched the street, questions without answers pounding her brain, twisting her heartstrings into anguished knots. Surely there was only one explanation for a man spending his nights away from his home—there was another woman, a rival. And how could she blame Edward? From the beginning he'd had a wife who was not a wife. Oh, dear Lord in Heaven, she prayed, please let it not be too late. Do not let him have given his love to another. Let me be Edward's wife.

How could she have been so foolish as to let the great love of her life slip away like this? She remembered the first night he had kissed her at her bedroom door, with an ardor she knew instinctively was real and wholehearted and for her alone. Slowly he had withdrawn his lips from hers, and he had waited, searching her face for some sign that she wanted him to love her, but she had given no sign. She recalled his almost imperceptible sigh as he left her to go to her lonely bed. But on the succeeding nights his bedtime kiss had been perfunctory, as if he were anxious to leave. As indeed, apparently, he had been.

Scalding tears slipped down her cheeks, and blinking them away she saw a pony trap coming up the hill. As it drew nearer she stared, hardly recognizing the unkempt, unshaven man who slumped wearily, the reins dangling from his hands, his head nodding over his chest.

Emily ran to the front door, down the steps, out onto the street. When the pony trap came to a stop, Edward looked at her with glazed, tired eyes, as though scarcely seeing her.

"Edward, oh, my dear, you look so weary! Where have

you been all night long?'' The question was out before she had time to wonder whether or not she should ask it.

He climbed down, attempting to give her a smile. She saw then that an Indian boy had been sleeping in the trap, almost hidden beneath a pile of blankets. The boy roused himself and rubbed his eyes sleepily.

Edward spoke to him in Spanish, which he seemed to understand, and then Edward turned to her. ''Carlos will take care of the horse and trap. Let's go into the house. We'll talk there.''

She walked beside him, feeling rising panic. Was he about to tell her their marriage was a sham, which it surely was, and send her packing? Even the deepest love could die from neglect, and he had loved her and waited for her for over three years. Perhaps his love had simply died and these past days all he had been feeling for her was sympathy that her father was dead.

By the time they reached the house, she had worked herself up into such a state she was trembling.

''Emily, I must bathe and change my clothes,'' Edward said. ''Wait for me in the morning room; I shan't be long.''

She wanted to cry out, no, let the ax fall now, I can't bear the waiting, but of course she did not. She waited patiently until at last he joined her in the morning room. Josefa poured a cup of strong black coffee and set it at his place and then, at his signal, left them alone.

''I was so worried about you,'' Emily said, close to tears. ''I know you've been spending many nights away from home, and I hear such frightening stories about the robbers and murderers who roam the streets at night, and—oh, it isn't right to torment me so!''

He sighed deeply. ''I should have explained my absences. I believed . . . foolishly, I thought you would be unaware of my activities if I left after you'd retired for the night. I'm sorry for worrying you, Emily. Please forgive me.''

''What activities? What do you do all night long?'' Emily asked faintly, fearfully. She remained standing, her fingers gripping the back of a chair as though to keep a barricade between them.

But he did not move toward her. He collapsed in near exhaustion into his own chair. "Do you remember the day you arrived, I insisted that I was now a businessman, and indeed I am. But old habits die hard. Although I told you I never wanted to practice medicine again, that the horrors of the war will remain with me forever, still I find myself unable to refuse to do what I can for the poorest and most helpless of our citizens . . . the Indian and Mexican children orphaned or separated from their parents by the war."

Relief washed over Emily in great cleansing waves. "Oh, Edward, that is wonderful of you! But why did you not tell me? And why do you go only at night?"

He smiled tiredly. "Your questions answer themselves— I went at night because I did not want to tell you."

"But why on earth wouldn't you want me to know you were engaged in such a noble endeavor? I am so proud of you."

"To explain fully I must go back to my army days, to the dusty hellhole that was Matamoros. The men died like flies—there was so little we could do. We lost ten men to sickness for every one who died in battle. Our hospital tents were little better than . . . But I will spare you the details. The doctors were overworked. Medical supplies, such as they were, arrived only sporadically. We were simply overwhelmed by disease. I believe we could have handled the war injuries had it not been for the rampant sickness."

"It must have been dreadful for you," Emily murmured. "How did you endure it for so long?"

"One does what one must. There was no time to give comfort to our patients. We performed amputations, gave only rudimentary treatment of illnesses, and so we were grateful to the local priests who not only comforted the sick and gave last rites to the dying but also spent time talking to the men who survived, writing letters home for them and so on. It was thus that I met a man who became a friend. He was a Jesuit."

"He spoke English? Or had you learned Spanish then?"

"He taught me to speak Spanish, but he was neither Spanish nor Mexican. He was an American."

Edward broke off in order to drink some coffee. In the bright morning sunlight the lines of strain and weariness were evident on his handsome features, and Emily considered again how much his wartime experiences had aged him. The blankness of youth was gone, replaced by experience and maturity.

He went on: "At least—I thought he became my friend. Perhaps I've acquired the cynicism of men who witness the unimaginable horror of war, but I do wonder if a casual conversation I had with him shortly after I met him might have been the reason he pursued a closer acquaintance with me than with any of the other medical officers. After I came here to await your arrival, he wrote to me a couple of times and I replied. So I know he was aware of your impending arrival, and that's what troubles me—you see, he came here, just a couple of months before your ship reached San Francisco."

Emily listened patiently, and when he paused to drink some more coffee, she asked, "And it is your Jesuit friend who asked you to care for the sick Indian and Mexican children?"

He nodded but did not speak again for a moment as he stared into space.

"Edward, I don't understand what the arrival of a priest just prior to my reaching San Francisco has to do with us. I don't know any Jesuit priests, although there were Jesuit missionaries in China, but I suppose they are all over the world?"

"The Society of Jesus was founded by a Spaniard, Saint Ignatius Loyola, and has indeed spread all over the world over the centuries. There are many Jesuits in Mexico."

"And here, in the United States?"

"Oh, yes, England, too."

"I sense it is important that I understand more about them."

"Yes, I think so. Although I may be wrong in my assumptions."

"And what are those assumptions?"

"That my friend came to San Francisco for a purpose.

But let me tell you more about the Jesuits. They take vows of poverty, chastity, and obedience. Recruits are divided into scholastics and brothers. The scholastics spend up to fifteen years studying philosophy, divinity, humanities. There is a year of mystical theology and intense study before they take their final vows and go out into the world. Many Jesuit missionaries have been martyred, including a group who suffered fiendish cruelties while attempting to convert the American Indians.''

''But, Edward, why are you troubled about this particular Jesuit coming here at this time?''

''I believe he came because I told him about you and that you might be bringing Phin Tsu with you.''

Emily stared at him, too perplexed to see any rhyme or reason in this.

Edward said, ''I have told no one about what happened to cause us to leave England, and no one knows our real names, please believe that. Of our group, only Phin Tsu uses her real name, because she has no reason to hide her identity, as we have. So when I told him—forgive me, Emily, but I must be quite honest with you—when I told him that I was concerned about your friendship with a beautiful Eurasian named Phin Tsu, who I believed might be . . . a pleasure woman . . . he immediately asked me an extremely troubling question.''

''What did he ask?''

''He asked if your maiden name was Faraday and if you were Emily, the daughter of Fletcher Faraday, a diplomat who had served in China.''

Emily felt all the color drain from her face. ''How could he possibly have known?''

''He said he might have known Phin Tsu in China.''

''But Phin isn't a Christian—and certainly not a Catholic.''

''Exactly. Not only that, but Phin's . . . profession seems to preclude any relationship other than that of a priest attempting to save a sinner. When I tried to question him, however, he became angry—almost distraught—and said that he had rebelled against the doctrines of his order for a time and had fallen from grace. He wouldn't say more, but the implications were obvious.''

"You think he and Phin . . . oh!" Emily's cheeks flamed.

"So you see why I am worried? He is a good and dedicated man of God now, and I do not wish to be instrumental in precipitating another fall from grace if Phin Tsu again casts her spell over him."

"Edward! How unfair of you to say such a thing! Surely your Jesuit is the one who should resist temptation! Why blame Phin?"

"Your loyalty to her is commendable, Emily. But there is something of which you are unaware. She has left Mrs. Ling's boardinghouse and moved into the Lantern House, a bordello so named because it is decorated with Chinese lanterns. The girls who live and work there are mostly Asians."

Emily turned away, too distressed to comment. At her request, Edward had brought Phin to see her after learning of their father's death. Phin had comforted her in her grief. They had not spoken of anything else. Now Emily resolved that she must meet with Phin again as soon as possible.

Chapter 30

• •

THE OLD ADOBE house retained few traces of its former grandeur, when it had been the *casa grande* of a *rancho* belonging to a *Californio* who had received a land grant for service to the Spanish king. The vaqueros' cabins were gone, and the house had been burned during an Indian raid, leaving only the adobe shell. Part of the tile roof had collapsed and only the charred remains of the olive trees and live oaks that had once shaded the *casa grande* remained.

Clad in the black robe of a Jesuit and seated on a wrought-iron bench beside the ruined remains of a fountain, Father Juan watched a pony trap climb the hill. Some of the older children who had been hoeing the small vegetable garden scratched out of a burned-out field saw the trap and ran to meet it. Señor Eduardo, as the children called Edward Dale, was a popular visitor to their remote haven.

Father Juan, who had been born Brent Ethan Carlisle, rose to his feet to go to meet Edward. The sun was climbing the summer sky, and Brent felt the urgency of time passing. Edward had spent most of the night at the bedside of a ten-year-old boy named Ramon and had informed Brent at dawn that he would have to amputate the boy's gangrenous leg. Recalling the hellish hacking off of limbs from screaming men in the hospital tents of Matamoros, Brent dreaded having to hold the boy down during the surgery but knew that this was the only way to save his life.

In the few short weeks since Brent had found a dozen starving and sick children living in the ruined *casa* in the care of an elderly Mexican woman, the number of his charges had doubled and, along with them, his problems.

Edward had at first been reluctant to resume any medical duties, but one visit to the children had persuaded him to change his mind. They were so helpless, so innocent and trusting.

Catching the pony's reins as Edward's trap came to a halt, Brent held up his hand to still the babble of greetings from the children. "Go back to your chores now. Señor Eduardo must take care of Ramon."

Edward climbed down from the trap. "Has there been any change?"

Brent shook his head. "Carlotta is with him. Did you bring all the necessary tools?"

Edward lifted his black medical bag from the trap, then picked up something wrapped in burlap. "I stopped to have this sharpened." Brent recognized the size and shape of a hacksaw and quickly sent the children back to their work. He fell into step beside Edward as they made their way to the house.

"I want to try something," Edward said. "I believe it will make the operation easier for Ramon."

"What can you do, other than use sharp cutting tools and be as fast as you can?" Brent asked. "The rest is in God's hands."

"When I was a medical student, some of my more reckless colleagues attended parties where a chemical was sniffed that produced an effect not unlike that caused by consuming spirits, but unlike the slower process of getting drunk, the chemical acted immediately. I was curious and went to one of those parties, and although I didn't try the stuff myself, I observed a rather odd side effect. Those who sniffed the chemical would frequently fall down or bump into furniture and so on, yet they appeared to feel no pain. Oh, they'd get bruises and cuts but didn't seem to notice them."

"And what *is* this chemical?" Brent asked, following Edward's line of thought. They had agonized all night long about the pain and shock that would be inflicted upon the boy.

"It's called ether."

"You have some of this substance?"

"Yes. I started dehydrating alcohol when I began to suspect that Ramon's leg would become gangrenous."

They were now inside the house. The adobe floor tiles had been swept clean, the walls scrubbed. A crucifix hung over the door of what had formerly been the *sala*, which they had converted to a sick bay. Brent paused, his hand on the rough door he had constructed to replace the burned one. "But surely using this ether to alleviate Ramon's pain during the surgery is a far cry from its use by healthy young men sniffing it for pleasure, don't you think?"

"Yes, it is. Ramon is undernourished and terribly weakened from the fever and gangrene. Frankly, I don't think he can survive the operation, no matter what I do. I do believe I can eliminate some or even all of the pain of the amputation and possibly the resulting shock, but will the ether itself kill him? I'm unsure how much would be safe to give."

"Only you can make that decision, Edward. I can pray to God to guide you, and I will help with the surgery in any way I can. Tell me what to do."

"My plan is to sprinkle the ether onto a cloth and place it over the boy's mouth and nose for a few seconds. If, as I hope, he falls asleep, I will quickly amputate the leg. If you would stand by with the ether-soaked cloth in case he begins to regain consciousness and again place it over his face . . ."

Brent felt his stomach contract. "I cannot administer something that might kill the child. You just said you didn't know fully what the effects of the ether would be."

"There's no one else here to assist me. Carlotta is too old and frail; her hands tremble constantly. My alternative would be possibly to overdose Ramon in the beginning, as once I start the amputation I can't stop. For pity's sake, for once don't think like a priest. I'm not asking you to break a commandment or dishonor your vows."

"Thou shalt not kill," Brent said through clenched teeth. "I might poison Ramon with the ether. You said so yourself—you have no idea how much the child could withstand."

For a moment the two men stared at each other in a silent battle of wills.

How could Edward know, Brent thought, that in China one moment of weakness had led to his fall from grace? And having committed a single forbidden act how swiftly his descent into sin and degradation had been? He had become a soldier of fortune, he had killed and plundered, he had broken his vow of chastity and fornicated with Phin Tsu. Perhaps he would have continued to do so, had she not wished to leave China to find her English father and half sister. He had compounded his sins by not confessing to her that he was a priest; instead he had allowed her to think he had a wife. He had traveled halfway around the world to find Phin Tsu to make amends to her.

But for now he must concern himself with these children, in particular Ramon. And never, by word or deed, could he ever again break his vows to the Society of Jesus. He said quietly, "I will hold the boy down while you operate, I will do anything you ask—except administer a possibly lethal chemical. I cannot kill."

"So be it," Edward said shortly.

Brent opened the door and held it to allow Edward to pass.

Tonia Bardine looked with distaste upon the sprawled body of Henry, who lay across her bed in a drunken stupor. His eye patch had slipped, and the sunken socket of his missing eye revolted her. Henry looked like the pirate he was. Oh, he'd never actually plundered unwary merchant-men, but he'd transported slaves, and she suspected he'd stolen and refitted at least one of his fleet of ships. Nowadays, with his properties in San Francisco and his mining shares, and with the *Antonia* making record-breaking voyages laden with profitable cargoes from the Eastern Seaboard, Henry no longer needed to resort to his former practices. But his newfound legitimacy had not changed his basic character, and Tonia would have left him but for the fact that he had threatened to kill her if she did so. He was the only man she had ever feared.

She pulled her wrap around her and tiptoed from the room. In her own room she rang for her maid, then went into her dressing room to wash away every trace of Henry.

Her maid, who had been expecting the midnight summons, appeared at once and showed no surprise that her mistress wished to dress and leave the house at such a late hour. The servants were all aware that Mrs. Bardine occasionally arose from her husband's bed in the small hours of the morning and departed for some mysterious destination. Only Cervantes, her coachman, knew where she went, and no one dared question him. She would return at dawn, before her husband was up, and be waiting at the breakfast table when Henry came downstairs.

"Hurry," Tonia said impatiently. "No, no, don't bother with my stays or petticoats, just give me my shift and the black wool gown with the matching cloak. Is the carriage ready?"

"Sí, señora."

Tonia pulled the hood of her cloak up over her tumbled hair and, the instant her maid finished buttoning her shoes, sped from the room. The carriage was waiting in the shadows, and as soon as she was inside, Cervantes snapped the reins, and they rolled silently down the hill into the creeping mist. He knew their destination without being told.

Cervantes had been hired by Tonia herself, not only to be her coachman but also to protect her. She knew he had ridden with Murrieta—indeed, might still be with the feared outlaw had the two not quarreled over a señorita. There was a cool insolence to the way Cervantes looked at her, and his lithe body, always clad in black, seemed poised to spring, like a predatory panther.

Henry had at first balked at hiring Cervantes, but she had pointed out that the streets of San Francisco were becoming dangerous as a lawless element bent on robbing and plundering arrived in the wake of the gold prospectors. There was even a band of Australian convicts who had escaped from the penal colony and called themselves the Sydney Ducks who terrorized the citizens. Surely, Tonia had urged Henry, it was prudent for the wealthy Bardines to have a coachman who was also a crack shot and who could throw a knife with deadly accuracy?

Inside the carriage Tonia leaned back and let out her breath in a long sigh. Despite Cervantes's less than satisfactory attitude toward his employers, she always felt safe with him. Unlike the violently unpredictable Henry Bardine, who was becoming more of a trial to her every day. She deeply regretted marrying him, but how could she have foreseen how swiftly the time would come when she no longer needed him? That she would become wealthy in her own right with the advent of the discovery of gold at Sutter's Mill?

She now owned two bordellos, and it was becoming increasingly difficult to conceal the riches that poured in. She didn't dare use a bank for fear Henry would learn of her private income, and she worried about the gold and other valuables buried beneath the live oaks in the rear garden of their house on Nob Hill. Cervantes had buried the tin boxes, and once a month he would dig one of them up and add to the contents. In addition, Tonia had bought the deed to a vast *rancho* in the south, a former Spanish land grant.

The time had come to get rid of Henry Bardine.

But he was crafty, cunning in a way that none of the other men in her life had been. Like herself he was from the gutter and as capable as she when it came to underhanded dealings or violent methods of getting his way. She would have to be very, very careful. Henry was no naive gentleman, as Fletcher Faraday had been.

She had been so obsessed with plans for ridding herself of Henry that most other concerns had been pushed aside. Only one other nagging thought intruded. Ever since the party Max Seadon had given at the Rosebriar—a combination celebration of the arrival of the clipper ship and welcome party for that snobbish and uppity Briony Forest's sister-in-law—Tonia had been troubled by a vague feeling that she and Mrs. Edward Dale had met before. But where? And was their previous meeting of any consequence?

Tonia's impression of the young Mrs. Edward Dale—what was her first name?—had been one of a too-thin, almost sickly looking young woman whose large pale blue eyes dominated her pretty but gaunt features. Her hair was true gold, with no hint of copper or flaxen. Tonia recalled thinking that Mrs. Dale looked vaguely familiar, but her overriding impression was that the ethereal creature would surely blow away in the first stiff breeze. Someone had commented that Edward's wife had been ill for most of the long voyage around the Horn, and that probably accounted for her present fragility. Tonia decided she would call on the new arrival when she had time, and perhaps a conversation would reveal where they had met before.

As the carriage approached the waterfront, a string of colored lights glimmered through the fog. The Lantern House was a two-story mansion decorated with cupolas and towers and cornices. The sea captain who built it had moved out when he realized his only neighbors were going to be warehouses, taverns, and bordellos. Only the paper lanterns strung across every window and adorning the front porch even remotely suggested that the Victorian mansion was a house of Oriental pleasures.

The doorman, a burly Chinese named Lee Wong, took charge of their carriage. It was understood that Cervantes never left his mistress's side, and so he accompanied her into the vestibule, which led to an open lobby where clusters of lanterns suspended from the ceiling created a rainbow of soft light. Carved ebony benches piled with silk cushions were artfully arranged so that waiting clients, who were being served expensive drinks, could watch the girls ascending the wide staircase to the upper floor and coming downstairs again accompanied by men wearing blissful expressions. Disgruntled clients were discreetly removed down a back stairway by Lee Wong. All of the girls had been taught to walk down the stairs in a graceful, sensual glide, never looking at their feet, their gaze fixed on the waiting clients below, seducing them before they reached the lobby. Tonia spared no expense when it came to maintaining the house and dressing the girls. Less than immaculate clients were directed to a bath house in the rear of the Lantern House before being admitted.

As Tonia crossed the lobby, her sharp glance took in the brocaded walls, the rococo mirrors, delicately painted shoji screens, and ivory-inlaid tables. She had cleverly combined a few real Chinese and Japanese pieces with American- and British-made furniture in the Oriental style, including Chinese-style beds in each room. These sat in the middle of the floor like complete little houses, with elaborate canopies, draped sides, and even small attached verandas. If some of the other furnishings were not authentically Oriental but rather a Western idea of Far Eastern decor, no one complained.

Tonia was extremely proud of the Lantern House, and her only regret was that her handiwork had to be a well-kept secret. She resented the praise heaped upon Briony Forest for her insipid Rosebriar Hotel when she could not take credit for the far more exciting Lantern House.

She paused before one very young Chinese girl who sat with lowered eyes and downturned lips. ''Smile, look at the gentlemen. Use your fan. How many times have you been upstairs tonight?''

The girl jumped, startled, and murmured something unintelligible but straightened up and smiled hopefully at a bearded miner nearby. Tonia continued on her way, and Cervantes opened a black lacquered door partially concealed by a screen.

This was the office of the mama-san, a tiny woman named Qing Chan, whose papery skin no amount of powder could whiten and whose coarse black hair was covered with ornaments, further shrinking her withered face. She was like a tiny yellow moth who fluttered about the house, but she ruled with the ruthlessness of Genghis Khan. According to her girls, Qing Chan's tiny slitted eyes could see around corners and through walls, and no one ever deceived her. She was kneeling on the floor beside a low ebony table set for tea and bowed her head in greeting as Tonia entered the room.

Unlike the opulence of the lobby, this room was comparatively bare. The low lacquered table, a pair of ivory-inlaid mandarin chests, and a mahogany carved console that served as a desk were the only important pieces of furniture.

Two Chinese folding stools were used for seating, a curtained alcove concealed storage shelves and cupboards. A jade Buddha in a wall niche surveyed the visitors with a sinister leer.

Tonia went straight to the console, pushed aside an abacus, and flipped through a ledger. She nodded, satisfied, then said to Qing Chan, "Tell me about them."

The mama-san poured tea into a tiny china bowl and offered it to Tonia, but she waved it away.

"Phin Tsu is perhaps the most beautiful Eurasian I have ever beheld," Qing Chan said, her voice as whispery as a zephyr. "And the man Kane is surely the ugliest creature ever to escape from a nightmare. A no more unlikely pair will you ever encounter."

"Then why did you not keep the girl and send him packing?"

For answer, Qing Chan picked up a small brass bell and shook it. A moment later the sad sweet strains of a love song, played by a master violinist, filled the room.

Even Cervantes, who lounged against the door, straightened up to listen. Spellbound, they listened in silence as the ballad faded and the unseen violinist flawlessly rendered a Haydn sonata, then blended the last notes into a rousing selection of Mozart's compositions.

When the impromptu concert ended, no one spoke for a moment. Then Tonia glanced quickly at the other two people in the room. The music had obviously touched them both. Tonia's mind quickly saw the possibilities. It was difficult to retain the services of any competent musicians, as when word spread that one of the bordellos had a good piano player or fiddler, he would quickly be lured away to a hotel or restaurant, or even to the theaters that were opening. There was not an establishment in town who could boast of a violinist of the caliber of the man now hiding in the curtained alcove.

Tonia rose to her feet and snatched aside the curtain.

He stood with his violin still nestled in the crook of his shoulder, his face tilted so that the cruelly scarred face was cast in sharp relief by the overhead lanterns.

Burns, Tonia thought, the lower part of his face had been badly burned. He's lucky one eye was spared. The mouth . . . oh, God, the mouth!

She asked, "Can you speak?"

The parody of a mouth moved painfully, but his words were clear. "I am not an animal. Of course I can speak."

"I will construct a place on the landing for you, at the top of the stairs, so that your music will be heard in the entertaining rooms and downstairs in the lobby. Since you'll need a place to eat and sleep, we'll give you the adjacent room presently used for gambling. It's large, with a balcony, and we'll have the landing door connected to your music chamber so that you can move about without being seen. You may advise the carpenters as to how best to conceal you without muffling the music."

Having thoroughly scrutinized his face, she lowered her gaze and continued, "You will stay out of sight—anything you need will be brought in for you. I will pay you in gold dust, and your stipend will be twice what you could earn in any hotel in town—not that any of them would hire you. In return I want you to sign a contract, renewable by mutual consent, agreeing to stay at the Lantern House for one year. You will have Sundays off, and if you wish to go some-where, Lee Wong will take you. Are you agreeable to these terms and conditions?"

His amber eye, which by some trick of the light appeared to be golden, drew her gaze back to his and held it there. "I will stay as long as Phin Tsu stays. No longer. All other conditions are acceptable."

Tonia hesitated. She had already recognized what an asset he would be to the Lantern House. When word of his music got out, the lobby would be filled with men hungry for the culture they had left behind in the East. The Lantern House would be the epitome of gentlemen's sporting houses, catering to their half-forgotten love of the arts as well as their baser instincts. She would push ahead with her plans to add an elegant dining room. No other establishment in San Francisco would be able to compete. Perhaps she would turn the Lantern House into a private club and demand hefty initiation fees.

She smiled sweetly. "I'm sure we will also be able to make Phin Tsu happy. We will offer her a generous contract. Where is she? I should like to meet her."

Chapter 31

• •

EDWARD STOOD ON a small rise just beyond Father Juan's *casa de niños* watching the sun rise over the rolling hills to the east. His body had long since shrugged off exhaustion, becoming numb, his limbs automatically obeying his brain's command. He felt as if only his mind remained alive and functioning, existing beyond the realm of physical needs. He would have to sleep soon, he knew, but he wanted to savor this moment, celebrating the victory of life over death.

Ramon had survived the amputation of his lower leg, he had felt no pain thanks to the ether, and he had lived through the night. Edward had not dared to hope for more.

Lost in the magic of the sunrise, he did not hear the approach of sandaled feet and started as Brent suddenly appeared at his side. "I thought you had gone to the chapel to pray, Father Juan."

"I have given thanks to God for delivering Ramon."

Edward felt his jaw move reflexively and resisted the urge to respond that God had had a little help. Instead he responded, "The child is not out of danger yet. You will have to watch him carefully, and I will have to come and check his stump every day for a while. When it is properly healed, we'll find someone to make a peg leg for him."

"We are grateful to you, Edward."

"Are you? Grateful enough to tell me why you followed me to San Francisco?"

"You do not subscribe to the belief that God called me here to care for the children and convert the heathen to the true faith?"

"No, I do not."

Brent turned away from the brilliance of the rising sun and walked a few paces along the ridge. Silhouetted against the sky he was an imposing figure, Edward thought. With his great height and robust build he seemed to belong to some other more-than-mortal breed of man. After a few moments' silent deliberation he answered, "I knew Phin Tsu in China."

"I surmised as much. But I can't fathom the serpentine path you trod to follow her here."

"I knew she had gone to England to seek Fletcher Faraday and his daughter Emily. Through diplomatic channels I learned that Faraday had been assigned to Mexico City and that he had departed before Phin Tsu's ship would have reached England. Therefore, I was sure she, too, would go to Mexico. I sailed to Mexico but could find no trace of them. The Americans and Mexicans were at war. I joined a Jesuit order and was sent to Matamoros, where I met you, and you spoke of your wife Emily and her Eurasian friend, Phin Tsu, who would be joining you when the war ended. If you do not believe God directed me to your hospital tent in Matamoros, then I pity your lack of faith."

Edward said, "You haven't explained why you wanted to find Phin Tsu."

"I must save her soul."

Edward wondered if Father Juan, rather than Brent Carlisle, had spoken.

Phin Tsu had no intention of spending any more time in the Lantern House than necessary. The idea of servicing barbarians was repulsive; indeed, to be forced to pleasure many different men with no right of selection or refusal revolted her. Her plan was to stay only long enough to learn how her father had perished and, if by the hand of his second wife, to see that justice was done.

But it seemed that Mrs. Bardine and the mama-san were extremely eager to please. Phin was given the best room in the house, the most generous clothing allowance, and free time, in addition to a higher percentage of her earnings than any of the other girls received. Still, Phin refused to sign a contract until she had, as she sweetly explained, "worked in the Lantern House for a trial period, to see if I wish to remain."

The tiny black eyes of the mama-san glittered angrily at this announcement, but Mrs. Bardine quickly agreed. "A month's trial, then? You do understand that some of our gentlemen prefer to spend time with the same young lady on each of their visits? We need the security of knowing you will stay."

"When I have reached a decision, I will let you know," Phin replied.

If some of her clients were barbarians of the lowest class, Phin accepted this, knowing that anyone could endure anything when it was known that there was a time limit.

Within days of her arrival Phin learned that Mrs. Bardine and the mama-san, although impressed with her beauty, had another more pressing reason to keep her happy.

The mama-san spelled this out clearly on Phin's first evening. "Your friend Kane," she said in her whispery voice, "may visit your room whenever he chooses, provided he tells you in advance. You may as well know, Phin Tsu, that I recognized you as a troublemaker the moment I saw you. You are beautiful, but you do not show the proper subservience and humble gratitude our gentlemen expect from Oriental girls. You, Phin Tsu, have the measured gaze of a brigand. You had better keep Kane contented; he is the only reason you are here."

Phin Tsu didn't know whether to be outraged or amused by this. She merely nodded and later decided that Kane could schedule visits whenever she decided she did not wish to pleasure some great oaf of a bearded miner.

She had grown accustomed to Kane; in some ways their platonic relationship reminded her of her friendship with the chief eunuch in the Forbidden City, for she knew he would not make any demands, yet offered companionship and concern for her well-being. Phin had long ago given her heart to a dashing soldier of fortune and knew she would remain untouched by every other man on earth; but it was good to have a man in her life she could trust.

A pagodalike structure made of wicker was placed at the top of the stairs, and Kane's music filled the lobby and drifted along the upper landing. The wicker walls of the pagoda allowed the clear sweet tones of the violin to escape, but Kane himself was only a vague, faceless shape.

Almost immediately both the magic and mystery of the unseen violinist created a stir. Men who formerly visited the upstairs rooms and promptly departed now remained in the lobby, buying drinks and listening to the music. Some evenings men came only for the music. Tonia hired a cook and began to serve dinner in a cramped room formerly used only by the girls. Carpenters arrived to build an addition to the house to accommodate a full dining room.

Phin observed all of this with interest, but her main concern was to learn more about Tonia Bardine. She questioned the other girls discreetly but was disappointed to learn that none of them had known Tonia before coming to the Lantern House. They were all more than happy to gossip about her life in San Francisco, however, and Phin soon learned that Henry Bardine was unaware of his wife's business, that he frequently beat and ill-used her, that she was afraid of him. She never visited the other bordello she owned, the one she had started with, because it catered to the worst type of client. It was rumored that she was in the process of selling it.

But the most important piece of information Phin gleaned came from one of the girls who had briefly worked as Tonia's maid in their Nob Hill mansion.

The girl, a shy young creature named Hou, had her career as lady's maid cut short when she was caught eavesdropping. She had heard a revealing exchange between the Bardines.

Hou had been cleaning Tonia's dressing room when Henry pushed his wife into the bedroom. Hou cowered behind the dressing room door and listened to the sound of Henry slapping Tonia.

She heard her mistress gasp in pain, and then Henry

growled, "Don't you ever look down your nose at my friends again, you slut. Who do you think you are?"

"Henry, they're so uncouth! I hate to have to take a meal with them. Their table manners—their language. Besides, while we associate with such people, we'll never make any decent friends."

"You don't seriously believe the society matrons are ever going to accept you, do you? Maybe you think if you were rid of old Henry, they'd invite you to their cotillions and soirees? Well, think again, because I'm going to be here for a long time yet, and you, my pretty, are going to be my dutiful wife. So don't plan any sneak attacks because I've got eyes in the back of my head. Besides, if anything happens to me, I've made sure that the British Embassy in Mexico City gets word about what really happened to your last husband."

"You're bluffing!" Tonia had cried. "You never even knew Fletcher."

"No, my love, I didn't. But I know a man who knows the men who made you a widow."

At that point Hou had accidentally nudged the china pitcher on the washstand, tipping it into the bowl with a loud crash. Tonia was livid. That night Hou was relegated to the Lantern House.

Phin absorbed this information with growing anger. So Fletcher Faraday had been the victim of an assassin. Had the killer been hired by Tonia? It seemed likely, but she would need proof of that.

There was one, albeit dangerous, way of probing Tonia's past life. To go to the source.

When Tonia arrived for her weekly midnight inspection and collection of receipts, Phin Tsu made certain that not only would Kane be playing Tonia's favorite Mozart when Tonia arrived, but also that she would be in the lobby.

As Tonia paused for a moment to listen to the music, Phin approached her and stood waiting patiently to be noticed.

When a pause in the music came, Tonia turned to her. "How lovely you look, Phin. I'm surprised to find you waiting in the lobby. I understood from mama-san that the gentlemen were clamoring for you.''

''Mrs. Bardine, if I could speak with you privately? It's a matter of great urgency.''

Tonia's calculating gaze flickered over Phin, then she pointed in the direction of her private office, a room tucked away at the rear of the house, to which Phin had not formerly been invited. Phin was very much aware of the presence of the black-clad Cervantes, who preceded them along a dimly lit corridor and examined the office before allowing them to enter. He then positioned himself at the door.

The office was furnished with a comfortable sofa, a pair of armchairs, and a substantial-looking desk. As soon as they were inside Tonia said sharply, ''If you are going to complain about Qing Chan, I must warn you that she is indispensable.''

''Not at all, Mrs. Bardine. It is you that I am worried about. You are in great danger.''

''What are you talking about?''

''In China we pay heed to our dreams, as you might know. I have had a disturbing dream about you, that you were being stalked by one who would harm you—perhaps even try to kill you.''

Tonia stared at her, but before she could respond, Phin pressed her advantage. ''I am the daughter of a spirit woman, and I have inherited my mother's gift of foretelling the future. If you would permit me, it would be my humble pleasure to give you a reading and thereby warn you of where to look for danger.''

As she spoke she held out her hand. On her palm rested two delicate ivory disks, one painted with a miniature figure clad in mandarin's robe and the other inscribed with death wearing a cardinal's hat and mantelletta.

''These are ancient Chinese fortune cards, from which your people derived both your playing cards and your tarot cards. The Chinese have used these cards since the seventh century. If you will permit me, I will bring to you the complete set, and we will find the source of the danger.''

Tonia looked at the ivory disks for a moment, then said, "Not now. I must leave shortly. I will speak with you again tomorrow. Meantime, don't speak of your dream or your fortune cards to anyone, do you understand?"

Phin nodded.

"Go back to the lobby now," Tonia said.

Phin slipped the ivory disks into the pocket of the silk robe she wore and left.

Outside the office door she was startled when mama-san stepped out of the shadows and seized her arm in a fierce, clawlike grip. "Why did you go in there? What did you say to her?"

Phin found herself being dragged through the lobby toward the black lacquered door of Qing Chan's office. Before they reached it, however, the strains of the violin stopped abruptly in mid-stanza. Phin looked up toward the wicker pagoda and hissed under her breath, "He sees you. Let go of me, old woman, or he will come down those stairs and frighten the wits out of everybody."

Qing Chan released her instantly, casting a fearful glance upward.

Phin said coldly, "My business with Mrs. Bardine has nothing to do with you or with the Lantern House. If you don't believe me, ask her. Now, I'd better go and speak with Kane, to reassure him that all is well."

She ran up the stairs to the pagoda.

Phin had been dreaming she was back in China watching her mother comb her hair, weaving blossoms and ornaments into the dark glossy mass, when suddenly her mother turned to her and said, "You must beware. He will harm you."

The dream faded and Phin sat up in bed, her heart beating fast. She pushed aside the heavy curtain that enclosed the bed just as her door was unceremoniously flung open and Qing Chan entered the room. "Get up at once," she hissed. "You have brought trouble to us. I knew it, expected it. I should never have told Mrs. Bardine about you—I should have sent you on your way."

Still only half-awake, Phin swung her legs over the side

of the bed. "What is it? What time is it? I feel I have slept only minutes."

"The sun has not yet risen—we are not open for business. But someone is here, asking for you. You must get rid of him and make sure he never returns."

"But who is it? Surely not Edward Dale?"

"It is a priest," the mama-san spat out the word contemptuously and turned on her heel. "He waits in the vestibule."

A priest? That was impossible. Why would a priest come to a house of sin and ask for her? She dressed quickly, selecting black silk trousers and an embroidered satin jacket with mandarin collar and gold tasseled closures. An interview with a priest seemed to call for her to appear as Chinese, and therefore as alien to his beliefs, as possible.

Crossing the lobby, she saw the black robed figure through the open vestibule door, and her heart stood still. She paused for a moment, staring at the priest's majestic height and bearing, the strength of the powerful shoulders, the tilt of the head; and knew before he turned to face her that the fates had brought her beloved barbarian back into her life.

She moved toward him as if in a dream, and a hundred memories returned, of the love they had shared, of the delight of being one with him, of creeping into the shelter of his arms and knowing that he would never hurt her, would protect and honor her.

When she reached his side and looked up into the brilliance of his eyes, it seemed that for an instant the earth stood still and all the stars in the heavens waited.

Then he spoke, and there was such sadness in his voice that a chill gripped her. "I cannot speak with you here, Phin. Will you walk outside with me in the fresh air?"

Wordlessly she walked through the front door he held open for her and out into a cold dawn. "So you became a priest," she said, unable to think of anything less obvious to say.

"I was a Jesuit before I knew you. I was sent to China to convert the people to the true faith."

"But—"

"Walk," he said harshly. "We are still too close to that evil place."

She hurried along at his side as he set a fast pace in the direction of the wharf. "But you told me you were not free to be with me because you were married—"

"I am married to the church."

"But—"

"I ask your forgiveness for not telling you the truth. I was a fallen priest, who broke my vows and sinned most abominably."

"Because you lay with me?" she asked miserably.

"My fall from grace took place before I met you. You were the only good thing that happened to me in that dark period of my life, Phin, please believe that. I think had I not known you, your bravery and stoic acceptance of life's cruelest blows, your sheer resilience to overcome adversity, I might have continued on my way to hell and damnation. But after you left, I realized that perhaps God would forgive a sinner who truly repented—that there would be redemption for me after all, if I returned to the true faith and rejoined the Jesuits."

They reached the wharf and stood looking out over the gray water of the bay. A chill breeze swept in from the sea, and the timbers of anchored ships creaked and groaned like arthritic elders. Phin shivered in her satin jacket and longed to press herself close to Brent's warmth, but he stood away from her, aloof and disapproving.

She asked softly, "If it was not I who caused your fall from grace, then what was it?"

The memory of suffering creased his face and lingered in his eyes for a moment. "Another Jesuit and myself were captured by river bandits and subjected to torture. My friend died, a true martyr, as I should have died."

"No!" Phin exclaimed.

"Better a martyr's death than my betrayal of my faith, of all I believed in and had vowed to protect. I wanted to live so badly that I renounced my God, cursed and reviled my faith, and swore allegiance to the heathen general who defeated the bandits and who gave me the choice of death or serving him.''

''But that was a sensible choice,'' Phin said, bewildered by his torment. ''Better to live than to die. Now you are a priest again, so the decision was a good one.''

''No, Phin, I committed mortal sins, for which I will do penance the rest of my life. Let us say no more, for it is imperative that we speak of you. You must leave that evil house immediately.''

For an instant Phin felt euphoria, coupled with an utter willingness to forgo all thoughts of revenge for her father's death, all ties to Emily, indeed to anyone else; even though, deep down, she realized the hope that had sprung within her was a vain one. ''You wish me to be your woman again?''

He took a step backward, away from her, and his expression closed as though he had mentally slammed a door in her face. He said, ''I am a priest. I have taken a vow of chastity. There will never be a woman in my life, not in the way you mean, ever again. This will never change, Phin.''

She felt her shame stain her cheeks. ''Then what do you care what I do?''

''I do care. Phin, listen to me, what you do in that wicked place is the worst sin a woman can commit.''

''Women do not sin alone, Brent. What about the men?''

''I am no longer Brent, I am Father Juan, and the men who use you are just as guilty. Phin, the Bible tells us that every other sin committed by man is done outside his own body, but this offense is against his own body.''

''You did not think so in China when we were together.''

''To my eternal shame, I knew we sinned. I shall spend the rest of my life attempting to atone. You must give up the life you are leading. What you are doing is the ultimate in human degradation and delusion. The joining of a man and a woman is more than a mere physical act. It is kindness, courtesy, gentleness, selflessness, and a commitment to each other to care, to share, to know that person in the deepest way possible and to give oneself wholly, completely. Phin,

you *must* give up your wicked ways or face eternal
damnation. It isn't too late to save your soul.''

"And what do you propose I do instead? Starve to
death?''

"God will provide.''

"I do not believe in your God, Brent.''

"Let me teach you about Him. I am teaching some
children at a place about two hours' ride south of the city—we
call it the *casa de niños*. You can attend the classes—you
can stay there if you wish and work with the children. The
greatest joy on earth is in serving others.''

Phin stared at him, feeling humiliated beyond endurance,
wanting to lash out at him and make him suffer as she was
suffering. She said, "Ah, but you see, *Father Juan*, I am
serving others—that is what I do at the Lantern House.''

She turned and ran blindly, away from him, away from
any hope of happiness, back to the house that was just as
evil as he believed it to be, back to plans to destroy the
woman who had killed her father.

Chapter 32

∙∙

EMILY WATCHED BRIONY pour tea from a silver pot into Wedgwood bone china cups decorated with English landscapes. The damask teacloth was crisply starched, the hotel's trademark roses in a silver rosebowl were pink and fragrant, tiny triangular cucumber sandwiches looked fresh and appealing, the tiered trays of petits fours and pastries mouth-wateringly tempting.

A circle of well-dressed women hung onto Briony's every word, studied her every gesture. But Emily's foot had fallen asleep and, oh, how she longed to go home to Edward!

He had returned from the *casa de niños*, as he called the house where his Jesuit friend cared for the children, exhausted but elated by the success of his experiment with the ether. Emily thought that, regardless of the method, the poor little Mexican boy had still lost his leg, but did not say so. Edward promptly retired to his room to sleep and was still there when Briony sent her carriage to pick up Emily for afternoon tea at the Rosebriar.

Wondering how soon she could politely excuse herself and return home, Emily was only vaguely aware of the conversation around her until Briony said, "There is something of importance I want to discuss with you ladies. I suppose you've all overheard the men talking about forming a vigilance committee?"

Annabelle Clark said, "And about time, too. We've got the scum of the earth pouring into San Francisco and virtually no law and order. Why, I heard of a lady who was accosted in broad daylight on her way to the emporium. . . ."

There was a collective murmur of outrage and excitement as everyone pressed for the identity of the unfortunate woman and details of her ordeal.

Briony put down her teapot and held up her hand for silence. "Please! Let's not show a prurient interest in such matters. Personally, I thoroughly disapprove of vigilantes—I saw enough of their handiwork in Texas to last a lifetime. Surely here in San Francisco we have the opportunity to create a more orderly society. We don't need to have our laws enforced by thugs who are little better than the felons they punish."

The other women fell silent, waiting for a cue as to the proper attitude to take. Emily regarded them with carefully concealed amusement. What sheep they were! So eager to be part of Briony's elite circle that they were even willing to let her form their opinions for them. Only Annabelle seemed to have the gumption to argue with Briony. She said, "All well and good, Briony, but we don't have a police force. Landsakes, we don't even have any formal municipal government."

"Don't you think it's time we did? You ladies must use your influence with your husbands to give up the idea of a vigilance committee and set up democratic courts, with judges and juries to deal with offenders."

"And in the meantime what do we do about the outlaws?" Annabelle asked.

Ignoring her, Briony continued, "There's to be a meeting tonight to discuss the formation of the vigilance committee. I want you all to go home and beg—no, strongly urge your husbands to do everything in their power to prevent what surely will be anarchy if such a committee is formed. At the same time they must set up an orderly city government and police force. Our leading citizens must become aware of their civic duties."

"There was another fire last night," one of the women put in. "A warehouse burned to the ground before the volunteers arrived. My husband said they were fighting three other blazes around town at the time. I'd say we need a proper fire brigade as much as a police force."

Emily sat very still, a memory returning. There had been an apartment house fire in New York, only two blocks from where they lived, and the smoke had enveloped the entire neighborhood in a murky pall. It was the only time she had ever seen Kane show fear. He had wanted to flee from the house and became angry and panic-stricken when Phin and Emily assured him they were in no danger and refused to go. Afterward, when the fire was out, he said, "What a coward you must think I am." Phin had made, for her, a curiously compassionate gesture. She had gently stroked his scarred cheek and murmured, "You would be a fool not to fear fire, you who know it more intimately than most."

Now Emily wondered how Kane was coping with the fires that frequently plagued San Francisco, and she realized with a stab of guilt that she had not even seen Kane since they arrived. Somehow the days slipped away, her hours occupied by shopping for furniture, running the household, or receiving the constant flow of visitors who wished to welcome Briony's sister-in-law to San Francisco. Whenever Emily had a free hour, Briony would either drag her off to call upon friends and neighbors, or to one of her afternoon teas.

An unusual heat wave had the city in its grip, and the ladies fluttered fans, which did little to stir the warm still air. Emily waited for a break in the conversation and then asked, "Briony, would you excuse me? Edward is home today, and I'd like to be there when he wakes up."

"Gracious! Why didn't you tell me he was ill in bed?"

"Oh, he isn't ill. It's just that he was up all night—" Emily broke off, appalled at her blunder. Edward had specifically asked her not to tell anyone he was caring for the sick children, fearing if Briony's friends knew of his medical knowledge, he might be called upon to treat their vapors and sick headaches. "I mean, he was working—" She floundered, aware of the curious stares of the circle of women, especially Briony.

"Oh, yes," Briony said smoothly, "I'd forgotten that my brother has been concerned about some of his investments. He's such a worrier, isn't he, Emily? But you really shouldn't allow him to sit up all night going over the books. If you ladies will excuse us for a moment, I'll see Emily out. Come along, Emily, I'll have my coachman take you home.''

Briony maintained her unconcerned manner until the two women were in the cloakroom, then Briony's deep blue eyes flashed her displeasure. ''Do watch your tongue, Emily. There's no need for everybody in town to know of your husband's nocturnal excursions.''

''You knew?'' Emily whispered, mortified.

''Josefa talked to Topaz. I squelched the gossip immediately, of course, and discounted it completely. Until now. Is there something I should know?''

Since she couldn't betray Edward's confidence, all Emily could say was ''I'm sorry.''

''Don't be sorry. Find a way to keep him at home,'' Briony said shortly. It was evident from her tone that she suspected Emily of failing in her wifely duties, and Emily had no defense to offer, since it was true.

Briony went on, ''Apart from the gossip, it is extremely dangerous for Edward to be out alone at night. Why do you think the men want a vigilance committee? The streets after dark harbor criminals of the worst kind. There is a part of town south of Telegraph Hill called Sydney Town—home of the notorious Sydney Ducks, who are all escaped convicts from the Australian penal colony, and then there is Chinatown and the waterfront and . . . Please at least assure me that my brother doesn't travel through the city's cesspits.''

''Edward doesn't stay in town, he goes to—oh, dear, I really shouldn't tell you. But, Briony, please believe me that what Edward has been doing is a noble endeavor. He helps a friend at a place well away from town, out in the countryside.''

''For heaven's sake, that's just as dangerous! Maybe even more so. Haven't you heard of the outlaw Joaquin Murrieta and his band of cutthroats? They have terrorized the countryside from here to the border and are as elusive as shadows. Max thinks there must be more than one *bandido* using the name Murrieta, as he couldn't possibly strike in so many different places almost simultaneously."

"Perhaps Edward himself will explain to you where he goes—I cannot betray his confidence. But be assured he is quite safe."

"No one is ever *quite* safe, Emily," Briony chided.

After Emily departed, Briony returned to the mezzanine but cut short her afternoon tea ritual and made her way to Max's office.

He was waiting for her and gave her an appreciative glance as she swept into the room in her afternoon gown of deep burgundy with a froth of ecru lace at the throat, the jabot pinned with a cameo brooch. "You look particularly stunning today, Lady Briony."

She stopped dead in her tracks. "*What* did you call me?"

He grinned. "I guess it was a slip of the tongue. I always think of you as Lady Briony, rather than Mrs. Forest."

"I would be called Lady Forest—not Lady Briony."

"Since you don't possess the title, it doesn't make much difference, does it? But you sure can act the part with your teatime cronies. Have you sent them all home to nag their husbands to give up on the idea of a vigilance committee?"

"You will be making a big mistake if you have anything to do with such a scheme, Max. But you know my feelings on the subject. Did you take care of that other matter for me?"

His grin widened. "You are now the proud owner of the sloop *Sea Dancer* and her entire cargo. Though what you intend to do with either is a mystery to me, since she's been abandoned by her crew, who took off for the goldfields. But even if you had a crew, the *Dancer* probably isn't seaworthy anyway, and she's anchored amidst other abandoned ships, with no way to unload her."

"I shall simply wait until the outward spreading shoreline covers the tidal flats and the ship is beached. In a town busy dumping sand, dirt, and unsalable goods into the bay, this will not take long. The ship will then become my store."

He shook his head disbelievingly, but there was admiration in his eyes. She was right about the spreading shoreline. In no time at all her ship would join up with the jerrybuilt banks and brokerage houses, interspersed with other beached hulks, that now made up Montgomery Street.

"Furthermore," Briony said triumphantly, "the cargo consists almost entirely of tools—hammers, saws, and so on—and case after case of *nails*."

Max now realized why she'd been so eager to buy a ship that wasn't seaworthy and which she had little hope of unloading in its present anchorage. San Francisco had grown from a sleepy village of a couple of hundred people to a city of twenty-five thousand and twice that number disembarked at the port en route to the goldfields. The city was growing by at least thirty houses a day, not to mention the construction of stores and warehouses and hotels, all infused by a steady stream of gold from the Sierra mines.

"Shall I remind you of the mad rush to build houses?" Briony asked.

"Strange how you see the need for nails, but not the need for a vigilance committee. The immigrants need houses, but they also need protection. Are you aware that there are at least two murders a day, and an arson-started fire, and more lesser crimes than anyone can count?"

"Yes, I am. It's time we had a police force and a fire brigade, and the place to start is with a city council. Max, I think you should be our first lord mayor."

He threw back his head and roared with laughter. "First of all, we don't have *lord* mayors in this country, and secondly I can't stand to be in the same room with politicians."

"I hate it when you laugh at me," Briony said crossly. "You know what I meant. I was going to suggest you help me celebrate my acquisition of the *Sea Dancer* by coming to the theater with me—there's a new play opening. But, of course, I'd forgotten you were going to organize your band of thugs tonight."

"I'd be happy to go to the theater with you."

Relief washed over her. "You're not going to get involved with the vigilance committee?"

"No, I'm not. But that isn't to say I don't understand the motives of the men who are, and my decision has nothing to do with your feelings on the subject, so don't congratulate yourself on that score."

Briony regarded him with a smug smile. "How you do like to pretend I have no influence on you!"

"Oh, I've never believed that, Bri," he responded easily. "By the way, there's a new restaurant opening tonight, too, out near Telegraph Hill. A small place and not in the best location, but the owner is a friend of mine. After the show maybe we could stop by for a late supper."

Pleased that she could be sure he wouldn't go near the vigilance meeting, and that she now owned the *Sea Dancer*, Briony's good humor knew no bounds. "I shall wear my new gown and bonnet, and you will wear my birthday gift to you, and we will dazzle everyone at your friend's café."

He gave her a mock scowl. "And when *is* my birthday this year?" It had become a standing joke between them that since Max refused to tell her either how old he was or when he was born, she selected one day each year and gave him a birthday gift.

"Today," Briony said. "You'll find your present in your room." She fled before he could question her further. She looked forward to seeing him in the embroidered velvet waistcoat and fine linen shirt she had bought for him. Such gifts were, of course, completely inappropriate for a woman to give to a man not her husband. But then, she and Max had never observed propriety.

Edward was still sleeping when Emily arrived home. She felt let down, as though she had been anticipating some momentous event that had been canceled. How silly you are, she told herself. He'll be down for dinner, and you'll see him then.

Josefa was on her way out and explained in her mixture of Spanish and English that she needed to buy coffee and would return shortly.

Emily went upstairs with the idea of taking a nap so she would be refreshed when Edward awoke, but after removing her gown, petticoats, and stays, the prospect of falling asleep seemed remote. She pulled on her dressing gown, then discarded it and fished in her wardrobe for the embroidered silk wrap Phin had given her. Phin had instructed her to wear it—and nothing else—should her husband ever have difficulties performing his marital obligations. At the time Edward had been far away in the army, and Emily had no idea the time would ever come when she would be scheming to have him consummate their marriage. She had donned the wrap several times since arriving in San Francisco, but it surely did little good when her husband never came into her room to see her in it. Still, it made her feel womanly and more than a little wicked.

For a moment she fingered the beautifully embroidered peacock on the back of the wrap, then pressed the tasseled sash to her cheek. How soft it was—how luxurious! She removed her shift and pantalets before slipping her arms into the wide loose sleeves. The delicate silk caressed her skin like a lover's breath.

Where had that simile come from? She felt herself blush. She sat at her dressing table and took down her hair, then rose and prowled restlessly about the room. She paused beside her tallboy and opened her jewel box. Edward had sent her several brooches and necklaces from Mexico made of silver and turquoise and had presented her with a string of pearls and a gold pendant upon her arrival. Phin had given her a set of jeweled combs, and Briony a pair of gold earrings, so her jewel box was filling up. But her searching fingers went straight to the brooch Edward had given her in England so long ago. She picked it up and held it for a moment before replacing it on the bed of velvet.

Not realizing she had left the jewel box precariously balanced, as she turned away she dislodged it. The carved wooden box and contents crashed to the polished wood floor. She bit back an exclamation and glanced in the direction of Edward's room, wondering if she had awakened him, then bent to pick up the fallen jewelry.

Her unpinned hair fell forward, obscuring her view. She did not hear the adjoining door open.

Straightening up, she caught her breath as Edward, wearing only his nightshirt, appeared on her threshold. "Are you all right? I heard a crash and was afraid you'd fainted. . . ."

He broke off as his gaze dropped to the silk wrap. Although Emily herself didn't look down to check, she was sure it must be gaping a little, thus revealing her nakedness.

Her cheeks flaming, she murmured, "My jewel box—I dropped it. Did you sleep well?"

He didn't speak, but the expression on his face was one of raw hunger. He moved toward her across the expanse of polished floor, and it seemed to Emily that he would never reach her side. When he did he wordlessly took her into his arms and kissed her. She made a small sound, deep in her throat, and flung her arms around his neck and returned the pressure of his mouth with her own yearning lips.

For a long minute they stood wrapped in each other's arms, their mouths connected and hearts beating in unison, then somehow the silk wrap was on the floor and Edward was slipping his hand under her knees, swinging her up into his arms to carry her to the bed. He paused only long enough to roughly pull off his own nightshirt, then lay beside her and took her in his arms.

His touch was gentle but firm, and where his fingers pressed against pliant yielding flesh, it seemed to Emily that her skin became incandescent as a star glittering in the endless universe, and the feeling of unbearable tension generated by the pressure of his hands matched that sense of eternity.

"Emily, my darling wife," he murmured against her mouth, and they were the last coherent words either of them uttered.

Briony did not hide her dismay when Max reached up to lift her over the muddy chasm between carriage and planked sidewalk in front of his friend's restaurant. The small storefront was crowded with tall lean men still wearing their Texas-style hats, a practice Briony found ill-mannered in the extreme. No gentleman ever kept his hat on indoors. Not only that, but they were loudly toasting one another with large glasses of whiskey and were already becoming quite boisterous, and, except for one flashily dressed señorita, Briony saw there were no other women.

She froze, her expression clearly disapproving.

Max said, "Oh, come on, it won't hurt you to go slumming for a little while. We won't stay long. I suffered for two boring hours through your totally incomprehensible play, didn't I? The least you can do is bring a little class to the clientele of my friend's establishment."

"I'm not going in there, Max. Look at those oafs— they're already drunk."

"That's just high spirits, Bri."

"We came to an agreement long ago that there were certain areas of our lives into which we would not force each other, Max. I don't expect you to sit in on my afternoon teas, and I am not about to attend one of your drunken brawls. No doubt soon this entire group will repair to the nearest bawdy house."

Max's expression suddenly became serious. "Five minutes, Bri. Just come in for five minutes. I'm going to try to talk this particular group out of riding over to the vigilance committee meeting. These boys are all former Texas Rangers." He paused, then added with a hint of a grin, "And if I'm not successful in persuading them that San Francisco doesn't need vigilantes riding the streets, then I thought maybe you could say a few words. God knows, when you open that pretty little mouth of yours, everybody listens."

Briony hesitated for a moment, then sighed. "Very well. Five minutes."

"Good." He clasped her about the waist and swung her from the carriage.

The noisy clamor inside the restaurant stopped the instant Max opened the door and Briony walked inside. Two men leapt to their feet to pull out a chair for her, another slapped Max on the shoulder, and a third pumped his hand. "Max, you old reprobate, good to see you."

A small swarthy man, wiry and sinuous as a whip, wearing a flour-dusted apron, emerged from the kitchen. He pounced upon Max, hugging him around the waist since Max's height precluded reaching higher. "Maximillian, *mon ami*! 'Ow kind of you to come!" He turned to Briony and exclaimed, "And zis is your lady! Ah, *sacré coeur*, she is even more beautiful zan you say!"

Briony's hand was seized and raised to his lips as Max said, "May I present Louis-Philippe Ramadier?"

They were given wine and delicious morsels to nibble while Louis-Philippe returned to the kitchen to put the finishing touches to the crepes he insisted upon serving to them. He had been a chef in Paris, Max explained to Briony, and had fled to Canada after an unfortunate incident with the wife of a government official, left Quebec under similar circumstances and drifted south to the Russian colony at Fort Ross.

"That little pixie of a man?" Briony whispered. "He doesn't look the part of a great lover."

Max grinned. "Perhaps it's his food. I met him up at the Russian colony, where he was cooking for a camp of trappers. I'd never eaten such food in my entire life, not even in France. I suggested he was wasting his talents on the Russians, and when he was ready to leave to let me know. He never made it to Texas, but when we arrived in San Francisco, I began a campaign to try to get him to come to the Rosebriar. He felt there would be too much temptation in a hotel—too many pretty women married to less than understanding men. So I offered to set him up in his own business. He turned me down. Now he's somehow raised enough cash to open this café."

Louis-Philippe stood by proudly while they tasted his crepes. Briony announced she was ready to swoon with ecstasy—the delicate crepes and subtle sauce quite literally melted in her mouth. Not even the noisy atmosphere of the small café or the rough-and-ready customers could diminish her enjoyment.

As their host went to greet a new arrival, Max leaned closer and said, "If we could get Louis-Philippe as a chef, and Kane to play his violin . . . can you imagine the business we'd do?"

"Kane? How could he possibly play in public?"

"He's playing at the Lantern House. Hadn't you heard?"

"I don't keep up with the happenings at bawdy houses," Briony said coldly. "But evidently you do."

Ignoring the taunt, Max went on, "He plays inside a wicker pagoda. But it isn't entirely satisfactory; it muffles some of the music. If we could get him to play in our restaurant, I thought of suggesting he wear a hood over his head to conceal his scars. It would also make him seem sinister and mysterious, therefore even more appealing to the ladies."

"What makes you think ladies like sinister or mysterious men?"

"Don't they? Aren't I sinister and mysterious? No one knows where I came from, or much about my past, but I'm constantly under siege by eager would-be brides."

"It's your money they're after," Briony answered matter-of-factly.

He laughed again. "You're the only woman I've ever known who is so brutally honest. Didn't anyone ever teach you the gentle art of flirtation? Of flattering a man?"

Before she could comment, one of the Texans called to Max, "We're riding over to the meeting now, Max. You coming along?"

Max jumped to his feet instantly. "Wait! Everybody—listen to me. I know you're sick and tired of murder and arson and thievery on our streets, not to mention the outlaws riding the length of California, but a vigilance committee isn't the answer—"

The rest of what he said was lost in an angry clamor.

Briony listened for a minute, then she, too, rose to her feet and held up her hand for silence.

She was ignored.

Max attempted to shout over the babble of protests and accusations that he was selling out to the lawless element, but it was clear that these former Texas Rangers were itching to clean up the streets, and the organizers of the committee had convinced them to become vigilantes.

Suddenly a gunshot exploded, stifling the angry voices.

Louis-Philippe stood on a chair, a smoking pistol in his hand. "*Mon Dieu!* Where are your manners, you misbegotten swine? A lady wishes to address you. You shut up your mouths, or you nevair eat at Louis-Philippe's again."

The threat had the desired effect, and the sudden silence seemed deafening.

Briony cleared her throat. "We *do* need law and order," she said. "And we definitely need men of your caliber to enforce the law."

There was a murmur of approval. Max grinned. Trust Lady Briony to know exactly the right way to capture their attention. When she wanted something, she sure knew how to get it.

"But San Francisco is going to become a city, and a city needs a proper police force and judicial system," she went on. "If you align yourselves with the vigilance committee now, you will never become real law officers because you will be tarred with the same brush as the criminals."

The men still looked doubtful, but they listened quietly as she went on to outline briefly the steps that could be taken to achieve their goal by legal means. Having been married to a lawyer with political aspirations, she spoke with confidence on the subject, and the men recognized the voice of authority, despite the fact that it came from a woman.

On the sidelines Max Seadon watched her with pride and knew his friends, at least, would not be on the vigilance committee.

"Let's go into your drawing room and have a nightcap," Max suggested when they returned to the Rosebriar.

Still buoyed from the evening and wide awake, Briony nodded and led the way to her suite of rooms on the second floor. Her bedroom, dressing room, drawing room, and office were situated at the end of the landing, and to prevent guests from stumbling into her private suite by mistake, Briony had installed stout double doors across the corridor, making it appear to end in a linen closet.

In her drawing room she poured a brandy for Max and a glass of sherry for herself and took them to the window alcove, where he waited until she was seated before taking a chair opposite to her.

He drained his brandy and stared at her. "We're quite a persuasive combination, aren't we? I figure we could have led those Texans out of there tonight and taken the city if we'd wanted to."

Briony smiled. "When we work together, we do seem to be able to move mountains."

"I wanted to talk to you about that." His expression changed and became unreadable. She had come to recognize that particular look. It was the one he wore when he played an American card game he called poker. "About how well we work together. I'd like it to continue."

She looked at him in surprise. "Why would it not? I have no plans to end our association if you don't. Oh, Max, surely my buying the *Sea Dancer* didn't bring this on? I just wanted to have an investment of my own. You've been generous and paid me a handsome salary and I've a bit put away in the bank, but I do have to think about my old age. I don't like relying wholly on a salary, so I wanted a business of my own."

"And when you've made a success of your ship-cum-emporium, what then? A small hotel maybe? Pretty soon you won't need my capital—you'll be investing your own. You're a mighty independent and ambitious woman, Bri. I've never met one quite as determined as you. You could have married any one of the richest men in town, but you're hell-bent on being independent, aren't you? You never talk about your late husband, but I reckon he must have had a lot to do with how gun-shy you are about marriage."

Briony sipped her sherry. "Where exactly is this conversation leading, Max?"

"Well, I've observed you for over three years now, sure that the next man who came along would be able to breach that barricade you keep around yourself. It hasn't happened, and I'm beginning to think maybe it never will. So maybe the time's come for me to step in and make an honest woman of you."

She almost dropped her glass. "What?"

"I told you I wasn't the marrying kind, I know, but well, we're a helluva partnership, and you do tend to curb my more primitive instincts and keep me on the straight and narrow. You must admit we make a handsome couple. You wouldn't have to scramble around buying derelict hulks to put away money for your old age if you married me. I'd settle half of everything I own on you, including the Rosebriar. So how about it? Will you change your name to Mrs. Max Seadon?"

Chapter 33

• •

"YOU'RE ASKING ME to *marry* you?" Briony repeated incredulously.

"That's right." Max still wore that impersonal expression, as though he were suggesting nothing more than a business arrangement.

Which, of course, he was, Briony thought. She felt a wave of conflicting emotions, the natural satisfaction of taming a previously untamable man, along with apprehension about his reaction when she refused him, as indeed she must.

During the time she'd known Max, their connection to each other had run the gamut from close personal friendship through easygoing camaraderie and business partnership to an adversarial relationship that occasionally came close to enmity. She had long ago learned to avoid being alone with him in any surroundings even remotely romantic, not for any fear that he might act inappropriately, but simply because she found him too attractive and feared where her own behavior might lead. There had been a certain type of male-female tension between them from the first, and Briony, well tuned to her own womanly desires, had missed the intimacy of marriage. Rupert had been a cad and a swine, but he had also been a perfect lover. She suspected that Max would be, too, and therein lay the problem. She knew intuitively any affair with him would be far too intense and would surely destroy their business relationship. The last thing on earth she had expected was that he would ever want to marry her. Indeed, hadn't he warned her at the very beginning never to set her cap for him?

Max gave her an enigmatic smile. "I wish you could see the conflicting emotions racing across that beautiful face of yours. You're as transparent as glass, Bri. You don't know whether to be flattered or outraged. But think about it, we do get along well together, we respect each other, and . . . forgive my bluntness, but a lot of tension between us would be dissipated if we were also sleeping together. Since I've come to realize you aren't a woman who would take a lover—I know many men have tried to convince you otherwise—I figure the only solution is to marry you."

The image of Rupert's face flashed into Briony's mind. Rupert, who had lied and cheated and tried to destroy her. Any warm feelings she had toward Max were obliterated by thoughts of her husband's perfidy, and the irrevocable fact that she was not free to marry anyone, since she was still married to Rupert.

"Max, I do have the greatest respect for you, and I value your friendship. I want to continue working for you. But I can't marry you, or anyone else for that matter."

Max was suddenly alert. "*Can't?* Or won't?"

She started to turn away, but he caught her wrist and stopped her. "You feel more than friendship for me, Bri, you know you do. Just as I feel more than lust for you."

"Lust, Max?" She attempted a light tone. "How romantic you are."

"Of course I want you. Desperately enough to end lifelong bachelorhood. What did you think this was all about?"

He had pulled her close and, before she realized what he was going to do, kissed her.

At the first touch of his lips Briony felt her breath stop, somewhere between her heart and her throat. Every instinct was screaming for her to pull away, to run, to hide, before it was too late. But his mouth was persuasive, insistent, and would not be deterred. She could feel her resolve melting away as she swayed against the lean length of his body, crushed in an embrace that left her lightheaded, her knees buckling. Not even Rupert at his most ardent had kissed her with such passion. It was a kiss that was almost an act of love in itself.

When, an eternity later, his mouth released hers, she clung to him until the world stopped spinning. She was too breathless to speak.

He regarded her with a wicked gleam in his eye. "As man and wife, we could have even more fun. I'm no callow boy, Bri, I'm a man who's always been fond of the ladies, and you know what they say about practice making perfect. Come on, say yes and I'll go find a preacher right now. We've both waited long enough."

Oh, how she longed to say yes! It took every ounce of resolve she possessed to disentangle his arms. "Max, I'm sorry. I won't marry you, now or ever."

Phin collected the ivory fortune-telling disks and replaced them in an enameled box. She looked up at Tonia Bardine, who waited expectantly. Phin closed her eyes in contemplation, deliberately drawing out the suspense.

The muted sounds of the Lantern House—laughter, conversations, creakings, and rattlings, all overlaid by the sweet clear notes of Kane's violin—drifted into Tonia's private office. Phin was on her knees on the floor, where earlier she had spread the ivory disks.

Tonia perched on the edge of a low sofa, wearing her customary stark black gown. She reminded Phin of a bat, and the image was disturbing, because in China the bat was symbolic of long life. Did she wear black in order to disappear into the night? Her only jewelry was a beautiful hair ornament that she often wore, a gem-encrusted gold filigree bird. Cervantes, like his mistress, was also clad in black. He had taken his usual position near the door.

"What did you see?" Tonia hissed.

Phin opened her eyes but affected a distant, trancelike tone. "I will burn the joss sticks to your Tai Kung—that is, your founding ancestor. You need much guidance and protection."

"What did you see in my fortune? I swear if you don't tell me this minute, I'll have Cervantes beat you."

"Beating me would serve little purpose. The demons of your past are rising up to haunt you. Someone who has knowledge that could destroy you is already seeking you out, is in fact close by and poised ready to strike. The key lies in exorcising those old demons."

Tonia's expression betrayed nothing, but her hand drifted to her side, pressing between the folds of her dress and seeking the flesh beneath.

The gesture was not lost on Phin, who quickly used it to her advantage. "The one who seeks you is already causing internal turmoil, which will become worse. A pain in the belly that begins as a niggling ache . . ." Phin allowed the seed to grow in Tonia's own imagination.

"How can I find this person who is after me?" Tonia asked, pressing her side even harder.

"That I do not yet know. But I saw in your cards that all of your troubles stem from a man who was once close to you. This man lived in China, did he not? There are ancient Chinese curses . . ." Again Phin's voice faded to a whisper, and she left the thought unfinished.

Tonia had grown pale. She darted a glance in Cervantes's direction, and for a moment Phin wondered if she'd gone too far and Tonia might direct the sinister former bandit to kill her. But she said, "I did once know a man who lived in China. But he is dead. He cannot have followed me here. There must be something else to indicate the identity of my enemy."

"Tell me about the man who lived in China. Where and when did he die?" Phin's voice was very soft.

"Why do you ask that?" Tonia said sharply.

"Your fortune seems to indicate that the person who pursues you is connected to him."

"That's impossible. His only relative is also dead."

Phin waited, her expression enigmatic, knowing that Tonia would find her silence unbearable and break it by answering the question. At length she did so. "He was killed by bandits."

"Where?"

"In Mexico."

"You were with him?"

Tonia hesitated. "No." She glanced at the ivory disks and changed her mind, evidently believing her future would not be revealed if she lied. "Yes. I was there. I suffered horribly at the hands of the bandits."

"But you survived."

"I was rescued by American soldiers."

"The bandits were caught—punished?"

"No."

Phin hesitated, then handed the enameled box to Tonia. "Reach into the box and take out seven disks without looking at them, then spread them before me. Let us try again."

Tonia had told her nothing she did not already know. She needed to persuade her to reveal more about Fletcher's death. At the very least perhaps she could learn the location of his grave so that she and Emily could pay their last respects.

As Tonia bent to place the seven disks on the floor, the filigree hair ornament she wore slipped from her head. Phin picked it up and her pulse suddenly quickened. The gold filigree bird was a phoenix, the gems polished but uncut. Phin had seen pictures of centuries-ago Chinese empresses wearing such pieces.

Phin held the ornament on the palm of her hand and looked up at Tonia. "This came from ancient Cathay—the man who was killed must have given it to you. I am surprised the bandits let you keep it—"

Tonia snatched it from her hand and leapt to her feet. "This is all nonsense. I don't know why I'm listening to you. Go—get out."

Phin hastily collected her disks and stood up. As Cervantes opened the door for her, his black-eyed stare flashed her a warning that she was playing a dangerous game.

Dawn was breaking and most of the Lantern House patrons had departed as Phin made her way up to her room. The mama-san watched her from the lobby as she climbed the stairs, and Phin knew the tiny woman resented her private audiences with Tonia but dare not question her about them.

Opening the door to her room, Phin started. Kane was seated at her dressing table, scribbling notes onto a sheet of music.

"You do not have my permission to walk in here uninvited," Phin said coldly. "You're supposed to make an appointment."

"You've been avoiding me for days. I wanted to talk to you."

"I don't feel like talking."

"What did you think of the piece I played last night? It was my own composition. I wish I hadn't played it. Or written it. How dreadful it was."

"Why do you have such contempt for your talent?"

"Perhaps the contempt I feel is for myself."

"Then take your contempt and leave me alone. I have no patience for it. Nor for your self-pity. You may have scars from your burns, but your blood is pure. Unlike mine. Don't you think I could feel sorry for myself if I chose? I must deal with the fact that I do not belong—to my mother's race, or my father's race and therefore am accepted by neither."

"We are the eternal outsiders, you and I, are we not? Destined to forever drift around the perimeter, just out of reach."

"Out of reach of what?" she asked indifferently.

"Life, I suppose."

"You're not making any sense, Kane. You aren't smoking opium again, are you?"

"No." He frowned at the sheet of music in front of him, then scratched out several notes and moved them up the scale. "Would Emily meet us somewhere, do you think?"

"No. We don't belong in her life now."

"*That* was what I was trying to tell you."

"Then why did you ask?" She walked over to the window. "I wish it would rain. I'm tired of the endless sunshine."

"Pretend the morning mist is rain. Fog and rain are first

cousins. You haven't told me about the priest. Why did he come here looking for you?"

"I knew him in China."

"My God, you loved a *priest*?"

"I said I knew him."

"I know what you *said*. Ah, Phin, what a pair we are."

"A pair, Kane? Hardly that."

"Tell me, when you service one of the customers, do you close your eyes and imagine you are in the arms of your priest?"

"As you imagined I was Emily, you mean?"

He studied his music morosely and didn't answer.

She moved closer and looked at his work. He had made many changes in the original composition, apparently not satisfied with earlier drafts; yet she had never heard him play anything that was less than haunting.

"Why do you waste your music in a place like this, Kane?"

"My music makes my surroundings disappear. I discovered that phenomenon when I lived in my father's cellar. By comparison, the Lantern House is a palace."

"Leave now, Kane, I'm tired. I must sleep."

As he departed, he waved the sheet music in farewell. "Perhaps this time I'll get it right."

Emily sat beside Edward as he guided the pony trap along a narrow trail slicing through the coastal hills toward the *casa de niños*. The morning fog had dissipated, and the sun shone from clear blue skies, matching her joyous mood.

She was so happy. Happy to be Edward's wife, happy he was taking her to meet his friend Father Juan and the children. The shadow of her father's death hovered in the recesses of her mind, but the wonder of being Edward's wife was so great that even her sadness over losing her father could not diminish her joy.

At the same time Emily felt strangely shy with Edward, and as he turned to smile at her, she felt her skin tingle and her cheeks grow warm at the memory of the intimacies they had shared. As if sensing her thoughts, Edward leaned over and kissed her cheek tenderly.

"Not much farther now, my dearest. Do you see those pines all twisted and gnarled by the wind along that ridge ahead? The *casa* is just beyond them; we'll see it in a moment. No doubt Brent and the children will be watching our approach."

"Shall we mention Phin to him? Is it all right to talk about her?"

Edward considered for a moment. "If he brings up the subject, I suppose we should answer honestly. But let's not mention her otherwise. The less we say about anyone's past, the better. Not that he would divulge our secrets to anyone, but it's just a good idea to be forever on our guard."

Small brown children who were working in a vegetable patch dropped their makeshift tools and came running to meet the trap, and long before they reached the *casa* a very tall, broad-shouldered priest wearing a black robe appeared. He was a giant of a man, surely at least six and a half feet tall, with a thick mane of black hair and, Emily saw as they drew near, remarkable silvery-blue eyes that flashed like sabers. Emily's first reaction was that he looked more like a pirate than a priest, but then she saw that his face was kindly, if somewhat stern. His features were striking, almost handsome, she decided.

"Señor Eduardo!" the children chorused, then spoke excitedly in Spanish.

Father Juan, or Brent, as Edward called him, held up his hand. "In English, please. The señora does not speak your language, and it is bad manners to exclude her from our conversation."

One frail little girl with enormous velvet brown eyes said shyly, "Welcome, señora, to our . . . house," she finished triumphantly.

"Well done, Felicia." Brent patted her head. He offered his hand to help Emily from the trap and added, "I am happy you came, Mrs. Dale. I have looked forward to meeting you."

"And I you," Emily murmured, awed by the strength of his grip.

"Go back to your chores, children," he instructed, and as they scampered away he said to Emily, "I am teaching them English. Some are doing better than others. But they must all learn the language of the conquerors if they are to survive. Come, let me take you to meet our miracle child."

Edward rolled his eyes at his wife as he jumped down beside her. Emily was already aware that Brent gave most of the credit for saving Ramon's life to the Almighty rather than to the physician.

The interior of the *casa* was cool and dark, the thick adobe walls absorbing most of the sun's heat. Brent said, "I moved Ramon into my room, in case he awakened in the night and was frightened."

"Has he been having nightmares?" Edward asked.

"He awakened the first night, screaming in terror when he discovered his leg was missing. That's when I moved him in with me. Apart from tossing and turning and a little whimpering, he's been all right since."

Emily's heartstrings twisted into a knot at the sight of the little boy lying on a pallet in the priest's bedchamber, which contained only a sea chest and a second, larger, pallet. Ramon quickly pulled a threadbare blanket over the blood-stained bandage on the stump of his leg as they entered, and seeing Emily with the two men, hung his head in an agony of shyness.

Edward spoke to him gently in Spanish, introduced Emily, and then suggested she leave the room in order to preserve the child's dignity while he changed the dressing.

"I will take you on a tour of the house," Brent offered, and she followed as he led her through one bare room after another.

Homemade benches and a long trestle table were the only furnishings in the dining hall. Pallets covered the floor in the two largest rooms, which were used as dormitories, one for boys and one for girls.

The kitchen had a worktable of scrubbed wood and a wood-burning stove for cooking. An elderly Mexican woman bent over a cast-iron pot, stirring the contents with shaking hands, and Emily wanted to take away the spoon and ask her to sit and rest, but Brent was already ushering her to the room he had converted to a chapel.

Emily scanned a makeshift altar beneath a carved crucifix, three rows of benches, two small statues of saints. How poor they were, how little they had in the way of worldly goods. Then her gaze returned to the niches in the wall that contained the carved wooden statues of the saints. There were three niches, only two statues. Fastened to the adobe in the third niche was a magnificently jeweled knife, with a curved and lethal-looking blade. Her practiced eye recognized instantly that the gems encrusted upon the hilt were real.

The knife was so incongruous in this place of worship that she gasped aloud. A jeweled chalice, she could have understood. Although gems of such worth belied the Jesuit's vow of poverty.

Brent said, "You are wondering about the dagger. It is a relic of a previous life, and I shall dispose of it shortly. But for now I need it here, where I come to pray, in order to keep before me the quest I have set for myself."

The impulse to respond was too strong to ignore, despite Edward's plea to her earlier not to mention Phin. Emily said, "I saw daggers like that in China. Does your quest concern Phin?"

He hesitated for a moment before answering. "Yes. Her salvation is, I think, irrevocably tied to my own. I wear the robes of a Jesuit, strive to live and work and pray as a Jesuit, but I have not yet attained the state of grace I once believed I had."

"Those jewels would buy a great deal of comfort for the children."

"Yes. And in time they will. For now it does the children no harm to work to support themselves."

Emily looked up at him, and although every nerve in her body cringed at her own temerity, she said quietly, "Why must you priests tell everyone else how to live their lives?

Phin is kind and loyal and has never hurt anyone. Can you say the same of all of your God-fearing Christians?''

The steely eyes seemed to bore into her very soul. ''Phin Tsu is that most depraved and pathetic of women, a whore. It is from that degrading existence I must save her.''

Emily's own loyalty to her half sister made her cast aside her natural deference toward a man of God. ''Why not save the souls of the men who use her? I once overheard my father ask a question a priest could not answer—he said he wondered why the Bible never fully explained the relationship between Christ and Mary Magdalene.''

''To think evil thoughts is as wicked as doing evil deeds. Your father blasphemed with such a question.''

Emily was trembling, as no doubt sturdier souls than she had trembled in the overpowering presence of this priest, but he had called her sister a whore, and that was not to be tolerated. ''It is neither wicked nor blasphemous to question dogma. My father never judged his fellow man—or woman. He believed no one had that right, as do I. You call Phin a whore yet have no name for the men who corrupted her—where is the fairness in that?''

''Ah, so you admit she is corrupt?''

''No! I—'' Emily broke off as footsteps echoed down the tiled corridor outside the chapel.

A moment later Edward appeared. ''Ah, there you are. I thought perhaps we might carry Ramon outside so he could be near the other children. There's no reason he must stay alone in your room during the day. The fresh air and sunshine will lift his spirits, and he'll have the others to talk to.''

''Yes, of course,'' Brent said. ''But I shall have to stay nearby so there will be someone to carry him back inside in case of danger. I saw the dust from several riders yesterday. There may be bandits in the area.''

''Surely bandits would not attack a man of the cloth and a handful of orphans?''

''Desperate times breed desperate men.''

''Emily and I must return to town, but we could stay with

Ramon for a little while," Edward said. "That is, if you have something urgent to attend to."

"It is time for my meditation and prayer."

"Who am I to question the demands of your faith?" Edward said. He took his wife's hand. "You don't mind staying a little longer?"

"No, of course not."

"We'll stay for an hour, then I must go back," he told Brent. "I've neglected my business these past days in order to treat Ramon. The lumber mill needs my attention. It's so difficult to find workers. They all want to go to the goldfields."

The priest regarded him accusingly. "Why do you deny your calling, Edward? Your true purpose in life?"

Edward looked at Emily. "He believes I should spend my life healing the sick. Despite the fact that I've explained to him a hundred times that I only entered the doctor's school in order to be close to you, and only became a medical officer in the army because I did not think I could bring myself to kill the enemy. What little I know about healing I picked up more by accident than design." Edward shook his head and returned his gaze to Brent. "Medicine is the last profession on earth I'd choose for myself. Why can't you understand that I merely stumbled into it?"

"In 1624 a Chinese philosopher named Cahnge Chieh-pin wrote, 'Medicine is not a petty thing,'" Brent responded. He looked at Emily as he spoke.

In that moment something flickered in his steely gaze, some barely veiled accusation that was directed at her. Was he blaming her for Edward's reluctance to practice medicine? Or was the reference to Cahnge Chieh-pin to turn her thoughts back to China and to Phin? Did he know she and Phin were half sisters?

Emily slipped her arm through her husband's and wondered uneasily if the Jesuit was her friend or her enemy.

Chapter 34

. . . .

THE CHIRICAHUA MAIDEN Fletcher called Sings Softly
regarded him with sad dark eyes as he pulled on his
buckskin leggings and then slipped his feet into knee-high
moccasins.

"You are leaving me," she said.

"We need meat. I go to hunt," he responded. Her
language came easily to him now, but there were words he
had not yet learned that he needed to assuage her fears.
Indeed, perhaps there were no Chiricahua phrases to comfort her. She had recognized the changes in him almost as
soon as his memory began to return, and she sensed his
turmoil.

"Soon you will leave forever," she said, and the misery
in her eyes was more than he could bear. He took her hands
and drew her to her feet, then wrapped his arms about her in
a comforting embrace. "I will return before the sun sets."

She clung to him until he gently pried loose her arms, and
she watched with drowning eyes as he placed a blanket on
the back of his horse and slipped his rifle into the hide case
he had fashioned to hold it.

He picked up his bow and quiver of arrows and slung
them over his shoulder. Ammunition was too scarce to
waste when an arrow would serve the purpose just as well,
but he carried the rifle because a marauding band of
Comanche had attacked one of the Apache hunting parties a
week earlier, and smoke signals carried warnings that the
old rivalries between Apache and Comanche were about to
erupt again. In addition, even if the bounty paid by the
Mexicans for Apache scalps had been rescinded since the

Americans won the war, that news had not yet reached the
Arizona Territory, and there were plenty of men, American
as well as Mexican, who still hunted for the most prized
trophies of all: Apache scalps.

Fletcher paused before mounting his horse, realizing that
once again he was thinking like an Apache. His metamor-
phosis from Indian to Englishman was moving very slowly.

"We do not need meat," Sings Softly protested. "The
antelope you killed is barely touched. Why must you ride
alone? Wait until another hunting party is formed. It is too
dangerous to ride by yourself."

He hated lying to her, but how could he tell her where he
was going? How could he make her understand the need?
He said roughly, "Do not question me, woman. I shall
return before nightfall."

Then he sprang up onto his horse, dug his knees into the
mustang's flanks, and galloped toward the narrow slit
between monolithic boulders that was the only egress and
ingress to the hidden canyon where the Chiricahua camped.

Out in the open desert he allowed his pony to set the pace,
staying up on the ridges where not only could he scout the
trail ahead to avoid ambush but also catch any slight
movement of air in the arid heat.

The chaparral smelled of baked sage and creosote, and
the rocks captured and radiated the heat of the sun although
it had risen only a short time before. Except for a red-tailed
hawk that still circled hopefully, all of the desert creatures
had found shelter from that blazing ball of fiery steel
climbing the sky.

Away from Sings Softly and her pleading eyes, away
from the Chiricahua chief and the shaman and the braves
who were beginning to eye him suspiciously, sensing with
that uncanny intuition of primitive people that he was no
longer completely theirs, he again began to reassemble in
his mind the pieces of his past.

He remembered the pain of burying his only daughter,
Emily, in that bleak cemetery in Liverpool, and he remembered as if through a misty veil Emily's mother and how he
had adored her. He also remembered small fragments of his

life in China, but they were even less clear. The dominating images that floated to the surface of the void that once had been the memory of his past life were of Tonia. Beautiful, deadly Tonia. Why did the mere memory of her cause him to feel fear? Not the normal caution that one reserves for known dangers, but the desperate terror of attempting to deal with a conscienceless, unpredictable madwoman.

Had he ever trusted her, really? Or simply been besotted by her? He couldn't believe what he had felt was love; how could anyone feel love for one who was so irredeemably evil? *What had become of her?*

Perhaps there would be an answer to that when he came to the place where the Comanche had attacked the stage-coach. Perhaps he had lived long enough with the *Tin-ne-ah* that he could speak with the spirits of the earth and the rocks and the animals and plants in that spot and find what he was seeking, some glimmer of memory that would tell him where he had been journeying before he was captured by the Comanche.

He was almost certain he had been pursuing Tonia, and now he knew why.

The pictures that flashed into his mind were brief and fleeting, but he collected them greedily, savoring each image, every snatch of remembered conversation.

From all of the fragments he had assembled a scene in his mind. They were aboard the ship sailing from England to Mexico. The rough seas of the Atlantic had been left behind as they moved into calm gulf waters. He was finishing packing in their cramped cabin, and Tonia stood at the porthole, searching for a first glimpse of land.

Thinking she would not turn and look at him again for a moment, he had taken the opportunity to slip the leather pouch from beneath the false bottom of his valise in order to check that the lock was still secure.

Tonia turned and saw what he was doing before he could return the pouch to its hiding place. "What's that?"

For an instant he considered telling her it was a diplo-matic pouch but hated the idea of lying to her. After all, she was his wife. He'd never fully understood why he hadn't told her about the contents of the pouch, and whenever the question arose in his own mind, he evaded it. Perhaps he'd kept the pouch secret in order to pass along the contents to his daughter, but now Emily was gone, and if anything happened to him, Tonia would be his only heir.

"Fletcher? Did you hear me? What is that?" Tonia prompted.

"Come and see for yourself," he answered and took the key attached to his watch fob and unlocked the tiny padlock that secured the pouch.

She moved to his side as he tipped the contents of the pouch onto the bunk.

Tonia gasped and her eyes widened as she stared, mesmerized, at the glittering jewelry.

He picked up a phoenix-shaped hair ornament of gold filigree, the bird's tail feathers studded with pearls and uncut but polished precious stones. "This was once worn by an empress during the T'ang dynasty."

Tonia fingered a brooch shaped like a dragon, with fiery rubies for eyes and a tail of diamonds and tourmalines. There were also two rings, one a cluster of diamonds surrounding a ruby and the other a large pearl set in silver.

"My God!" Tonia exclaimed. "Did you steal them?"

Fletcher smiled. "No. I came by them honestly. The hair ornament, the brooches, and the pearl ring I purchased in China. The ruby ring I bought in England. I suppose you're wondering why I haven't mentioned them before. . . ."

"I'm wondering why I haven't been given the opportunity to wear them," Tonia answered, her eyes narrowing.

"My dear, the ancient Chinese pieces are priceless—far too valuable to wear."

"Then what good are they and why are you carrying them in your valise, which could be snatched from you by any passing thief?"

"I acquired the jewels—except for the ruby ring, which belonged to my first wife—during a time of great upheaval in China. As an investment, you understand. I wanted something of value that I could carry with me and convert immediately into currency or transport, in case we had to beat a hasty retreat from the embassy. You see, I've seen the families of diplomats stranded without the means to escape countries torn by internal strife—months away from their superiors in England or any hope of receiving funds with which to travel. I've never trusted foreign banks. I wanted something I could trade for my daughter's safe passage home should the need arise. I must confess that when I bought the T'ang dynasty pieces, I had no idea of their true value.''

"You don't trust English banks, either?"

"I did think of leaving the jewelry in England, but then there were rumors of war in Mexico and I worried about getting you out of the country quickly, should the need arise." There was no need to tell her that he never intended to return to England and that the jewelry was destined for deposit in an American bank at the first opportunity.

Tonia picked up the hair ornament and held it against her black hair, peering at her reflection in the mottled mirror fastened to the bulkhead. "Look how perfect it is against my hair. Do I look like an empress, Fletcher?"

"You look quite enchanting, with or without the ornament. The bird is a phoenix, by the way, the emblem of immortality.''

"I know what a phoenix is, Fletcher. It lives for five hundred years, burns itself on a funeral pyre, then is reborn young and beautiful, isn't that so?''

He smiled. "More or less, I suppose." He picked up the other pieces and returned them to the pouch, then held out his hand for the hair ornament.

Reluctantly she returned it to him. "Are you sure the pouch will be safe in your valise?"

For answer he showed her the false bottom of the bag and the chain on the handle of the valise that attached to a steel cuff around his wrist. "When we land in Mexico, I will keep the valise attached to my person—a not unusual way for diplomats to carry confidential documents. Our nest egg will be perfectly safe.''

Tonia's gaze grew languid, inviting. She moved closer to him and played with the buttons on his shirt. Looking up at him from beneath a thick fringe of curling lashes, she said playfully, "We have time before the steward comes for our luggage. . . ."

Looking back, it was easy to discern that her excitement—and oh, how frenzied their lovemaking had been—had been generated by the discovery of a fortune in jewels in his possession. When he married Tonia, she had been deeply in debt, and it had taken virtually all of his available cash to pay off her creditors.

When had the doubts about Tonia begun? When had he first questioned whether she was as passionately in love with him as he was with her? When did the suspicion surface that he had merely represented the money she needed quickly? Did he recall several instances where she had expressed disappointment that a diplomatic career was not as financially rewarding as she had first believed? And had her attitude changed after the discovery of the jewels?

In the heat of the Arizona desert the Chiricahua brave he had become stroked his horse's neck reassuringly as a snake slithered across their path and disappeared into a clump of mesquite. The mustang hesitated but did not panic, recognizing, as he did, that the snake had been harmless and not a deadly rattler.

Before the sun reached its apex, he found the canyon where the Comanche ambush had taken place. The war party had chosen the place well, coming up out of the sun along a ridge to the west, with a sheer granite cliff to the east. They had driven the stagecoach into a box canyon.

He rode into the canyon and dismounted. The searing heat enclosed him as the movement of air was shut off by the canyon walls. His mustang wandered over to the scant shade offered by a tall saguaro. For an instant he grappled with a sense of doom but forced himself to descend farther into the canyon.

A jumble of boulders lay in his path, and he scrambled over them. Immediately in front of him lay the wrecked coach and the bleaching bones of the horses, picked clean by coyotes. Several mounds of smaller rocks nearby testified to the fact that other white-eyes had stopped long enough to bury the dead.

He stood beside the overturned coach. The wheels were gone, and one side of the coach was caved in by the crash, but the dry desert air had preserved the remaining splintered wood and brass fittings. Everything that could be carried off had been removed, but he sifted through the gravelly sand around the coach searching for any small item that had been missed.

His mind felt like the honed edge of a blade, eager to strike out at any hint of a clue that might reveal his destination aboard that doomed stagecoach. His searching fingers closed around an arrowhead, buried in the sand. He pulled it free and looked at it. It told him nothing.

A moment later he felt something metallic, buried even deeper and wedged under a rock. It took a minute to work free a chain. Slowly, link by link, he pulled it from the ground until it refused to come any farther. Using his knife, he carefully pried the rock loose. The chain was attached to a watch.

Wrapping the chain around his fist, he clutched the watch and closed his eyes, feeling rising excitement. Another memory was flooding back into his mind.

The watch had belonged to a traveling companion—he could even see the man's features, lean, swarthy, with half-closed eyes. He couldn't recall a name, but he remembered something else that was perhaps even more important. The owner of the watch had been a gambler, and on the long journey he had taught his traveling companions, including Fletcher, to play both faro and poker.

The rules and nuances of the card games crowded into Fletcher's mind, and he had to reluctantly make himself push them aside in order to open his thoughts to more productive memories.

The gambler must have buried his gold watch under the rock in some vain hope he would survive the Comanche attack and return for it. Fletcher pictured him lying behind the fallen coach, digging up the rocks as the others frantically loaded and fired, fighting for their lives. Had he buried anything else of value?

As he painstakingly probed every inch of the ground, he unearthed several coins, more arrowheads, spent bullets, and finally a gold watch fob.

The fob had undoubtedly been attached to the gambler's watch chain, but as Fletcher looked at it, he thought again about his own watch fob, to which he had attached the key to the jewel pouch.

A memory returned, hitting him like a kick to his gut. The image filling his mind was the stuff of nightmares and, in its sheer cruelty, even more ghastly than what the Comanches had done to him.

In shocking detail he saw Tonia standing over him as he lay sprawled on the ground, semiconscious, frantically trying to bring her into focus and understand what was happening.

Flanking her were two dark-skinned men, wearing serapes and the side-buttoned trousers favored by Mexicans. He could hear other men and the nickering of horses in the background. A third man, an American, pushed one of the Mexicans aside and stood beside Tonia.

Her voice floated down toward him, as though through thick fog. "Is he dead?"

"Near enough," the American answered.

"What are you waiting for? Get the valise. You'll have to shoot it off him. It's fastened by a chain to his wrist."

"Hell, we shoot it off and we might blow away anything of value, too. Where did he carry the key?"

"On his watch fob," Tonia answered impatiently. "Hurry, get the valise, but don't open it in front of the others."

Fletcher's sight had been fading as she spoke, and pain radiated from the back of his head in sickening bursts, like the pounding of a hammer. Someone had hit him from behind, and he was lying on a dusty street. They were in Mexico. They had disembarked from the ship only days earlier and were awaiting a coach to take them to Mexico City.

As his vision blurred, he felt hands roughly remove his

watch and chain, fumbling at the cuff on his wrist, then
yanking away the precious valise.

Then Tonia's voice again. "Finish him. Go on, put a
bullet into his brain."

"Hell, he's dying, why waste a bullet? Besides, somebody might hear a gunshot. There are soldiers not far
away—do you want to bring the army after us?"

"Get one of your *bandidos* to cut his throat, then. I want
him dead."

The American gave a hollow chuckle. "God's blood,
woman, remind me never to cross you." He said something
in Spanish, then added in English, "Carlos will take care of
him. Come on, let's see the treasure you promised."

Their voices drifted away into the night, and Fletcher lay
absolutely still, staring unblinkingly up into a black velvet
heaven filled with stars that glinted like scattered diamonds.

The vague shape of a man bent over him, seized his hair,
and raised his head. He saw the gleam of a knife in the
starlight and prayed the end would be quick, but one last
hope for survival made him relax completely and hold his
breath, feigning death.

The point of the knife touched his throat.

Someone shouted something in Spanish, and Fletcher's
head was slammed back down to the ground as his would-be
assassin let go and fled.

Fletcher's last conscious memory that night had been of
the thunder of approaching hooves, shouts, and gunshots.
Then someone dragging him out of the path of the galloping
horses.

Chapter 35

• •

THE DELICATE CHINA cups rattled against their saucers, spilling tea on the damask cloth. The most recent arrivals to San Francisco looked up in alarm as the chandeliers swayed overhead and a picture slid down the wall, crashing to the floor behind Briony's table.

She stood up, feeling the mezzanine tremble under her, and said calmly, "It's all right—just an earth tremor. It will pass in a moment."

Another picture fell, then a vase of roses toppled. One woman cried out in fear, and several of the others attending the afternoon tea whimpered in fright.

Briony laughed. "Goodness, this one is lasting longer than usual. Hold on to your cups, everyone; it will take months to ship in replacements."

Some of the women smiled nervously, and Annabelle grabbed the crystal vase on her table and cradled it to her ample bosom. "Lord, don't let my new Italian mirrors break, that's all I ask!" she cried. She added, to no one in particular, "They just arrived, and I haven't had a chance to admire myself in them yet."

A little of the tension dissipated. The shaking gradually subsided, and Briony began to pick up cups and mop spilled tea with her napkin. She rang the bell to summon help.

Annabelle commented, "That was a strong one."

"It's passed now," Briony said. "Did any of the tea stain your gowns, ladies? If so, please allow the Rosebriar to have them laundered for you. As we're drawing to the close of our teatime, perhaps we should send Annabelle home to check on her mirrors, and the rest of you might also want to go home and calm your servants. They do tend to get a little excitable, don't they?"

The inference was that the ladies of her tea party were above becoming excitable over such a minor incident as a tremor and knew there had been no real danger. The shaking earth was as much a part of life in California as the endless sunshine. There was rarely any real damage, and except for a waiter who had once been cut by broken glass, no one had ever been hurt in the Rosebriar.

The mezzanine emptied rapidly. Everyone knew the safest place to be was outside, away from falling ceilings and chandeliers . . . just in case the tremor had been the precurser to a stronger earthquake.

Annabelle was the last to leave. "Haven't seen your sister-in-law lately. She isn't ill, is she?"

From Annabelle's arch tone, Briony translated *ill* to infer *enceinte* but didn't give Annabelle the satisfaction of rising to the bait.

"No, she's quite well. She and Edward have been helping a friend who runs an orphanage for Mexican and Indian children, I believe. Somewhere between here and the Spanish mission. My brother and his wife are inseparable, you know. It's really quite charming. Now, if you'll excuse me, I have several errands to attend to."

Briony went to her room, put on her bonnet, and picked up her gloves and reticule. She went outside into the late afternoon sunshine, reflecting that her small circle of respectable friends was increasing to the point that the afternoon teas might soon lose their intimacy. Although prostitutes from all over the world had poured into the city, at first only a handful of married women had followed their husbands to the boomtown.

Most troubling were the numbers of very young Chinese girls who had arrived and were set up in parlor houses and cribs on Grant Avenue, Waverly Place, and Ross Alley. The parlor houses were a Caucasian's idea of China, decorated with poor-quality teak, tawdry silk hangings, and grotesque gods, scrolls, and paintings, where the clientele choked on musk and sandalwood fumes. Some of the slave girls were as young as twelve years old.

Lining Jackson and Washington streets and the adjacent alleys were cribs housing the lowest denomination of slave girls. Slatted cages about twelve feet wide were divided by a drape into a front and back room. As many as half a dozen girls, wearing only short silk blouses, usually black, sometimes decorated with flowers, worked in a single crib. In the back was a pallet and washbasin, occasionally a chair. In front a rug and mirror. The door was barred. The girls clung to the bars like prisoners, calling out to passing men.

Briony avoided going anywhere near what the Chinese called *Tong Yung Gai*, or Chinese Street. She'd heard that joss houses were also springing up. These were Confucian, Taoist, and Buddhist temples. It was clear that San Francisco would soon have a sizable Chinatown.

The Chinese were avid gamblers and played fan tan and poker like madmen. Max had said that all the parlor houses catered to gamblers and opium smokers as well as providing prostitutes, and he had his doubts about the joss houses, too.

In a class by itself was the Lantern House, which was currently the most high-class brothel and gambling establishment in the city. Unlike the clapboard shacks and tents of the parlor houses, as well as many less exotic businesses in the city, the Lantern House was a real house. No one knew who the owner was, but it was rumored to be a respectable citizen.

As Briony made her way to the newly opened post office at Clay and Pike, she wondered again if Max could be persuaded to go to the Lantern House and entice Kane to come and play his violin at the Rosebriar. Surely a screeching fiddle would suffice for a bawdy house, and Kane's talents should be displayed in the proper setting.

Briony was annoyed with herself for not thinking of concealing him in some way so that he could play at the Rosebriar before the Lantern House owner had the idea, but she wasn't above stealing both the idea and the musician.

The trouble was, she had seen very little of Max since she refused his proposal of marriage. He'd left the following day to go to the goldfields to check on his mines and said he might also go hunting up north near the Russian settlement. If only he would return!

Edward was just leaving the post office as she arrived, and catching sight of her, he made his way through the throngs of people waiting in line. "Hello, Bri—I wish I'd known you needed to come here. I just spent over an hour waiting to get to a window. I could have done your business for you, too."

"I shan't wait," she replied. "I'll send Topaz tomorrow. Come back to the Rosebriar with me, and we'll have a glass of sherry. I haven't seen you for ages."

He fell into step beside her and glanced admiringly at a new brick building going up, a stark contrast to the two tents that flanked it. Across the street a wooden storefront was half finished but apparently abandoned.

"Do you believe the pace of this city's growth?" he remarked. "I've run out of lumber at the yard until the next shipment gets here. We even dismantled a couple of hulks and sold the planks. I need to talk to you about buying some of your nails, Bri. Are you ready to sell yet?"

"Not at the price you want to pay," she answered, her dimple appearing. "Yesterday I saw a man set up a stand to sell toothpicks—twelve of them—for fifty cents, and he sold out by the end of the day. If you have any wood left, perhaps you should make toothpicks—*then* you can afford to buy some of my nails."

Edward laughed. "Listen to us! Our parents must be spinning in their graves to see what skinflint merchants we've become. Bri, I'll walk you back to the hotel, but I really must go home to Emily. I've been out since dawn."

"How is she? I can't persuade her to come to my afternoon teas nowadays. She isn't . . . you know, is she?"

"In the family way? Not to my knowledge. She's become obsessed with planting a garden at the house. She wants flowers and grass and shrubs like the English gardens."

Briony raised an eyebrow. "If she does you'll have the only house in town with a garden."

"Where would I find a gardener in this city of argonauts?"

"At least we have a town council at last. And a new alcalde."

"Did you hear the statement he made? He said there isn't a dollar in the treasury, there are no public edifices, no police officers or watchmen, and even if there were, nowhere to confine felons—in short, San Francisco is without a single requisite for the protection of property or the maintenance of order."

"I do hope you carry a gun, Edward. Everyone does, you know. We always have at least a couple of Max's Texas friends with their Colt revolvers strolling about the Rosebriar, in addition to the doormen. And I have a derringer in my reticule."

"My God, Briony! Now I know for certain that Mother is spinning in her grave."

They reached the Rosebriar and lingered for a moment at the door. "I haven't seen Max about town lately," Edward said. "Is he out checking on his mine?"

She nodded. "He and some friends went hunting, too. Edward . . . I do wish you'd come in for a moment. I have an enormous favor to ask of you."

"A favor, Bri? Anything, you know that. What is it?"

"I want you to visit the Lantern House."

Qing Chan fluttered about her office in her yellow silk blouse and black trousers like an angry little bee, occasionally raising a pointed claw to point at Phin. "Do you want to be sent to the parlor houses? Maybe even into a crib? That's where you are bound, you wretched creature, if you don't mend your ways."

"What have I done now?" Phin asked tiredly. She ached to curl up in bed and sleep but obviously was in for another of the mama-san's tirades.

"You refused a gentleman's request. He complained to me."

Phin's nose wrinkled. "He was dirty. I sent him to the

bath house. He demanded that I beat him first. I do not do that.''

"You will end up as a crib girl, Phin Tsu, you arrogant, disobedient girl. Shall I tell you what happens to the crib girls who displease a gentleman?'' Qing Chan thrust her long yellow fingernail in Phin's face to emphasize her words. "She is starved, beaten, sometimes branded with hot irons. If she becomes too much of a problem, or is diseased or broken-minded, then she is sent to what they call, sarcastically, a hospital.''

The mama-san paused for breath, her pigeon chest wheezing, then went on. "Let me tell you about the hospitals, Phin Tsu. The Chinese physician notifies the girl that she must die. She is taken at night to the 'hospital' and made to lie on a shelf. A cup of water, a little boiled rice, and a small oil lamp is placed beside her. The door is locked and she is left alone. Those in charge of the establishment know how long the oil should last, and when the limit is reached, they return and unbar the door. By then the girl is dead, either by thirst or starvation, but often by her own hand.''

Phin suppressed a shiver but said calmly, "Why do you tell me these things, old woman? I shall refuse all the barbarians I wish so long as Kane plays his violin, and you know it.''

"Hmmph! You think Kane will stay? Already everybody in San Francisco is talking about him. The fact that no one has seen his face gives him an air of mystery and romance that make him irresistible. Some say he is a world-famous violinist who hides his identity to shield his family and that he is here because he is besotted by a whore. Everyone agrees he will come to his senses as soon as she begins to lose her looks, as all whores do. So play your little games, Phin Tsu, while you can. Your days are as numbered as any wretched crib girl. Go now, get your beauty sleep. Keep your looks as long as you can.''

Phin made her way up the stairs to her room. The nagging feeling of apprehension she'd felt constantly since coming to the Lantern House had now blossomed into an ever-present premonition of doom. It was time to leave. She was probably not going to learn any more about her father's death from Tonia, who had not visited the house since their last session with the fortune-telling disks.

Perhaps, Phin reasoned, she had already sewn the seeds of vengeance for her father's death. Despite Tonia's protestations to the contrary, she was worried and fearful that someone was after her. Phin knew that the fear contained in one's own mind was the most deadly enemy of all. It had destroyed more people than any assassin.

Mama-san knew this. Hadn't she just raised the terrible specter of the crib girls in Phin's own mind? She shivered. Yes, it was definitely time to move on. Fortunately she had carefully hoarded all of her earnings. The pokes of gold dust, along with her jewelry and other valuables, were stitched into her mattress.

Despite her fatigue, she bathed and changed into street clothes, then packed her two carpetbags. She would send for her trunk later. For the time being she would return to Mrs. Ling's boardinghouse, then decide where to go next. Perhaps it was time to return to China. She had enough money to support herself for a considerable period of time. A business, she thought, I shall invest in a business. Perhaps I shall become a dealer in fine gems and antique jewelry.

She felt a surge of anticipation that helped dispel some of her exhaustion. A new life lay ahead.

As she carefully slit open the side of her mattress, she allowed herself to think briefly of Brent Carlisle. Perhaps before she left the country, she would dress in her finest clothes, visit his children's home, and make a handsome donation. She would be Lady Bountiful, bidding him goodbye and showing not one scrap of regret or hint of the yearning she felt for him. He would not have the satisfaction of knowing he had ruined all her chances of loving any other man. She giggled to herself. Perhaps she would rub salt in his wound by telling him she was going to open her own House of Delights and live off the earnings of other depraved women—wasn't that what he said they were?

She slid her hand into the feathers of the mattress, but her

searching fingers did not connect with the soft leather of the
gold dust pokes or her jewel cases.

Minutes later she was enveloped in a swirling cloud of
white feathers as she ripped the mattress apart.

They were gone. Everything was missing. Someone had
stolen her new life, and now she was at the mercy of the
mama-san and Tonia Bardine.

Chapter 36

. . . .

"YOU AIN'T GOING down to the store at this time of night?" Topaz, aghast, asked Briony. "Ma'am, it ain't safe with them Hounds roaming the streets."

Briony adjusted her hat and regarded her maid's reflection in the dressing table mirror. "I shall have Arnold take me." Arnold was their doorman, a former bare knuckles boxer left slightly bewildered by one too many bouts, who adored Briony. He was good with horses and handled her carriage well. She had unofficially made him her coachman. "Besides," she added, "we now have a paid police force *and* a jail."

Topaz rolled her eyes heavenward. "That ole brig anchored at the intersection of Battery and Jackson? They done filled it up already. And there's more Hounds than police anyhow. One coachman—I don't care how big he is or how well armed—ain't going to fight off a whole crew of Hounds. Ma'am, they're vicious men."

"Don't fuss, Topaz. I shall be quite all right."

Briony thought, but didn't mention, that the infamous Hounds preyed mostly on the town's foreign colonies. Their favorite target was the camp of the Chileans at the base of Telegraph Hill. The Hounds would raid the camp, tear down the tents, beat the occupants, and take whatever they wanted, then set fire to whatever remained.

Max was still away, or she would have asked him to accompany her to the beached ship that was now a thriving store. She had intended to go there during the daylight hours, but with Max away there simply hadn't been time during her busy day, and she needed to pick up the store's receipts for deposit in the bank. If too much cash was allowed to accumulate, it might be a temptation for her manager, a taciturn individual named Nate Craw, whose foot had been mangled in an accident at the goldfields, thus ending his prospecting career. He could hobble about but no longer stand in icy-cold water panning for gold. She paid him a generous salary and hoped he wasn't cheating her. He lived aboard the ship and refused to visit her at the Rosebriar so, since she didn't trust anyone else, she was forced to collect the receipts, which frequently consisted of large quantities of gold dust.

Arnold had her carriage waiting at the entrance to the Rosebriar and hovered protectively as she emerged from the hotel. Briony dismissed any fears she had. After all, the streets were brightly lit and filled with people. Rich miners came into town every evening in pursuit of pleasure, drinking, gambling, whoring. Several drunken miners called out to her as she lifted her skirts above the muddy street, but they backed off when Arnold turned on them threateningly.

The night air was damp and chilly. The heat wave had ended, and San Francisco's more typically cool summer weather had returned. She regretted not wearing warmer clothes but told herself it was unlucky to turn back having once begun a journey, a superstition whose origins she couldn't recall.

Arnold avoided the more unsavory parts of the city, taking a long detour to the waterfront. Since most of the merchants had closed their establishments for the night, by the time they reached her store, there were few people on the street that so recently had been tideland, but the glimmer of a whale oil lamp in the converted ship testified to the fact that Nate Craw was still at work.

Briony told Arnold, "Wait here. I shall be in and out in a moment. There's no need to come with me."

She picked her way through the maze of cargo crates and barrels to the counter Nate Craw had built of deck planks and which was now piled high with merchandise. He was perched upon a high stool, a cigar clamped between his teeth, scribbling in a ledger. He looked up at her, squinting

in disapproval, his long-jawed face and downturned mouth
looking dismayingly sharklike.

"Evenin', Miz Forest. Didn't expect you to come for the
receipts this time of night."

She kept her distance from the noxious cloud of cigar
smoke. "Good evening, Nate. Is the pouch ready for me?"

He hefted a bulging leather pouch from behind the
counter and dropped it in front of her. "You want to go over
my figures? I haven't finished balancing yet."

"No. But I do want to take a box of nails with me for my
brother. You haven't sold any of them yet, have you?"

"You told me not to until the price goes up some more."
He disappeared into the dim recesses of the ship, and she
heard him dragging his injured foot over the rough wooden
decking.

Briony glanced at the open ledger, quickly adding up a
column of figures and finding it accurate. She had always
been good at arithmetic. One governess had told her that
with her head for figures, she should have been born a boy.
Although the governess had not meant it as a compliment,
Briony had been pleased.

When Nate Craw returned with the box of nails, she
asked him to take it out to the carriage.

He dumped it on the counter. "Send your man in for it.
I'm not going out carrying goods this time of night."

"But there was no one in the street."

"You didn't *see* nobody. I figure in here I got a chance.
I got a loaded shotgun under the counter. Out there in the
dark with a lame foot and a heavy box in my arms is a
different story."

"Oh, very well." She picked up the leather pouch of
receipts and left, pausing at the door to glance up and down
the still-deserted street.

"Go inside and fetch the box Mr. Craw has for us," she
told Arnold as he helped her into the carriage.

A worried frown creased his battered features. "Hadn't
you better come back inside with me?"

"Mr. Craw has been smoking one of his foul cigars

again. I'd rather wait out here, despite the dampness. Just be quick, Arnold, there's a good fellow.''

The instant he disappeared through the door carved into the hull of the former ship, Briony regretted her decision to remain in the carriage. Every shadow seemed menacing, and the night was filled with scurryings, rustlings, and creakings.

She pushed the leather pouch under the carriage seat and slipped her hand into her reticule, finding the derringer. The cold feel of the small gun offered little comfort. It had been a mistake to come here at night. Damn Max. Why didn't he return? How did he expect her to run both the hotel and her own thriving business?

Arnold returned a minute later. The box of nails, although not large, was heavy, and it shook the carriage as he placed it on the floor at her feet.

She gave a sigh of relief when they were again moving, but her resentment about Max's prolonged absence grew. As they reached the brightly lit square it occurred to her that someone had mentioned that Louis-Philippe Ramadier had made a brief trip to the goldfields but was now back in town. The little Frenchman's café was apparently thriving, and for a price he would deliver food to the hostesses of fancy soirees who wouldn't dream of visiting his establishment. Rumor had it that a mine owner had persuaded him to go out to his diggings and cook a gala meal to celebrate the unearthing of a gigantic gold nugget. The mine owner had not wanted to go into town to Louis-Philippe's café and interrupt his search for further riches.

As Arnold helped her from the carriage at the Rosebriar, she said, ''I shall need the carriage tomorrow at noon.''

Louis-Philippe's dark eyes were wide with surprise and delight when Briony arrived at his café the following day. He tripped over his feet, attempted to smooth back his hair and left a floury wake through his dark mane, kissed her wrist, ordered two clients from a choice table in the window, and pulled out her chair with a flourish—all while expressing his great joy at seeing her again, complimenting her on her gown, her bonnet, her incredible eyes and fiery hair and complexion fair as lily petals.

"Ah, Madame Forest, if only I had known you were coming! I would 'ave prepared a feast fit for a queen. What honor you do my 'umble café! But this is a bad part of town for a lady to be. If you 'ad sent zee word, I would 'ave brought to you any dish your heart desires!"

He snapped his fingers, and a diminutive Mexican, even more slight of stature than Louis-Philippe himself, appeared at his elbow with a bottle of wine.

"If you're not too busy," Briony said, glancing at the crowded tables, "perhaps you could join me for just a moment?"

Beaming his pleasure, Louis-Philippe whipped off his flour-dusted apron and handed it to the Mexican waiter, then took the wine and poured two glasses before taking a seat opposite to her. "I 'ave a chef in zee kitchen I am training, and Manuel 'ere will take care of the tables. It is not often I 'ave the pleasure of eating excellent food with a beautiful woman."

Noting that many of the other patrons were glowering in their direction, no doubt resentful of the attention she was getting and worried about service to their own tables, Briony said quickly, "Oh, please—I would be uncomfortable taking you away from your other customers. Allow me to eat alone. I assure you I am not one of those shrinking violets who can't even eat a meal without an escort. Let us have a quick toast to your continued success, and perhaps you can also tell me if you saw Max on your recent trip out to the goldfields."

A comical pout contorted Louis-Philippe's finely chiseled features. "*Sacré bleu*, but the love of my life comes to inquire about another man! I am broken in pieces—'ow you say it, shattered! And all zee while I think you come to see me, or at least enjoy my *carte*."

"Oh, but I did," Briony said hastily. "It's just that I haven't heard from Max and had some questions about the Rosebriar. I just wondered if he'd mentioned to you when he might return."

His deepset eyes bored into her knowingly. "You and Max, you 'ad a quarrel, no?"

She felt herself color slightly but shrugged. "Not really."

"'Ow very strange that he would leave suddenly without telling you when he would return. I did see him, just before he left the goldfields to go north to see his Russian friends. He did not say when he would be back in town. I am sorry, *chérie*. P'raps there is something I could do to 'elp?"

Always ready to seize an opportunity, Briony answered without hesitation. "Why, yes, indeed, Louis-Philippe. You can come to the Rosebriar and run the kitchens and hire entertainers for the dining room. I can't seem to keep a chef or a pianist."

For a second she expected him to laugh and treat the suggestion as a joke, but he squinted at her with his dark eyes as though assessing her need for him over his own desire to be independent. At length he said, "I will come to zee 'otel and 'elp out—but only until Max returns."

Briony couldn't believe her luck. "Bless you! I can't tell you how grateful I am. We shall have to discuss remuneration, and with Max gone—"

"We talk money later." The Frenchman waved his hand airily. "For now I wish to eat lunch with my lovely companion and flirt with 'er outrageously."

Chapter 37

• •

CLASPING HER HANDKERCHIEF to her mouth, Emily lay back weakly on her pillow as the bedroom slowly revolved around her. At least, it felt as though the room were spinning. She looked up apologetically at her husband, who placed the breakfast tray onto the chest of drawers and then sat on the edge of the bed beside her.

"I'm sorry . . . ." Emily whispered. "It was the sight of the food . . . the congealing egg yolks."

Edward picked up her limp hand and cradled it in his. "Don't think about the food. Perhaps you could drink a little tea? I'll have Josefa make you some plain toast."

"No—please, just let me lie still for a moment. I'll be all right. If you could stay with me for a few minutes?"

"Of course I shall stay, my darling. I'm so sorry you feel ill. Emily . . . I know a husband isn't supposed to ask such things, but, well, I am a doctor of sorts, and I can't help wondering . . . have you had your monthly cycle?"

Emily blushed to the roots of her hair. She shook her head. "Do you think . . . ?"

Edward's handsome face broke into a smile, his eyes lit up, and he gathered her into his arms. "My dearest darling wife, yes, *yes*, I *do* think. The extreme fatigue you've felt lately, the nausea you've been suffering . . . You are with child. I'm so happy, Emily, I can't find the words to express my joy and gratitude."

She struggled against the weakness she felt and attempted to respond to his kiss but was relieved when he laid her head gently down again. How unfair it was, Emily thought, that just when they could enjoy the physical bonding of marriage she should find her body so unwilling to respond to her mind's desires. She had never known such overwhelming fatigue, or the constant churning of her stomach, or the aching tenderness of her breasts that almost caused her to shriek in pain if they were touched, however lovingly. Although she, too, longed for a child, she wished she and her husband could have had a little more time alone together.

"Edward . . . did you have my note delivered to Phin? I can't understand why she hasn't called to see me."

"There's a whole avalanche of calling cards downstairs and several letters. I'll look through them to see if anything came from Phin," Edward said. "But some of your other friends might be hurt if you receive her and not them."

"I'm just not up to having visitors. Did you explain that I wasn't feeling well?"

He nodded. "Your friends understand."

Her eyelids fluttered wearily. "I'm . . . so very tired."

A moment later her even breathing signaled sleep, and he tiptoed from the room.

Downstairs, he went into his study and retrieved the envelope he had pushed under his blotter. The note had arrived from Phin a few days after he reluctantly posted Emily's letter to her. He told himself that it was his concern for his wife's feelings that caused him to open Phin's letter, but he felt guilty nevertheless. He had certainly not been prepared for the contents and knowing Phin's declaration would upset Emily, he had awaited the right moment to give her the letter.

Phin had written:

Dear Emily,

I cannot visit you. Nor do I wish you ever to come to see me. There is a time for everything in life, and our time together has now ended. For you it is now time to be a wife and soon, I hope, a mother. But the time we spent together will always be a part of us, living on in memory. How I shall treasure, always, my memories of you, little sister, and your sweet and gentle ways.

Only one thing remains to be said. As we both feared, I am now convinced that the woman we suspected of causing your father's death is indeed guilty. But rest assured that justice will eventually be done and she will pay for her crimes. This I swear to you.

Ha yung chi! (Good luck)
Phin Tsu

Edward held the letter for a moment. At least Phin had the good sense to recognize that their association must end. Upon their arrival in San Francisco he had immediately paid Phin back all the money they had borrowed, with a generous interest rate, and had hoped that would be the end of her. He wished Emily were not so devoted to her. He was sorry Phin had mentioned Fletcher Faraday's death, as that was bound to upset Emily. Still, Phin's decree that their friendship was over was too important to destroy the letter.

He put the letter back into the envelope. He would give it to Emily when she awoke. She would be hurt, but he could not shield her from her hurt, and it was time to close the episode with the Eurasian girl.

Henry Bardine rammed himself into his wife with a fury, his weight almost suffocating her and the brass bedstead rattling as if in an earthquake. His sweat dripped on her, and the sour taste of his saliva made her want to retch.

Tonia gritted her teeth and forced herself to move her hips and use her hands and tongue to bring him as quickly to climax as possible.

Sometimes, especially after he'd beaten and abused her during their sexual encounters, she would think about the contrast between Henry and Fletcher Faraday. But she was not one to dwell on the past; she lived for the moment and the immediate future. Her fantasies nowadays revolved around watching Henry Bardine die. She would like his death to be slow and painful but would probably have to settle for it to be swift and undetected.

She could, of course, have simply run away, taking her buried treasure with her. But the trouble was, she loved San

Francisco. It was a wild, free, exciting town, with the men outnumbering the women by the hundreds. The climate was mild, the bay beautiful, and the steep hills gave the growing city a thrilling texture. Everything here was new. Nobody had a past, and everyone could choose to be whatever he or she wished. She loved the sweeping view from her house, she loved being rich, and most of all she loved owning the Lantern House.

No, she wasn't going to run. Henry was going to make her a widow, and then she'd give Briony Forest a run for her money. She'd show San Francisco who was going to be the leader of society.

Grunting, Henry collapsed on top of her. When his breathing began to slow down, she said, "Darling, if you could get off me—"

He raised his head and looked at her with his single eye. She sometimes dreamed of that eye, disembodied, following her along endless dark corridors, forever watching her. "I've decided to sail back to New York on the clipper. You're coming with me."

Pinned beneath his weight, Tonia found it difficult to speak, and she hoped her breathlessness did not give away her shock and dismay at his announcement. "But, Henry—why would you want to spend all that time at sea? It's so nice here in San Francisco."

"I want the record for making the voyage from the Eastern Seaboard. By God, I *will* have the record. We're going to make the voyage faster than any other clipper ship or die trying. I reckon the only way to get every last ounce out of the crew is to be aboard myself."

"Darling, I really dislike long sea voyages. Would you mind terribly if I stayed here?"

"Yes, I would. You're going along. We leave in three days, so pack your trunk." He rolled away from her and seconds later was snoring loudly.

Tonia lay beside him in silent fury. She was tempted to slip down to the kitchen and return with a meat cleaver. But Henry Bardine could not only fall asleep in an instant, he could also be snoring one second and wide awake the next.

Once she had stood over his sleeping body and wondered about smashing in his skull with a heavy brass candlestick. Without changing the pitch of his breathing, or opening his one good eye, he had suddenly said, "I sleep with the other eye open, darlin'. Wide open under that patch, seeing everything that goes on. Funny thing, ever since I lost that eye, I can see more with the empty socket than I ever could before. You ever think of walking out, I'd find you and drag you back by the hair."

She had been relieved that his assumption had been that she had been standing beside him contemplating flight. If he knew she was thinking about murder . . .

Three days. He wanted her aboard his damn clipper ship in three days. Henry Bardine had to be disposed of immediately.

Chapter 38

∙∙∙

FLETCHER SLIPPED INTO the wickiup and crouched beside the sleeping squaw. He tapped her cheek. "Sings Softly—wake up."

She sat up, pushing her long plait of black hair back over her shoulder. Flickering firelight from the campfire lit the interior of the wickiup, and the sound of the drums and chanting warriors testified to the fact that the tribal council had reached a decision to go on the warpath.

Surprised that her man was not participating in the dance to ask the spirits to protect the braves, Sings Softly asked, "Something is wrong, yes?"

"The chief has learned that a white-eyes wagon train is coming this way. The braves will ride at dawn and lie in wait along the ridge overlooking the plain. I cannot go with them."

"But you must! If you refuse, you will be cast out—or worse, killed. Oh, my husband, you cannot defy the chief's order."

"I cannot kill and plunder my own people."

"The *Tin-ne-ah* are your people. You became a Chiricahua brave of your own free will."

"When I became a brave, I had no memory of my own race. I had only knowledge of Indians and Mexicans. I was born, full grown, when your shaman rescued me from the Comanche. I had no compunction in stealing horses from the Mexicans, nor in killing them when the need arose, because I had seen Mexicans kill the *Tin-ne-ah*. But it is different now. I remember parts of my past, and now the

White-eyes are crossing Apacheria in even greater numbers. I cannot—will not attack the wagon trains.''

"I have seen your torment. I knew you would leave soon. My heart cries bitter tears that I must part from my people, but I will go with my husband.''

He kissed her forehead, then her lips. "I do not know where I will go, what I will do. I am not yet ready to return to my own people. I still seek the man I was. So much of my past is lost to me. I know that I came to Mexico, and that I was to take a post with the British Embassy. But I was attacked, robbed, and left for dead. I shall return to Mexico, attempt to retrace my footsteps from there. I may have to go back to England. My plans for the future are vague. I have a compelling need to find the one who betrayed me. Can you understand? Until all of the questions in my mind are answered, I feel cut adrift, unfocused. Until I have finished piecing together my past and decided upon my future path, I must travel alone.''

"Please, don't leave me,'' she begged.

"As much as I want you by my side, Sings Softly, I cannot take you with me, nor ask you to share the dangers and uncertainties I will face. You would be deprived not only of the companionship of the other women but also the protection of the tribe. I care too much for you to ask such a sacrifice of you. But I swear to you I will return for you when my life is in order.''

She pressed her face to his chest and wept, and for a moment he considered asking her to share his exile. Then his Chiricahua training warned him sternly that not only would he travel faster alone, but his quest would be hampered if he had to constantly watch over the woman. How could he leave her alone in camp while he hunted? How could he move unobtrusively through unknown territory and enter Mexican villages or American settlements with a squaw at his side? No, she had to remain with her own people, for her own safety as well as his.

Pulling free of her arms, he gently pushed her away.

Swiftly and silently he gathered up his belongings.

"Goodbye, Sings Softly. I will come back for you as soon as I can. Until then I will keep you in my heart."

She took a step toward him, one hand raised. "Wait. The braves must not see you leave. They will kill you. Let me go to the ramada for your horse. I will meet you away from camp, on the other side of the pass." She smiled sadly. "They will not see me. A squaw is always invisible, yes?"

Between Apacheria and the Mexican border he caught two mustangs and traded them at the first Mexican village he came to for boots and a saddle, the first accoutrements of a non-Indian. He considered asking the old man who agreed to the barter for some clothes that would make him less conspicuous, but he was reluctant to give up the comfort of soft buckskin for the cumbersome serape and *calzoneras* the old man wore. His filthy shirt was out of the question. The Apache, Fletcher had found, were a clean people. They bathed frequently and washed their hair with a shampoo made from the pulp of various cacti.

His most pressing need, for ammunition, the old man could not fill.

In a mixture of sign language and the little Chiricahua dialect the Mexican farmer understood, Fletcher asked if he knew of any American trading post where he might find clothing.

The old man regarded the tall, blue-eyed Apache with a mixture of curiosity and fear, recognizing that this white man was a Chiricahua brave, and therefore to anger him would mean instant death. He indicated that the nearest Americans could be found at a stagecoach station, some distance west. He did not add that Murrieta and his men were only hours ahead in that same direction, riding to plunder a new American settlement. After all, he reasoned as he watched the blue-eyed Apache ride away on his ancient and battered saddle with its silver trappings, the prowess of the legendary Chiricahua warriors was almost supernatural. Besides, the old man was glad to still be alive and now in possession of two fine horses.

* * *

Fletcher observed the camp from a ridge just above the great river. Twenty men, several women, an impressive ramada. Their campfires lit up the night, and their music echoed across the valley. Sentries were posted, but it was obvious that these men had little fear of being attacked. They strolled about the camp, clearly silhouetted against the leaping flames, and even slipped out of camp alone to answer the call of nature. They were heavily armed. He recognized them for what they were.

Just after midnight he left his horse tethered up on the ridge and slipped down to the camp. When he left he had a new American-made rifle, bandoleers of cartridges, a handsome silver-studded sombrero, and a pouch of what looked like gold dust, although he didn't take the time to examine it closely.

He had removed the clinking silver trappings from the saddle and so detoured silently around the bandits' camp a short time later.

As the first streaks of dawn lit the horizon, he approached the stagecoach station. A youth leading a horse to the water trough stopped to stare in amazement at the approaching rider.

Despite his weariness, Fletcher smiled to himself. What a sight he must present, wearing his Mexican sombrero and crossed bandoleers over Apache buckskins, astride a Mexican saddle on an Indian pony, bristling with weapons.

Before the boy could panic Fletcher called out to him. "My name is Fletcher Faraday and I am an Englishman, despite my appearance. I've come to warn you of an impending attack by bandits."

There had been time to ride to an American settlement nearby and to round up outlying farmers.

Murrieta and his men were astonished to be met by a well-prepared group of citizens firing from every vantage point. Surely every tree and boulder concealed a sniper, while the stage station had armed men at every window.

What was worse, Murrieta's bandits were suddenly

attacked from the rear by Apache. The bloodcurdling war cry of the Chiricahua struck more fear into the *bandidos* than the hail of bullets, and when two riders in rapid succession were felled by arrows, the raid quickly disintegrated into a rout.

That night Fletcher feasted on roast beef and yams and fresh-baked bread and listened in amazement as the settlers spoke of the changes that had come about during his years with the Chiricahua.

He had known that the war between the United States and Mexico had come to an end, and now learned that the Mexican territory of Alta California had been ceded to the United States. The news that the discovery of gold at Sutter's Mill had precipitated a mass migration from all over the world certainly explained the increase in wagon trains crossing Apacheria. Furthermore, train tracks were being laid to link the western settlements with the East, bringing still more settlers. Fletcher had a sudden disquieting vision of hordes of whites engulfing the *Tin-ne-ah* and wondered if, so vastly outnumbered, they would survive.

The men seated about the dinner table in the stagecoach station dropped fascinating bits of information into the conversation, and he would have liked to press for more details, but they were too curious about his life with the Apache and asked so many questions he spent most of the evening answering them. He was given sympathetic but somewhat doubtful looks when he told them that he remembered little of his life before joining the Chiricahua Apache.

Fletcher felt ill at ease, not only because he was out of touch with the world beyond Apacheria but also because he was unaccustomed to being confined inside a building. The wooden chair upon which he sat felt uncomfortable, the air in the log cabin overheated and stale.

For the first time since leaving the Chiricahua stronghold, he realized fully what lay in store for him. There would be no simple transition from Apache brave to English diplomat. Indeed, he might never be able to resume the life he'd known before, nor even want to. He felt no connection to these men, although physically he resembled them and spoke their language.

One burly farmer said, "Well, we'd best get you into some decent clothes right away. Somebody's going to bushwhack you if they see you dressed half 'Pache and half Mex. My oldest son is about your size. You come by my place, and we'll take care of it."

"I'm very grateful to you, sir."

"If you're looking for a job, I'll hire you on," another farmer said, and the others joined in a chorus of agreement.

"No, thank you," Fletcher said quickly. "I must continue on my way to Mexico City. That's were I was going when I was attacked. You see . . . I must find my wife."

Chapter 39

. . . .

"YOU SENT FOR me?" Phin asked dully. "How shall I pleasure you?"

Kane took her arm and pulled her closer to the circle of light created by his bedside lamp. "Something happened to you. What happened, Phin?"

She stared at him uncomprehendingly for a moment and then, as if he had not asked the question, said, "Edward came to see you, did he not? No doubt to ask you to play your violin at his sister's hotel. You should accept their offer, Kane. Leave this house before it is too late."

"I'll leave at once, if you come, too."

"You must go first. There is no time to lose."

"Tell me what happened to you. Suddenly all the life went out of you. I would ask you to look at yourself except that I harbor no mirrors in my room. But then, I suspect you must also have discarded every looking glass you own. Your hair has lost its gloss, there are circles under your eyes, and your generous application of Blanc de Perle doesn't disguise the fact that you have not bathed for days."

Phin walked unsteadily toward the window. "This house—this town—cannot endure. Not the way they are building. Everything is all wrong. So many buildings are not aligned properly. There is bad *fung shui* here."

"*Fung shui*?"

She waved her hand in a vague gesture. "Wind and water. The right balance with nature. This house should have been built with the hill behind and the water in front, not the opposite as it is. The windows should be arranged so that good spirits can get in, but the bad ones cannot."

"What nonsense. Besides, if this *fung shui* is so critical to you, why did you come here in the first place?"

"I put a *baht qwa* in my room. It is an eight-sided mirror to reflect and frighten away evil spirits. But it didn't work. The evil ones got into my room anyway."

"This cursed house is turning you into a superstitious China girl, and dammit, you're not. You're as much European as Asian."

He crossed the room and stood behind her. The window opened onto a narrow balcony strung with the house's trademark paper lanterns. His room was at the back of the house, overlooking the water. "Let us leave together, Phin," he said urgently. "Now. Tonight."

She turned to face him and spoke with a hint of her old fire. "No. I will not be your slave."

"I'm not suggesting it. For God's sake, tell me what's wrong!"

"How much did they offer you to play at the Rosebriar?"

"Edward asked what I was paid here. I told him, truthfully, three ounces of gold dust a night. He said he would be back with an offer as soon as Max Seadon returned."

"So you *are* thinking of leaving?"

"I was going to talk to you about it as soon as I had a definite offer from Seadon. There have been many other offers, but I thought perhaps I could persuade you to come with me if I went to the Rosebriar."

"Oh? Why?"

"Because of family connections. Your sister's husband and her sister-in-law—"

"Hush! You are never to speak of my ties to Emily. Never, do you hear? No one must know." She hesitated a moment and then asked wistfully, "Did you ask Edward about her? Is she well? Is she happy?"

Kane thought of his brief meeting with Emily's husband. Edward had been cordial but businesslike. His sister would like to hire Kane's services and wished to know how much he was paid at the Lantern House. Almost as an afterthought, as he was leaving, Edward had added, "By the way, Phin sent my wife a letter, formally ending their friendship."

To Phin, Kane answered, "No. I didn't ask. But he mentioned that you had written to her."

"Yes. To say goodbye. As I now wish to say goodbye to you. Please, leave this house while you still can. I have looked into the future, and all I see is darkness and demons. If you stay, I will drag you down into the fires of hell with me. I saw it in my fortune-telling disks."

"Those same disks you were using to frighten Tonia Bardine, you mean? Come on, Phin, it's all nonsense and you know it."

She sighed deeply. "The Occidental half of me thought so, too, but the Chinese half now knows differently. Ah, how often our own worst schemes are turned against us! At first I practiced telling my own future in order to be credible when I told hers. But then, each time I sorted the disks, the same pattern emerged—no matter how I tried to change it. Every day I tried again and every day the same thing. The two of us—who came here together—I see us lost in this house, lost in impenetrable darkness. We can't find our way out. I do not know when the end will be, but I believe it will be soon. But there is a faint hope. The disks show us being lost together, so we may escape our fate if we separate. Perhaps we can trick the evil spirits if we are not together. You must leave, Kane, I beg you to go."

"At least leave with me—you don't have to stay with me. I just want you away from this house, this life."

"There is something here I must find. I cannot go until I find it."

"What? What have you lost?"

"Everything of value. All of my jewelry, my money, gold dust, everything. Stolen from me."

He gave a sigh of relief. "Is that all? Phin, I'll buy you all the jewelry you want, give you all the gold dust your heart desires. I've been paid so handsomely I believe I'm fairly well off. I deposited most of my money in the bank, which is what you should have done with yours. But in any case, there's more than enough for both of us.''

"You don't understand. Some of my jewelry I brought back with me from China, and I feel as if my past were stolen along with it, and the money I saved for my future has been taken from me also, leaving me trapped in this horrible present. But there is more to it than that. I have a demon gnawing at my vitals. He is called vengeance, and I must appease him.''

"Acts of revenge usually have a nasty habit of backfiring, Phin. Besides, how are you going to find the thief? It could be anybody, from one of the other girls to any of the customers.''

"The thief is Qing Chan. No one else would dare enter my room; no one else hates me as she does. It is not only because she was forced to take me into her house and dare not question anything I do because Tonia Bardine has ordered her to keep me happy so that you will stay. No, there is much, much more to her hatred than that. She hates me for my mixed blood. You believe your people look down their long noses at Eurasians? Ha! Their contempt is nothing compared to the utter disdain of a Chinese for one with the tainted blood of a barbarian in her veins.''

The merest hint of a smile twisted Kane's scarred mouth. "Don't you think—given your current occupation and that of the mama-san—that the matter of mixed blood is somewhat inconsequential?''

"I am too tired to argue with you. Will you leave? Please.''

"Phin, I came here to try—in my own rather useless way—to protect you. If I left now and something happened to you, I'd never forgive myself. Let's go together, make a new start.''

"No! I will not go with you.''

"Then leave by yourself. If you won't accept help from me, then go to your Jesuit. He will be more than happy to provide for you when you renounce your evil ways." His voice was harsh and filled with fear for her.

Not recognizing his genuine concern for her, she cried angrily, "*My* evil ways? Who are you to judge me? Who is he? You are men, nothing more. Goodbye, Kane. I will not willingly come to you again."

Before he could stop her, she darted under his arm and raced from the room.

Cervantes slid from his bed, his fingers closing around his revolver, as his door slowly opened. He drew in his breath sharply as he recognized his midnight visitor. Tonia, wearing a thin silk dressing gown, her black hair streaming loosely about her shoulders, stepped into the room and closed the door behind her.

She carried a candle in a pewter holder and set it down on his dresser. "You can put the gun away, Cervantes. For now, at least."

"What is it you want, señora?"

"To talk to you."

"In my bedchamber? With the señor upstairs asleep? If the señora wishes to die, there are less painful ways, and for myself, I have no wish to be caught by your husband."

"He's dead drunk, passed out completely. He'll sleep until morning," Tonia lied. Henry Bardine never slept deeply, no matter how drunk.

She looked at her bodyguard, who had stripped off his shirt. His pectoral muscles were well developed for one so lean, and his chest was smooth and hairless, unlike Henry's gorilla-like mat of coarse hair. She had an immediate impulse to run her hands over Cervantes's chest, to encircle his nipples with her mouth, to press her body to his. She had seen him as only a hired protector, a Mexican bandit to be used as a shield between herself and others, but not looked upon, or treated, as a man in his own right. Now in the intimate caress of the candlelight, with his smooth olive skin so temptingly near, she felt a warmth radiating within her, and when she spoke again her voice was low, inviting. "He wants to take me away with him, Cervantes, aboard his new ship. I would be gone for months. I don't want to go. I don't want to go anywhere with Captain Bardine.''

"So.'' Cervantes slid the revolver back under his bed and moved so close to her she could feel his breath fan her cheek. He regarded her with a bold stare that sent shivers rippling along her spine. "You come to Cervantes to ask him to kill your husband for you, *sí*? *Caramba*! You think I did not expect you to ask me this? You think I did not know from the beginning why you hired me?''

He picked up a strand of her hair and brushed it back over her shoulder, taking her silk robe with it. She held her breath as his warm hand closed over the cool flesh of her shoulder, then slid to her breast.

She stared at his mouth, at the thin cruel lips curling back over feral white teeth, felt her own lips part and grow moist. She swayed forward against him, feeling as if she were in a trance, unable to speak or think or even feel anything beyond a white-hot surge of desire.

Then his mouth took hers, and his hands were under her robe, exploring her body. Roughly he pushed her back onto his bed and fell on top of her.

She was aware of his eyes and his lips and the insistent probing of his hands. He was not rough in the same way as Henry, his demands were more subtle, but just as compelling as the brute force of her husband. She felt overpowered, swept away by the molten lava of passion flowing from his body to hers.

She cried out, heedless of the danger of alerting others to her presence in her servant's bed, as his manhood found the core of her need. Then all rational thought ended, and she lost herself in delicious, forbidden rapture.

There was no more conversation until, an hour before dawn, she forced herself to break free from him. "Cervantes, please . . . my God, you are magnificent, but we must talk now . . . ah! Oh, that feels wonderful! But listen . . . oh, oh, oh! Ah, where did you learn to do that? Listen, darling, we must make plans. Henry is so crafty, he has only one eye, but I swear he can see in his sleep and certainly out the back of his head, so we shall have to be very careful . . ."

Cervantes raised himself on one elbow and looked down at her. "And when your husband is dead, señora, what then? You keep Cervantes here in the servants' quarters, your trained wolf, to kill any man who angers you, take you to your whorehouse, and bury your money in the ground? To escort you about town with his gun and his knife at the ready? Maybe, when you feel the need, you slip into his room with your hair down and your nakedness hardly covered and tempt him? Tell me, señora, this is your plan, sí?"

"My dear, no, of course not. You will share everything with me. Naturally, I could not marry you, but—"

"Why not?" His voice was silken soft. "Because I am a—what do you call us? A Mex, a greaser?"

She cleared her throat nervously. "We would have to keep up appearances. But I would make you a very rich man, Cervantes."

He laughed and buried his face in her breasts and did not give her another opportunity to speak.

Just before dawn she crept from his room, feeling sore and sated, and unsure who had been in charge of the encounter.

That day Henry insisted she accompany him to the clipper *Antonia* to supervise the loading of her trunks and personal belongings. After that he kept her with him while he checked on the provisions being loaded for the long sea voyage around the Horn.

It was late when they returned to their house, and she was tired and irritable. There was so much to be done and only two days left to accomplish everything. She really needed to go to the Lantern House and check on her interests there, and it was essential that she speak with Cervantes again, to see if he had a plan for disposing of Henry. Her secret inner places trembled in anticipation of being with Cervantes again, despite her fatigue.

But on this night Henry seemed insatiable, and no matter

what she did she could not seem to satisfy him or get him to fall asleep. At length it was she who drifted off to sleep, out of sheer exhaustion.

She awoke to find a sullen dawn breaking, the streets shrouded with mist. Henry was not in bed with her.

Donning a dressing gown, she hastily pushed her feet into slippers and rang for her maid.

Minutes later she asked the girl, "Is Captain Bardine having breakfast?"

"No, señora. He said to tell you he was going to the ship and then he'd stop at the bank on his way home."

"Very well. You may go. Have a pot of coffee sent up and then come and help me dress. And while you're downstairs tell Cervantes to bring the carriage around."

"He is not here, señora."

"What do you mean, not here? Did he go with Captain Bardine?" It was unlikely, since Henry disliked the former bandit and rarely even spoke to him—a fact Tonia felt would further convince Cervantes to kill him.

"No, señora. Captain Bardine left by himself."

"Then Cervantes probably went on some errand. Send him to me when he returns."

"Not coming back, señora."

"Of course he's coming back."

"All his things are gone from his room. His horse is gone. He is gone."

Tonia pushed the girl aside and raced downstairs to the servants' quarters.

The door to Cervantes's room was wide open. All of his personal possessions were gone.

Tonia leaned weakly against the door. Damn him. Damn him all to hell, the coward. He'd left her rather than face Henry Bardine. Well, she didn't need any man. She'd never needed a man, not since the day her father had sold her to his creditors, two ugly old men who had used and abused her for hours before she crawled out into the alley and hid from them. She had been twelve years old.

She returned to her own room, calmer now. After all, there were murders every day in San Francisco. The

fearsome Hounds and the Sydney Ducks ruled the streets of
some parts of town. It would not be too difficult to find
someone else to do what Cervantes had been afraid to do.
Not every ruffian in town was aware of Captain Henry
Bardine's fearsome reputation. Surely two or three men
would be a match for him, for the right price.

Chapter 40

• •

PHIN TOSSED RESTLESSLY on her bed, unable to either fall asleep or come fully awake, caught in the terrifying web of her own fear and dread. Everything was building to some cataclysmic conclusion, she was certain, and she felt powerless to stop the tidal wave about to engulf her. She had sprinkled camphor and rose petals around her bed to ward off the night spirits but realized it was a futile gesture.

She could hear the sounds of Kane's music and the giggles of the other girls as they led their clients to their rooms. But Phin had no clients. The mama-san had told her curtly, on the day following her discovery that she had been robbed, that she was not to join the others in the lobby.

Deprived now of the means of earning even enough for a humble new beginning, Phin knew she was lost. How long would it be before Qing Chan sent her to a crib or a parlor house—or, worse, to the "hospital" to die?

Occasionally a weak but urgent voice in the back of Phin's mind strove to be heard. That voice asked her to look for answers to the question of how and why her present malady had come about. That malady was her total acceptance of defeat, something she had never experienced before. Why was she unable to see a way out of her present dilemma?

This fearful lethargy, which had begun about the same time she had decided to leave the Lantern House, left her unable to think clearly. It was almost as if she were under the influence of opium.

Some of the girls had said Lee Wong would provide a pipe and *gow* pills for a price and suggested to Phin the smoke would help get her through a night's work. Phin refused. She had used the drug only once, a long time ago in China, and had been put off by the dreamy stupor and lack of control it produced. When she later observed how some people became utterly enslaved by the drug, she had vowed never again to use it.

The nagging inner voice persisted in calling her attention to an incident that had occurred several days earlier. She had been eating the main meal of the day, which was served in the early morning just before the girls retired to bed. As the maid had started to place her plate in front of her, Qing Chan had said sharply, "No, not that plate. There is a special plate for Phin Tsu. She is looking sickly and I have ordered especially nutritious food for her."

Phin clutched her abdomen in realization of what was happening to her. Her nightmare fears and lethargy were not of her own making. She was being fed opium or some other drug with her food.

Tonia was in no mood for the performance of Oriental business rituals. She said impatiently, "No, I don't want any tea. Finish totaling the receipts so that I can go over the books."

Qing Chan's withered fingers rapidly moved the beads of her abacus. "If milady will permit, is necessary to discuss the girl Phin Tsu."

"I don't want to hear any more complaints about Phin Tsu. You know very well that Kane will only continue to play for us if she remains. Besides, she is very attractive. You must put aside your prejudice against Eurasians."

The crafty eyes of the mama-san glittered like the small black beads her finger manipulated. "She is slipping more and more under the influence of the magic smoke. She has already used all of her earnings to buy it and now is stealing from the other girls. She is lost in a dreamworld from which it is impossible to arouse her. Most nights she is unable to service the clients."

"Then cut off her supply of opium, you old fool. Confine her to the house. Insist that the other girls give you their valuables to put in the safe or take them to the bank. You must keep Phin Tsu healthy and happy at all costs.''

Qing Chan decided it was time to speak boldly. ''The music maker Kane would perhaps follow Phin Tsu if she left to go to another house, but if she no longer existed . . . he would stay here, I am certain. He is accustomed to us, he is comfortable here, he has everything he wants. One of the other girls would soon catch his eye.''

Tonia regarded the mama-san with a knowing stare, understanding the need to be rid of someone. Sometimes there was no other way. Tonia herself now felt the need to be rid of Henry, just as once Fletcher had stood in the way of the life she wanted to lead. She had quickly decided she did not want to live in Mexico among people whose language and culture were alien to her, nor did she intend to remain with a man who would never be wealthy. The discovery of his nest egg merely hastened the end she had been planning anyway. Just as Henry Bardine's proposed voyage to set a clipper ship record now made his demise imminent. Qing Chan had run the Lantern House as efficiently as Henry ran his ships, and Tonia did not want to lose her services. But this obsession to be rid of Phin had to be nipped in the bud.

''If anything happens to that girl, I will hold you responsible, Qing Chan. I do not agree that Kane would stay on. I want him to stay happy and her to be healthy. Do you understand?''

The mama-san nodded silently, and only the shaking of her fingers on the abacus hinted at her inner rage.

Tonia, who had other things on her mind, quickly forgot the subject of Phin. When the matter of the receipts was disposed of, she said, ''Go and fetch Lee Wong now, then leave us alone. I must hire someone to replace Cervantes.''

When her doorman appeared, Tonia waited to be sure Qing Chan was out of the room and then said, ''I need two—no, three men for a special task. I want you to find them for me. They must be men who have no qualms about what they do. I am prepared to pay them handsomely. I

believe a good place to look for these men would be among
the Hounds or the Sydney Ducks.''

Lee Wong's enormous moonlike face showed no reaction, but the flicker of his slitted eyes told her that he
understood perfectly the type of men she required.

''Naturally, there will be a bonus for yourself for discreetly finding these men,'' Tonia continued. ''I must meet
with them no later than tomorrow at midnight. Have them
waiting for me in the bath house when I get here, and be
sure no one disturbs us.''

Edward and Brent watched Ramon hop down the steep
slope on one leg, expertly balanced on the crutch Brent had
fashioned for him.

''Look at that agility!'' Edward exclaimed. ''Ah, the
remarkable healing power of the human body—especially
when it is young.''

''God answered our prayers,'' Brent said. ''Now, if you
would only open your mind and soul to listen to His plea
that you dedicate your life to caring for the sick and
afflicted.''

''Let's not spoil this happy day with that old argument,''
Edward replied. ''I have no intention of becoming a doctor.
There are enough quacks in San Francisco, dispensing their
sugar pills and snake oil. In fact, now that Ramon is
obviously well on the road to recovery, I came to tell you
that I shall no longer be traveling out here to see you.
You're too far from town, and I have too much to do there.
Besides, my wife is in poor health, and I do not wish to
leave her alone.''

Brent's brilliantly blue eyes flashed in his direction.
Edward had often felt that those eyes could draw a man's
secrets from his very soul. Brent smiled. ''She is with
child?''

Edward nodded, but his expression was troubled.

''Why such a woebegone face? Surely you are happy that
you will be a father?''

''Yes, of course, I'm delighted. But Emily is so frail. I
should have taken care to postpone motherhood until she is

stronger. Her months of poor nutrition and slave labor in the doctor's house left her weakened. Then the rigors of the long voyage around the Horn took their toll. She suffered terribly from seasickness—she was just skin and bones when she arrived. Now with the demands the developing baby is making on her . . . I'm worried about how she will withstand the pregnancy, and even more worried about her ability to deliver the child. Her hips are so narrow.''

"She is in God's hands, Edward.''

"She was in *my* hands when it came to preventing pregnancy.''

"Edward! Mind your tongue. You're speaking to a priest. It is a sin to try to prevent your wife from conceiving.''

"I am not a Roman Catholic, Brent, so spare me the sermon. But—well, I would appreciate your prayers for Emily and the child. I must be going. I probably won't see you again.''

"Don't be too sure about that. I have a young Jesuit en route from Mexico to take over the mission here. I shall be doing God's bidding in San Francisco. There are many souls to be saved there, much missionary work to be done.''

"Starting with Phin Tsu at the Lantern House?'' Edward asked dryly. "You'd be wasting your breath.''

"If necessary, I shall burn the cursed place to the ground, but yes, save her I will. Along with the other sinners.''

"Fighting words, coming from a priest.''

"Our founder, Saint Ignatius Loyola, urged us to go, set the world on fire.''

"Surely the admonition was intended to be symbolic.''

"We Jesuits are perhaps more aggressive than other orders, Edward. You see, our work as educators is centered on our reverence for knowledge, but our mission as priests is first concerned with virtue. So we constantly deal with the tension between knowledge and virtue. It is a moral battle that has created the most dynamic of Christian orders.''

"From what I've observed,'' Edward remarked, "you Jesuits are a mass of paradoxes. You seem to thrive on tension, drama, tragedy. I've heard that you deliberately seek martyrdom. Look what happened to your priests at the hands of the Indians.''

''We do not shrink from danger, if that's what you mean. We do not believe we must sacrifice our masculinity for the sake of our piety.''

Edward grinned. ''Perhaps I'd better hurry back to San Francisco and warn everyone to repent before it's too late. To be honest, I've never seen a city that needed saving more. My sister serves afternoon tea to the respectable women in town, and at last count I believe there were only about two dozen of them.''

''Come back into the *casa* for a moment. I'll have Carlotta pack some cheese and tortillas for your journey back to town.''

''I shan't be hungry after that meal she just served us, but perhaps some of her cheese might tempt Emily's appetite. She can't keep anything down except a little weak tea and desperately needs nourishment.''

They were in the kitchen watching Carlotta wrap cheese in a cloth when they heard excited cries and the sound of footsteps on the tiled corridor. One of the Mexican boys came running into the kitchen. ''Father! Come quickly.''

''What is it, my son?''

''A man—hurt—bleeding!'' the boy cried. ''His horse brought him, and he fell off and lies in the cornfield.''

''American? Indian?''

''No, Father. He is Mexican.''

Brent looked at Edward. ''You'd better come, too.''

''Do you have a gun? I left mine in the pony trap outside.''

''A doctor doesn't need a gun, and neither does a priest.''

''They do if your visitor is a bandit, which is more than likely, and probably with the rest of his gang hard on his heels,'' Edward answered, but Brent was already following the boy outside.

Edward's worst fears were confirmed the moment he saw the visitor's lathered horse with the bloodstained saddle. The man lay on the ground on his back. He was unconscious, a gray cast to his swarthy skin and blood soaking his shirt, oozing up between crossed bandoleers of cartridges.

"He's been shot, perilously close to the heart," Edward said, bending over him. "I doubt he'll regain consciousness."

Wordlessly Brent slipped his powerful arms under the man and lifted him into the air. He strode back toward the house, carrying his burden as easily as if the grown man were a child.

Resigned to at least attempting to treat the bandit, Edward went in search of his medical bag. By the time he joined Brent in the sickroom, he was administering last rites.

Edward paused and was about to leave and let the priest perform his ritual, but then a stubborn denial to meekly permit death to have its way surfaced. Or was it, he wondered as he rolled up his sleeves and fished in his bag for a probe and scalpel, a need to compete with Brent in that ancient conflict between men of God and men of science? To save a man's body instead of his soul?

Chapter 41

· ·

EMILY CLUTCHED HER dressing table as waves of weakness and nausea assailed her again.

Behind her, Josefa said again, "Please, señora, don't go. You are not well enough. Ah, *Madre de Dios*, the señor will kill me when he finds you gone."

"Edward won't know," Emily replied. "I shall be home long before he returns. He has gone out to the *casa de niños*. He won't be back before nightfall, I'm sure."

She tied the strings of her bonnet. "Bring my wool cape, will you, Josefa? I feel so cold nowadays."

Josefa's reluctance to be a part of such a foolhardy venture was written all over her lovely face. "I am afraid to go with you," she said miserably. "They will take me and make me into a whore."

"No one can make you do anything you don't want to do, and I certainly can't insist that you go with me. But at least tell me how to find the Lantern House."

"No decent señora goes there. They won't let you in."

"Josefa, please stop arguing with me. It's near the waterfront, isn't it?"

"*Sí*. But those places don't open in the daytime. They'll all be sleeping. You're wasting your time." Josefa's English was not good enough to translate all of her thoughts, and so she spoke in Spanish, but it was a useless gesture anyway, as Emily was already plodding resolutely down the stairs. Josefa was far too fearful to follow.

Edward had taken the pony trap and both horses, leaving one at the blacksmith's for shoeing, so Emily had no alternative but to walk, since she had been unable to persuade Josefa to go to the livery stable and hire a horse and trap for her. Josefa's command of English deteriorated rapidly when she was asked to do something she did not want to do. Under ordinary circumstances the walk would not have been a problem, but early pregnancy caused such dizziness that Emily worried about fainting and harming the baby. Still, she simply had to see Phin and learn why her half sister had turned so cold toward her.

Going downhill was fairly easy, but she dreaded having to climb the steep slope to their hilltop home. Perhaps Phin could arrange to hire a conveyance for her. Emily was unsure just what privileges the girls of the Lantern House enjoyed, or even, as Josefa had suggested, if she would be admitted.

Emily had no trouble recognizing the house. Strings of paper lanterns, unlit as it was morning, adorned the eaves, windows, balconies, and veranda. The red lacquered front doors were emblazoned with white Chinese symbols and were flanked with a pair of more permanent wrought-iron lanterns. She raised a brass doorknocker in the shape of a rearing dragon and let it fall.

After several minutes the door yawned open to reveal a very young Chinese girl, rubbing sleep from her eyes.

"Good morning," Emily said, distracted by the fact that the girl wore only a tangerine-colored silk jacket which barely reached the tops of her bare legs. "I wish to see Phin Tsu. Will you tell her Emily Dale is here?"

The girl looked at her blankly.

"Phin Tsu," Emily repeated firmly and stepped into the vestibule before the red door was closed in her face.

The girl hesitated, then turned and slipped through an inner door, closing it behind her. Emily leaned weakly against the vestibule wall. There was nowhere to sit.

A few minutes later a tiny Asian woman, thin as a stick and with skin like wrinkled parchment, opened the inner door and regarded Emily with tiny crafty eyes. "No visitors. You go now."

"I must speak with Phin Tsu. I know she is here. Please inform her that Emily Dale is waiting and . . ." Emily faltered as through a stained-glass panel in the inner door she saw that a Chinese man of enormous size was now standing motionless, watching them. She wondered for one panicked instant if he would pick her up bodily and remove her.

The old woman said, "Phin Tsu is ill. See nobody. You go now."

Although Emily felt faint, she forced herself to return the woman's stare unblinkingly. "I'm not leaving until I see her."

For a moment they fought a silent battle of wills, then the old woman shrugged and withdrew. The huge figure of her manservant remained just inside the lobby.

Emily waited, unsure if anyone would return. She could feel perspiration forming on her brow, but she was icy cold.

She was about to give up and leave, so much time had passed, when at last the Chinese man stepped aside, and Phin entered the vestibule, moving so slowly she seemed almost to be sleepwalking.

Emily caught her breath at the sight of her half sister. Phin did indeed look ill, far more ill than Emily herself felt. Her formerly translucent complexion now had an unhealthy cast, the whites of her eyes had yellowed, and the pupils were unnaturally large. Phin had always been immaculately clean and took pride in her luxurious black hair, which now was matted and unkempt. Her trousers were creased and her silk blouse soiled. She swayed on her feet as if in a trance, and her gaze was unfocused.

"Oh, Phin!" Emily attempted to embrace her, but Phin pulled away, pressing herself back against the door.

"Don't touch me!" she whispered. "I am unclean. Why did you come here? To shame me, as the priest shamed me?"

"Father Juan came here? Edward didn't tell me that. But, Phin, whatever he said to you, please believe that I came only out of a desire to see you. I've missed you so much. When you wrote that dreadful letter, I was devastated. What have I done?"

"You are an ignorant barbarian," Phin said, but her voice

was gentle, belying the words. "A barbarian who does not understand the grand design of life. The arrivals and departures, the beginnings and the endings. You should not have come here. You must never seek me out again. You are embarrassing both of us. Let us save face now by parting cordially."

"But why? *Why*?"

"Do you want the world to know that your sister is a Chinese whore?"

"Please don't call yourself that."

"Why not? It's true. And even if I were not a whore, I still would not be acceptable. Don't you know how the citizens of San Francisco feel about even the most respectable and industrious of my people?"

"Phin, I'm with child," Emily blurted out.

"That is an even stronger reason why we must part."

"But you are the baby's aunt. Oh, Phin, I do so want my child to know you. You are the only blood kin I have."

Phin swayed drunkenly, and Emily instinctively put out a hand to steady her, despite her own weakness. "Phin, you're ill. Please, come outside into the fresh air—perhaps we could go somewhere and have tea?"

"No, I cannot go outside. I will never leave this house."

"What are you saying? Phin, you only came here to find out about . . . you know who. From what you said in your letter, you have learned that what we feared is true. There is no reason for you to stay longer. Besides, you are ill. Please, come home with me. We can take care of each other, just as we did in New York."

"Go home to your husband, Emily. I shall not see you again."

Phin pulled free of Emily's supporting hands and disappeared through the inner door before Emily could react. She found herself looking up into the solemn face of the Chinese man. He opened the red lacquered door. "Missy leave now."

"I will speak with Mr. Kane!" Emily cried desperately. "Please summon him."

"Missy leave now." He did not touch her, but somehow

she was propelled outside and found herself standing on the street.

Briony sighed in blissful contentment and patted her lips with a damask napkin. "Louis-Philippe, you are the greatest chef who ever lived. That was the most delicious meal I have ever eaten. Soon I shall be as big as a house."

The little Frenchman refilled her wineglass. "Not if you drink wine with your meals. Zee wine eats up the fat."

She laughed. "It also makes me act in a rather giddy manner most unbecoming to my position here."

"Ah, but you are far too beautiful to work! You should marry a man who adores you and let him spoil you." He paused and affected a mock-serious expression of great concentration. "I believe that man should be my 'umble self."

"Oh, Louis, you'll never know how much I've enjoyed your company, even your outrageous flirting. I can't remember when I laughed so much before you came to the Rosebriar. I'm so grateful to you for all you've done."

It was true. He had taken immediate and efficient charge of the dining room and the private banquets. He had hired musicians and kept them happy with his cuisine. He could bully, cajole, or flatter anyone into doing his bidding. In a few short days he had made himself indispensable. Almost to the point that Briony no longer watched anxiously for Max's return.

Briony leaned back in her chair, holding her wineglass up in front of the candelabra to admire the clear amber liquid. "This wine is wonderful. French, I suppose? But the color reminds me of California sunshine."

"Someday I believe there will be vineyards in California. The climate is right. Ah, Briony, how fortunate we are to be 'ere at this time. A whole new country, p'raps a new kind of life, is being born."

They were alone in the smallest of the private banquet rooms, and a fire blazed in the hearth to ward off the chill of the evening. Briony felt no inclination to retire to bed, despite the lateness of the hour or the strenuous workday she had just completed. She was sated by the fine food, the smooth wine, the warmth of the fire, and not least, Louis-Philippe's stimulating company.

She dreamily admired the images captured in her wineglass, which transformed the firelit room into something as mystically surreal and lovely as an El Greco painting. How perfect every detail of the Rosebriar was! It occurred to her that she could not have loved the hotel more had it been her own home, as indeed it was, but made more exciting by the continual stream of guests and visitors. A queen in her court, Max had joked, but no royal lady commanded more respect, nor enjoyed her subjects' devotion more than she did.

Louis-Philippe began to tell one of his ribald stories of the latest exploits of the newly rich miners who came into town determined to spend money like water, and Briony was laughing helplessly when the doors to the banquet room were flung open.

She looked up in surprise as Max Seadon seemed to burst into the room. Louis-Philippe swiveled slowly in his chair to look over his shoulder. "Ah, *mon ami*, you 'ave come back at last."

Max had obviously come looking for them the moment he reached the hotel. His clothes were rumpled and trail-dusted, and he was badly in need of a shave and a haircut. There were tired lines around his eyes, and his expression was anything but cordial. He growled, "Well, this is a cozy little scene."

"Come and join us, *mon ami*," Louis said easily. "I will pour you some wine."

For some unaccountable reason, Briony felt a pulse begin to flutter in her throat. "Max, Louis-Philippe has been a godsend. He relieved me of so many duties. I don't know how I would have managed without him. We must persuade him to . . ." Her voice trailed away under Max's impersonal scrutiny.

He tossed his coat and hat to the nearest chair and stood with his back to the fire. He was wearing a gunbelt, Briony noted, with a pair of Colt revolvers prominently on display.

He said shortly, "Will you excuse us, Louis? I have to speak to my hotel manager in private."

Briony stiffened. So she was to be relegated to the role of employee, and no doubt chastised for sharing a late dinner with their chef. She tried to contain her anger, although a voice inside her head cried out *Why, that arrogant bastard! After all I've done to create the finest hotel in town!*

The Frenchman rose to his feet immediately, gave Briony a sympathetic glance, and picked up her hand. He brushed his lips over her wrist without haste. "*Bon nuit*, Briony. Remembaire what I told you. And don't let this 'ombre bully you. I shall see you in the morning."

His footsteps fell quietly on the carpeted floor, and only the gentle click of the door closing and a slight shifting of ash in the grate broke the silence.

Briony took another sip of wine.

"Don't you think you've had enough of that? When I came in you were giggling like a schoolgirl."

"Welcome home, Max." Her voice dripped with sarcasm. "I see you've returned in remarkably good humor."

"And I see you lost no time in turning your charm on Louis-Philippe. I couldn't pay him enough to come and cook for us, but you flutter your eyes and smile invitingly, and lo and behold, here he is."

"Surely all that matters is that he's here, and if we make him a handsome offer, I believe he might stay," Briony replied. "Max, you're obviously tired and out of sorts. Why don't we wait until morning to discuss business? I have a feeling that anything either of us says tonight is going to be the wrong thing."

"My announcement can't wait. Tomorrow I expect to pack my belongings and leave the Rosebriar for good."

"For good?" Briony repeated faintly. "You . . . haven't sold the hotel?"

"No. But I am going to rent it to some investors. They'll run the hotel and restaurant, but my real profits will come from the gaming tables I intend to lease. I've been offered ten thousand dollars a month for each table, which together with the hotel rental will give me an income well into six figures annually. Why bother with the work and trouble of running the place myself?''

Briony sat quite still, letting his words sink in. At length she drew a deep breath and, unwilling to confront the worst possibility, brought up the least. ''Gaming tables, Max? You're going to turn our lovely hotel into a sporting house?''

He raised an eyebrow. ''*Our* hotel, Briony?''

She flushed. ''Are you telling me that you no longer require my services?''

He shrugged. ''You might apply for a position with the new people, see if they need a manager. Or maybe you could learn to deal faro, if you feel you must stay on. But I doubt the roughneck miners who are taking over will be interested in afternoon teas and violin recitals. Besides, you've got your store to run. You aren't going to be left high and dry without the means to support yourself.''

Briony stood up and faced him across the remains of the late supper she had shared with Louis-Philippe, realizing all at once how intimate it must have appeared to Max. Even though she knew it was the wrong thing to say, she could not resist remarking, ''Was it Mr. William Congreve who wrote that hell hath no fury like a *woman* scorned? I believe he had the wrong gender. This is unworthy of you, Max.''

''You flatter yourself, Briony. This decision has nothing to do with you. It's a business matter, pure and simple.''

''There's nothing pure or simple about it. You say you are leaving tomorrow. Does that mean I must move out, also? We have no written contract, but even the lowliest scullery maid is usually given adequate notice.''

''There'll be a generous severance payment for you, and you can occupy your suite until you find other accommodations, providing you do so within a reasonable length of time.''

Pride did not permit her to question him further. She said quietly, ''Then there's nothing more to be said. Good night.''

Kane had become accustomed to the crowds of men who jammed every inch of the Lantern House where his music could be heard. Many came to drink and gamble, or eat in the newly opened dining room; not all took advantage of the erotic pleasures provided by the girls; but all listened in rapt silence when Kane placed bow to strings and filled the air with the magic of his music.

After peering through the wicker trelliswork of the pagoda to assure himself that once again Phin was not seated with the other girls, he forgot all about his mesmerized audience and began to play a favorite Mozart selection.

He was worried about Phin. On the one hand he was glad she was no longer servicing the throngs of lonely men who nightly lined up outside on the street waiting to get in, but she also refused to see him, and he worried about the state of her health. The last conversation they'd had disturbed him greatly. He hadn't wanted to force his way into her room to see her but decided that tonight after his performance that was exactly what he must do, to reassure himself that she was all right.

When he finished his recital in the early hours of the morning, he slipped through the private door into his own quarters with the intention of going straight to Phin's room. But to his annoyance, Qing Chan was waiting for him. He disliked the tiny woman intensely and was especially annoyed at her intrusion into his personal quarters.

"Will you see a man who says he is an old friend?" Her whispery voice made every utterance sound furtive.

"I have no friends," Kane said shortly.

"This one says to mention some names to you. Emily. Edward. Briony." She paused. "Phin Tsu."

His attention captured, Kane asked, "Who is it who wishes to see me?"

"Max Seadon. He is one of the wealthiest and most influential men in town. Our very existence and livelihood depend on keeping his goodwill. He has friends on the town council and police force. He is the owner of the finest hotel in town, the Rosebriar, and, I believe, several gold mines."

"Yes," Kane said slowly, "I know who he is. You can send him up."

Waiting for his unexpected visitor, Kane recalled their

brief acquaintance after they had all disembarked from the ship in New York. He'd barely exchanged a dozen words with Seadon at that time but knew Emily's sister-in-law had worked for him ever since. He remembered a tall, rangy, silver-haired man who exuded self-confidence and fearlessness; qualities that Kane, newly thrust into the world, had envied greatly. He recalled, too, that Seadon had an easy charm that seemed to appeal to both men and women. Kane had believed, erroneously it seemed, that Seadon had long ago forgotten all about him, if indeed he'd ever really noticed him in the first place. But perhaps no one ever quite forgot features quite as scarred as his.

A few minutes later there was a knock at his door.

He felt the impact of Max Seadon's presence instantly. Wearing a well-cut jacket over a fine linen shirt, Seadon looked just as strong and in charge of the situation as he had nearly four years earlier, and not a day older.

But there was something different about him, Kane decided as he motioned for Seadon to enter. Something lurked in the depths of his eyes that Kane understood. Max Seadon, for all his wealth, good looks, and easy charm, had recently suffered a loss.

"Thank you for receiving me, Mr. Kane."

He offered his hand, but Kane did not take it, nor did he acknowledge the gesture. No one was allowed to touch his hands.

Instead he said, "You can sit down if you wish."

"Thank you." Max searched the near darkness of the room to find a chair and eased himself into it.

Kane didn't apologize for keeping his lamp turned low; he wasn't even aware of it since he had always shunned bright light.

"I enjoyed your music very much—"

"Mr. Seadon, it's very late. I would appreciate your getting to the point with as few preliminaries as possible."

"Very well. I believe you were acquainted with Mrs. Briony Forest and her brother in England."

"That is so."

"And, I assume, you also knew Mr. Forest. That is, her husband?"

"No. I never met the man."

"But he was, as far as you know, still alive at the time she left England?"

Kane remained standing, keeping as much distance between them as possible. "Why ask me such a question? Why not ask her?"

"She never speaks of her past, and I'm quite sure she'd tell me, if I inquired, that it was none of my business."

"My sentiments entirely."

"Look, I'll lay my cards on the table. I want to find out if her first husband is still alive—"

"Her *first* husband?"

Max grinned. "A slip of the tongue, I guess. Mr. Kane, I'm prepared to pay handsomely for any information about her marriage you can give me—and I swear to you I'll never reveal the source or use any such information against her."

"You're trying to bribe a man who already has more money than he knows what to do with." Kane walked to the door and threw it open.

Max rose to his feet but made no move to leave. "You could save me a long trip to England if you'd at least confirm whether her husband is dead or alive."

Kane hesitated, then slowly closed the door. If Seadon began to investigate, he would undoubtedly uncover the fact that not only Briony, but he, too, was a fugitive from British justice. That being so, there was one outstanding matter that had preyed on his mind since leaving his father's cellar.

"You're going to England? I will answer your question, in return for a favor."

"Anything, name it."

Kane briefly explained about his father's research and medical school, and how he had lived shut away from the world in the cellar, along with the laboratory animals. "There was a half-witted youth named Dudley, who cared for the animals. I suppose you could say that apart from my father, Dudley was my only companion. From time to time I conspired with him to save a dog he had grown fond of from the research knife. My father left me all his worldly goods, but since no one knows where I am, I expect the school is being run by the executors of the estate. What I am concerned with is the boy, Dudley. I didn't think too much about his predicament when I, too, was a prisoner of the cellar, but since coming here I feel a great deal of remorse for my father's treatment of the lad. Will you set up a trust fund for him, at my expense, and find him a good home?''

''Tell me what I need to know, and I'll take care of him myself.''

''No, he is my responsibility. But since I am a fugitive from British justice, I cannot help him. Besides, there is very little I can tell you about the husband of the lady in question.''

Chapter 42

••

THE BARDINE HOUSE had been built at the crest of a hill and, like most of the newly built residences in San Francisco, rose from the bare earth without benefit of landscaping, since everyone was too busy to lay out formal gardens. However, the Bardine house was lucky enough to have a grove of live oaks in the rear, and it was here Tonia had had Cervantes bury her secret fortune.

Dawn had broken with a veil of fog wreathing the bay, and Henry Bardine had again departed early to supervise the fitting and loading of the clipper ship for what he hoped would be a record-breaking voyage. Tonia, carrying a shovel, made her way to the live oaks.

The previous midnight she had met with three of the most disreputable-looking ruffians ever to cross her path, and they had agreed to dispose of Henry Bardine. Their price was even higher than she anticipated, but she decided it was worth it. However, they had demanded gold, and the only way she could pay it was to dig up some of her buried treasure. With Cervantes gone, she decided not to let anyone else know of the secret cache.

As she reached the hollow where the live oaks grew, she stopped abruptly. A shovel and a pick were propped against the nearest tree, and an empty sack lay on the ground nearby.

She scrambled down into the deepest part of the hollow and uttered a sharp animal cry of rage as she saw the ravaged ground. The piles of earth glittered with spilled gold dust where one of the pokes must have broken open. Cervantes had not bothered to scoop up the spilled dust;

why should he bother with so little when there was so much more to steal?

What a fool she'd been! That damn greaser bandit had stayed around long enough to steal her money. To add insult to injury, before walking out on her, he had taken her to his bed. She didn't stop to consider that it had been she who seduced him. Her anger boiled up inside her, and she wanted to shriek her fury into the swirling fog, but she managed to control herself.

Perhaps he'd overlooked one of the boxes they'd buried. She fished around with the shovel, tossed some earth aside, then dropped to her knees and scrabbled in the dirt with her fingers. There was nothing left. Her only other asset was the deed to the Spanish land in the south, but the Hounds were scarcely likely to accept a musty document instead of the gold they'd been promised and there wasn't time to sell the deed, not with the *Antonia* ready to set sail.

She stood up, panting. What to do? What to *do*?

After a few minutes she was calmer. She made her way back to the house and, ignoring the curious stares of the servants at the sight of her muddy shoes and dirt-sprinkled clothes, went upstairs to change.

An hour later she arrived at Edward Dale's emporium, which stocked the largest selection of goods in town. She went to the counter and whispered to the clerk, "I've been bothered with rats lately. I must get rid of them."

"We have some very fine traps, ma'am—"

"No! I mean, my husband is away so much and I don't have any menservants. My maids and I simply couldn't bring ourselves to remove rat carcasses from traps. Don't you have any poison?"

"Oh, yes, ma'am. I'll get you a tin. It's in the back of the store. I won't be a moment."

Tonia strolled down one of the well-stocked aisles while she waited. She paused before a display of pans and skillets. Movement out on the street caught her eye. A carriage had stopped in front of the emporium and Edward Dale alighted. She heard him greet his clerks as he came in, calling out that he needed lamp wicks and to please hurry, as his wife was waiting in the carriage.

Tonia peered over the display of skillets and saw the ethereally lovely Mrs. Edward Dale seated in the open carriage.

The girl turned her head, and at that instant the sun broke through the marine layer of cloud and fog and shone full on her face. Caught in that clear light, it was easy to superimpose the face of an adolescent girl upon the face of the young woman.

Tonia Bardine had her second shock of the morning as she realized why at their first meeting Mrs. Edward Dale had looked vaguely familiar. Why hadn't she recognized Emily Faraday? It was her stepdaughter, she was certain. Not dead and buried in a Liverpool cemetery as she believed, but alive and well in San Francisco.

Tonia ground her teeth in a frenzy of anger. She had been tricked. Martin Crupe had sworn to her that the girl was dead—he'd even provided a body! No doubt of some pauper saved from an unmarked grave.

The clerk had returned with her tin of rat poison and was looking at her oddly. She realized she was still crouching furtively behind the display of pans and straightened up. She made her way back to the counter.

Fumbling in her reticule for money to pay for her purchase, she whispered, "Is there a back way out? I don't want to speak to someone out on the street just now."

"Yes, ma'am. I'll take you through the stockroom."

On her way home Tonia began to analyze the situation in regard to her stepdaughter. Somehow Emily Faraday had escaped death. Undoubtedly she had then attempted to find her father. Somewhere along the way she had met and married Edward Dale. But what was she doing in San Francisco? It was possible, of course, that like everyone else Edward Dale had come here to seek his fortune in the goldfields. But what if Emily had learned how her father died, put two and two together, and decided to follow her stepmother? What if even now she was planning to accuse her of being involved in his death? The girl looked fragile as a butterfly, but appearances could be deceiving. Didn't Phin Tsu warn her that someone from her past was seeking her, with vengence in mind?

When she arrived home, Tonia immediately dismissed her servants, a personal maid and two housemaids, for the day. "I shan't need you, you may take the day off," she told them. "We've finished packing, and I shall cook dinner tonight."

Alone in the kitchen, she opened the tin of rat poison and looked at the white crystals speculatively. What tasty dish should she prepare for Henry's dinner? He was inordinately fond of spicy Mexican foods, which would probably disguise any odd taste caused by the arsenic. She wasn't sure whether or not it had a strong taste, or how much to use to ensure Henry's swift demise. She'd heard it was possible to poison a person over a period of time with small doses, making it appear they had died after a prolonged illness, but she couldn't wait for that. The departure of the clipper ship *Antonia* was too close.

What a pity she couldn't invite Emily for dinner, too, and take care of two problems at once. But even if she accepted, which was unlikely in view of the Bardines' lack of social standing, perhaps two sudden deaths would be a bit obvious. She would deal with her suddenly resurrected stepdaughter later. Once the uncouth, ill-bred Henry Bardine was out of the way, Tonia knew she could inveigle her way into the Nob Hill crowd. Some well-publicized donations to charity and a pet cause—perhaps a public library or museum— would work wonders.

Tonia put red beans in a pan to soak and then began to crush some dried chile peppers. How would she explain the fact that she was not eating the same food as Henry? She would have to remove her portion before adding the arsenic. If she kept Henry in the parlor until the meal was on the dining table, he wouldn't notice.

When Henry Bardine arrived home that evening, he was pleasantly surprised to find his slippers and a large glass of whiskey beside his favorite armchair, his wife wearing a becoming low-cut gown, and for once not complaining bitterly about the forthcoming voyage.

The aroma of spicy beef and beans drifted from the kitchen and he sniffed the air appreciatively as Tonia said in her most seductive tone, "I sent the maids home so we could have the entire house to ourselves, darling. After dinner I'm going to delight you in every room."

It was late when Edward arrived home. He had stayed with the wounded bandit after removing a bullet from his chest and had finally managed to staunch the flow of blood. Miraculously the bullet had missed the heart, but the man had lost a great deal of blood. When the man's eyes flickered open and he whispered, "*Gracias*," Edward left Brent and Carlotta to care for him and hurried home to Emily, worried that he had been gone for so long.

A frightened Josefa greeted Edward at the door when he arrived home. "The señora . . ."

He didn't wait to hear more. Tossing his hat to her, he raced up the stairs.

Emily lay in bed, her red-rimmed eyes and tear-streaked cheeks making her appear more pale and wan than ever.

"Oh, my darling, what is it? What happened?" Edward gathered her into his arms and held her. "My God. You haven't had cramping pains—bleeding?"

She shook her head. "Don't be cross with me, Edward. I went to the Lantern House."

All the breath left Edward's body. "Oh, dear lord!"

"I had to see Phin."

"But to go to a house of prostitution! Why didn't you ask me to go to see her? You know there's nothing in the world I wouldn't do for you. Emily, dearest, I thought you'd accepted her edict that your friendship is over."

"Edward, she is my sister."

"I know you feel as close as a sister—"

"We are half sisters. My father was also her father. He had an affair with a Chinese woman before he met my mother."

"I see," Edward said slowly. "That explains a great deal. But why did you keep this from me?"

"Phin insisted I tell no one. I couldn't break my promise. But now I must, because she is ill and confused, and we must take her away from that dreadful place."

"Yes, of course. But that might be easier said than done."

"You must go and get her—now, tonight. Please, Edward."

"Darling, I can't get her if she doesn't want to leave. What did she tell you today? I assume she refused to come home with you."

Emily nodded. "I am so afraid for her. We must think of a way to get her out of that house. I keep remembering being a prisoner in the doctor's house . . . the helpless feeling, the terror. I'm sure they have done something to her. She seemed so bewildered, at the point of collapse, both physical and mental."

"I don't see how I can go storming into a bordello and remove one of their girls, Emily. But perhaps there's hope in another direction."

"What do you mean?"

"Brent told me he's coming to San Francisco to save the sinners here. I have a feeling his main concern is Phin. He's just staying on at the *casa* until another young Jesuit arrives from Mexico. Perhaps when Brent gets here, he can persuade Phin to leave. I believe they were once very close."

Emily thought of the tall, broad-shouldered priest with the brilliantly blue eyes and thick mane of dark hair. It was easier to imagine him clad in chain mail and wielding a broadsword than wearing the black robes of a man of God and carrying a Bible. Yes, if anyone could save Phin, it was he. "Oh, I do hope he gets here soon," she breathed fervently.

There was a tentative knock on the bedroom door, and Josefa's voice called, "Señor—there is a lady here asking for you. She says it is a matter of life and death."

"Not my sister?" Edward leapt to his feet.

"No, señor."

"Who could it possibly be?" Emily asked.

"I'd better go and find out."

At the top of the stairs he looked down and saw a well-dressed woman waiting in the hall below. As she raised her head he recognized Captain Bardine's wife. He felt a flicker of annoyance that she would presume to arrive uninvited. But as he descended the stairs, he saw that she wore a terrified expression.

Before he reached her side, she cried out, "Forgive me, Mr. Dale, but your maid told my maid that you had medical experience in the army and that you've been treating sick children here. I have tried to get several doctors to come to my husband, but they all refuse."

"Mrs. Bardine, I am not a doctor—" Edward began firmly.

But she interrupted. "At least give him something to calm him down, I beg of you! He's rampaging through the house, destroying furniture, smashing everything in his path."

"I am even less capable of treating mental illness. It sounds as if you need the police more than a doctor, to restrain him. What caused this outburst?"

Tonia Bardine had strangely oblique eyes, not quite Oriental, but slanted rather in the manner of a cat's. Edward found himself staring into her eyes as she spoke, feeling almost mesmerized.

"He ate something that disagreed with him," she said. "I don't know what, it must have been aboard his ship, because we had the same thing for dinner and I feel all right. He began to have violent pains in his belly, then he vomited and screamed that his mouth and throat were on fire. He was having trouble breathing, and after a time could not utter a coherent sound. That was when he seemed to go mad. He knocked me down, and then started crashing about the house. At first I thought he was just colliding with the furniture, but then I saw that he was deliberately smashing things. A great rage possessed him, I suppose because of his pain. He seemed to want to take it out on everything in his path. I feared for my life, so I crept out of the house without his seeing me and hurried to the nearest doctor. But when I described what was happening, he wouldn't come back with me."

She paused for breath and then added, "Please, at least give me a draft to sedate him. I heard you were able to put a boy to sleep while you amputated his leg."

Edward sighed. He'd hoped with the remoteness of the *casa de niños* that news would not have traveled to town, but Carlotta had probably told one of her relatives, or Josefa might have overheard him telling Emily about the operation. "I'll come and look at your husband, Mrs. Bardine. Perhaps a dose of laudanum might help. I believe there's some in my medical bag. But I have no more of the chemical I used to put the boy to sleep, and the process of making it is slow and arduous."

He went upstairs to explain to Emily that he must go out again, but found she had fallen into an exhausted sleep.

Wearily he donned his coat again, picked up his medical bag, and, accompanied by Tonia, set forth once again to offer services he had never intended to perform. He recalled someone had once told him that every gift came with a price and every misfortune concealed a gift. Meeting his beloved Emily at Dr. Stoddard's house had been the most wondrous gift, but the price had been his enrollment in the doctor's medical school, where the knowledge he'd acquired had subsequently shaped his life. At this point he felt it unlikely that his reluctantly acquired medical knowledge concealed a gift.

"I gave the maids the day off, so there was no one in the house with me this evening," Tonia told him as they went up the veranda steps to the front door of her house.

She had left the door unlocked, and he pushed it open slowly. A lamp with the wick turned down low shed a meager pool of light on the marble floor of a circular hall, and an undraped window on the upstairs landing sent a pale beam of moonlight down the staircase. The house was eerily silent.

"Where did you leave him?" Edward whispered.

"He was upstairs, smashing all my perfume bottles."

She turned up the lamp and Edward gasped.

The hall was littered with broken glass, splintered wood, and torn cushions. A grandfather clock had been toppled, pictures torn from the walls, and, most curious of all, a trunk standing near the front door had been opened and its contents, which appeared to be Tonia's clothes, ripped and scattered. She had not exaggerated her husband's rampage, and Edward tensed, knowing people who destroyed property in this manner were also quite capable of violence toward others.

Tonia clutched his arm. "Look!"

It was then that Edward saw the crumpled form of her husband at the foot of the stairs, his face on the marble floor, arms outstretched as if clutching the stairs to halt his fall, one leg twisted awkwardly under him.

Edward ran to his side and eased him over onto his back, then felt for a pulse. He was aware of Tonia approaching. "Is he dead?" He was repulsed by the eagerness in her tone.

"No, he has a strong pulse. I believe the fall knocked him unconscious. It looks as though he struck his head." Edward carefully examined Henry Bardine's twisted leg. "Broken, I believe in two places. We shall need help to get him into bed."

"I'll go and wake up my neighbors," Tonia said.

"First get me a pillow and some blankets."

She was unbelievably slow in fulfilling both requests, and Edward had the uneasy feeling her disappointment at finding her husband still alive was great, indeed.

He was unaware of the passage of time as he helped carry Henry up to an equally ravaged bedroom, then set his leg using broken table legs as splints.

As he worked he was vaguely aware of voices and movement around him as Tonia managed to recruit her neighbors' servants to help pick up the debris Henry had left in his wake.

Edward considered using smelling salts to jolt Henry out of his unconscious state but decided it would be prudent to leave well enough alone. Henry seemed to be breathing normally, and there was no sense subjecting him to the pain and discomfort of having his bones set. The bump on his forehead meant he would also awaken with a monumental headache, to add to the miseries of his stomach. Henry was a big man, and Edward had no desire to have to wrestle him into submission while he set his leg.

Daylight was seeping into the bedroom when at last Edward turned to Tonia. "He's quiet and reasonably comfortable now. I see you've removed most of the evidence of his violent loss of control. This would be a good time to bring your own doctor to check on my handiwork. You might also wish to have a couple of sturdy attendants on hand when Captain Bardine wakes up."

Edward snapped his medical bag shut. "Your husband will probably be all right after whatever upset his stomach works its way out of his system, but it will take a couple of months for his bones to mend."

Tonia wrinkled her nose as she surveyed her husband but said with some satisfaction, "At least he won't be able to sail aboard the *Antonia* with a broken leg."

Eager to be gone, Edward responded, "Your family physician will probably advise you to keep him on a bland diet."

Tonia's catlike eyes seemed to become opaque, and her voice purred, adding to the feline illusion. "Oh, don't worry. I shall prepare his food myself with the utmost care."

Part III

Chapter 43

· ·

THE APPROACH OF winter had brought heavy rain, transforming the unpaved streets of San Francisco into quagmires, and Briony was forced to walk the entire length of the block in order to cross where the mud was only ankle-deep. In common with all the other women in town, she had shortened her skirts and now wore high-topped boots. The men tucked their pantaloons into their boots, recalling their grandfathers' knee breeches.

Although the temperature never dipped below fifty degrees, to stand still for even a moment brought a deathlike chill to the feet, and so Briony hurried toward her destination without glancing at anyone she passed.

At the corner of the street she suddenly found herself caught in the wiry arms of a slightly built man bundled up in a voluminous overcoat. "Brionee, *ma chérie*, where are you off to in such an 'urry?"

"Louis-Philippe! You startled me," Briony said breathlessly. "I was so intent upon getting to the bank before it closes, I wasn't looking where I was going. Forgive me, but I can't stop now, not even for you, my dear."

He took her elbow. "Then let us go, I will accompany you. You 'ave been avoiding me, Briony. I did not know where you went when you left the Rosebriar. I searched for you—I even went to the 'ouse of your brother, but he tell me if you want to see me, you will call on me."

Briony laughed. "Cautious Edward, that's exactly what he'd say. But I haven't been staying with him. My brother and his wife are so completely wrapped up in each other that one feels like an interloper. I have a place of my own."

They waited as a powerful London dray-horse pulled a loaded wagon through the mud in front of them. Mules could no longer drag even empty carts along the muddy streets, and it was not unusual to see Chinese workmen carrying bricks and mortar, slung by ropes from long bamboo poles.

"And where is this place of your own?" Louis asked as they continued across the street.

"I have a room at the City Hotel. It isn't the Rosebriar, of course, but I'm comfortable enough." She bent her head before the biting wind and thought ruefully that her room was little more than a garret, but it was all that was available as the great tides of immigrants continued to pour through the Golden Gate. "Besides, I'm just staying there until my house is built. The foundations have been laid and if the rain holds off we hope to begin raising the walls. Ah, here we are."

Inside the bank Louis-Philippe waited as she deposited the receipts from her store, withdrew some currency, and chatted briefly with the manager.

When she rejoined Louis, he scowled in the direction of the bank manager. "That man is in love with you."

"Ssh!" Briony blushed. "He'll hear you! Louis, I know you are only joking, but you really must stop this nonsense."

He held the door for her. "Nonsense? I do not think so."

"Of course it is. Not every man in town is in love with me."

Outside, a gust of wind caught them, obliterating Louis-Philippe's response. But as Briony was about to bid him good day, he said, "Come to my café—let me prepare dinner for you. We must talk. I have news of Max Seadon."

Could there have been a more compelling reason to accept? Briony nodded her agreement, and they battled their way back across the muddy street.

The rains had driven deer and other animals down from the mountains and game of all kinds was abundant. They passed butcher shops with fat elk and black-tailed does hanging from the doors, the windows packed full of wild geese, duck, large California hares, and even choice cuts of grizzly-bear meat.

A young man pushing a wheelbarrow moved aside to allow them to pass. Louis greeted him and, as they went on their way, said to Briony, "Some of the gold seekers are not succeeding in their quest. That young man shoveled up no riches, but now he earns ten dollars a day pushing his wheelbarrow. However, it costs him six dollars to live and he loses the other four at monte."

"Everyone in town has gambling fever," Briony said. "I can't bear to think about the gaming tables Max installed at the Rosebriar."

It was a relief to reach the café and step into its fragrant warmth. Delicious aromas filled the room. There were now three hurrying waiters attending to the packed tables and a number of people patiently waiting to be seated, despite the fact that it was not yet the dinner hour.

"Louis, please don't ask anyone to give up his table," Briony whispered, recalling her last meal at the café.

"Nevaire fear, fair lady. This way, *s'il vous plaît*." With a sweeping bow he indicated that she should go into the kitchen.

Two cooks stirred pots, checked ovens, and chopped vegetables. The sizzle of meat and the delicious aroma of herbed sauces made Briony's mouth water.

In a corner of the already crowded kitchen Louis had set up a small table for two, curtained off for privacy. Linen napkins, silver place settings, and a pretty porcelain candle holder were set upon a damask cloth. Briony hid her smile as the Frenchman helped her remove her coat. He had undoubtedly entertained other female guests here. Louis-Philippe's reputation as a ladies' man was already legendary.

Pulling out a chair for her, he said, "I, too, am building a house and a larger café. But *sacré bleu*, the workmen, they are slow as treacle in an ice storm. For now this is the best I can offer."

Briony knew he had left the Rosebriar the moment he heard Max had dismissed her, and ever since he had been besieged with offers from other hotels.

He poured wine for her and then bustled off to select the food, fussily tasting and rejecting several of the chefs' dishes before choosing breast of game hen in a subtle cream sauce, with tiny whole carrots and crusty bread, preceded by oyster soup.

Recalling Louis-Philippe's hurt—perhaps feigned, but possibly real—when she had inquired about Max in the past, Briony was careful to allow the meal to progress at a leisurely pace and make small talk until he was ready to bring up the subject closest to her heart. For the truth was, she had missed Max terribly and had not even seen him in passing since leaving the Rosebriar. Of course, since he had leased the hotel, there was nothing to keep him in San Francisco, but somehow she had not expected him to drop off the face of the earth.

She was halfway through a wonderful chocolate gateau when in the middle of telling her about the masquerade ball that was to be held at Christmastime, he suddenly brought up the subject of Max.

"P'raps Max will 'ave returned by then. I expect it depends on the route he takes. A man told me he left New York less than two months ago aboard a steamer and transferred to the *Panama* at the Isthmus. Of course, there is also the voyage from Europe to be added . . . and what am I thinking of? I 'ave not considered that first, Max must travel there before he can return."

The mousse, light and airy as it was, all at once felt like lead in her mouth. She swallowed. "Are you telling me that Max has sailed to *Europe*?"

He nodded. "He has gone to your homeland."

She should not have been surprised, of course, since she had first met Max aboard a ship plying the Atlantic; but somehow the sheer distance of their separation overwhelmed her. Perhaps it was true after all, that absence made the heart grow fonder.

Louis-Philippe was watching her closely, and he gave a long sigh. "So. It is as I feared. You 'ave given your 'eart to that rogue and vagabond. Ah, Briony, you would do better to try to tame a Bengal tiger."

She smiled sadly. "He asked me to marry him, you know, but I turned him down."

The Frenchman's surprise was almost comical. "Max? *Max Seadon* proposed to you? *Sacré coeur*! Do you know how many ladies he has loved and left? I do not understand. 'Ere you sit looking so sad it break my 'eart, yet you did not accept his proposal. Do you 'ave any idea 'ow he must feel? He waited his whole life for you, and you reject him. No wonder he take off for Europe."

There was something about Louis-Philippe, aided and abetted by his fine food and wine, that always caused Briony's defenses to crumble, inviting confidences. Today, his empathy combined with the shock of the news of Max's departure caused her to fling discretion to the wind. Almost before she realized she was going to say it, she whispered, "I could not accept his proposal. I am not free to marry."

Louis-Philippe's dark eyes gleamed. He pounded the table with his fist, rattling the delicate china. "I knew it! I knew it all along! When Max tell me 'ow the air crackles when the two of you are together but you put up a wall to keep him out—and I know from my own observations that no woman alive can resist the sheer charm of the man—I say to 'im, she 'as a husband somewhere. P'raps she fears 'e may one day find 'er—and you."

His words were like a cold splash of water in her face. How foolish she'd been to admit she wasn't free to marry. What if Max were to check on her past—dear Lord! What if that was the reason he'd sailed to England?

The same thought had evidently occurred to Louis-Philippe, because he said in a voice of doom, "Max 'as gone to find your 'usband, Briony, for what purpose I dare not guess. But the night before 'e left, we dined together, and 'e said 'e had put all of 'is affairs in order here, leasing out the Rosebriar and giving a power of attorney to his lawyer, so that 'e could be away for an extended period. And I ask why 'e wants to go back to Europe when I know everything 'e wants is 'ere, and 'e said—"

He broke off, biting his lip.

"What, Louis? What did he say?"

" 'E said 'e was going to find the man who stood between 'im and what 'e wanted most in the world.''

The mysterious Mexican who had arrived at the *casa de niños* with lead in his chest had made a remarkable and rapid recovery. When Father Juan's replacement arrived, and he announced that he was leaving for San Francisco, the man, who had given his name as Gregorio, promptly asked if he might accompany him.

"Please, Father, let me help you with your work. Your prayers saved me from certain death, and I wish to dedicate my new life to God's work."

He refused to be dissuaded by descriptions of the spartan life a Jesuit must lead, or the disciplines that would be required of him, and so when Brent departed for the city, Gregorio accompanied him. He left all of his weapons behind and was unaware Brent still carried the jeweled dagger that was a memento, and a stern reminder, of his fall from grace in China.

Brent agonized over his need to save Phin's soul. Was it, he wondered, actually a need to save his own? He had long ago confessed the sins he'd committed in China, especially toward Phin, and his penance had been years of servitude in the poorest, most disease-ridden cesspools of South America, culminating in his wartime service in Matamoros. But in the deepest part of his conscience he knew it was not enough. Not while Phin still sold her body.

He and Gregorio moved to the poorest part of the city, working mainly with non-English-speaking immigrants, the Mexicans, Chileans, Chinese. Brent conducted Mass in tents, on the streets and waterfront. He baptized babies and adult converts in the cold water of the bay. He heard confession wherever the sinner found him. He set up a school for the children, he scavenged for food and clothing for the destitute, and he began an aggressive campaign to eliminate the blatant importation of Chinese girl-children for the brothels that sprang up like mushrooms in the Little China section of town.

The priest and the former bandit became well known after

an incident that took place shortly after they arrived in San Francisco. Receiving word of the impending arrival of a shipment of young Chinese girls, the two men borrowed a longboat and rowed out to the anchored vessel.

The startled crew were confronted by a fearsome sight as a black-robed giant swung over the side of the ship, accompanied by a slender, swarthy-skinned Mexican.

Towering over a diminutive Chinese captain, Brent demanded, "Where are the girl slaves?"

"No savvy." The captain shook his head so violently his queue whipped back and forth.

"We'll check the hold," Brent told Gregorio.

Two crewmen, brandishing knives, attempted to bar their path. Both were disarmed and flung aside. A third sailor with a hatchet in his upraised hand hurled himself at Brent, and a moment later found himself flying over the side into the bitterly cold water.

Although the boarding party was unarmed, it seemed no one could stop them. The ship was searched from stem to stern, but no sign of a human cargo was found. Brent began to wonder if the information he'd received was valid.

He was about to give up searching for the girls when Gregorio said, "Father Juan, wait!" He went back to the shipping crates stacked in the hold. The crates were marked "fine china." Placing his ear close, Gregorio's dark eyes gleamed. He rapped the side of the crate with his fist, then picked up a crow bar and pried it open.

Twenty-five girls, ages nine to thirteen, were packed inside the crates. By the time Brent returned with sufficient lawmen to remove the pathetic human cargo, all of the crew had fled the ship and were no doubt headed for the goldfields.

Brent arranged for the older girls to be taken to various households and businesses to be trained as servants and clerks. The younger ones were dispatched to the *casa de niños*.

Within a matter of days of arriving in town, the reputation of the tall Jesuit and his unlikely companion was firmly set.

He had followed the order's founder's edict to "Go, set the world afire."

Brent was less successful in his efforts to save Phin Tsu. He visited the Lantern House frequently, calling at different times of day. He even attempted to get in during the evening. He was always refused admission, and the Chinese doorman would not take a message to Phin.

Gregorio, for whom old habits died hard, did not understand the priest's patience. "Do not bother with that China fella, Father Juan. Let me go into the house and bring out the woman."

"No, Gregorio, we will use force when it is necessary, as with the slave-girls in the china crates, but in this case the woman must come to us of her own free will."

There was, Brent decided, another way to reach Phin. He would call upon his old friend Edward and enlist the aid of Phin's half sister, Emily.

Chapter 44

IT WAS TAKING Henry Bardine an interminably long time to die. True, he was growing weaker from his daily ingestion of arsenic with his food, but unfortunately he refused to eat more often than not, due to his constant stomach distress. Tonia had to beg and plead with him to take tiny quantities of food in order to "build up his strength."

Then an announcement about the planned masquerade ball to be held at Christmas caused her to reconsider her impending widowhood. After all, if she were in mourning she could hardly attend the ball, but with Henry still alive, she could certainly attend a charity event. Henry Bardine had just, unknowingly, been given a reprieve until the new year.

He watched her warily, but had no choice but to submit grudgingly to her care since she allowed no one else to enter his room. She also took care of business for him, but after the *Antonia* sailed without him, he expressed little interest in other matters.

With her husband confined to his sickbed, Tonia no longer worried about concealing her mounting profits from the Lantern House, which were now openly deposited in several banks and brokerage houses. Having persuaded several doctors that Henry had trouble sleeping, she also had on hand a stock of sedatives with which to knock him out during the evening so that she spent more time at her pride and joy. Nowadays she did not think of the Lantern House as being a bordello, but rather a fine private club. And with Briony Forest no longer reigning at the Rosebriar, Tonia felt her time as queen of high society had come. To that end, she immediately put into effect her plan to give large contributions to charity, making sure that her donations were well publicized. She also spread the word that she intended to recruit a committee to raise funds for a public library.

There was that other little matter. The question of Fletcher Faraday's brat, Emily. But the frail Mrs. Edward Dale apparently was enduring a hellish pregnancy and rarely left her house. Tonia decided that she, too, could wait for the new year.

As Christmas approached, Tonia concentrated on planning how to be the star of the masquerade ball. She decided to go as Cleopatra. With her black hair worn loose, a filmy costume, loads of gold jewelry, and her striking eyes emphasized by kohl, she was sure no other woman would even be noticed. Briony Forest did have an interesting fiery glint to her auburn hair, but she was too much of a lady to wear a daringly revealing costume like the one Tonia instructed her seamstress to make.

To Tonia's surprise, she was invited to tea at the home of Annabelle Clark, who had recently announced her impending marriage to a banker. When Tonia arrived, she found the former members of the Rosebriar afternoon tea group seated in Annabelle's attractively furnished drawing room. Notable by her absence was Briony.

Annabelle led her into the exclusive circle and said, "I believe you know everyone. You see, we all missed the afternoon tea parties at the Rosebriar since the new people took over. So we decided to get together in our own homes. We take turns."

"I'm honored that you invited me," Tonia murmured, thinking that *shocked* was perhaps a better word.

"Tonia, we want you to know that we all admire you tremendously for being such a devoted wife to Captain Bardine. It can't be easy caring for an invalid, especially one . . . well, he always was rather difficult, wasn't he? Why, we heard that you cook special meals for him yourself and won't let your servants near him. And you've been so generous to the charitable causes so dear to our hearts.

Frankly, my dear, we never understood why you were excluded from Briony's afternoon teas.''

Crossing her ankles primly and lowering her eyes modestly, Tonia settled into a brocaded chair, her triumph complete. She accepted a cup of tea and knew better than to inquire about Briony's absence. The ladies had made their choice. A devoted wife, active in charitable causes, over an unmarried working woman who no longer enjoyed the protection and patronage of Max Seadon. The queen is dead, Tonia thought. Long live the queen!

The nausea and weakness that plagued Emily did not abate. In fact, as her pregnancy advanced, she felt even less inclined to eat, although forced food down at Edward's urging. Most of the time she was too tired to do more than lie on the chaise longue Edward had placed in the bay window so she could enjoy the view from the top of the hill. She made a desultory attempt to knit baby clothes, but it was really too much of an effort.

Naturally they did not entertain, except for Briony's brief visits, and so Emily was both surprised and dismayed when one morning Edward announced that Father Juan would be calling on her that afternoon.

"Calling on *you*, surely. I am not receiving, not even a priest. Especially not a priest. I am not Roman Catholic."

"No, actually he wants to see you," Edward said apologetically. "He wouldn't take no for an answer."

Emily had heard of the exploits of Father Juan and his Mexican disciple. They had stirred up a great deal of controversy by forcing the good people of the town to face the problems caused by rampant prostitution and gambling and had exposed the even more evil practice of importing Chinese slave girls. Josefa had told her that among her people Father Juan was heralded as a saint for his work with the poor and the sick.

"Why does he want to see me?" Emily asked. "Did he say?"

Edward frowned. "No. But I think it's probably about Phin Tsu."

"Then I'll be glad to see him. I've been worried about her, too. She hasn't answered any of the letters I've sent to her."

From her vantage point at the bay window, Emily saw the Jesuit arrive. He came striding up the hill, walking like a man with a purpose, his bare feet hardly protected from the mud or the elements by his handmade sandals, and his mane of dark hair sprinkled with dew drops from a cold drizzle of rain that had started to fall.

Josefa had been so excited by the prospect of the priest's visit that she had prepared a tempting array of snacks to serve to him. Emily heard Josefa's joyous greeting as she opened the door and admitted her beloved Father Juan. Minutes later Edward escorted him into the room.

"How nice to see you again, Father Juan," Emily said.

His penetrating gaze locked with hers, and she had the distinct feeling he saw through the falsehood.

"Edward tells me you have not been well. I pray you'll soon feel strong again."

"Thank you. Edward, would you mind pouring the tea? My hand is a little unsteady."

"Allow me," Brent said and picked up the silver teapot. He filled the china cups and passed the milk and sugar. "I've always felt that the Chinese and English practice of serving tea is a highly civilized one. Perhaps it would have become an American tradition but for the unpleasantness in Boston."

Edward watched with a bemused expression. "One tends to forget that you're American born, Brent. I suppose it's the combination of the priest's robe and your world travels, and not least your command of foreign languages. Emily, did you know that Brent speaks fluent Italian and Spanish as well as Manchu and Mandarin?"

"If we are to list accomplishments," Brent said dryly, "let's talk about yours, Edward. How many men survived the war who would not have but for your care? Which other doctor in town could have spared Ramon the agony of amputation?"

"You forget the presence of my wife when you bring up

such matters, Brent,'' Edward said sharply. ''In her present delicate state of health there is no need to conjure up such images in her mind.''

''I'm sorry, Emily,'' Brent said at once. ''It's just that I mourn the waste of your husband's gift of healing. I especially become incensed when I consider the reason for it.''

''And what is that?'' Emily asked.

''Oh, not lack of compassion for his fellow man, nor even the fact that he has made a fortune here and could if he chose live the life of the idle rich. No, the reason is much more infuriating. Edward came from the most privileged class of England, and aristocrats consider the medical profession beneath their dignity.''

''Damn you, Brent,'' Edward said hotly, ''that's not it at all. I do not practice medicine because I do not have sufficient knowledge. You speak of my army medical service. Do you know how many men in my care died? Do you realize that the only female patients I've ever seen were the streetwalkers in the charity hospital where I studied?''

Brent looked at him in surprise. ''How many doctors do more than prescribe tonics or cough medicines for even decent women? Midwives take care of childbirth. You're making excuses, Edward.''

''I'll thank you to drop this subject right now,'' Edward snapped. ''You told me you needed to speak to Emily. I would never have agreed to this visit had I known you were going to try to enlist her as an ally in your misguided campaign to get me to hang out a shingle.''

Brent looked undisturbed. ''Not that I'll ever give up my efforts in that direction, but I didn't come to appeal to your better nature, Edward. I came to enlist Emily's aid in rescuing her sister.''

Emily twisted a lace-edged handkerchief between her fingers. The handkerchief was delicately scented with lavender water. She found the fragrance helped a little to dispel her constant nausea. ''Father Juan, I have repeatedly invited Phin to come and stay with us. She refuses even to speak with me and does not respond to my letters, although I write almost every day.''

"And have you told her of your ill health?"

Emily blushed. "I am not ill. . . ."

"Brent—" Edward warned.

"Phin would come to you if you were to tell her you need her," Brent said. "That's all I ask. Send word that your strength is waning and you must see her. I feel sure that once she is away from that evil house, we can persuade her to give up the life she is leading."

Edward was on his feet. "This is an outrage, Brent. You want my wife to pretend she is dying, is that it?"

"I cannot lie to Phin, Father Juan," Emily said. "I will not stop my efforts to try to see her. But I won't prey on her sympathy."

"I am not asking you to lie. Isn't it true you have been ill? You could tell her the truth and ask her to come to see you. If I could just speak to her, away from that house, I believe I could convince her never to return."

"Then devise your own method of getting her away from the house. My wife and I have done all we can for Phin Tsu. She doesn't want to be saved. Face it."

"There is no sinner alive who does not, even if only in his secret heart, desire redemption."

"You're wasting your time here, Brent," Edward said. "We are not members of your flock."

The warrior priest's expression changed to that of the kindly father. "But you are members of the human race, Edward."

"Where have you hidden the pipe, Phin?" Kane demanded. "Damn you, where are the *gow* pills?"

He emptied the contents of her chest of drawers, flinging silk garments on the floor. He had already searched the rest of her room, which now lay in ruins.

Phin stood by the window, watching impassively, waiting for him to calm down.

At last he turned to her and asked in a more mollified tone, "If not the smoke, then what? I've just been told that

Qing Chan intends to send you away. The girl who told me said if you're lucky you'll go to a crib house, but she was afraid you were destined for the hospital.''

''And you feel that justified your bursting in here and laying waste to my belongings?'' Phin asked coldly.

''I was afraid you were being sent away because you were using opium,'' Kane said sheepishly. ''You know that several of the girls were banished because they were caught. Since our proprietor has such lofty ambitions for the Lantern House, she won't tolerate any hint that we are an opium den.'' He paused. ''You do look better than the last time we talked, but Phin, you've hardly any flesh on your bones.''

''Qing Chan was giving me a drug in my food. When I realized it, I stopped eating what she served. I didn't trust anyone, so I've been slipping down to the kitchen when everyone is asleep.''

''For pity's sake! Why didn't you tell me? You could have shared my meals. Or, for that matter, why didn't you simply get up and leave?''

''I told you why. I have been robbed. When I have recovered my possessions, I will go. Kane, when we last talked I know I was bewildered, drugged—I probably did not make much sense. But now I know what to do. If you will kindly pick up all my things and put them back where you found them, I will tell you my plan.''

As he began to replace her clothes in her drawers, she sat on the edge of her bed and continued in a low voice, ''One of the younger girls whom I befriended told me that she had overheard Tonia Bardine tell Qing Chan that on the night of the masquerade ball she is coming here to put on her costume, as she doesn't want Captain Bardine to know what she intends to wear. She had brought her costume and asked Qing Chan to put it away. Then Qing Chan told her that one of the girls had some long gold necklaces that would be perfect with the costume.''

Phin paused, feeling her anger suffuse her again. The girl had seen Qing Chan produce the necklaces for Tonia to admire and had instantly recognized them as belonging to Phin.

Relating the incident to Kane, Phin concluded, "Tonia—being the magpie she is—immediately wanted to take my necklaces home with her in case she had an opportunity to wear them before the night of the ball. So you see, I now must stay here until the masquerade ball, when she will come to dress in her costume. Then I can recover my property."

Kane finished picking up the shoes he had scattered. "And what will you do then? Walk up to Mrs. Bardine and rip the necklaces from around her throat? Or perhaps strangle her with them? And what would that accomplish? You would be taken away to prison, probably hanged. I understand there have been several vigilante hangings recently."

"Do you see why I don't confide in you, Kane? You never see my side of things."

"On the contrary. I see the danger you place yourself in only too clearly. Phin, you're still looking for a way to avenge your father's death. Your conflict with Tonia Bardine isn't about your stupid jewelry—Qing Chan evidently stole it anyway—it's about Tonia depriving you of a father."

"Why are you still here, Kane? Playing your violin like one of your Christian archangels. And for what purpose? To drown out the sound of whores. I thought you had an offer from the Rosebriar. I thought you were considering it."

"The offer never materialized. Max Seadon has rented the hotel to some investors and left the country. He fired Briony Forest before he left, so we no longer have a connection there."

Phin pricked up her ears at this announcement. She had never been particularly fond of Briony, perhaps because she sensed they were too much alike, far too independent for the world they lived in, but Phin thought Max was a fool to let Briony go.

"Will you go to Tonia Bardine and tell her of Qing Chan's intention to send me away?" Phin asked. "The mama-san won't dare banish me if you intercede on my behalf.''

"Yes, of course. But it would be so much better if we both simply left.''

"Let's stay until the masquerade ball," Phin said. "I read my fortune today. Long before the new year there will be monumental changes.''

"The new year?" Kane asked. "Our new year or the Chinese new year?''

"It has just occurred to me," Phin said. "It will shortly be the year of the dog. That is indeed ominous. You see, I was born in the year of the dog. Perhaps my life has come full circle.''

Chapter 45

● ●

FLETCHER FARADAY SAT in a dimly lit cantina in Veracruz, trying to blend with the other patrons but knowing he was not succeeding. He had found lingering resentment and animosity directed toward *gringos*, which was natural in view of the outcome of the war. The Mexicans had fought bravely, stubbornly, frequently skillfully, but they had been defeated by the superior leadership and better weapons of the northern republic.

He was waiting in the cantina to meet an American. He did not know the American's name but hoped he would be able to provide the missing pieces to fill in the details of what had happened to prevent the arrival in Mexico City of a British diplomat and his wife.

A visit to the British Consulate had helped a little. The consul general had been in Mexico at the beginning of the war. "Those were chaotic times," he'd said. "But I remember very well our shock and horror upon hearing that one of our people had been attacked by bandits between here and Veracruz. Communications were very slow, and the information we received was sketchy at best, but we immediately dispatched a man to Veracruz to assist Mrs. Faraday, intending to get her aboard a ship back to England. But our man returned with word that she had dropped out of sight. He assumed she had made her own way home."

The consul general paused and cleared his throat. "You must understand, with the war and troop movements and so on . . . our man was perhaps not as diligent as he might otherwise have been. He ascertained that the local people had buried the body."

Fletcher had not identified himself. He was still unsure whether or not he wanted to be resurrected from the dead.

"I assume Mr. Faraday was a relative of yours, sir? I didn't catch your name."

For so long he had been known to the Apache as white-eyes, and since it appeared he would not be given any further information unless he introduced himself properly, Fletcher replied, "My name is White. I was a close friend of Fletcher Faraday. Since I found myself in Mexico on business, I decided to try to find out what had become of him. I was distressed to learn of his death and wondered where his wife—or rather, his widow was now living."

"She did not return to England, I do know that, Mr. White. I'm sorry I can't be of more help to you. But . . ."

"Yes?"

"Well, the man we sent to assist Mrs. Faraday spoke of an American in Veracruz who was rumored to be running a pack of Mexican *bandidos*. The brains of the gang, so to speak. Our man heard that nothing happened to travelers arriving in that city that the American was not aware of. Apparently he befriended new arrivals, offering to help translate their wishes to the locals or deal with currency and so on, then later some of the more wealthy travelers were waylaid and robbed. I mention this American to you because our man was informed that Mrs. Faraday had been seen in conversation with him the night before the Faradays departed for Mexico City. Frankly, Mr. White, neither Mr. nor Mrs. Faraday was seen after that. One would hope that the bandits spared the woman, but . . . well, I would not want you to search in vain."

Fletcher had journeyed immediately to Veracruz, with the faint hope that the American was still there, or someone who knew him could be found. Perhaps there was still a way to find Tonia.

The stiflingly hot and humid port of Veracruz seemed vaguely familiar but only in the manner of a place dreamed about. But as soon as he reached the waterfront, he remembered the American. The man had been hanging about as they disembarked from the ship, and he offered to find a conveyance to take them to a hotel. He spoke Spanish fluently, he said, and had lived in Mexico for several years.

That memory immediately connected with Fletcher's recollection of lying on his back on the ground as Tonia urged his unseen assailants to kill him. One voice had been American. Had it been the voice of the man on the quay? If so, would the man recognize him four years later?

He learned that a *gringo* who "helped" travelers usually could be found in this waterfront cantina, but after an hour of pretending to sip tequila, Fletcher was beginning to think he was wasting his time.

Just as he was about to give up for the night, the American arrived. A tall, gaunt man wearing a black frock coat, he greeted the other patrons as he made his way to the bar. He was the same man who had approached them on the quay four years earlier.

As always when memories of the past returned, Fletcher felt his head begin to throb. He sat with his back to a wall and a clear path between his table and the door. He wore the clothes the farmer's son had given him, and four years of strenuous outdoor living had tanned his skin and weathered his features. His hair was both sun-bleached and streaked with silver, whereas four years earlier it had been uniformly brown. Then he had worn a well-tailored suit and, he was sure, had presented an entirely different facade to the world. Perhaps he had changed sufficiently that the American would not recognize him.

The American took a position with his back to the bar and finished a drink while surveying the other patrons speculatively. Then he made his way toward Fletcher's table.

"Evening, sir. Always glad to see a countryman. Not many *gringos* are brave enough to drink alone in a place like this."

"Won't you join me?"

"Thank you."

As the American sat down, Fletcher saw a revolver tucked into his belt under the frock coat. He squinted through the smoky gloom. "Have we met before?"

"I don't believe so."

A bony hand reached across the table. "Ezra Gant, glad to meet you."

"John White—how do you do?" They shook hands briefly.

Gant's eyes flickered over Fletcher's clothes. Was he deciding this particular *gringo* was not worth robbing?

Drinks were ordered, and Fletcher told of living in the Arizona Territory.

"A farmer?"

"Yes."

"But you weren't always a farmer. You sound like an educated man."

"Mr. Gant, let me lay my cards on the table. I came here specifically to see you in the hope that you can help me find a woman who disappeared four years ago."

Even in the dimly lit cantina it was obvious that a mask instantly descended over Gant's features.

"I am willing to trade a good horse, a saddle, and a turquoise and silver Indian amulet for the information," Fletcher continued. "And give my word that I will use it only to find the woman. Perhaps if I describe her, you will remember something about her. She is very beautiful, black hair that comes to a widow's peak over a high intellectual forehead. Her eyes are her most striking and unusual feature. They are slightly slanted and appear to change color—green, gold—and her eyelashes are very dark, very lustrous. She has a pale complexion that contrasts with her dark hair. Her name is Antonia Faraday, although she prefers the shortened form of Tonia. Four years ago she arrived with her husband from England, en route to Mexico City—"

Gant leaned forward. "I thought you looked familiar. You're him, aren't you? How come you're here again after all these years?"

"Before you reach under your coat for that revolver, Mr. Gant, please be advised that I have a Colt forty-four in my hand under the table. I hope I won't have to use it."

Gant shrugged. "Hell, I've no quarrel with you. But what

I don't understand is, why are you asking me these same questions again?''

Fletcher blinked. "I've asked them of you before?''

"You don't remember?''

"No. Until recently I had no memory of anything that happened to me at that time. Then the memory of my wife telling someone to kill me . . .'' His voice trailed away. It still cut to the quick that she had betrayed him.

Recognizing the sincerity in his voice, Gant said slowly, "I reckon one of the señoritas must've took pity on you, pulled you into her place, and nursed you back to health. About a month after we left you on the street, you came in here, all decked out in a wide-brimmed sombrero and serape. You were a man with a mission. All you wanted was to find your wife. I guess nothing else mattered. You put a pistol to my head and demanded to know where she was.''

"And what did you tell me?''

"That she was a cold-hearted bitch who used me as bad as she used you. She got your money and goods *and* mine. She was gone before daylight the next day. Then, a couple of weeks later, we heard of a family of Spanish *Californios* who were returning to their *rancho* in Alta California who had hired an Englishwoman to teach them English. From the description, weren't no doubt who that woman was.''

"This is what you told me?''

Gant nodded. "You hightailed it out of here. Last thing I said to you was to give her hell for me, too. You sure you don't remember any of this?''

"So I was on my way to Alta California when the Comanche attacked the stage,'' Fletcher said. "Do you have any idea where the *rancho* is?''

"Was, you mean. Somewhere near the Mission San Juan Capistrano was what I heard. I ain't been north of the border for ten years on account of a little trouble with the law. But hell, I doubt the *Californios* are still there. At the end of the war the treaty of Guadalupe Hidalgo gave upper California and New Mexico to the United States. The treaty was supposed to honor all titleholders, but the old Spanish land grants were in trouble even before the war—the Mexicans wanted the land. From what I've heard, the *ranchos* are already being carved up and sold to the newcomers. The hacienda days are over. Damn funny how the United States grabbed California at practically the same minute gold was found at Sutter's Mill.''

''But that *rancho* where my wife went with the *Californios* would be a place to start looking. Do you recall the name of the family she went with?''

Gant shook his head. ''You can probably find out from the fathers at the mission which *rancho* had an Englishwoman in the hacienda and what became of her.''

Fletcher stood up. ''You'll understand if I don't thank you for your information. But I will show my gratitude for your putting me on the trail of my wife. I will spare you a swift Apache-style death.''

Chapter 46

••

BRIONY DECIDED AT the last minute that she would attend the masquerade ball. All work and no play was taking its toll, and Louis-Philippe had begged her to accompany him to the charity event of the season.

There was no time to have one of the town's overworked seamstresses make her a costume, but she had noticed two items of interest. First, that Louis-Philippe was—if one subtracted her bosom—just about the same size as herself, and second, that he was a splendid dresser.

"I'll go with you if you'll lend me one of your suits," she said. "If I add a ruffle or two to one of your shirts to make it fit, nip in the waist a little, don a black satin mask, I believe I would make a dashing rogue at the masquerade ball."

"*Sacré bleu!* A woman in man's clothes! A daring idea, *ma chérie*—I like it very much. You shall have my best suit. But my shirt? I think not. You are too well-endowed, dear heart. We shall buy a new shirt in a larger size."

"You won't mind dancing with a man, then?" she teased.

He laughed. It was a fact of life in the new city that many men did indeed dance together, for the simple reason they outnumbered the women by the hundreds. "No one is going to mistake you for a man, Briony, even if you wore a suit of armor."

"I do wish Emily felt well enough to go," Briony said, frowning. "I wonder if I could persuade Edward to come without her? He spends every moment hovering over her, as if by watching he could prevent . . ." Her voice trailed away.

Her brother was so afraid he was going to lose Emily that he had sent to the country's most renowned medical schools for every book, journal, and paper written on the subject of obstetrical and gynecological problems and had been incensed when he discovered the medical profession virtually ignored women's ailments, especially those pertaining to childbirth.

He had told Briony of his frustration and added, "The only female patients I've ever dealt with were at the charity hospital in Liverpool, and they were streetwalkers in the final stages of their filthy diseases—they didn't come to us unless they were dying. We simply gave them salves and sedatives, and they treated themselves."

"Perhaps one of the other doctors in town . . . ?"

"They'll direct me to a midwife. Bri, I know you lost a baby, but no one ever told me the details. I don't want to embarrass you, but if you could tell me what happened, perhaps I could help Emily."

"I had more than one miscarriage, Edward," Briony replied. "In the early weeks of pregnancy. There was no warning, and I hadn't fallen or anything like that. I didn't even have the morning sickness. Don't worry, dear, Emily is further along than I was when I lost my babies. I know of several women friends whose pregnancies also ended in the early weeks. Perhaps as the baby develops in the womb there is less chance of miscarrying?"

"Did you see Dr. Stoddard at the time?"

"Good Lord, no! The midwife came. Darling, I've never had my female parts examined by a doctor, and I don't know any woman who has. When a woman visits a doctor, she is usually given a fully dressed doll and asked to point to the place on the doll that is hurting her."

"And then the doctor treats the doll, I presume? I'm beginning to wonder how the human race has survived. Do you think any of the midwives here—or perhaps more to the point, their patients—would allow me to be present during their deliveries? I need to make a real study, so that when Emily's time comes I'll at least have some experience."

"You surely don't intend to deliver your own child?" Briony was shocked.

"We'll have a midwife present, but I'm going to be on hand, too."

"Oh, Edward, does Emily know how much you adore her?" Briony asked wistfully. She could not imagine Max Seadon caring that much and wondered why Max always came to mind whenever she contemplated her brother's devotion to his wife. She added, "But I can't imagine any midwife, or mother-to-be, allowing such a thing. However, I will inquire for you. You might also ask your Jesuit friend to speak to some of the ladies of his flock—from what I've heard, they would all die for him if necessary."

Later Briony learned, to her surprise, that several midwives and their patients had been glad of Edward's help with difficult deliveries.

She reflected that, despite Edward's protestations to the contrary, he was honing his medical skills to the point that he was probably more qualified than most of the former barbers and traveling medicine men in town who called themselves "doctor."

Tonia had increased prices to the point that only the most wealthy men in town now visited the Lantern House; therefore on the night of the masquerade ball, the mama-san expected few customers and told Kane he could take the night off if he wished.

He immediately went to Phin to tell her he would be available to be at her side when she confronted Tonia to demand the return of her stolen jewelry.

Phin gave an enigmatic smile. "Tonia will come back here after the ball, to change from her costume before she goes home. I can get my jewelry at the end of the evening. Let's go to the ball, Kane. For one evening let us be carefree citizens of San Francisco—no, don't looked shocked! It is a masquerade ball—we can both cover our faces with masks, since my features betray my unacceptable racial background and you do not wish to show your scars, although I am unsure why you feel ashamed of them. After all, your scars are visible proof of pain endured and wounds healed. They are a tribute to your courage.''

Kane bit back a protest when it occurred to him that at least he could get Phin away from the Lantern House for a little while. Besides, perhaps Emily would be at the ball, and oh, how he longed to see her again!

He was just one more immigrant, a new arrival who had sailed up the coast from Southern California, indistinguishable from the hundreds of men burning with gold fever who paused briefly in San Francisco before rushing out to the Sierra Nevada foothills.

But a close observer might have noticed that he showed none of the wide-eyed wonder or greenhorn clumsiness most immigrants displayed. He was not a sailor, nor a businessman, nor a fugitive from the Australian penal colony. Nor was he one of the mountain men who drifted into town, reeking of animal skins and frequently spoiling for a fight. He was a white man yet seemed as silent and stoic as any Indian. He was not young, nor was he old.

If anyone had had the time or the inclination to care, they might have noticed that each evening at dusk he headed out of town to camp in the hills, scorning the overcrowded hotels and boardinghouses.

Fletcher Faraday could no longer stand the close proximity of his fellow man; he loathed the teeming, mud-choked streets of the city, the constant noise, the drunkenness and debauchery. He longed for the peace and quiet and unspoiled vistas of Apacheria, for the simple life he had lived there, and, most of all, for Sings Softly.

But he could not return to the Chiricahuas. He had broken his vows to them, deserted the tribe. How could he ask Sings Softly to exile herself permanently from her people?

He had truly loved two other women in his life. He

realized now that his infatuation with Tonia had not been love; he had succumbed to what had aptly been described as the "dark gods of the loins." Long ago he had loved a Chinese woman. She had warned him that their love was forbidden and would end sadly, but he had not believed it until she vanished from his life. Then he had been blessed by finding Priscilla, who gave him Emily, but tragically he had lost her, too. Now he realized that Sings Softly combined the exotic appeal of his first love with the gentle patience and understanding of his second. Every instinct urged him to return to her, but was that in her best interests? Was he being selfish?

It seemed ironic that just when he was surely about to track down Tonia, he no longer cared about taking her to task for her perfidy. All he truly wanted was to return to Sings Softly.

He prowled the streets of San Francisco in an agony of indecision, only halfheartedly searching for Tonia, still unsure whether or not he would confront her. He was sure she was here somewhere, since the fathers at the mission in the south remembered her very well. She had run off with a sea captain, they told him, and they'd heard she was living in San Francisco.

As his memory returned fully, he recalled his ill-fated journey from Mexico to Arizona, and, in startlingly clear detail, the gambling tricks his traveling companion had shared with him. They had whiled away hours, days, playing cards. That knowledge, along with the ability to conceal his emotions, learned from the Chiricahua, now provided him with a way to support himself. He discovered he had come to a town where the cost of living was incredibly high, where gambling was a way of life, and rich miners played for high stakes. Although he didn't particularly enjoy the card games he played, it was an easy way to make the money he needed while living in the city.

"Now if you want some real high stakes," one faro player told him, "and a nice place to stay, you either go to the upstairs rooms at the Rosebriar Hotel or the Lantern

House. Only it's pretty tough getting a table at the Lantern House. You'd never know it's a sporting house. They got a fiddle player straight off the concert stage, and—except for Louis-Philippe's café—the best food in town. They specialize in Oriental girls, real high-class, and make so much money from the whores that they don't have to cheat on the gaming tables, so you'll get an honest deal.''

Fletcher knew that most dedicated gamblers had little interest in other pursuits; their opiate was the thrill of the game. He wasn't particularly interested in playing at the fanciest whorehouse in town, concert level fiddler notwithstanding, until a snatch of conversation at the next table caught his attention.

''. . . Yep, couldn't believe my eyes when Tonia Bardine slipped into the private room at the Lantern House and told us to deal her in. I reckon since her old man is laid up with his busted leg and a chronic bellyache, she figures she can get away with it. I wonder what the Nob Hill ladies she takes afternoon tea with would think if they knew?''

Tonia Bardine. His Tonia had been deeply in debt from gambling when he met and married her. She'd claimed that her first husband had forced her to play.

When the player who had spoken eventually dropped out of the game, Fletcher was waiting to buy him a drink.

''You mentioned a woman named Tonia . . . Bardine, wasn't it? Is her husband a sea captain who traded for hides down the coast?''

''Henry Bardine's an old sea dog, right enough. Though nowadays he's the owner of a fleet of ships, including a fast clipper ship.''

''And his wife gambles in a whorehouse?''

''From the rumors I've heard, her connection to the Lantern House is more interesting than that.''

''How so?''

''Well, nobody knows for sure, but there's always been a mystery about who owns the Lantern House. It was built by a seaman who wanted a quiet place to retire, but then gold was discovered and the rush was on, so he sold it and took off for the Sandwich Isles. That's when somebody strung up the lanterns and brought in the China girls. The question is, who?''

''Tonia Bardine?''

His companion grinned. ''Why don't you ask her? I heard she's going to be at the masquerade ball tomorrow night.''

Chapter 47

A GLITTERING ARRAY of costumed revelers assembled in the young city for the masquerade ball. The largest of the Rosebriar banquet rooms was decorated with holiday garlands and fir boughs and filled to capacity with every imaginable character, real, fiction, and imagined. Buccaneers, Cossacks and toreadors whirled gypsy girls, Hindu maharanis, and French courtesans about the polished parquet floor. But the two most eagerly awaited guests had not yet arrived. Everyone waited with baited breath to see which of the two rivals, Briony Forest or Tonia Bardine, would succeed in outshining the other.

Since everyone wore masks, some more concealing than others, as the champagne began to flow and couples spilled onto the dance floor, few people gave more than a passing glance to the sad-faced clown who sat on the sidelines with a twelfth-century monk, hooded, masked, and, as the clown had pointed out, looking vaguely like an executioner.

"The hood covers my hair," Phin had told him.

"Then go as Little Red Riding-Hood," Kane suggested.

"I'll go as a priest. I like the irony."

"He won't be there to see you."

Ignoring the taunt, Phin waited until they were at the ball and then took some satisfaction in telling Kane that his true love would not be attending, either.

"Emily is with child and won't be coming. So don't bother to search for her."

With his face plastered with greasepaint and almost hidden by an outsize false nose and downcast lips, it was difficult to tell whether this news caused him distress or not.

But Phin knew he was uncomfortable with the crowds and suggested that they take their glasses of champagne to a corner that was shielded by a marble column entwined with fir boughs and dried grasses.

"I don't know why we came," Kane grumbled, "other than to satisfy your prurient interest in the social activities of the so-called respectable citizens."

"Tonia Bardine will be here, and I want to keep an eye on my jewelry," Phin reminded him.

She didn't add that since making her first lighthearted decision to attend the masquerade ball, more compelling reasons to be here had arisen. First, her fortune-telling disks had warned of imminent disaster. Then, only this morning, one of the other girls had told her of overhearing Qing Chan tell Lee Wong to send word to the "hospital" to expect another "patient." Phin decided then that as soon as she retrieved her gold jewelry, which she needed to finance her journey, she would leave the Lantern House. With that decision made, she wanted Kane at her side this evening. She didn't question her reasons for needing to keep him nearby; they were too complex. He had been a part of her life for so long that it was unthinkable to make plans that did not include him.

"Why did I let you talk me into coming?" he muttered. "Now I shall have to listen to that miserable excuse for a violinist murdering the Strauss waltzes. I shan't dance, and I doubt anyone is going to ask you in that forbidding costume."

But he was wrong. Even in her monk's robe it was evident that Phin was female, and women were too scarce to be left on the sidelines. She was whirled onto the floor by a spangled Harlequin, and Kane watched, amused, as she followed her partner's clumsy waltz steps.

It was good to see her in this setting, enjoying the harmless flirtation of the dance like any young unattached woman. For a little while he could imagine her to be chaste, untouched. Besides, with Phin occupied, he could allow thoughts of Emily to creep into his mind.

So she was to be a mother. He thought of her slender

body and fragile bones and tried to feel hopeful that she was strong enough to endure the rigors of pregnancy and childbirth.

Uniformed footmen announced each new arrival, not by name but by the character they represented, and there was a stir among the crowd as Cleopatra, Queen of the Nile, appeared in all her glory. Her costume was revealing in the extreme, her breasts barely covered with jewels, filmy harem trousers clearly showing her well-shaped legs, her long dark hair caught up in a jeweled ornament, then falling down her back in a shining cascade. She wore several long gold necklaces, with matching bracelets. Her mask was attached to a jeweled wand, and she made no real effort to conceal her identity. Everyone knew that Tonia Bardine had arrived. She was immediately surrounded by eager partners.

Kane searched the floor for Phin, hoping the sight of her gold jewelry adorning the alabaster throat of the woman who had conspired to have her sister murdered and probably killed her father did not precipitate a public confrontation. But Phin, whose monk's hood had slipped back to reveal her own luxurious black hair flying free, was smiling at something her partner had said and apparently was ignoring Tonia's arrival.

How good it was, Kane thought, to see Phin, whose youth had been stolen from her, enjoying a brief carefree interlude.

"The pirate Jean Laffite," a footman announced, "with a mysterious companion who wishes to remain incognito."

The legendary buccaneer was easily recognizable as Louis-Philippe Ramadier, whom Kane had seen in his audience at the Lantern House on several occasions. A gasp whispered through the crowd as he and his companion stepped into the brightly lit hall. The man's suit, with its narrow trousers and fitted jacket, seemed to emphasize the curves of the woman who wore it. All heads swiveled in her direction and Jean Laffite was pushed aside in the stampede of partners wishing to fill her dance card.

On the other side of his concealing column Kane heard a woman say, "Why, that clever minx! What a daringly different costume. How better to call attention to her figure than to dress as a man! She makes Tonia Bardine look like a strumpet, while she is as regal as ever.''

''Who is she?'' her male companion asked in a spellbound voice.

''Briony Forest. Look at that fiery hair. I don't know anyone else with exactly that shade.''

Cleopatra and the Jean Laffite's dashing companion did not come face to face until the orchestra took a short break and the guests trooped into the adjacent dining room to help themselves to refreshments from the long buffet table.

Tonia, who sat at one of the small tables provided while an army of admirers picked up delicacies to bring to her, looked up as Briony passed by on the arm of Louis-Philippe. Tonia's mask lay on the table beside her, but Briony still wore hers.

Addressing Louis-Philippe in ringing tones, Tonia said, ''Why, M'sieur Laffite, I see you brought one of your lackeys with you. How kind of you to let him wear one of your cast-off suits. If you can spare him, I could use a handyman at my house.''

A silence fell in the immediate area as everyone waited for Briony's response.

Behind her mask, Briony's eyes were an almost metallic blue, and Louis-Philippe could almost feel anger radiating from her, but she spoke in her usual calm, well-modulated voice, looking at him, rather than at Tonia. ''I had no idea when you suggested we come tonight that the bordellos would send one of their girls. If they wished to advertise their wares, I'd have thought they could have selected a more attractive costume—one that revealed fewer flaws.''

A gasp whispered among the nearby guests. Several of Tonia's bruises, fading legacies of her husband's rough lovemaking, were still visible through her filmy costume, despite generous applications of Blanc de Perle, the body powder favored by prostitutes. It was well known that such bruises were the badge of the whore.

Several men nudged one another, expecting the two women to fly at each other with teeth and claws. Tonia did leap to her feet, but Briony said smoothly, "Your costume is a success, Mrs. Bardine, you have accurately portrayed the pathetically tawdry dress of the ladies of the night in their desperate bid for male attention."

"*C'est la guerre!*" Louis-Philippe muttered and grabbed Briony's arm to propel her swiftly out of range. Two of Max's Texas Rangers moved to block Tonia's path, and one of the ball's organizers quickly announced that the orchestra was returning to the dais.

A lanky Robin Hood immediately bowed to Tonia and asked for the dance. Casting a venomous glance after Briony, now being greeted by several friends, Tonia accepted his hand and was led back into the ballroom. Moments later she was waltzing again.

Kane had remained in the ballroom during the refreshment break, as one of Phin's partners had accompanied her to the buffet. She was now dancing with him again. When the musicians resumed playing, Kane started toward the now deserted buffet table. He was transversing the parquet floor when he saw a man walking, without a partner, through the dancers. He was not in costume. Despite the time of year, he was deeply tanned, and he wore his sun-streaked brown hair longer than was fashionable, almost as long as native Americans wore theirs.

Tonia had dropped her partner's hand and spun around to face the uncostumed man. Her naturally pale face seemed to drain of all color, and her rouged lips parted in what appeared to be shock and horror.

She reeled backward, colliding with her partner, who tried to pull her back into his arms. She pushed him away and stumbled from the floor. Kane's last glimpse of her was as she disappeared through the French windows that opened to the veranda. The tanned stranger followed without haste.

At the same time Kane saw that Phin had been close to Tonia at the time of the confrontation, and now she withdrew from her partner, and she, too, disappeared through the veranda doors.

Phin had seen the man striding across the dance floor and wondered about his grim expression and the look of flint in his eyes. He appeared to be oblivious to the curious stares and stared at someone to Phin's left. Following his gaze, she saw Tonia's head slowly turn, as though pulled by invisible strings. As she caught sight of the approaching man, a look of incredulous disbelief gave way to panic. She turned to face him, then reeled backward against her startled partner.

Phin stopped dancing to watch. Everyone in the vicinity also paused in midstep and conversation died. Something about the approaching man and Tonia's frightened expression spoke of a drama about to enfold.

Then the man, looking at Tonia, said distinctly, "No, my dear wife, I am not a ghost."

Tonia's lips moved, and Phin saw that they formed the single word *Fletcher*. Then she was fighting off the restraining arms of her partner and stumbling from the dance floor. The man followed. Other couples resumed dancing.

"Come on, let's dance. It's all over, whatever it was," Phin's partner said.

"Excuse me," Phin said and quickly left the floor.

Phin felt as though she were gliding after the man and woman, moving as if in a dream. The dancers in their colorful costumes, the gaily decorated hall, the music and laughter, had all faded into a misty void. Thoughts of getting her stolen jewelry back from Tonia dissolved.

Fletcher. No, my dear wife, I am not a ghost.

My father, Phin thought. That man is *my father*. It seemed a giant gong was being struck inside her head, driving the words into her brain, but she knew it was only the blood pounding in her ears. Her father was still alive—he was here. The barbarian her mother had loved and longed for all the days of her life, he was here.

Unsure what she would do or say when she caught up with him, Phin reached the doors and stepped out onto the veranda. Coach lanterns cast a faint amber glow on the two figures who stood at the top of the veranda steps.

Phin drew back against the French door. She could not hear properly the frantic, furtive whispers that Tonia uttered, but the man spoke in a normal voice. "Save your breath, Tonia. Your denials are as stupid as you are. Nor do

I want your tainted money, although you can return the phoenix hair comb you're wearing. It was meant for a nobler head than yours.''

Tonia quickly pulled the ornament from her hair and thrust it at him, again imploring something of him in hoarse whispers.

He responded, ''I didn't come to blackmail you nor to punish you for your perfidy. Perhaps if Emily were still alive, I might be more inclined to see justice done. Oh, yes, I am convinced now that it was you who drove my beloved daughter to her death. But she's gone, and frankly I no longer care what happens to you. Besides, it's been my observation that most people get what they deserve in the end.''

Tonia attempted to place her hands on his chest, but he pushed them away and the next instant he was walking back toward Phin.

In that split second Phin knew this was not the time to reveal herself. How could she, when he still believed Emily was dead? He must first be reunited with his true daughter, the child he had loved and cared for and brought up to young womanhood, not she who was no more than the result of the careless spilling of his seed.

Phin pulled the monk's hood up over her head, and as her father reached her, she stepped forward. ''You must come with me. Someone is waiting for you.''

Emily had begged Edward to accompany his sister and Louis-Philippe to the masquerade ball, pleading with him that she felt guilty for keeping him at her side when most of the time she was too tired even to hold a conversation.

He had smiled and sat down in his armchair in her bedroom and said, ''There is nowhere else on earth I'd rather be than with you, dearest. You don't have to converse with me. I shall read to you. I found a complete set of the periodicals containing the serial story *Oliver Twist* by Charles Dickens.''

He had scarcely begun to read when Josefa knocked on

the door. "There is a señor and a señorita to see Mrs. Dale. The señorita asked me to say her name is . . . Pin?"

Emily sat bolt upright. "Oh, tell her I shall be downstairs directly! Edward, quickly, pass my velvet housecoat. Josefa, make a pot of tea, will you, please?"

"The señorita—Phin—she has gone. I showed the señor into the *sala*."

"But—"

"I'd better see what this is all about," Edward said. "Josefa, stay here with Mrs. Dale."

He was gone for so long that Emily had time to dress and have Josefa comb her hair. When Edward returned, she saw that his expression was carefully controlled. He said quietly, "Sit down, Emily. I must prepare you for your visitor."

"Who is he? What an odd time to come calling. And why did Phin bring him and then leave?"

"First of all, I must tell you that he doesn't know who Phin is. You must keep that in mind and respect her wishes to remain anonymous for the time being. You see, I believe your father is waiting for you downstairs."

He caught her as she swayed as though about to faint. But she drew a deep breath and whispered, "I'm all right. Oh, dear God in heaven, can it be true?"

"Just as you believed him to be dead, so he believed he had buried you back in England. Are you sure you're up to this? Perhaps I should ask him to return after you've had time to digest this news."

"No!" Emily cried. "I must see him—help me downstairs, Edward."

He slipped his arms around her, and together they made their way down the stairs. When they reached the drawing room door, Emily gave a small cry and broke free of Edward. She ran into the waiting arms of the man whose eyes closed in a silent prayer of thanks as he held her.

Emily was weeping joyously. "It's you! It's really and truly you! Oh, Father, I can't believe it—am I dreaming? Where did you come from? How did you find me?"

"I was brought here by an apparition—a girl dressed as

a monk—who gave your maid a Chinese name and then vanished into the night. Who was she?''

"Emily—'' Edward warned.

"Could we sit down?'' Emily asked breathlessly.

"Of course. You look very pale, my dear. This has been a shock to you.''

"We have so much to tell each other, Father. But first of all I must give you our wonderful news—you are going to be a grandfather.''

Edward saw the tear slip from Emily's father's eye and course down his cheek. For a moment he was too overcome to speak. Edward said, ''I'll leave you two alone while you catch up. Josefa will bring in some tea. Ring if you need anything.''

He was quite sure neither of them noticed him slip out of the room.

Kane had waited in vain for Phin to return, but neither she nor Tonia nor the mysterious man came back. When it was obvious she had abandoned him, Kane made his way as inconspicuously as possible through the dancers and searched the veranda. There was no sign of any of them, nor of the carriage that he had hired to bring Phin to the Rosebriar. He set off for the Lantern House on foot.

He had traveled only two blocks when an acrid odor drifted toward him, and he stopped dead in his tracks, turning to sniff the wind to find the source of the smoke.

Almost at once the alarm bell of the Montgomery engine house rang its urgent warning, confirming his suspicion. He felt an acute stab of fear, not knowing which way to run from his old enemy.

Within minutes billowing clouds of black smoke filled the streets on the east side of Portsmouth Square. As engines dashed down the hill, the square filled with people, and he was caught up in the rushing throng.

Storekeepers heaved chests of gold dust out into the street to drag down to the pier, where as a last resort the chests could be thrown into the water. Kane stopped to help one man heave a chest from his store and into a carriage, only to see the horse bolt in fright as flames roared up over the roof.

A second glow, this time to the west, lit the night sky. Kane stared in horror, paralyzed by the thought that one blaze was racing in the direction of the hill where Emily lived, while the second had to have broken out near the Lantern House.

''Hey, you—clown! Don't stand there like a fool. Grab a bucket,'' a voice yelled at him out of the smoky confusion.

But Kane was already pushing through the milling crowd, his own fear of fire forgotten in his desperate need to reach the woman he knew he must save.

Chapter 48

· ·

ALL THE WAY from Emily's house back to the water-front Phin thought of her father and wondered why she felt no blood bond with him.

Fletcher Faraday seemed an honorable, compassionate man. He had at first doubted her word that his daughter was still alive but had been willing to go with her to see for himself. This, Phin felt, showed courage, since it was well known that many men were lured to dark places by whores and then set upon and robbed.

He had questioned how Phin knew Emily, and she had replied merely that they had traveled together from England, she knew the story of his disappearance, and had overheard his exchange with Tonia.

Her father had looked at her long and hard, and Phin had held her breath, wondering if he would guess her identity. But he did not. The realization struck her then, like a blow. Why should he recognize her? She did not look like him, nor did she look like the Chinese woman he had loved.

For so long she had yearned to meet her father, had imagined what their reunion might be like, but now she felt curiously let down. Was it because her father, like Brent, was a Caucasian, and therefore the nemesis of her people? Or perhaps she had simply lost respect for *all* men. They were either unattainable or nothing more than passing faces etched with lust.

At least Emily and her father were now reunited, and Phin had learned a valuable lesson. Despite seemingly incontro-vertible proof, nothing in life was certain—nothing was ever quite as it seemed. She had been so sure that Tonia had killed their father, and obviously this had not been the case. Still, if Tonia was not a murderess, she was still guilty of attempting to have Emily killed. She was also still in possession of Phin's gold jewelry, her only ticket out of her present life.

When Phin reached the Lantern House, she saw Tonia's carriage outside. She considered going in through the tradesmen's entrance at the side of the house in order to slip unnoticed up to her room and pick up her packed bags before confronting Tonia. But if Tonia had come straight here from the Rosebriar, she could now be ready to leave for home, possibly taking the jewelry with her. While Phin was entering the side door, Tonia could be leaving through the front. Phin decided to go directly to Tonia's private office.

Despite the small crowd of men in the lobby, their voices seemed raucous, their presence more uncouth and threatening than usual, and Phin realized that Kane's music caused the men to lower their voices and behave in a more gentlemanly manner.

The door to Tonia's office was slightly ajar, and Phin could see that Tonia had already discarded her costume and was dressed in street clothes. Qing Chan fluttered about in the background, folding and packing the Cleopatra costume into a box. Phin's necklaces were still dangling from Tonia's throat.

Knocking lightly on the door, Phin said, "Forgive the intrusion—"

"So it *was* you at the ball," Tonia said, her eyes narrowing. "When your hood slipped and I saw your hair, I suspected it. Did you go there to spy on me? I saw you lurking on the veranda. Do you think what you learned can now save your miserable skin?"

"Mrs. Bardine, I have learned only that you are, according to your peculiar laws, a bigamist. That is no concern of mine. I am aware you have committed other crimes, but it is not up to me to judge you. I believe, in fact, that ultimately we all pay for our transgressions. Someday you will have to face your ancestors, as I will have to face mine. I came back here tonight only because you are presently wearing my gold necklaces and bracelets, which were removed from my room. Will you please return them to me now?"

"She is lying!" Qing Chan spat out. "The jewelry does not belong to her."

Ignoring her, Tonia regarded Phin coldly. "How dare you threaten me? Are you aware that none of the other Chinese girls in town are paid for their services? Only the girls of the Lantern House receive a percentage of their earnings. I have been a most generous employer. In the parlor houses and cribs the girls are slaves owned by their masters. They are taken straight from the ship to the auction block, paraded naked, examined, and bid for like animals. You are an extremely ungrateful girl, Phin Tsu. You owe me a great deal, yet Qing Chan tells me you refuse to work, and now you are making wild accusations. Frankly, I fear for your sanity. You must have taken leave of your senses."

"She lured Kane away tonight," the mama-san said, her small eyes glittering with anticipation that the hated half-breed was at last about to receive her just deserts. "Perhaps he won't come back."

"Get Lee Wong," Tonia snapped. "Have him take her to the hospital." Before Phin Tsu could react, Qing Chan darted past her into the lobby.

Phin reached out and grabbed at her gold necklaces. The clasp of one broke, and she pulled it from Tonia's neck, then turned and ran.

She saw Lee Wong and the mama-san coming across the lobby, and since there was nowhere else to go, Phin raced up the stairs and into the wicker pagoda where Kane played his violin. The connecting door to his room was unlocked, and she slipped inside, locking the door behind her. Oh, if only Kane were there!

Moments later the door rattled, and Lee Wong demanded that she unlock it. When there was no response, he put his massive shoulder to the wood and came bursting into the room.

Phin looked around wildly. Kane had one of the best rooms in the house, with an attached balcony. She pushed open the window and stepped outside. She felt the night breeze, freshening with the incoming tide and stirring the string of paper lanterns so that their multicolored lights danced along the balcony rail.

Now she was trapped on the narrow balcony, and if she were to attempt to jump to the street below, she would surely break her legs, or worse. If she could have gone to her own room at the back of the house, she might have been able to jump into the water.

Lee Wong paused before stepping through the window, regarding her malevolently. Phin felt like a small creature pinned to the spot by a serpent's stare.

Tonia, breathless from running, appeared at his side. "Seize her! Get the necklace away from her before you take her to the hospital." Bristling with rage, she shook a finger at Phin. "You are already dead, Phin Tsu. How dare you lay your filthy hands on me! You will pay dearly for attacking me."

Phin backed away as far as she could, until the palm of her hand connected with the warmth radiating from the candles inside the paper lanterns.

As Lee Wong stepped out onto the balcony, Phin's fingers closed around the string of lanterns, breaking a portion loose. Some of the lanterns fell to the wooden floor, and she flung the rest at Lee Wong, hoping to distract him long enough to get back inside and make her escape.

She was unprepared for what happened next. One of the candles flew from a lantern and struck Lee Wong's chest, immediately igniting his Mandarin jacket.

He paused, looking down as if not believing what he saw, as the flames, fanned by the breeze, shot upward toward his face. He beat at them with his hands, but his sleeves caught fire. For a second he stood immobilized by the sight of his burning clothes, then he gave a cry of fear and stumbled back toward the window, the wind whipping the flames. By the time he climbed back inside the house, his clothing was fully engulfed.

Tonia screamed as he crashed into the room, a human

torch spewing sparks that set Kane's bedcurtains ablaze. Tonia attempted to run through the door to the wicker pagoda, but in his panicked flight Lee Wong lurched into her, and for a few seconds they struggled to be first out of the burning room. By the time Lee Wong pushed her aside, Tonia's clothes were also alight.

Still outside, Phin was grateful that the recent rain had saturated the balcony and the candles that had spilled went out without igniting the sodden wood. But inside Kane's room the fire was spreading, and now Lee Wong and Tonia, both with their clothes on fire, were in the pagoda. The dry wicker exploded into flames, and Phin heard screams and shouts as the blaze spread to the landing.

With no way to escape through the house, Phin looked down again at the street. It was simply too far to jump. Smoke was now billowing from the window. Quickly discarding her monk's robe, she climbed up onto the balcony rail. Could she reach the window of the next room? She stretched as far as she could, but the next window was too far away.

Then her groping hand connected with a drainpipe running from the eaves but stopping well short of the ground. Could she jump from the end of the pipe? Looking down, she saw that the drainpipe was directly above the pointed spikes of an iron railing. If she were to jump, she would be impaled.

The roof then? Could she climb up the pipe to the roof?

As flames shot out of the window, Phin didn't stop to wonder what she would do if she were able to reach the roof. She grasped the drainpipe with both hands and swung free of the balcony.

For a terrifying instant she hung suspended above the spiked railing, feeling her fingers slip down the rusty pipe, then she kicked off her sandals, seeking footholds in the clapboard wall.

Clinging like an insect to the drainpipe and poking her toes into every available cranny, it occurred to her to be grateful again for her long, flexible feet. She said a silent prayer of thanks to Kwan Yin that her feet had never been bound.

Kane's lungs burned and he had lost his clown's wig, false lips, and nose. The greasepaint had melted into a sticky mask on his face. His costume was torn and scorched, but for once no passerby turned to stare in either shock or horror as he fought his way through the smoky confusion. There were too many other odd sights as the costumed revelers rushed out to help battle the fire.

The night was filled with the roar of the conflagration as flames swept from one building to another, devouring street after street. The crash of falling timbers and hissing steam were joined by what he at first thought was the pop of Chinese firecrackers. Then he heard someone yell that a warehouse filled with loaded muskets was going up in flames. What he was hearing was the staccato crack of discharging guns. Fortunately the muskets must have been in perpendicular racks, as the shells were thrown upward.

The wind had picked up, and now a vast sheet of flame extended for half a mile in length. Fire engines were driven back. Horses released from a livery stable bolted through the streets, maddened by the fire. Hospital patients laid on the street were trampled by people forced back by the flames.

Kane felt as though he were running through his own vision of hell, created from nightmare and fear and guilt and remembrance of past sins. But nothing imagined could approach the horror of a city turned into Dante's Inferno, filled with the screams of the burnt and injured, the thunder of collapsing brick buildings, the blinding glare as spirits ignited, and the explosions as gunpowder was used to blow up houses in a vain hope of stopping the rampaging monster that was destroying the city, whipped from one street to the next on a wind that was now near gale force.

He was showered with burning splinters as he ran, and the smoke felt like needles pricking his eyes. When firefighters threw water at red hot walls, it returned as a scalding steam, and coming upon a cloud of it, he panicked momentarily as he recalled the exploding chemicals in his father's laboratory so long ago.

At last he reached the waterfront and looked longingly at the safe haven of dark sea but forced himself to turn toward the Lantern House. He could not hide until he was sure Phin was safe. He had given Emily's safety only a passing thought, quickly deciding that her husband would protect her. Phin was his concern.

He realized with a jolt that no one was more important to him. Phin had been both his tormentor and his savior, infuriating him, healing him, challenging him, and worrying him; he had hated her and he had loved her. For Emily he had felt only love, and perhaps that had not been enough.

Long before he reached it, he saw that the Lantern House was engulfed in flame. The entire front and most of the roof was ablaze. Silhouettes on the street dashed about in the red haze, and as he drew nearer they materialized into scantily clad girls and men passing buckets of water.

He caught one girl by the shoulders and spun her around to face him. She screamed at the sight of the melting greasepaint on his scarred face, but his fingers bit into her flesh and refused to release her. "Phin Tsu? Have you seen Phin?"

She shook her head. He grabbed another girl, but the response was the same. Then he saw Qing Chan, standing alone in the middle of the street, clutching her abacus as though to count the fleeing girls. Rushing to her side he asked hoarsely, "Did Phin come back here? Did she get out all right?"

The mama-san turned slowly to look up at him. She seemed to be in a trance and didn't speak. Kane grabbed her and shook her. "*Where is Phin?*"

"Inside. She is inside," Qing Chan hissed. "Up in your room."

Kane raced around the house, looking for a way in, a pathway through the bonfire. On one side was the tradesmen's entrance, the door and corridor beyond spewing smoke but not yet any sign of flame.

He plunged into the smoky darkness, shouting Phin's name.

Briony sat in the blackened shell of the Rosebriar, feeling scorched, half-blind from the smoke that still rose in red columns from piles of lumber that would burn for days. Her hair, white with ash, straggled over the shoulders of Louis-Philippe's best suit, and her face was soot-streaked.

In the surrounding debris she could see that spoons, forks, and knives had melted together in surreal sculptures, broken crockery resembled crushed bones, and iridescent pools of melted glass reflected rainbows of color.

Last night when the fire alarms sounded, everyone had poured out of the Rosebriar to help fight the flames. When Briony realized that the hotel itself was about to be engulfed, she had tried to go back inside to save some of the priceless works of art. But brawny arms held her back.

She hadn't given any thought to her own ship store until dawn, and it occurred to her then that she had been more worried about Max's hotel than her own possessions. She soon determined that her half-finished house was gone, and a brief visit to the waterfront confirmed that there was nothing left of her store. She found Nate Craw poking about among the ashes. Their precious nails were now welded together by the heat and standing in the shape of the kegs that had held them. Gun barrels were twisted like snakes. She had lost everything she owned, but her greatest heart-break was the destruction of her beautiful Rosebriar.

The crunch of boots on debris caused her to look up, and at first she thought she must be imagining the figure picking his way through the ruins toward her.

When he reached her she said tonelessly, "I thought you'd gone to England."

"I started to . . . changed my mind."

Briony gestured about her. "There isn't anything left. Everything burned."

Max lifted the blackened remains of a support beam with the toe of his boot. "I seem to recall your architect designing the Rosebriar to withstand an earthquake."

Briony sighed. "We never seem to worry about the right things, do we? I worried that you'd go to England and discover I'm wanted for murder."

The tight lines around Max's mouth eased. "So that's your deep dark secret. Hell, I was afraid you really had something to hide—like a husband."

"There's a husband, too, Max."

"You're a long way from England and British law, Bri."

"But not from my own conscience. Oh, I didn't kill anyone, but I am married and I do stand accused of murder. I've been looking back over my shoulder for four years. How could I burden anyone—least of all a man I cared about—with that?"

Hope leapt in Max's eyes. "Do you? Care?"

"Of course. I've been hiding my feelings for you for years, even from myself. I know that now."

He offered his hand to help her to her feet, then pulled her close to him. "After you turned me down, there didn't seem to be any point to anything. Not even getting up in the morning. I started out on journeys and then forgot where I was going. Nothing I began seemed worth finishing."

She nestled her head into his shoulder, drawing comfort from his sheltering body. "I worked every minute of every day to try to forget you. Now all I worked for is gone. My store, my half-finished house, all my belongings except for what I'm wearing." She paused, remembering that she was still clad in the tattered remnants of Louis-Philippe's suit.

Max grinned. "I noted your new style of dress. Whatever you wear it's okay with me, just so long as you don't intend to change into a man in other respects."

"I went to the masquerade ball—it seems like such a long time ago, and so inconsequential now. What a fright I must look."

"You'll always look like the most beautiful woman on earth to me."

"I'm so glad you're here, Max. Nothing seems quite so bad now."

"I looked for you all night long—well, between trying to douse flames and helping people haul their goods down to the pier. Then on my last trip to the wharf the fire cut us off, so all we could do was watch that monster devour the city. I was frantic with worry. I was afraid one or both of us would die before I got a chance to tell you how much I love you. I do, Bri, more than you'll ever know."

Briony raised a soot-streaked face toward him. "And I love you, Max. But I'm still not free to marry you."

"Does that matter? It doesn't to me."

"No," she said softly. "Nothing matters so long as we're together. But . . . well, I suppose I wish I didn't have a past."

He chuckled. "You think I don't have one?"

"I should have told you that I was still married. I should at least have been honest about that."

"I knew about your husband before I left. I guess I had some idea of going to England and bribing him to give you a divorce. Then I realized he wasn't the obstacle."

"Oh, Max. Did two people ever try harder to deny themselves happiness? I should have trusted you enough to confide in you. Perhaps I'd better tell you now that I was accused of the murder of my husband's mistress."

Max whistled. "I'm impressed."

"Max! I didn't kill her."

Slipping his arm around Briony's shoulders, Max said, "Let's not worry about the past; we've too much future ahead of us to discuss. Come on, let's go find a hot bath and a large breakfast someplace, then talk about rebuilding our hotel."

Phin had plunged from the roof of the Lantern House into the cold water of the bay. For a while she clung to a pier piling watching as the house was consumed by fire. Then, as the flames rapidly spread to the waterfront warehouses, she swam out to an anchored fishing boat and pulled herself over the side. Shivering, she lay in the boat for the rest of the night as the sky was bathed in a bloodred glow filled with golden sparks.

At first light she swam to the shore. A few people still wandered up and down the street, searching for loved ones or rooting through piles of ash for anything to salvage.

She saw Qing Chan sitting on the ground, her fingers moving the beads of her abacus, her tiny eyes staring straight ahead. A row of bodies, hastily covered with tarpaulins, lay nearby.

Phin walked on, unsure where to go, what to do. She must assure herself that Emily was safe, and then find Kane. Luckily he had still been at the Rosebriar when the fire started.

Through the gray blur of smoke ahead she could make out a group of people crouching over others lying on the ground. One of the figures stood up, and Phin's heart leapt. There was no mistaking the broad shoulders and impressive height of Brent.

Very much aware that the thin silk blouse and trousers she had worn under her monk's robe were now wet and clinging to her body, Phin approached the priest.

As she drew nearer she saw he was administering last rites to a badly burned man who appeared to be already dead. She did not at first notice that some of the prone bodies were still alive, and that Emily's husband was moving among them, binding up their wounds, attempting to ease their pain.

She paused for a moment, watching the two men, feeling pride in being connected to them, however tenuously. Then Brent turned and saw her.

There was no mistaking the relief and joy on his face, and she caught her breath with the realization that he must have feared that she had perished. Surely he did love her, after all. She ran toward him, loving him more than she had ever loved him, needing him more than she needed air to breathe.

Her headlong dash was stopped when he caught her and held her at arm's length. "Thank God," he breathed.

"I will never go back to that life, Brent, I swear it."

He nodded. "You must atone, Phin, you do know that?"

"Anything. Just let me be with you."

"If you wish to do God's work, you can take the veil. I have given my life to serving God, Phin. The only real joy we can find, the only real truth, lies in service to Him. I am a Jesuit; I must look for Christ everywhere, not just in cathedrals and churches. I must spread the word and teach the most humble among us. I will go wherever I am needed. I've been ordered to leave San Francisco."

"Please, take me with you."

"I cannot. But you will find your own way now." He reached under his black robe and pulled out a sheathed dagger. The hilt of the knife was encrusted with gems that glinted imperially in the murky air. "This will help you begin a new life, Phin. Sell the stones individually; they will be worth more. I took that dagger from the river pirate who kidnapped you in China. In a way it has always been yours."

Phin held the dagger, a vision of her magnificent barbarian leaping aboard the river pirate's boat flashing into her mind. How very long ago it seemed now.

"God be with you, Phin," Brent said softly. He turned away, bending over one of the burned men.

Phin stood uncertainly, watching him lean close to hear the dying man's confession.

A blanket was slipped around her shoulders, and a voice spoke beside her. "I'm glad you're all right, Phin."

"Edward . . . is Emily safe? Where is she?"

"Your father took her out of town when we saw the fire was out of control. They're up in the hills somewhere."

"So you know we are sisters?"

He nodded. "Phin, I couldn't help but overhear what Brent said to you. Believe him. He's never going to change. There is no more dedicated disciple than the redeemed sinner. Let him go. Don't humiliate yourself any further. You can stay with us; our house was spared."

Phin began to shiver uncontrollably. "I must find Kane. Then I will decide what to do."

Edward unaccountably took her hands in his, gripping them tightly. He regarded her with eyes red-rimmed from the smoke. "Phin, I'm so sorry . . ."

She felt an almost uncontrollable impulse to run away before he could confirm her worst suspicions. But he was already saying the words. "When I heard that a clown had run into the burning Lantern House, I didn't know at first—"

A low moan escaped Phin's lips. "No, no—it was not him! There were other clowns at the ball. He was deathly afraid of fire."

"He wanted to save you, Phin," Edward said gently. "His concern for your safety was far greater than his fear of fire. One of the girls overheard the tiny Chinese woman tell him that you were still inside. He must have loved you very much, Phin."

She almost blurted out that Edward was wrong in assuming Kane loved her enough to give his life for her; she almost said the unthinkable, that Kane had loved Emily. But despite the whirlwind of grief sweeping over her, some last speck of reason prevailed and she did not. After all, Emily was Edward's wife. Instead Phin whispered, "I can't bear it. He didn't have to die—he didn't have to save me. I saved myself."

"As you can save yourself again. Make a new life, Phin. Let us help you. I see now how wrong I was to fear Emily's attachment to you. I worried about other people's reaction to your mixed blood and how it would affect my family. I am bitterly ashamed for that and beg you to forgive me."

"There is nothing to forgive, Edward. How can I censure you for feeling what everyone else feels? I think including me."

"Doc . . ." a feeble voice interrupted. "You got any water?"

"I must do what I can for the injured," Edward said. "Go to our house. I'm sure Emily and your father will return soon. Tell Josefa I sent you."

Phin shook her head. "Thank you, but you see, everything has changed now. If Kane gave his life for me, then I must learn what that means and find a way to live my life that will justify his sacrifice.''

She didn't look back at the black-robed priest as she made her way through the smoke-shrouded dawn. Her head seemed to be filled with Kane's music, and rather than being a dirge, it was joyful, as though his spirit had at last been set free.

Afterword

· ·

AFTER THE FIRE the town council passed an ordinance levying heavy fines on anyone who refused to join in fighting fires or removing goods from the path of the flames. The ordinance also provided for the digging of artesian wells and the building of reservoirs. Before the ordinance could be put into effect, however, an even more destructive fire raged for three days, and recurring fires continued to plague the city for several more years.

Early in the spring Emily delivered a healthy seven-pound boy. Edward, who had been at his wife's side during the twenty hours of her labor, deferring to a midwife, eventually sent the woman away. He was able to turn his son from the breech position, possibly saving the life of both his wife and child. They named their son Fletcher Ambrose, his middle name to honor the memory of Kane, whose real name had been Ambrose.

Fletcher Faraday, who had searched in vain for the Chiricahua squaw he called Sings Softly, at last learned that she had been killed by soldiers in a raid that was retaliation for an Apache attack on a wagon train. His grief was intense, but the birth of his grandson brought solace, and although he never could bring himself to settle in the burgeoning city by the bay, he visited Emily and Edward and the boy frequently.

After a time Edward disposed of all of his businesses in order to devote his life to treating the sick. He lived long enough to see ether used routinely to anesthetize surgery patients but not long enough to see women breach the bastion of male-run medical schools to become doctors, or to have their ailments treated with the same care afforded to male patients.

Louis-Philippe Ramadier built a magnificent restaurant, and people traveled for miles, then waited for hours for a table; but it burned to the ground in the great fire of May 3, 1851, which destroyed virtually the entire city.

Captain Henry Bardine recovered from his illness shortly after the death of his wife, but was lost at sea attempting to break the record for clipper ship voyages around the Horn.

Max and Briony built a new hotel, even more splendid than the Rosebriar, but it, too, was destroyed by fire in 1851. They promptly broke ground for a third hotel, which endured until the great earthquake of 1906. After several years of "living in sin," Max and Briony heard that Sir Rupert Forester had been murdered by a disgruntled legal client in England. They were quietly married.

Father Juan, accompanied by Gregorio, left San Francisco shortly after the Christmas fire of 1849.

Phin Tsu also left immediately after the fire. Although Edward had expected that Emily would be deeply distressed by her half sister's abrupt departure, to his surprise she accepted their parting philosophically.

"Phin has to deal with her grief over Kane," Emily said. "I know how much his sacrifice must have affected her, because I know how acute my own shock and sadness are. And the one person on earth who could comfort her—Brent—has gone. Apparently he believes that now she is no longer working at the Lantern House, her soul is saved. Your priest does not concern himself with her broken heart."

"She left about the same time as Brent," Edward pointed out. "Perhaps she has joined him?"

"No, I don't think so. But Phin will return some day. For now, like our father, she must follow her own star. I wish Father and Phin could have got to know each other. In many ways she is more his daughter than I am."

Edward did not tell Emily of her father's shock upon learning, not that he had a Eurasian daughter, but that she had been raised to be a pleasure woman and had been the main attraction at San Francisco's most infamous bordello. Still, to his credit, Fletcher Faraday immediately asked to see Phin in order to welcome her as his long-lost daughter. But she had left town the moment she learned of Kane's death.

When a safety deposit box leased by Kane at his bank was opened, a will was found, leaving everything to Phin Tsu with the exception of a sum set aside for a trust fund, to be set up by Max Seadon for Dudley in England. Unfortunately no copies of Kane's music were ever found.

But no one ever forgot Kane, or his music.

National Bestselling Author
PAMELA MORSI

"I've read all 'ier books and loved every word."
—Jude Deveraux

WILD OATS

The last person Cora Briggs expects to see at her door is a
fine gentleman like Jedwin Sparrow. After all, her more
"respectable" neighbors in Dead Dog, Oklahoma won't
have much to do with a divorcee. She's even more
surprised when Jed tells her he's just looking to sow a few
wild oats! But instead of getting angry, Cora decides to get
even, and makes Jed a little proposition of her own...one
that's sure to cause a stir in town—and starts an unexpected
commotion in her heart as well.
__0-515-11185-6/$4.99

GARTERS

Miss Esme Crabb knows sweet talk won't put food on the
table—so she's bent on finding a sensible man to marry.
Cleavis Rhy seems like a smart choice...so amidst the
cracker barrels and jam jars in his general store, Esme
makes her move. She doesn't realize that daring to set her
sights on someone like Cleavis Rhy will turn the town—and
her heart—upside down.

__0-515-10895-2/$4.99

448